DEMON'S ANGEL

HARPER DAKOTA

WARNING:

This book contains mature themes and is intended to be read by ages 18+. Contains curse words, sex, tail play, paranormal creatures, magical and fated mate themes, m/m relationship, BDSM elements (all adult/consensual). Graphic scenes of torture and sexual assault. Mentions of people doing evil things and being punished for it.

Trademark Acknowledgements:

The author acknowledges the following trademarks and trademark status of these items mentioned in the book, including: Monopoly, Furglars, Sprite.

Cover Design by: Artscandare Book Cover Design

Editing by: Lori Parks

Formatting by: Leslie Copeland

To my family. I love you all.

To the wonderful people who help make my books happen: my beta readers, proofreader, formatter, and cover designer. A big thank you to all my readers who called out for Uncle Luc's book!

Thank you to everyone who reads and reviews.

SYNOPSIS

Luc has his job and visits from his favorite nephew. He has a few friends, but in general, no one wants to get close to him. All they see is his job. He's more than his role as *Lucifer*, ruler of Netherworld, but it keeps people at arm's length. After being alone for centuries, he fears that the Fates may have forgotten him when they were pairing mates. To be fair, he certainly doesn't give many opportunities for his mate to appear, given that he never leaves his realm.

When his angel appears, will he be Luc's salvation or his downfall?

AUTHOR'S NOTE

This book can be read as a standalone. However, there are some characters that appear from the previous book in this universe, *Demon's Mate.*

- Mac: demon, Luc's nephew, Enforcer
- Viv: human, Mac's mate, librarian
- Declan (Dec): Mac and Viv's baby
- Thomas: human, Viv's best friend, mate to D, teacher
- D: demon, Mac's best friend, works in Intake on Netherworld side, mate to Thomas
- Faolán: hellhound, raised/trained by Luc, given to Viv

This is a paranormal/fantasy romance. There are three realms/planes: Earth, Netherworld (aka Hell, Underworld, etc.), and Arlysium (Heaven). Angels and demons are simply another species, neither inherently good nor bad; some work as Enforcers protecting those on Earth, Netherworld, and Arlysium. Nonhumans can travel between the realms, as well as their human mates. God and Lucifer were appointed to their roles and act as leaders, similar to a CEO in the human world.

Being the leader of Netherworld has its dangers. Please read the trigger warnings on the copyright page.

PROLOGUE
LUC

Luc stood over the body of his predecessor, standing straight despite his exhaustion. Blood dripped from his body, his clothes coated with both his and Satan's. His entire being ached, muscles sore, cuts and wounds scattered over his body. He was pretty sure the last knife Satan had drawn had been coated in poison based on the smirk on his face. It had been a great knife, although he suspected it was also spelled. His own blade had been made of the strongest metals, but it snapped the second it hit Satan's blade. He had thrown his to the ground, moving in close and using his strength and speed to wrestle the blade away from his opponent. The smirk had quickly faded from Satan's face as Luc used the blade to finish the fight.

The arena was quiet, no one moving. He could barely hear a sound. He thought everyone was shocked that he had won. The Fates walked over to him, healing his wounds with a touch to his shoulder.

"You're going to be perfect for this role," they told him, three voices speaking as one. "Never forget we picked you. I chose you and God to rule the nonhumans together. You each have your place and your gifts. Your personalities and abilities make you the perfect ruler. I know it was a long time getting here, and I appreciate that you entered the challenge when I asked. Wait here a minute while I get God. I only want to make this announcement once."

Luc waited, breathing heavily, still winded after the hours of fighting despite his wounds being healed. He caught sight of his brother walking toward him through the crowd. At least there was one friendly face nearby. His brother stopped at the edge of the ring and nodded to him with a small smile. Luc was exhausted and wondered how his life had taken this crazy turn. Of course he knew. The Fates.

The Fates had thrown their world into a tailspin months ago when they announced that God's predecessor, Yahweh, had retired. Word was it had been strongly encouraged. When Satan had refused to step down, the Fates had announced his removal and had set up the challenges themselves. Satan wasn't used to being told no and had seemed to think if he won the challenge he would keep his job; he didn't accept that the Fates were going to remove him one way or the other. No one had ever wanted to go after him before; the few that had tried ended up dying after watching their entire family being publicly slaughtered. All before the challenge had even been made public or taken place.

Luc had stayed out of the challenges; he didn't want to lead. Honestly, almost anyone would be better than Satan. He was sick of fighting. He'd had enough in the wars. He was tired and just wanted some peace. All he wanted was to live out his life, spend time with his brother, maybe find his mate. It had been years since he'd seen his brother; they had both been in the wars and had made it through intact, although the same couldn't be said about their parents.

He was at his home one day, attempting to plan out a garden and wondering if he could keep some animals when the scary-ass Fates arrived. They had insisted very politely that he enter the challenge.

"We know you are who is meant to be in the position. You have everything needed to be a great ruler. You will bring order to your world and God will rule Arlysium. Together I see you bringing all nonhumans together, peace, and so many babies will come," she said gleefully.

Luc had bitten his lips shut to keep from telling her that he actually preferred men.

A twinkling laugh sounded. "No, not you, silly boy. You'll have puppies."

Luc had stared at them in shock. "What?"

"Hellhounds. You will raise and train so many of them to help Netherworld. Just remember; this is only one of the futures that I see and it's the one I want to exist. This is the best for everyone, but you still need to fight to prove yourself, to earn the position in the eyes of all nonhumans. I can see into every aspect of your soul, I know every little bit of your being, even parts of you that you haven't discovered yet. It all makes you perfect to be ruler of Netherworld. Remember that when it gets hard."

He'd had no idea how to respond to that advice, so he had simply nodded. He didn't think he was the smartest demon out there, but he was smart enough to know that when the actual fucking Fates asked you to do something, you better do it. They were the real ones in charge and had more power than any of them combined. It had taken months of fighting, challenging others, being challenged, working his way up the list of those who were also fighting for the position.

Through the course of the challenges, he had met God. There was something comforting about the other man and they had just clicked. Despite the fact that his predecessor had retired, and the Fates had appointed God to the position, there were still challenges thrown at him daily. Today was the end of it; they both had their final fight today. He hoped God was doing well.

Luc had a natural skill for fighting, even though he didn't enjoy it. After he accepted the Fates' request, he trained and learned as much as he could. His brother helped him, teaching him things he had learned during his time in the wars. He and God had also trained together, each one having a different style of fighting that taught them new things and made them both better fighters.

All the pain and blood, the cuts and broken bones had led to today. Despite the Fates declaring Luc the last one standing, as Satan was not eligible to win, he had accepted Satan's challenge, knowing that many wouldn't accept his leadership unless he won this last fight. He had locked away every bit of himself, focusing only on the fight until he finally stood over Satan's body.

"Hey," a tired voice said next to him.

Luc startled, looking over to see God had ported in. His clothes were torn, blood everywhere, but it looked like his wounds had also been healed.

"You okay?" Luc asked.

"Yeah. Glad this is about to be done. How'd it go?"

Luc shrugged. "He fought dirty like we thought he would. But no matter who you are, cut their Achilles tendon and they're not walking away." Hobbling Satan had given him the advantage he needed to finish the fight. He hadn't felt any remorse when he grabbed his head, tilting it back to slice his throat; after all Satan had played dirty by bringing a poisoned weapon and had killed countless innocents during his reign. Most of the wars had been because Satan had limp-tail-syndrome and had to feel superior.

"Nice." God nodded in approval. "Want to come over for a drink after this? Maybe play a game or something that isn't fighting and death?"

"I'd love to," Luc said honestly. It'd be nice to make a friend, and he had a feeling that once they were fully granted their positions real friends would be hard to come by.

A static buzz filled the air, gathering everyone's attention. The challenges had been public, and it now looked like the people who'd gone to witness God's final fight were now here as well.

The Fates stood in the field, their voices loud enough to carry everywhere. Luc wondered if they were using magic to make it carry so far.

"Listen up. Lucifer and God are now the rulers of Netherworld and Arlysium. I chose them myself for these positions. They will lead the realms into a new era of peace and balance. They earned their spots through blood and sacrifice, as you all witnessed in the challenges." They laid their hands on Luc and God, a golden sheen filling the air, power like nothing he had ever felt swarmed his body, filling it up until he thought he would burst.

When the shimmer faded, he was left with new powers. As the knowledge of everything good and bad the people standing in the field had done flooded his brain, he looked over at God and saw the same horror reflected in his eyes.

Fuck his life.

PROLOGUE
BERT

Bert stood amid the crowd of Enforcers waiting near the outside door. There were some stationed inside already for crowd control, but most were going to be porting to the stage at the same time as a show of brute force. He was waiting for Mac to let him know he had reached the area. They would walk in the serial killer together. He had sealed his fate by targeting an Enforcer's family. Tonight, both sides were coming together to show a united front. Even God, who hated the sight of blood, was coming. Bert would bet that he would leave before any blood was shed though. His boss had a serious blood aversion. Which was kind of ironic since he had gained his own position through a barrage of challenges back in the day. Or maybe that's where it came from. He wasn't brave enough to ask.

Tonight was to make a statement, and he could only hope that it did what they wanted it to. They wouldn't have many Enforcers staying or even new recruits if they feared their families would be targeted. They needed to protect their own. He was fully behind supporting Mac, who was becoming a good friend.

While most people on Earth thought that angels were good and demons were bad, it couldn't be further from the truth. They were just different species, and as in all groups, there were good and bad among each of them. Take the angel who decided to be a cult leader that he and Mac had recently stopped. Demons weren't the only bloodthirsty and violent ones; angels could be just as bad. Both sides worked to maintain the balance and protect those who were weaker from those who were more powerful. Nether-world, or Hell as humans called it, dealt with punishments of evil souls. Arlysium, or Heaven, dealt with rewarding those who led a good life. That could be being reincarnated, floating along as a spirit, or staying in Arlysium. The Enforcers helped track down evildoers of any species in Netherworld, Arlysium, and Earth. Both sides had their own Enforcers, but they worked together. It was how he had met Mac, actually. They worked on a couple of cases together.

Looking at his phone as it buzzed with a new text message, he slid out to meet Mac. Minutes later, he was helping Mac drag in the prisoner. The man was evil to his core and made his skin crawl. He deserved whatever he got tonight. As they stood on the stage surrounded by their fellow Enforcers, Bert watched as Mac gestured to another Enforcer to reveal the contraption designed just for this event. The man was going to get a taste of his own sick preferences. He'd find it wasn't fun being on the other end. It was going to be messy and horrific, which was why they had banned all children from the event. He took a deep breath to settle himself, helping Mac strap the man in.

What...What was that smell? Over the odors of the

many in attendance, over the body odor and fear of the prisoner, one stood out. It was similar to a smoky caramel; both sweet and a little savory. His angel side was saying *mate*. How crazy would it be if he found his mate here? Bert looked out, searching the crowd, trying to find someone that stood out. He recognized a lot of faces; none of them had smelled like this before.

"...And that will not be tolerated," a deep husky voice stated firmly off to the side of the stage. That voice. His cock twitched and he forced his burgeoning hard-on away before anyone noticed. That was his mate. Too bad he had been ignoring the first part of the speech; he had been focused on the prisoner and what Mac was whispering to him.

His head whipped around, looking for the speaker. He was gorgeous, taller than Bert, slender but clearly muscular, dark hair pulled back into a manbun, strikingly bright blue eyes. He wondered how long his hair was. He loved gripping hair in his fist during sex. His heart froze when God ported in, standing next to his mate, showing a united front. Oh shit. There was no way. He watched as his boss made a speech, patted the other man on the back, and left. That had to be Lucifer. His mate.

He was screwed.

Luc watched as his nephew said "I do" to his lovely mate. He was happy that they had chosen to have the ceremony in Netherworld so he could attend, but also ashamed of himself that he couldn't bring himself to Earth so they could have it there. Viv had assured him that they were happy to have it at his home; they had their best friends and D's parents there and would have a vow renewal on Earth so Thomas' parents could attend. He thought it sad that her own parents didn't seem too involved in her life, Thomas and his parents were more her family than her own parents. Their loss. He was happy to have her in his and would make sure nothing harmed her ever again.

They deserved their happiness after Mac took forever to claim her as his mate and that was after she had been kidnapped and tortured. It was unfortunately a demon that had kidnapped her, although there were other nonhumans involved in the torturing. They had made sure that everyone had been eliminated who had taken part. Then there had been the stalker serial killer that Mac had been hunting, who had tried targeting Viv thinking she was an easy target because she was human. He had been executed in quite a spectacular fashion, making a statement that the

Enforcers' families on both sides, Netherworld and Arlysium, were off limits. Mac had created the plan, both he and God had been present to show their united front. His nephew had rage carry him through most of the torture part of the execution, but he didn't have quite as many years to have been hardened like he had and eventually Luc took over and finished the execution.

As he had been wiping the blood off his hands, he... unlocked himself. To be in his position, it meant dealing with the worst of all species and that required a certain strength and brutality. He had learned over the years to lock most of himself away so he wasn't as effected by it. There was probably a special term for it now, dissociative something. At this point, he could turn off most of his senses, he tuned out noises, he breathed through his mouth to help eliminate any smells. Before he even walked into the stage area, he had locked himself down and didn't come back to himself until the end. It was then that he noticed a presence in the room. The sensation flowing over him was everything he had heard finding your mate would be, an extra awareness, a special scent, but it had disappeared as soon as he began looking around the room, breathing deep to try to scent them.

He would have dismissed it as wishful thinking, but his demon was quite adamant and was bordering on pouting at this point. Considering he never left Netherworld, it seemed unlikely he would ever find his mate if they didn't live there. He would have liked someone to come home to at the end of the day, someone to help share the burden of his life. Not that his life was a burden, but at times his job definitely felt that way. But this was his role in keeping the balance and it was an important one. Maybe the Fates would put his mate in his path again one day.

It had been about a month since Bert had seen his mate at the execution. He kept trying to forget but his mind and body would send images of Lucifer at random moments. He'd given up eating caramels because the smell reminded him too much of his mate.

Today he was drinking himself stupid, hoping to dull the one memory he had of his mate. His angel was ready to track him down, but Bert knew it couldn't be. Pouring himself another glass, he slouched down in his chair, his brain replaying the day of the execution.

He had tried to stay out of range of Lucifer, only moving closer when it was his part to play in the execution. The smell of blood and other bodies was overwhelming at that point, and he had hoped it would cover his own scent, especially since he had been splattered in it. When Mac had stepped back, Lucifer had taken over to finish. The man had been glorious, full of power and confidence. Bert had retreated to the shadows, putting as much distance between them as possible.

Watching Luc, Bert had realized just why he had stayed in power all this time and was spoken about fearfully by some. The man was brutal in his punishments and gave no quarter. He was absolutely coated in blood and gore by the end, so much so that Bert had been shocked the prisoner had that much left in him after everything else.

As he observed his mate, a stray thought had entered his head. It was almost like Luc wasn't really there. He'd heard stories from Mac about a loving uncle, but there was certainly none of that there. His eyes and face were completely blank. He took his time, but eventually Luc finally allowed the flames to consume the entire body, putting the man out of his current misery. That wasn't the end of course, his soul would still be in punishments.

His mate was everything he could have asked for and he'd wanted nothing more than to rush toward him. But Bert realized that by being with him, it'd put Luc in danger. Luc had to be the strongest one, the alpha as it were. Anyone who knew Bert, would realize that maybe Lucifer wasn't as dominant as they had thought. It could lead to assassination attempts, challenges, riots or civil war among the demons. He didn't want to do anything that could harm his mate.

Bert had stared at Lucifer for several minutes, memorizing his face. He caught the subtle signs that Luc was becoming more aware of his surroundings. When Luc's nostrils flared and he started looking around the room, Bert had quickly teleported to the showers. He wanted to check on his friend before he went home so he made it quick. He was sure Lucifer would also be stopping by to check on Mac and he didn't want to run into him.

His angel wanted their mate, but Bert didn't see how they could make it work.

Stop your whining, he told himself. His angel was really being a pushy asshole, urging him to claim their mate. The situation wasn't as simple as that. His calling in life was to protect others, and in this case, he believed that included staying away.

Sitting on the couch, stewing and fighting with himself,

Bert decided that maybe a quick peek wasn't bad. He knew from Mac that Lucifer had a full day of meetings and punishment hearings. Bert ceded to his urges and ported to Netherworld, specifically the office building that housed the Enforcers and dealt with the intakes.

The offices occupied the top floors, while the main level housed Intake, which was the initial processing. Both Netherworld and Arlysium had an Intake office and Enforcers generally sorted souls out before bringing them to either place. What a lot of people didn't understand was that they also dealt with physical-bodied souls. If a person was dark enough and had caused enough problems, the Enforcers would grab them while they were still alive to save the lives of future victims. The personnel in both Intakes would verify the person was where they belonged and send them to the other office if needed. In Netherworld, the souls then went to another stop which was similar to sentencing. The people who worked there would review the cases and decide on the punishment level needed. There were always Enforcers nearby to help assist moving souls to their assigned level. No one wanted to go, and some decided to fight back. Then there were the actual punishment levels, although some of them required teleportation to get to. Different Enforcers were in charge of handing out the punishments. Bert knew that Lucifer helped his people from time to time in the levels and also decided the outcomes for the worst of the bunch.

He fiddled around on his phone for a few minutes until a large group walked past him, heading toward the doors. He followed them in, sticking to the shadows to hide. Not that anyone would think it was odd he was here; as an Enforcer he visited both the Netherworld and Arlysium offices. Bert stood in the back corner, far enough away that his mate shouldn't see or smell him. It helped in this case that he was shorter than the normal demon or angel.

His mate was delicious looking. He sat tall in his throne-like chair, the black wood complemented by a deep, almost black, red leather. Lucifer was wearing a black suit with a deep burgundy pinstripe and as he shifted in his seat, Bert could see the interior of the jacket was lined with a burgundy silk. A black shirt and tie completed the look. Following the line of his man's body, he loved what looked like dressier biker boots for the footwear.

Bert looked over every inch, eager to have this image for his spank bank later. As the door opened, a gust of air moved past him toward his mate. Luc abruptly stood, searching the crowd, causing his guards to surround him, cutting off Bert's view. Bert sighed, disappointed that his time was over so soon. He quietly teleported out.

It had been another month and Bert was beginning to itch to see his mate again. Mac had mentioned they were taking Faolán to Netherworld to play with the other hellhounds. It was hard for him to find pups to play with at the dog park, most avoided him due to his sheer size. Bert thought they could probably sense he wasn't a normal dog either. Viv didn't want him to miss out on playing and being near other canines, so she had tried the park a few times to help him get doggie friends.

Bert decided to stop by Mac's house in Netherworld and return the casserole dish. Mac had made some amazing demon goulash awhile back and he kept forgetting to return the dish they had sent home filled with leftovers. He'd just...wander around and hope to get a glimpse of Lucifer. If not, he'd try again later.

Luc stayed in his seat. He knew his mate was somewhere in this room; his demon was going crazy, urging him to lock the room down and search each person until he found him. He took long measured breaths, filtering out familiar scents to find the one that called to him. His eyes looked over the crowd, trying to find him. There was a light, bright smell, like a combination of fresh air and when you had clothes in the dryer. His demon wanted to roll around in it. As he focused on narrowing down where it came from, it suddenly disappeared. Luc sighed. If his mate had been here and had disappeared again without talking to him, he could only think his mate was shy. Or the more likely reason was that his mate wasn't interested in becoming full mates with him, the pessimistic part of him pointed out.

This was becoming quite the habit, Bert thought to himself in mild disgust. Month three and he was officially stalking his mate. This time he was following him as he went to the grocery store. Bert cloaked himself, not wanting to draw any attention to himself as he followed his mate through the store. He had also coated himself in a spray to keep Luc from catching his scent.

Everyone stopped to talk to Luc; some simple hellos, some asking for help with a problem. It seemed like Lucifer was well-liked, maybe even loved. He wore a pair of dark wash jeans that perfectly cupped his small bubble butt. It looked tight enough that when Bert smacked it, his hand would bounce back. He couldn't wait. No. No. He would wait. That wasn't going to happen.

Bert frowned as Luc only got a few things, people not giving him space to get any real shopping done. It was a constant interruption. An hour into the grocery store trip, Luc finally checked out with only a frozen pizza, ice cream, scotch, and some junk food thrown in at the end from the check-out lane. Luc teleported out, Bert assuming to his home since he had frozen items. Bert followed, porting to his favorite tree. It was technically not on Luc's property, but with a pair of binoculars, it provided the perfect view into Luc's kitchen and Bert was kept out of view. When one demon Enforcer spotted him last time, he simply said he was doing a favor for Mac and that had been the end of the questions.

When he was done stalking his mate, he would pass on the message to put a film over that window that didn't allow people to see in, but for now it was the one window that allowed Bert access to his mate. He watched as Luc threw the pizza in the freezer, frowning as Luc pulled out a huge bowl and proceeded to fill it with ice cream. When the next thing he poured was a glass of scotch on the rocks, Bert wrinkled his nose at the combination. Dark chocolate peanut butter swirl ice cream and thirtyish-year-aged scotch did not go together. Was that really what Luc was eating for dinner? That was unacceptable.

Okay, this was getting ridiculous, Bert told himself. It had been six months and he was still finding ways to stalk his mate. Now he was watching him get his hair cut. He hoped Luc didn't take too much off, he loved the longer hair and the manbun he wore. It would be great for gripping when—No, he told himself. He still sighed in relief when Luc only got an inch trimmed off. Of course, he may have used his magic to move the barber's hand up a couple inches.

Luc eagerly started his day, hoping for a sensation of his mate again. He internally slumped down when there wasn't a trace to be found. It had been quite a while since he had sensed his mate in the hearing room. At first, Luc thought maybe his mate was shy about approaching him due to his position, so he had made it a point to come in early and stay after most people had cleared out to give his mate the opportunity to approach him. He took walks outside more often than usual, including at lunch. No one had approached him that smelled like his mate and he hadn't sensed the other person in months. The only thing that made sense at this point was that his mate didn't want him. He couldn't say it was a huge surprise, but he'd be lying to himself if he said he wasn't disappointed. He supposed it was asking too much to find someone to stand with him. It was a lot of scrutiny and drama. He had his family and his hounds. That would be enough, he told himself firmly as he tried to bury the sadness.

This was the riskiest, Bert thought. Although if he was caught, he'd use the excuse that he was visiting Mac. He cloaked himself, right around the corner of the waiting room doorway. That way he wasn't in the room, but close enough to keep an eye on his mate.

He was really concerned at the look in Luc's eyes. They were panicked and desperate, things that didn't make sense necessarily when waiting for a baby to be born when there had been no indication of problems. When Thomas came over and began to distract Luc, Bert wanted to cheer.

It took longer than Bert thought it would, but they were finally told the baby was born and everyone was healthy. As they were led back to the room, he saw Luc jerk his head back, eyes searching the room. He had thought the nasty cologne he had sprayed on before coming would have covered his scent, but it seemed like his mate still sensed him. He teleported home alone again.

Luc was about to claw his own skin off. He forced himself to keep to his seat, keeping his calm face on. His great-nephew was about to be born, and he wanted to be here to provide his support. They had already talked about him marking the infant with his seal, marking the baby as under his protection. While things had calmed down and it seemed like no other Enforcer families were being targeted, having that mark should put fear in even the most crazy and hardened criminals.

He stared at his phone, wishing it would provide enough distraction that he could behave normally. It wasn't working, but he was still staring at the screen. Maybe he could turn on one of his shows, if that wouldn't be considered rude. His heart was racing and he was doing his best to keep his breaths even. Thomas wouldn't notice, but D certainly could.

He was beginning to worry about how long this was taking. He didn't remember Mac's birth taking this long. His brother and mate had both been demons, so it could be because Viv was human. As a cold sweat tried to make an appearance, Luc closed his eyes, picturing his room at home. He wasn't even far from home, he chided himself. This was the nonhuman hospital, which resided in an in-between plane between Netherworld, Arlysium, and Earth. There were special teleport pads scattered about the realms, making it accessible to everyone, especially those who couldn't teleport themselves. Well, everyone who was nonhuman or part of a nonhuman family like a mate or adopted child. Regular humans wouldn't be able to access it.

"Luc? Do you want a drink? D's going to run to the vending machine," he heard Thomas ask him.

"A Sprite would be lovely, thank you," he replied, hoping it would settle his stomach. "How are your parents?" he asked, trying to distract himself. See, this was normal, it was fine, he tried to convince himself. He knew Thomas and D. Mac and Viv were just down the hall. All normal-ish and safe.

"Good. They're eager to meet their grandson," he said with a smile. "For now, they're babying the dog."

"He's good with them?" Luc asked, eager to check up on one of his pups. He had trained Faolán himself, but he hadn't really exposed him to a regular not-mated-to-a-nonhuman human.

"He is. He's very gentle with them and he seems to know not to do anything hellhound-like near them," Thomas replied. "I think he's going to be glued to the baby. He's been very curious about Viv's belly, always laying his head near it, sniffing."

"I think they'll be great friends. Mac loved having the hellhounds around growing up," Luc said, smiling as he remembered tiny Mac running with the pack. His nephew had been glued to the dogs from the time he was born. He didn't have Luc's ability with them, but they had all adored him. It had been quite the fight to get him to go to school instead of staying with the hounds. Luc had finally told him one would be coming with him to school and that had made Mac agreeable to go.

They both looked up as they heard footsteps coming toward them. They were the only ones in this waiting room, as a deference to Luc's position and Mac's own in the Enforcers.

"Everything ended up going great. Mom and baby are both healthy. The little dickens was shifted, so it made delivery a little harder. Thank goodness for magical medicines. You all are welcome to go visit. Congratulations, sir," the nurse said before walking away.

Thomas ran to the end of the hallway, poking his head around the corner, yelling for his mate. "D! Hurry up, the baby's here! I'm not waiting for you," he said. But Luc could see the smile on his face and knew he was teasing his mate.

Luc started toward the room but turned when he heard Thomas yelp. Laughter exploded out of him, making him a little more comfortable when he saw D barrel toward his smaller mate and toss him over his shoulder before sauntering over to join him. Luc shook his head but was thrilled one of his favorite people had found happiness.

As he began to follow them, the air conditioner turned on and he thought he caught a scent. It was buried under the smell of a horrible cologne that had been giving him a low-grade headache, but his demon swore it was the smell of his mate. Luc looked back, searching the room. When he didn't see anyone in the waiting room, he sighed, but put on his happy face and followed everyone back.

As they entered the room, he could see his nephew beaming with happiness. Viv looked tired but she was focused on the tiny, for a demon anyway, bundle in her arms. As they walked closer, Luc fought back tears as he saw how much the baby looked like Mac when he was born, who looked like his father. He hoped that the souls of his brother and mate were able to see this. They should have been here. He pushed the old anger down, locking it away again. This was a happy day. There was no place for anger or sadness.

"He looks just like you did when you were that age," he said softly to his nephew. He gasped in surprise when the baby opened his eyes. "Well, except for those blue eyes. Those are all your mate. Congratulations! He's perfect," Luc told them. He was adorable with little tiny horn nubs, the coloring and pattern of his demon markings making him a dead ringer for their family.

Now that he knew they were all safe, his skin was crawling with the need to be home. He forced himself to stay a few more minutes before he gave them all a kiss and marked the baby with his seal. Mac quickly swiped a healing salve over it as the baby whimpered.

"Congratulations. He's amazing. I wish I could stay, but work calls me back," he said sadly. It was a total lie. His stupid anxiety over leaving Netherworld was dragging him back home, not work. How fucking weak was that? He couldn't even stay to celebrate his great-nephew's birth for long.

"We'll be there to visit soon," Viv promised him.

Luc gave them one last hug, sending a protective spell over them before leaving the room. He quietly shut the door behind him, checking in with the Enforcers he had called in to protect his family while they were more vulnerable. If he couldn't be here, he wanted to make sure someone he trusted was watching over them. Mac and D were incredible fighters, but they were distracted right now.

As he moved to a corner to teleport home, his nose caught the same intriguing scent his demon had been hunting. He hadn't been imagining things before. *Mate*, his demon clamored. Luc walked around the room, subtly sniffing. He found the scent in an opposite corner, but there was no one there. He wondered if he was just looking for things that smelled similar at this point. What were the odds that his mate had been here, at this specific hospital, in a restricted area? None, that's how many. He needed to accept that his mate didn't want him.

He hadn't told anyone else about sensing his mate. He wished he could vent to someone besides Bal, his hellhound, but there was no need to let anyone else know just what a loser he was that his own mate didn't want him. God would try to tell him it was on the other person, not him. Mac would tell him he was amazing and the best uncle and anyone would be lucky to have him. Viv would hug him, which he needed right about now, and tell him it was their loss. They loved him, so of course they would say something nice. But he knew. If his *fated* mate, the one meant just for him didn't want him...well, he thought that was a pretty clear sign.

His shoulders dropped and he took himself home. Landing in his den, he felt like he could fully breathe again. The evening had pulled on him, even as joyous as it was. The den was warded, so while his Enforcers would know he was home they wouldn't be able to hear him unless he pressed an emergency button.

Grabbing a drink, he collapsed on the couch, Bal porting in to snuggle next to him. Memories flooded him. All the death and fighting from the wars, meeting God, his position appointment, his brother's wedding, Mac being born, his brother's and sister-in-law's deaths. No rhyme or reason, images flashed in his brain, out of order and chaotic. The deaths though, those kept repeating.

Seeing his brother's broken body, his sister-in-law's body ravaged, their breath stopped, with blood pooling around their bodies had broken something in him. He used to travel to all kinds of places and dimensions. He had always been more of a homebody, but he had been able to travel and even enjoy it. The next time he had tried to leave Netherworld after their murders, he had been crippled by a panic attack. He hadn't left since, until tonight. When Mac had first bought the house on Earth, Luc had opened a portal right next it and stood there to examine the wards and reenforce them with his own. He hadn't stepped out of the portal, so he was pretty sure that didn't count as leaving Netherworld.

No one else knew; he worked hard at hiding it. God was the only one in on the secret; he had witnessed Luc's first melt-down when he had tried to go to a meeting in Arlysium. He was a good friend; he had calmed Luc down and had never brought it up again. He simply moved their meetings to Luc's home or office.

He forced those memories away, giving Bal a final scratch behind his ears before standing. Moving to the sink, he washed his face, forcing his expression into work mode before stepping out of his room. The Enforcers would be eager for news on Mac's baby. They were a type of family after all.

3

This was stupid, he thought to himself. He wasn't in a position to take a mate, especially not *The Lucifer*. He had certain needs and tendencies that didn't lend themselves to most relationships. It was why he belonged to exclusive clubs and why he was currently alone. There was absolutely no way Lucifer, the ruler of the Underworld, aka Netherworld, aka Hell, would be into what he was, not in the way he needed. That was a man who had to rule with an iron fist, to be in charge, to apply punishments. No one with even a hint of submissive tendencies would be appointed to that position, much less last so long in it. The Fates had a twisted sense of humor sometimes, but that role would be an enormous strain on that type of personality. Especially to do it alone all these years.

Bert had walked away when he had first seen him at the execution, knowing that this mating had nowhere to go. It didn't matter what he told himself after that, once he had caught the scent of his mate, his body and mind kept reminding him that Luc was right there for the claiming. Heaving a deep sigh, he gave in, teleporting to Netherworld to spy on his mate again. It was judgment time, so he knew where Lucifer would be. It had been months since he had been in the room itself. After the last few times Luc seemed to sense him, he had stayed outside of any building Luc was in and looked through windows. And didn't that make him sound like a creeper peeping Tom?

A few Enforcers saw him, nodding in his direction, assuming he was there on official business. He waited until no one was looking, cloaking himself and following the next group in. He stayed in the far corner, hopefully far enough away that Luc wouldn't notice him. Studying his mate, he frowned in concern. He stayed the entire day, watching as his mate heard the cases. The morning seemed to consist of punishment hearings, but Bert was surprised when later in the day the hearings changed into personal matters. They varied quite a bit; some were demons running ideas by their boss, others asking permission for something, seeking approval for different things. Some were just petty arguments that somehow had made it in front of Luc.

He had no idea how something so stupid as a tree over-hanging a neighbor's yard was Lucifer's job to take care of. There should be someone else to handle the trivial things like this. The Dom in him wanted to storm over and shut it all down and whisk his mate away. He didn't think anyone else noticed, but Luc was clearly tiring, his eyes showed it the most. He soldiered on, the mask never cracking. Bert saw it though. And he wasn't quite sure what to do about it. As the day ended, he waited until Luc was safely out of the room before teleporting to his own home. Luc was looking more tired each time he saw him. It wasn't obvious to others he didn't think, but he was certainly noticing changes in the man. Changes he wasn't happy to see.

His heart tried shoving out a bit of hope. Maybe his mate did need him. Maybe the Fates hadn't fucked up their pairing. This was either the most brilliant or the most stupid thing he had ever done, he thought to himself as he pulled out his phone.

"Mac, it's Bert. Can we talk? I hate to bug you when you've got a newborn. But I really need a friendly ear for advice," he said as his friend answered. He had grown pretty close to the demon after working together on the serial killer case. He didn't have many other close friends, a few work friends, which meant they hung out at lunch if they were in the same area, but that was it. Plus, given that Lucifer was his uncle, maybe he could give some insight.

"Yeah, of course! He just went to sleep. Could you come over here? I told Viv I'd take the night feedings tonight so she could sleep," his friend replied.

"Yeah, that works. I'll teleport in so my bike doesn't wake him. Need anything before I come over?"

"I don't think so," Mac replied.

"Be there in a few," Bert said, hanging up the phone. How stupid was this?

He shook his head at himself, teleporting to Mac's front porch, knocking softly.

The door swung open, Mac standing there. He could feel a similarity, a sense of family, coming from Mac. He could now tell that Mac was related to his mate. It was crazy that he had been here multiple times before, but it wasn't until he smelled his mate that he could actually sense the family line in Mac.

"Hey," Mac said with a smile. "Thanks for the gift card and the baby basket. I haven't gotten around to sending out the thank-you notes yet. They're still sitting at the front door," he said, rolling his eyes at himself.

"You've been a little busy," Bert replied, shaking hands.

"I've got coffee, water, soda, beer…" Mac offered.

"I'll take a beer," he replied. He waited, standing, until Mac handed him his drink and sat.

"Viv and the baby are asleep. Thomas and D are having a date night out, so it's just us," Mac told him. "What's up?"

"I found my mate," Bert began then paused, not sure how to quite tell Mac it was his uncle.

"That's amazing! Congratulations! Who is it? Do I know them?" Mac asked, a huge smile overtaking his face.

"Yeah, well...about that. Okay. So first. Yes, you do, but I haven't talked to them yet."

"Why? Are they human? Don't do what I did and stay away," Mac warned him.

"No, he's nonhuman."

Mac waited a few seconds before asking, "What's the problem then?"

"I have a few tendencies that make it hard to find someone to have a relationship with," he started. "It's not just work," he said, holding up a hand when Mac opened his mouth to talk. "I'm a Dom. And not the Daddy type, although I do enjoy caring for my partners. I enjoy giving out spankings or whippings, having orgasm control, that type of thing. If I fully trust my partner, I can be vers, but I really prefer to top."

"I'm glad you know what you like, buddy. But I don't think I needed to know all of that," Mac said dryly.

"For this, you do. I scented my mate at the serial killer execution. I left before talking to him. He's in a position of power. There's just no way he could meet my needs, right? But then I visited him at work. I was cloaked and stayed in the back so he wouldn't notice me—"

"That sounds familiar," Mac muttered.

Bert had to laugh. Mac had done his own bit of stalking Viv before finally getting his head out of his ass.

"Yeah, yeah. So anyway, I noticed it was wearing on him. No one else noticed, but I could tell. His face never changed, always calm, but his eyes showed me the strain as the day went on. And my stupid heart is trying to tell me that maybe he does need me, but I just can't see how his job and my needs meet up."

"How many times have you spied on him?" Mac asked.

"A few," Bert muttered. More than he felt comfortable admitting.

"I can give general advice like talk to him and listen, but unless you tell me his name, I can't really give better advice."

"I'm not sure you really want to know," Bert warned him.

"It's up to you," Mac said, shrugging.

Bert drew in a deep breath, hoping he wasn't going to lose a friend. "It's Luc."

Mac stared at him blankly, not speaking, not even blinking.

"Your uncle," Bert clarified, although he didn't think there was another nonhuman named Luc that they both knew.

He watched as Mac abruptly surged to his feet, his muscles tight. Bert was ready to take a punch, and he really wouldn't blame him. He basically told his friend that he would want to spank or whip his uncle and fuck him. Instead, Mac walked to the kitchen, pulling down two short glasses, popping a round ice cube in each, before filling one with whiskey. He downed it in one shot, filling it back up, drinking that one as well, before filling both glasses and walking over to the couch. He silently handed a glass to Bert.

Grateful, he took a bracing sip. Oh, this was the good

stuff. He decided he had said enough and waited while Mac processed. He saw Viv poke her head out of the bedroom, Faolán standing with her. He waved, and after she waved back, she went back inside. She had probably felt Mac's turmoil over their bond.

It was several minutes before Mac spoke, which gave Bert time to look around the room. There were now outlet plugs, a baby swing, bottles drying on the kitchen counter, a play mat in the corner, dog bowls by the kitchen, and a basket of dog toys by a plush bed. His friend had clearly settled into family life and he was incredibly happy for him. Although he didn't see kids in his future, he was hoping he would eventually have a home life like this. A partner to share his day with, family stopping by. Dogs would be nice.

"I'm trying really hard not to punch you right now," Mac said in a very calm tone. "The execution was almost a year ago. I've noticed Uncle seemed sadder, but I thought, probably self-centeredly, that it had to do with me moving away and spending most of my time on Earth. It didn't occur to me that his mate had found him and left him alone."

"I didn't want to fuck up his life, Mac. I don't see how this ends well."

"I'm glad that Fate hasn't forgotten him," Mac said slowly. "I'll even be happy that he has you as a mate, after I'm done being mad at you. You're strong enough to help support the burden of his position, you're in a job that enables you to understand his to a point. You know that it will be a huge part of your lives, that it's not one he can quit. How important it is. You're a great friend, and you've been there for me at some of the worst moments.

"I've only seen Uncle as a leader, or as a father figure. I honestly don't know what his sexual tendencies are. I've never seen him bring anyone home. If he had lovers, he met with them somewhere else. But since everyone would know him, even if he did have sub tendencies, he probably wouldn't have acted on those with strangers. He needs to keep up appearances and I know he's had to defend his position many times, although not in my lifetime that I can remember.

"I know he needs someone to support him, someone he can talk to, someone to lean on. Everyone needs that. I know he's lonely. Have you never really met him before? Seriously? I know you've been in Netherworld multiple times."

Bert shook his head. "Never. I don't think I've even been in the same room until the execution. I've mostly visited the Enforcer offices or a few punishment levels. It is really odd that we haven't met before now."

"As much as I hate to say it, my best advice is still to talk to him. He's kept that part of his life away from me, so I really don't know. I believe that the Fates wouldn't fuck him over on his mate, especially after all this time, so you must be compatible. Which I don't need to know about since he's my uncle and helped raise me. You will have to go to him. He usually doesn't leave Netherworld so he can be ready if work needs him," Mac cautioned.

Bert downed the rest of his drink. "Damn it. I don't even know what to say to him. How do I bring that up? 'Hey, I'm your mate. Want to kneel for me?'"

Mac gagged. "I don't want to know!" he said loudly. "Maybe start with just 'Hi, I'm your mate. My name is Bert. I'm an Enforcer.' Something like that," Mac said. "There's got to be a way for you two to work it out."

"Yeah. Maybe."

ert needed to clear his head. The talk with Mac helped a little, but he still wasn't convinced claiming his mate, or at least introducing himself was the best move for either of them. It's not like his tendencies weren't known in certain circles, and the last thing he would want to do is bring trouble to his mate's doorstep. He didn't have any spurned lovers or anything stupid like that, but if the people who knew about him being a Dom saw him with Lucifer as his mate, they might talk. The clubs had a contract everyone signed, but he was sure that didn't stop people from gossiping. Gossiping could lead to someone challenging Luc for his position. Unless the contracts were magically enhanced. Huh. He had never thought about that possibility. Maybe he could ask the owners of the clubs he visited; all the ones he was a member of were nonhuman ones.

He nodded to himself, happy to have a place to begin. One that didn't involve confronting his mate. They could build their own room at home, but it might be nice if he could bring Luc to a club to show him all the different possibilities. Which would only work if there was a magical silencing clause; he would never endanger his mate. He changed into his tighter leather pants, his biker boots, a snug black t-shirt, and finished it with a wide leather cuff watch. He thought about adding a leather vest, but since he wasn't planning on playing, left it off. He took one last look in the mirror and teleported to his favorite one.

"Hello, Mr. Bert!" The attendant smiled in his direction.

"Hello, Hailey. Is Charles in tonight? I needed to talk to him."

"Yes, he is. He should be in his office. It doesn't look like he has meetings tonight. I'll call and let him know you're coming," she said.

"Thanks." Bert pressed his hand to the scanner, the wards letting him in. Looking around, he saw a lot of familiar faces, some looking to catch his attention to play. He hadn't visited since he realized he had a mate; he didn't feel comfortable having a scene, even if it wasn't sexual. He stopped briefly to watch a flogging on the Saint Andrew's cross in the middle of the room. His cock didn't even twitch. Huh.

He continued down a hallway, knocking on Charles' door, waiting until he heard an 'enter.'

"Good evening, Bert. Please have a seat. Hailey said you wanted to see me?"

Bert nodded, and noticed the sub sitting at Charles' feet. He looked at them and then back up to Charles, who nodded.

"Could you give us a few minutes, love. Wait in our room. I'll call you when I'm done," Charles said.

As the door shut, Bert spoke up. "Sorry to interrupt your night, but I have a delicate situation I wanted advice for." He had known Charles for many years, in fact he had worked with him in the Arlysium Enforcers for a while before Charles retired and opened his club. He could consider him one of his friends even.

"It's no bother. What's the matter?"

"I met my mate."

"Congratulations! Is that why we haven't seen you lately?" Charles exclaimed, smiling. When Bert didn't smile back, Charles' dropped off. "Or not?"

"Do you have a silencing spell on the office?" Bert asked.

Charles nodded looking concerned.

"I have a lot of things to run by you, but first—and do not take this the wrong way—are there magical components to the nondisclosure part of the contract, including members, staff, contractors, anyone who might see into the club or its records?"

"There are," Charles said, drawing out his words. He looked confused. "Has someone broken your trust here?"

"No! Nothing like that. I promise it will make sense soon. If I brought him here, I'd need to know those are iron-tight, that no one could take a picture, speak or write of it outside of the club, anything like that."

"I will go over it again to make sure, but the way it is worded no one would be able to say anything about what goes on in the club. Not even drawing or pointing or pantomiming," Charles confirmed.

"Okay, good. Thank you. My second problem ties into the first a little bit. I haven't introduced myself to my mate yet. He isn't known as being submissive and I'm worried that if I make myself known to him and we do become official mates, then it could cause problems for him. Hell, I don't even know if he has submissive tendencies."

"If he's your mate, you must be compatible in some way," Charles pointed out. "You may need to teach him about BDSM, but that could be a lot of fun," he said, winking.

Bert laughed. It would be fun rediscovering things with Luc.

"If you think it would be a huge problem, maybe you could speak to God or Lucifer to see if they could maybe subtly have your back? Or something to make it seem like no matter what, he's perfect at his position or whatever you're worried about, no matter what he likes in his personal life," Charles suggested.

Bert paused. Charles had always been truthful with him and had had his back on several occasions when they worked together. "I need a blood vow that what I'm about to tell you will not be shared," he said, staring right at Charles, letting him know how serious he was.

Charles looked at him closely, nodded once, and grabbed a dagger from his desk. Slicing across his palm, he let it drip on a piece of paper as he chanted in Entiretium. There was a flash as the vow concluded.

"My mate is Lucifer."

"Well shit. That does change things," Charles admitted, sitting back.

"Yeah. He's held his position for a long time and he's great at it. I don't want to jeopardize that. He hasn't had a challenger in years, but if they got wind that he might be less dominant than they expected, there could be problems. People not in the lifestyle automatically think subs are weaker, which we know isn't true."

"That's true," Charles agreed. He looked thoughtful though. "After the execution, I think that many would hesitate. He was brutal as he killed that man. And I've heard stories of some of his other exploits. Luc has a reputation for a reason. You would have to be insane to challenge him. Especially since it was made clear that God and he were united. They get along well, I can't imagine God would want another demon in his place. I really believe that God and Lucifer are meant for those roles; I even question whether the Fates would allow them to be dethroned so to speak.

"Mates are also allowed to protect each other. I think that having you as his mate, would actually strengthen his position. Someone would have to be willing to take on both of you."

"Mates aren't allowed to join in the challenge," Bert pointed out.

"Ah, that's true," Charles said with a smile, "but they are allowed to avenge their mate. There's no clarification that excludes challenges from that. So, they would have to be willing to take on Lucifer, knowing they could lose and die, or win and face you and die then. I'd bet Mac wouldn't let it go either. And D would totally help him. They're practically brothers. Someone would have to be willing to take on the whole family. Not that there isn't someone that stupid, but I don't think he would lose and if he makes it an event, like the execution was, no one would be stupid enough to try it again. Don't let the possibility of assholes steal your mate from you. At least talk to him and get his opinion. He deserves to have a say.

"As far as taking him to a club, I would stay away from the other two you frequent. I've heard rumors about a change in management that might be happening and I think it's going to lose them a lot of members, especially those who value their privacy. You make me wonder who else might be afraid to come here. I think it's time to up the club's wards and make the contracts iron tight, maybe include a blood vow. We can always reserve a room for you so you're not out in the main areas, or if you wanted to come before opening so you're alone. You need a safe place to show him the lifestyle and there's no way you can fit all the equipment available here in your place," Charles laughed.

"No, it's pretty small," he admitted. Luc's was of course bigger, but then again if they were exploring things, he didn't think Luc would want others to overhear or see anything. There were Enforcers nearby at all times, either guarding the house, stopping by, or those who lived on the street. "Thanks. You're a good friend," he said, standing and holding out a hand to shake.

"There's not many of us with our experiences. We need to stick together," Charles replied. Bert knew he was referring to the combination of being Enforcers and Doms. Some were one or the other, but not many had been both. Fighting together had formed its own kind of bond as well. "Good luck. I'll say a prayer for you."

Bert gave him a quick back-thumping hug before teleporting to his place. Now to create a plan to speak to his mate.

L uc walked through the ward, eager to get a shower. He had been visiting the punishment levels and had made a stop at the cells that held the men who had participated in Viv's kidnapping and torture. Most of them had been killed during the rescue, other than the mind bender and the big guy who had left before Mac got there. The mind bender had already been taken care of, as per the agreement Mac had made with him. His soul had been destroyed. The others were souls that he had locked away for their punishments, which was less messy, but not quite as satisfying.

The big one that had left early and evaded capture, he had been brought in alive later. For as much as he hated the wars, there was something about beating the shit out of someone who deserved it that made him feel calmer and he had come down here to try to work out some frustration. No matter what he did tonight, the guy only felt regret at getting caught, not regret at his actions. There really was no hope for some people. Luc had killed the man's physical body, leaving the soul trapped in the room.

His demon side had been moody and angry for months now, convinced they had been near their mate and they must have rejected him. Which he could understand; his job wasn't normal, it was on-call all the time, he sometimes came home bloody. He didn't want to lose his edge or to have his men believe he thought he was above them, so he made it a point to visit the punishment levels and assist at least once or twice a week. Although lately, his time there had been pretty limited; there had been an increase in hearings for him to oversee, both in punishments and disputes, he had a few rising Enforcers he was helping to mentor, Mac and Viv had been visiting with the baby, and he had a new litter of hellhounds.

Speaking of which...he looked down as he felt a pop of air next to him.

"Don't give me that look, Bal. I wasn't gone that long," Luc told his hellhound. He raised and trained all of them, but there were a few that he just bonded to more deeply. Bal was one of those and while he wanted to go everywhere Luc did, for now he was usually restricted to home. He was still very much a pup, barely old enough to be considered full grown.

He got a doggie huff in return. He dropped his clothes down the chute; each of the shower rooms on the punishment levels had one and they led directly to the incinerator. Blood and guts really didn't come out of clothes well. It's why he paid for uniforms for his men. There was no use having them ruin their own clothes. They could wear whatever they wanted, but after a week of being on the job, they tended to switch to the uniform.

Luc grabbed the nail brush, making sure to clean under his nails. You would think that shifting would help, but nope. Stuff that got under his demon nails stayed there unless he really scrubbed. The loofa was soaped and he started scrubbing his horns. His were a little bigger than his nephew's, both thicker and in length. They curled and twisted in a double loop, reaching down to his ears. The twists meant that he needed to really scrub well, or he'd be left with bits and pieces.

Luckily his wings usually only needed a good spray of water to rinse off. They were the easiest thing to clean. He grimaced as a piece of goop fell to the shower floor. He needed to wash his hair again apparently. Thank goodness they didn't get diseases or it would make his job much harder with blood-borne pathogens. Switching to his human side, he gave himself a once-over before deciding he was probably clean.

"Good enough, Bal?" he asked as he stepped out of the shower. Getting a rumble of agreement, he grabbed the change of clothes he kept here. "Ready to go home? I think I have some steaks for you guys." He wasn't above bribing his dog. Bal could hold a grudge.

He teleported to the edges of his land, Bal following him. He wanted to walk the rest of the way home, be visible to his men, make sure he was available if they needed to talk to him.

"Good evening, sir! How's the baby?" one of the mates called out as she watched her kids play in the front yard.

"Adorable! He looks so much like Mac. Although he has blue eyes like his mom."

"And you," she pointed out.

"True." He smiled. "Everything going well? Do you guys need anything?"

"Oh, no. We're great, thank you for asking."

"Can we have a hellhound?" a smaller voice piped up. Luc saw one of her youngest hiding behind her, just peeking her face out to stare at Bal.

Luc glanced up and saw Elaine's wide eyes and the subtle shake of the head. He knew they had four young ones and a puppy, even a well-trained one, would be hard on them.

"All of the pups have homes right now, but maybe when you're older," Luc said. He watched as the girl's face fell in disappointment.

"But...I do have something you can have now," he said, crouching down to her level. He clicked his fingers behind his back, drawing the object from his stash. Pulling it out from behind him, he gave her the hellhound stuffed animal. It was almost as big as her. She squealed and grabbed the plush, hugging it tight.

"Thank you, Mr. Lucifer! Thank you, thank you, thank you!" She threw herself at him in a quick hug and ran off into the house.

"Thank you for not saying yes. I don't think I could handle a pup on top of these guys," Elaine said gratefully. "The stuffie was a nice touch, you made her day."

"I'm glad it made her happy. Let me know if you all need anything, even if it's a date night." He'd babysat in the past for a lot of his Enforcers, especially those in his personal guard.

"Thank you. I may take you up on that; our anniversary is coming up." Elaine grinned.

"Just let me know when," Luc replied before continuing down the street.

He waved hello to a few other families who were out and crossed the boundary of his own yard. Almost home, he thought to himself.

"Sir. There's an angel here to see you," Alan said, stopping him before he opened the front door.

Luc frowned. He wasn't expecting anyone; he didn't have any meetings scheduled or any open collaborations with Arlysium. "Do you know who it is?"

Alan nodded. "Bert. He's an Enforcer on the Arlysium side. He worked with Mac on the cult case."

"Where is he?"

"The front sitting room."

"Thank you, Alan." Luc couldn't think of a reason why he would be here, especially this late at night. He glanced up at the green moon as it began to rise, noticing it was almost full. He took a deep breath in. Just one more thing and he'd be done for at least a little while. He let it out slowly, opening the door.

As he stepped inside and shut the door behind him, his demon roared. He was here. His mate. The mate who had stayed away from him for almost a year. Well, fuck him. He could just stay away longer.

"Don't, mate," a deep voice commanded him. Luc hadn't even realized his hand was back on the doorknob about to turn it.

Luc frowned as his body automatically stopped and a tingle went through him. Well, that was new. He'd had people tell him what to do before but had never had that reaction. He thumped his dick, telling it to stay down. Now was not the time.

Lucifer straightened his back, threw on his work face and slowly turned around, his body tight with tension and anger. His mate was handsome, he'd admit, as Bert came out of the sitting room. He allowed himself a quick glance over the man. Shorter than him, probably around five foot eleven or so, bald head, dark eyes, scruffy beard, and covered in muscles and tattoos.

"I don't think you get to tell me what to do. Mate. It's been a year, so any input you may have had a right to has since disappeared. Kindly fuck off," Luc said before porting to his den. No one could enter without his permission. Only a very few had permanent access, like Mac and Viv. His den had everything he needed, so he could stay here until Bert left. If he didn't leave soon, he'd tell Alan something had come up and have him ask Bert to leave, that he couldn't meet with him today. As much as he was hurt and angry that his mate had finally decided to show up, he knew Bert was great at his job and didn't want to make waves with that. He'd keep it polite. While he didn't want to jeopardize his job, he also didn't want anything to do with him.

"He's avoiding me, Mac. I went to his house and he teleported to a room I couldn't enter. I waited but the Enforcer there politely asked me to leave when it looked like he wasn't coming back. I tried catching him after work, same thing. One time he had the hellhounds surround me until he got away.

"He, um. He's known all this time that he ran into his mate and now he's pissed that I stayed away for so long."

"He's kind of right to, Bert. I get you were trying to protect him, but this year has been the hardest on him that I've ever seen. And yeah, there was lots going on with me and Viv, but I think knowing he had a mate out there that he believed didn't want him, played a big part. I know you do, but I don't think he does."

"I need to actually talk to him, to explain at least. I don't want him thinking it was him or something equally stupid, but I can't even get one word out before he disappears again," Bert said, frustrated.

"You need to catch him by surprise," Mac said.

"Mac," Viv warned.

"You know it's true. You agreed to being my friend and

seeing how things went after I was an idiot, so I could show up and be there, support you, send you gifts. If Bert can't even get an apology in, I doubt any gifts would be welcomed."

Viv sighed. "Probably," she reluctantly agreed. "You could try sending him a letter?"

"I did," Bert admitted. "I had a pile of ash sitting on my desk the next day. God was laughing at me, so I think he knows at least a little bit."

"Oh," Viv replied. "I still don't think surprising him is the best idea. He's made it this far in life by not being surprised, and I can't think he'd react well," she cautioned. The baby made a whimpering cry from the other room and she jumped up.

"That's the 'I am wet and uncomfortable and I'm about to scream this house down until I'm dry' sound," Mac said dryly.

"Fun?" Bert wasn't sure how to answer that.

"Look. I'm going to suggest something, but if you fail at getting his forgiveness, it's going to really fuck up my relationship with him. So don't fail, got it?"

Bert nodded. "What is it?"

Mac sighed. "I can't believe I'm going to do this. I can get into his den and let you in. It's his safe room, as it were. I have access to get in and can voluntarily bring another person with me. It was for when I had D over when we were kids and Uncle wanted me to be able to find a safe place if an attack ever came, but he knew I would never leave a friend behind. I don't know why he warded it that way, but it's a loophole we could use.

"You're going to have to find a way to keep him there long enough to explain yourself and get his forgiveness. I never thought I'd say this sentence, but it may be time to treat him like your sub and not the leader of Netherworld."

"So, what's the plan?"

Bert waited nervously in the den. He wasn't sure when Lucifer would be home, but Mac assured him he almost always came in here to decompress after work. Bert had Luc's favorite drinks and snacks ready, flowers hidden, and a plan of attack. As well as a tube of lube. Just in case.

He stayed hidden, feeling the flex in the wards as Luc ported in. He watched as the man poured himself a drink and took a sip, while slipping out of his boots. His mask fell away and Bert could see the tension and exhaustion he was really feeling.

For a moment, Bert again wondered if this was the right thing to do, but when Luc looked up, finally catching his scent, he knew he didn't have another option. Bert stepped out of the shadows, letting his mate see him.

"How did you get in here?" Luc asked, his voice furious, his eyes burning with flames.

That was kind of hot, Bert thought.

"We need to talk, and you need to listen," Bert said.

He watched as Luc shook his head, his lips firmly pressed together. He mentally sighed knowing his man was about to teleport out again. As he felt the change in air pressure, he dove forward, tackling Luc to the ground, holding his wrists above his head, straddling the amazingly hard body. His mate was dressed in a dark burgundy-brown suit with cream pinstripes. He wanted to slide it off and explore but he didn't have the right to. Yet. He held on as Luc fought back. Luc had the advantage of being taller, but Bert probably had close to the same muscle mass and was equally determined.

Luc wrestled one hand free and Bert saw the fist coming at him. "No, mate," he commanded, putting every little bit of Dom he had behind it. He was honestly a little shocked when the fist stopped. Maybe Luc did have what he needed after all, maybe he wasn't going to screw everything up.

The fight went out of Luc as confusion took over. "Why did that work? No one's ever been able to stop me with words. What type of magic do you have?"

"Did it feel like magic?" Bert asked, gently easing the hand back with the other, holding them both loosely against the carpet.

"No," Luc replied. He was squirming slightly. Not enough that you could see it visibly, but with Bert straddling him, he could feel it. Ah, someone was getting aroused, Bert thought as he felt Luc's dick begin to press against him.

"I know why it worked and I can explain, but I need you to stay here and actually listen," Bert told him firmly.

When Luc nodded, Bert loosened the grip on his wrists, keeping one hand gently resting on them and placing his other hand on Luc's sternum, fingertips brushing his throat.

"I saw you at the execution and thought you were exceptional. I had to hide my hard-on. You were utterly amazing and I wanted you." Bert stopped when Luc snorted in disbelief.

"Stop. You were and are. I'm getting there. I was horrified when I realized who you were. Not," he said strongly when he felt the muscles underneath him tense, "because of who you are, but because of who I am and the combination. I didn't want to hurt you or cause you problems."

"What problems?"

"What problems?" Luc asked. He didn't really want to listen, but his demon had firmly planted its ass on the ground and wasn't helping him fight back. If he was so amazing, he couldn't think of why Bert had stayed away. He also couldn't figure out why being held down was arousing him; he had never let anyone have this kind of power over him before and other than them being mates, he wasn't sure why he was allowing it. He hadn't even fought that hard, he could easily have flipped the situation if he had tried.

"I'm a Dom. As in Dominant. As in—"

"I know what a Dom is," Luc said. That was…not what he expected to hear. He knew of BDSM of course, even knew some people who were in the lifestyle. You'd be amazed at who he knew who was in it. But he had never experimented with it.

"Don't interrupt," Bert chided. "I'm not exactly hiding that part of myself. I don't have it as a bumper sticker on my motorcycle, but it's not a secret either. I worried that if you were known to be my mate that it could cause you problems. You've held your position for longer than anyone else. I didn't want to be the reason why the challenges started again."

"You think they'll see me as weak," Luc said flatly.

Bert shrugged. "I was also worried that you wouldn't be into the lifestyle, which is something I need on a deep level. I need to be in charge and help. I prefer to top. I think people would assume you were a sub and yes, that some stupid people could use that as an excuse to challenge you. You are strong, whether you're a sub or not. You've proven that over and over and that doesn't change because of your personal preferences."

Luc tried to listen to what Bert was really saying. But he kept getting caught up on the fact that if Bert was here, he must think that Luc was a sub in some way.

"What about you?"

"What? Think of you as weaker if you were a sub?" Bert asked. When Luc nodded, Bert leaned down, staring him in the eyes. "No. Never. I want to make you happy, keep you safe. I would never tell you how to do your job. Subs can stop a scene with one word, they hold power. It's simply that you want to give up control part, or in some cases all, of the time. That you want someone to carry the burden for a little bit, to have someone support you and that can include telling you what to do in the bedroom or in the privacy of our own home. I would never do anything to undermine you in public. I understand the importance of your role in our world and don't want to interfere with that at all. I need to feel needed, to care for someone."

"How would this work then?" Luc asked. He had yearned for someone to share the burden with, and Bert's words seemed a dream come true. He knew he should still be mad at him. It had been almost a year since they had realized they had a mate. A year that they could have been together. A year of Luc thinking he wasn't good enough for his mate. Logically, he should be furious. His heart though, that yearned for a partner and for someone to lean on. The Fates gave him Bert. He was tired of being alone and was cautiously optimistic that Bert could be the mate he needed and wanted. He was old enough to know not to let his anger and hurt blind him to what could be. He had preached to Mac not to let the past ruin his future, and it would be hypocritical of him to not follow his own advice.

"You learn to trust me. We try scenes together, figure out what you like. First, we need a safe word for you. Humans like the traffic light system: red for immediate stop, green for good to go, and yellow to slow it down, pause and talk. But if you're not used to those things, we can come up with something else that you can easily remember. Second, while I prefer to be called Sir or Master, neither one of those will work in public for your position, so we need to find something else that we will know means the same thing."

"I thought you said you wouldn't interfere with my job?"

"I won't. But I've watched you and there's been times I wanted to jump in and make you take a break. That's where our titles will be useful; if I use it, you know to pay atten-tion. The usual Boy or Pet or Sub doesn't work for you in public and I don't want to have two different sets of names. It needs to be something we can use in public and private, that way neither one of us inadvertently blurts it out and causes people to question you. For example, if I noticed you were getting overwhelmed, I could say 'Boy, I need your advice/there's a call for you/someone is here to speak to you.' You would reply with 'Yes/I need one moment/I'll be right there, Sir.' But the boy and sir need to be our words.

We'd take a quick break, no one would be any wiser, and you could go right back to work like nothing happened. Or if I'm not there, you could call and use the word we pick for Sir and I would know you need me."

Luc nodded. It made sense when he said it that way. But could he really give up control and submit to someone? It had never been in his mindset to have that ability to let go. That had been drilled into him from the time he had been born.

"What if I'm not a sub?"

"I don't think the Fates would have messed with us like that. I think it's something you have, but probably never thought of. We can take it slow, try new things. This type of relationship requires complete trust. If that means we date a bit like humans do, that's what we do. I don't expect to complete the mate bond without you fully trusting me. Even though I was doing it to protect you, I know staying away caused a break in our trust."

Luc took a minute to think over his response. He had been fully prepared to live the rest of his life alone, both when he hadn't found his mate and also when he had sensed him but thought he had been rejected. It would be so nice to have someone to share his life with. And to be able to lay down the burden of his position for a little bit sounded like a dream come true. Mac knew a bit of his job, but he kept the worst of what he had done away from his nephew, even though he was an adult now. He had his den as his sanctuary, but he only allowed himself to be in here for brief moments since he needed to be accessible for his people and Enforcers.

"I would like to explore this with you. I do need to keep it separate from my work. Not that I want to hide you, but our private life needs to stay private. I have no intentions of stepping down from my role, nor do I want to bring trouble to my family. People may make assumptions, but if we keep personal things quiet, it may help with speculation and gossip. I also will not back down from challenges. God and I have kept a good balance and I don't want that disrupted. If you have a problem with me fighting, then we should just stop here." It would suck, but better to know now than later.

"If it comes to that, I'll be there to cheer you on," Bert promised. He sat back, letting his hands rest on Luc's chest.

He kind of missed his hands being held down. Weird. He let his hands move to grip Bert's hips. How long had it been since he'd held someone like this? Probably before Mac had come to live with him. Once he had custody of Mac, he hadn't wanted to bring anyone into their home and in the beginning he was a bit of a helicopter parent. Which he supposed was understandable with the circumstances. Then he just got used to being alone. It was hard to know who to trust even for one-night stands.

"Let's grab a drink. We can go over any questions you might have, talk about basic rules, and I'll reward you when we're done," Bert said, smirking down at him.

A reward? "What kind of reward?" Luc asked, curious. His dick twitched, knowing what kind of reward it wanted.

Bert ground his ass against Luc's groin, grinning at the moan that escaped Luc. "One you'll like." Bert climbed off him, holding a hand out to help him up, which made Luc snort when they stood. He was easily a head taller than his mate. When he shifted to his demon form, he'd be a giant. Angels sometimes bulked up, but not as much as demons.

Luc walked over to the small bar he kept in here, feeling his mate behind him. He really had no idea how they would pull this off. Handing off his stress to someone else even for a little while seemed like a dream come true, but there needed to be a clear distinction. His job was never up for debate, not with so many lives riding on his decisions.

Pouring a drink for both of them, Luc took one corner of the couch. He needed some space to process. His body wanted to be close to its mate, but his brain was using some caution. While he could understand the logic of why Bert stayed away, that didn't erase the hurt he had felt.

Luc watched as Bert took a sip of his drink, watching his throat swallow. He held back a groan wondering what that would feel like against his cock. He wanted to find out, but for now he was content with allowing himself to study his mate. When they stood together, Bert came to around Luc's chin, making him a little under six feet tall. Luc himself was around six foot seven, taller when he was in full demon form. Bert had a shaved head, so no hair to grab on to, but he had a scruffy goatee and beard. He had large biceps, a clearly defined six-pack even through his shirt. Luc could see the tattoos peeking out from under his shirt on his chest, not to mention the arm tats. Not quite a full sleeve, but they were covered pretty well. He had a deep commanding voice, strong thick thighs, and a lovely bubble butt that Luc really wanted to sink his teeth into.

"How much do you know about BDSM?" Bert asked as he settled down into the couch. He gave Luc room but was close enough to reach out and touch.

"About the same as most not in the lifestyle, I guess. I know a few people in it, but we don't really talk about it."

"If you trust them, they're probably a good resource to talk to besides me. I can give you some websites to look at. Not all online information is great, so try the ones I give you first. The way it is supposed to work, subs hold the power. Everyone not into kink thinks differently, but a sub can stop a scene with a single word and the Dom is supposed to listen. That's why you need to come up with a word you will remember, no matter what. It should be uncommon enough that it won't be something you would normally say so it catches attention, but easy to remember."

"Can we stick with the traffic lights?" Luc asked. He didn't want to worry about what word to pick and the people he knew in the lifestyle had talked about it before so he should remember them. He knew enough not to pick 'stop.'

"That works for me. I'm going to give you a starter list of things to go over. Mark if you are interested, if you're a maybe, or if they're a hard no. If it's a no, it's a no. I'm not going to try to change your mind. I have some of my own that I'll share after you make your list," Bert said, handing over the sheet.

Luc looked it over, his nose wrinkling at some of the items in the bodily fluids section. While he didn't mind cum on him, urine and other things were a hard no. Bert handed him a pen, laughing.

"I can tell you found a no already," he said. "That's also one of mine," he added when Luc marked the page.

Luc paused when he got to the bondage section. The idea of it was sexy, but he had no idea what the actuality of it would be.

"What's that look?" Bert asked.

"I think I would be interested, but I'm not sure. It would also need to be somewhere where no one could interrupt us," Luc replied, his face heating. He didn't want Bert to think he was ashamed of them, of trying this. He certainly didn't want to make his mate feel bad for what he needed, but there were some things he didn't think the nonhumans he was in charge of would accept. Their big bad scary leader tied up and helpless was one of them, even if it made arousal course through him as images flooded his imagination.

"I understand that. I truly do. We would figure out something for in here or at the club I mentioned earlier. You're a private person to start with and your job has probably only increased that. As long as you don't deny we're mates, I can keep everything else private," Bert reassured him. He could even think of a few people himself who would probably think mean thoughts or change their opinions of Luc if they even had an inkling that they were talking about this. People needed to learn to stay out of other people's bedrooms, and he had no problem reminding them of this if needed. He quickly schooled his grin when he saw Luc eyeing him.

They went over a few more things before Bert called an end to their conversation. He didn't want to overwhelm Luc and he also wanted to give him time to think things over on his own. "I think that's a good start for today. Plus, you need your sleep for tomorrow. But first, let me give you your reward," Bert told him, sliding a hand toward his pants. When he rested it on Luc's belt, he looked at Luc for permission. They were nowhere close to having assumed consent for things like this yet. Luc lifted his hips, begging for a touch.

"I need the words, mate."

"Yes, please," Luc said, his voice husky with want. He watched with eager eyes as Bert undid his belt and zipper, keeping his hips in the air to help slide his pants off.

"Hmm. I love boxer briefs. They look amazing on your legs," Bert said, running a nose along the growing bulge. Taking a deep breath, he relished the smell of his Luc. A bit smoky, a bit of musk, and all male. He drew the long, thick shaft out, a bead of precum already on the tip. Luc was uncut, his cock gorgeous, and Bert was struck by a vision of Luc with a Jacob's Ladder. They could have so much fun with it, and with a demon's increased healing, not to mention healing potions, they wouldn't even have to stop playing for more than a day. Something to bring up later.

He ran a tongue along the underside, watching as the foreskin disappeared as Luc became fully erect. It had been many, many years since he had bottomed, but Luc's dick made him think about trying it again. Luc was big enough that it would cause him to walk funny; it would feel incredible. He closed his fist around Luc's shaft, dragging his hand slowly up and down, pulling the foreskin with each tug. His other hand wasn't idle, moving to lightly run his fingertips across the drawn-up balls. The shiver in Luc's thigh muscles meant he must be close and Bert quickly wrapped his fingers tightly around the base, creating an impromptu cock ring. It wouldn't last for long, but it would be enough to draw Luc back from the edge.

At Luc's whine, Bert told him, "Not yet. You can come when I decide." It was a little heavy-handed maybe for their first time together, but he wanted to give Luc a taste and also test him to see what his limits might be. He watched as Luc's pupils blew at his words, little flames dancing inside them. Ah, he did like that. "Green?" he asked, just to make sure.

Luc nodded, panting. "Yes, Green."

Bert nodded, keeping his fingers wrapped tight, sucking Luc down deep until his nose hit the dark wiry pubic hair. He kept a steady rhythm, his tongue worshiping the taut skin, drawing Luc closer to the edge again before letting his grip around the base loosen. He pulled off, tracing a line down the thick shaft. He was surprised to see the demon markings on his cock especially since Luc hadn't shifted yet. Usually those didn't show on human skin. He traced the swirled markings, loving how they looked like a tattoo. He deep throated his lover's cock again, gently pulling Luc's balls away from his body to keep his orgasm at bay.

After the third round of edging Luc, he pulled his mouth away, spitting in his hand. Wrapping it firmly around Luc's dick, he set a hard and fast rhythm, twisting his hand just a bit at the tip. "Come," he commanded. Bert watched eagerly as Luc exploded. He licked his hand clean, enjoying the salty slightly bitter taste of his mate. "Mmm. Thank you," he told Luc, gently tucking him back inside his clothes and laying him down.

Luc fumbled around, searching for Bert's zipper, but he stayed him with a hand. "Not this time. This one was for you. Go over your list, think of what you might want to call me or me you. If you need anything, give me a call. Open your phone and I'll put my number in," Bert told him. Luc drowsily opened his phone, handing it over. Before Bert had even finished putting in his number, Luc had drifted off to sleep. He grabbed a nearby blanket and draped it over Luc, setting an alarm on Luc's phone for a half hour so he wouldn't sleep through dinner. He sent himself a text so he would have Luc's number; he could have asked Mac, but he had already involved him too much.

Luc picked up the phone, calling his nephew. He could understand why Mac went behind his back on this, but that didn't mean he wasn't going to give him some shit over it.

"Uncle, I can explain—" Mac started before Luc even said hello.

"I know why you did it. I'm torn between being angry at letting someone in my personal space or happy because it worked."

"It worked?" Mac said incredulously.

"Yes, but I'm still a little pissed at you." Not really, but Mac didn't need to know that.

"Am I on dog duty?" Mac asked a little morosely.

Luc bit his lip to keep from laughing. He had forgotten that when Mac had misbehaved, he'd been put in charge of cleaning the dog kennels and the backyard. Hellhounds could produce quite a lot of waste. "Sure," Luc agreed.

"Wait! I wasn't even going to be punished, was I?"

"Nope," Luc laughed. "But since you offered, I'm going to make you do it. I think you should bring Viv and Declan. We'll play and you can work. Faolán too, he can play with the rest of the hellhounds."

"Alright. Does this weekend work? I think I'll be done with the rest of my paperwork by then," Mac replied.

"That's fine. I wanted to...do you know why..." Luc had no idea how to talk this over with his nephew. Although he had never really discussed his own sexuality, it wasn't the mated to a man thing he was worried about. Afterall, Mac's best friend D had been attracted to men since he had hit puberty and was mated to a wonderful man, who just happened to be Viv's best friend. It was the possibility of Luc being a sub that he was tripping over.

"I know why Bert stayed away. As much as I disagreed with how long he did it for, I believed his heart was in the right place when he finally told me. All I want is for you to be happy, and I think having a supportive mate will help that happen. Don't be dumb like I was," Mac teased gently. "You are a badass, no matter what you might end up liking in the bedroom. That doesn't change anything."

"We love you no matter what," he heard Viv shout in the background.

Mac laughed. "What she said. Plus, if anyone decides to open their mouth, D, Bert, and I will show them how to shut up and mind their own business."

Luc laughed, a little wetly. He must have done something right to have such a great nephew. "You don't care if I'm..."

"Nope. I don't need to know about the details, but your private life is yours to live how you want. No one else's business. It doesn't change how I see you, other than in an 'eww, my parent has sex' type of way."

"Love you," Luc said.

"I love you too. I've got to run to work, but call us if you need anything," Mac told him.

"Be safe," Luc replied, before hanging up the phone.

He sighed, glad that was one thing off his shoulders. He knew he shouldn't have worried, but Mac was his only family and for some reason that had twisted things around in his mind. He turned to his closet. Time to get ready for work. He was feeling optimistic this morning, so he pulled out a lighter red shirt, a charcoal suit, and a black tie. Not quite as dark as he normally wore. He slid into what he considered his dress boots. Dress shoes just didn't have the right amount of traction if he needed to kick some ass.

Lacing up the combat-style laces, he made sure his pant legs were in place. Standing, he looked at himself one last time in front of the mirror, making sure everything was perfect. Grabbing his phone, he ported to his office. His personal assistant would have the cases he was supposed to review today on his desk. Part of being in this role, was the gift to see everything a person had done. Most of the employees in the Intake and Punishment offices and the Enforcers could see the evil someone had committed, could see the balance of bad and good in their soul, but true insights were usually limited to the bad deeds. He didn't have that limitation; he could see everything. From the time they were born to the time they were brought to him, he could see every time they sneezed without covering their nose, every time they smiled at someone, anything at all in their life and he could see it with a thought.

Everyone had assumed that it was something he and God had been born with and that was why they had been chosen for the job, but it was the opposite. When they had been appointed to their positions, the Fates had given them the ability. It had been a bitch to get used to. Now he had developed the skills to block it unless he was extremely tired and then things could slip through. He still wasn't sure what had made him 'perfect' for being the leader of Netherworld, but he was still here all these years later.

Luc settled into his chair, sighing a bit at the thick files in front of him. So much for an easy day. Opening the top file, he pinched the bridge of his nose. Was there nothing this one hadn't done? Seriously, killed children, their own nonetheless, killed their spouse, committed fraud by pretending he was still alive and collected their money. Whoever thought women couldn't be just as devious as men, had clearly never met some of the ones he dealt with.

The second case file was a serial killer of the human variety who had managed to evade law enforcement until the day he died of old age. That certainly wasn't fitting justice for all those poor souls he ended. Luc would have fun with that one.

Case files three, four, and five were all similar. There was a knock on the door and Margo stuck her head in around the doorframe.

"Sir, I have your coffee for you. The Enforcers are here for the day. You have Greg and Steve in the room today. Brandon is on hallway patrol," she told him, handing him his favorite mug.

"Thank you, Margo," Luc replied, taking a sip. It was perfect like always, with a hint of sweetness. "Can you tell them I'll be down in about five minutes? I'm going to enjoy my coffee before I start the day."

As he finished the last sip, he began his daily meditation. It helped him lock away the more…sensitive wasn't quite the right word. Normal maybe. Compassionate possibly. Now that he met Bert, maybe it was more submissive tendencies. Whatever the right word or words were, he had learned a long time ago to shore them up and lock it away. When dealing with the types of people he did, those types of feelings were only a weakness that they would try to exploit. He had learned that lesson very quickly his first few days on the job; he had listened to someone's pleas for mercy saying they would reform. He granted that mercy, and the jackass had gone on to escape holding and killed two more people. Those deaths were on his head, and he had vowed never again. He had gotten much better at digging into the depths of a person's soul and had zero compassion for those who harmed others.

He placed his cup at the edge of his desk, knowing Margo would come get it later. He had tried washing it up himself when she first came, but she had very nicely scolded him for doing her job. Luc had tried it a few more times before he finally gave up.

"I'm off to the hearing room, Margo. The coffee was wonderful as always, thank you," Luc told her before he exited.

Just before he entered the hearing room (he refused to call it the throne room even if his chair looked like a throne), his phone vibrated in his pocket. Luc felt a smile come over his face when he saw Bert's name.

Good luck today. Dinner tonight?

Luc took a minute to type a quick reply. *Yes. My place, 8:00? Be safe today.* That should give him enough time to finish for the day, shower, and do a quick cleaning. He had someone who helped keep the front of the house clean for official business, but the family side of the house was locked and he took care of that himself.

Sounds good. You be safe too.

Luc grinned one more time. When was the last time someone had told him to be safe? Probably back when he was a child. His parents had passed away before Mac had been born and Mac seemed to think he was invincible. He hoped he never fell from that high position in his nephew's mind.

Putting his phone away, he schooled his face, putting on the work mask, and dramatically shoved the doors open. The huge wooden monstrosities groaned as they opened, announcing his arrival. Walking into the large room, his chair sat at one end, centered against the wall. It meant no one could sneak up behind him, especially with a hellhound stationed in the back corners watching the room.

Settling into the ornately carved chair, he looked out over the area. There was an energy today that he was not a fan of. He could see the defendants kneeling in the center of the room, an Enforcer keeping watch. The bench seats were mostly empty today, only a few people there. Some days the Enforcers who had been involved in a prisoner's case came to watch the hearings, the more well-known cases often brought in spectators, if it was a nonhuman matter then the victims' families often came to see justice. Sometimes those who had disputes would come early and watch the punishments. He usually allowed it, as it helped reinforce his position. When he had first taken over, he had made the hearing rooms open to the public, as he had wanted full transparency after his predecessor had kept everything closed and manipulated things for his own gain. Luc had wanted to work to help his people, not work against them.

'*Be on guard,*' he told his hellhounds. He'd always had an infinity for them, able to communicate telepathically. It wasn't strong enough to hear words back, but he usually was able to get feelings and sometimes images. It had helped immensely when he took on this position, just like the Fates had told him.

When he got an affirmative sensation, he sent the go-ahead signal to the lead Enforcer for the day.

"Good morning, sir. We have five cases today for punishment. The first is Patricia Darling. Human, aged 54. Charges of murder and fraud."

"You can't prove it," the woman sneered. She wasn't afraid yet. She would be.

"Hmm. That's not all though. Is it?" Luc asked.

"Fuck off," she scoffed.

As she began to spew vitriol and nonsense, Luc focused on the soul in front of him, tuning out the sound of her voice. He felt his body lock in place, his mind leaving his body spearing into her soul. So much filth. She had definitely killed her own children, drowning them in the pool to make it look like an accident. She wanted the attention and sympathy and hated being a mother. She had thought it was only fitting to get rid of the kids in the stupid pool. She hated it, she had never wanted a pool and had been livid when her husband put it in despite her wishes. He did it for the kids, convinced it would be a great family experience. After the 'brats' were dead, she had assumed that she would be able to get rid of it. But no, he wanted to keep his memories alive through the pool, he had told her tearfully, the stupid whiny bastard.

She had assumed that it would eventually deteriorate since she refused to maintain it and she could get her way then. Her husband however had different plans; when she came home and saw the brand-new pool liner, it broke something in her and set her off on the course for her last murder. It took a while, but she planned it all. As much as she hated the liner, she had been ecstatic when she found that her 'save it just in case' spouse had kept the extra pool liner in the shed. She drugged him to keep him asleep and drained the pool. Once it was empty, she beat him with a hammer in his sleep. Her rage kept her going, wrapping his body in part of the liner, dragging him out of the house, and dropping him into the now empty pool. She had already arranged for it to be filled in with concrete. Now he could have his stupid pool forever.

She had pulled the body to the deep end, arranging extra pieces of liner so it blended with the bottom. Luckily her husband was a skinny thing and his body didn't look too out of place. She glued down the edges of the cover, making sure it wouldn't blow away. The concrete truck was due to come at dawn, so the low light would help conceal it as well. She could always say he was a rock. She had almost danced in glee as the liquid concrete began to hide his body, but she had kept herself contained until they were done. A few artful tears about getting rid of the thing that had taken her children from her, and there weren't many questions from the crew about why she was filling it in.

She had married an older guy on purpose, so she didn't need to worry about calling into his work. He was retired, pulling social security. For years, she had kept up the appearance of him being alive, using the money in the accounts, taking his social security payments. She had been in the process of trying to figure out how to sell the house without him being there to sign off on it, when she had been in a car accident. She'd cut off a semi-truck; she had done it on purpose trying to get in an accident so that she could sue for damages. She'd seen the idea online on how to get some easy extra cash. She wanted to take a cruise. Instead, now some poor truck driver was stuck with the knowledge he had accidently killed someone. Luc made a note to have one of his people look into it and make sure the driver wasn't being held accountable. The accident hadn't been his fault, he hadn't had enough time to stop even though he had tried.

Going further back in her life, Luc saw more and more misdeeds. She was a truly awful person. Coming back to himself, he realized she was still talking to him.

"I'll sell you my soul," she bargained. "Let me go back, sell the house, do all the things I wanted to do. Give me ten more years."

Luc looked at her. She really was delusional. "I already have your soul," he replied, gesturing at her. "I have no need to buy it, nor would I want to. Selling your soul is a made-up story told to keep people in line with the fear of Hell when they misbehave. The consequences for your actions are very real, but we have no need or desire to bargain with people for their souls or to further the evil in the world. We help keep the balance. My part of that is to punish those that do wrong, of which you have done plenty. Level eight," he told Steve, who dragged her out while she was screaming curses and threats at him.

They got through one more hearing before hell broke loose. Well, not really hell, but certainly chaos. He should have been paying more attention, especially since he had felt the energy when he had entered the room. The next three to be judged were a human, a demon, and an angel. Steve had just left, bringing the last case down to punishments, Brandon was patrolling the hallway, and Greg was standing at the side door consulting with Margo on how many disputes were up for the afternoon. At least those were more trivial and not murder and mayhem.

Luc really wanted the day to be over quickly so he could get to his dinner date. He could get started on examining the men now, he thought to himself, instead of waiting for Steve to come back. As he centered himself again and sent his mind out to rifle through the souls in front of him, Luc noticed a few looks exchanged between the three men but tuned it out. He had only been out of it for a minute when Bal popped in front of him growling, bringing him back to himself. He really should have waited, he thought dryly as he looked down at the knife sticking out of his shoulder. His hounds behind him screamed in fury, their bodies moving forward.

Seeing the three men rushing toward him, a woman standing in the doorway with another knife in hand, Luc roared, his demon side ripping through him. There goes that suit, he thought as the shirt and jacket ripped. The knife blade ripped at his body as he grew in size. Greg had turned at the sound of the hounds and was running toward him, his body leaving the ground as his wings spread out. Margo hit the silent alarm, calling all Enforcers nearby to the room, before shutting the door. No one but him and a few others could open that particular door, and she would be safe.

His hounds tore at the first attacker, the demon. "You really should know better," Luc scolded, a grin on his face, as he plunged his hand into the demon's side, his claws slicing through the skin easily. Calling on hellfire, he burned the demon from the inside out. While normal hell-fire wouldn't burn a demon, his family line carried a special type and he would absolutely use it if needed.

The angel was fighting with Greg, but it looked like Greg had it in hand. One of the hounds ran over to assist. Bal pouted at his side, clearly looking to join the fight but unwilling to leave him.

As the human came closer, Luc realized this was the serial killer. Nasty piece of work. The woman at the doorway moved further into the room, a nonhuman. She called out to the human, tossing him a knife while throwing another one straight at Luc. Greg threw the angel in the path of the knife, the body falling as it lodged in his skull. Bal lunged forward, attacking the human, ripping him to pieces. The woman screamed in fury and began to run toward him. The third hound rushed toward her as Steve and Brandon burst through the door, trying to grab her from behind.

She popped out of sight, porting to stand behind him, a knife ripping into his wing. Luc swallowed a shout, spinning, his wings flaring out, their razor-sharp edges ripping through her throat. Bal came over, sniffing the body, making sure she was dead.

"Sir! I am so sorry," Greg began, kneeling at his feet, head bowed. When the other two joined him, Luc sighed.

"It's alright," Luc interrupted. They had all gotten complacent, including him. "We've gotten used to it being relatively calm. It's a good reminder to stay on guard."

"I would suggest we add another Enforcer stationed in the hallway at the door," Steve suggested. "They can be in charge of transporting the prisoners to the punishment levels. That way there's always two Enforcers with you in the room and one in the hallway. Maybe have all prisoners held outside the room, only allowing one in here at a time."

"Sure," Luc agreed. He really wanted to go home and wash the blood off him, but he knew he needed to make a statement after today's incident.

"Leave the bodies," he instructed. "Bring in everyone waiting for dispute hearings. Let's make this quick."

His hounds circled behind him, keeping watch. They were good protectors. He would need to spend time with them later, reassure them they did a good job. He could feel their sadness at letting him get hurt through their bond. He had thought that having them stationed in the corners would be a better option than having them at his chair.

This whole debacle was really his fault; the hounds were fast, but he had moved farther away from them when he had moved closer to the prisoners. As people filed in, he saw Mac slip through the side door and move to stand in the corner behind him, watching his back.

"Dispute hearings are cancelled for the day," Luc said, his voice cold and carrying throughout the room. He was still in demon form, bleeding, knife stuck in his shoulder. "This will not be tolerated. My job is to distribute punishments to those who have earned them, as is the Enforcers'. We will meet all attacks with deadly force. If you arrived here with your body, it will be eliminated. Your souls will be sent to the deepest pits or destroyed. You will not win. Understood?" He watched as the crowd took in the blood covering him and his people, the bodies on the floor.

"Dismissed," he ordered. He stood rigid, his arms crossed, legs wide, staring unmovingly until everyone had left. "Thank you for your efforts today," he told his people. "I apologize for the mess. Mac, with me."

He walked through the heavy doors, head held high until they closed and it was only Mac and him in the hallway. "Home?" he said, knowing he probably needed someone else to look at the wound and he wasn't about to go to the hospital.

"See you there," Mac said, looking worried. Luc knew he wanted to say more but would wait until they were home safe.

Luc breathed deeply, letting it out slowly before porting to his den. Mac was there waiting.

"What happened?" Mac asked, moving to gently prod and examine his shoulder. He waited until Luc was finished with the story to suddenly pull out the knife. Luc shouted, grabbing at Mac's shoulder as spots danced in his vision.

"Sorry," Mac apologized. "It didn't hit anything vital. I thought it would be better to do it without telling you."

"Probably," Luc agreed, sitting down heavily, his wings folded in. He would have tensed up if Mac had said something. "Thanks. I'm going to grab a shower and I'll throw on some healing cream I have here when I'm done."

"Do you want me to wait?" Mac asked.

Luc shook his head. It wasn't the first time he'd been injured, he even created a device to help him apply healing cream to his back; it wasn't fancy, just a sponge attached to a back scratcher, but it worked well enough. "No. Thank you though. Go home to Viv and the baby. Give them a kiss for me," he said.

Mac leaned down to give him a careful hug. "Love you, Uncle," he said before porting home.

Now to drag himself into the shower.

"What the fuck happened?" Bert asked, furious as he took in the state of his lover. He had been working on paperwork when he got a text from Mac. It didn't say a lot, just that Luc had a rough day and Bert should check on him. He made himself finish his report and ported to his mate, who happened to be in the bathroom, about to get in the shower. He needed to talk to Mac about what a rough day was; he had been thinking mentally taxing, but he was clearly not on the same page as Mac, even if he appreciated the heads-up.

He was not pleased to see blood and what looked like knife wounds on Luc's body. He was still in his demon form and one side of Bert took notice of the changes in his mate. He had grown several inches in height, his muscles bulked up, his skin darkened to a tan and he could see more of the demon markings on his skin, not just the arm bands that were normally there. Some led down into the remnants of the suit pants. Black wings, tail, and horns completed the transition to full demon. His tail was marked as well, swirls of red decorating the smooth black skin. The end looked like a double-tipped arrow, ribbed for his pleasure, he thought jokingly to himself. He was trying not to lose his shit, especially since he had just reassured Luc he wouldn't interfere with his job. They also hadn't established their boundaries, so he was hesitant to pull the Dom card quite yet.

"I was complacent. Steve had left to take a prisoner to the punishment levels, Greg was talking at my private door to Margo about the upcoming dispute hearings. I thought I could speed things along so I could get to our date quicker by starting a reading. The three of them joined together and tried to rush me. The hellhounds and Greg joined in the fight. The wounds actually came from a woman who was trying to help them. She snuck in after Steve left and Brandon was down the hall. Not sure who she is. I'll pull her soul later. I called in the dispute attendees, let them see the bodies, told them the rest of the day was cancelled, and that this was what happened when you tried to attack me. Mac came when he heard the alarm, and I was about to get in the shower and put on the healing cream," Luc told him slowly, his words starting to slur.

As he grabbed his lover's arm when he swayed a bit, Bert was shocked to realize that not all of the red swirls were demon markings, a lot of that was blood. He should have been starting to heal by now, Bert thought with concern. He kicked his shoes off, bending to unlace Luc's.

"Grab on to the counter and lift your leg," he instructed. He pulled one boot and pant leg off. "Next one." As soon as Luc was back on two feet, Bert ripped his own pants down, keeping his underwear on. He needed to focus on helping his mate, not lusting after him.

"Okay, into the shower for a quick rinse off. How do you feel?" he asked.

"Dizzy," Luc said, his wings drooping as he leaned heavily against the shower wall.

Bert quickly got the loofa soapy, running it over Luc's body, making sure to get the blood off. He was grateful that not all of it smelled like Luc. He urged Luc to sit on the built-in bench seat so he could reach his hair. Luc moaned, his dick twitching as Bert brushed against the horns. It said something about the state of him that Luc didn't even get to half-chub. He turned off the water, pressing down on Luc's non-injured shoulder when he tried to get up.

"Stay there." He quickly grabbed two towels, wrapping one around his waist and using the other to dry off Luc. With the smell of blood gone, other than what was still weeping from Luc, Bert could smell something was off. Leaning closer, he sniffed Luc's shoulder.

"I think you've been poisoned." Fuck. "Let's get you to the hospital," he said, trying to manhandle Luc up off the seat.

"No, no hospital. I have some healing potions and creams here. Should work," Luc slurred, shaking his head. That movement almost sent him to the floor, but Bert caught him. Luc felt his feet moving as Bert guided him to sit on the edge of the bed.

"Okay. For now. Where is it?" Bert asked.

"Den," Luc struggled to get the words out. "In desk. Top right." The den was the safest place in the house.

Bert made sure Luc was somewhat stable before running into the den. Luckily, it seemed like Luc had added Bert to the wards. Otherwise he would have had to call Mac as Luc was in no position to be moving. He searched through the desk, quickly finding a healing potion and a cream. He'd start with one and see where they got to. He didn't want to deplete Luc's supply if he didn't need to. As he rushed into the bedroom, Luc's eyes were closed, his breathing heavy and he was beginning to list to the side. He slid under Luc's arm, holding him up.

"Drink this," he said, adding a little command to his voice to get Luc to listen. He'd give it a half hour but if he wasn't getting better, he was dragging Luc to the hospital.

Bert watched, making sure Luc swallowed all of the potion. He awkwardly maneuvered so he could kneel up on the bed, still supporting Luc's weight, but able to reach the injured shoulder. He'd normally slap some healing cream on and superglue it shut, but with the poison in Luc's system, he thought it better to let it drain. He ripped his towel off, holding it against Luc's shoulder to save the bedding from getting bloody and helped him lie down on his stomach. He wouldn't have to worry about Luc falling over this way and he could reach the wing easier. As he applied the cream, he noticed that this wound didn't have the same smell, so he was hopeful Luc only got a single dose of whatever poison there was.

As he finished doctoring Luc, he noticed the eyes staring at him from the corner. How the hell had he missed the hellhound there?

"You must be Bal. Can you watch him while I wash up? Come get me if he seems worse." Bert felt silly for talking to the dog, but he knew the hellhounds were very intelligent.

The hellhound moved silently and climbed up onto the bed, laying his huge head next to Luc's. Bert made it to the bathroom before it caught up to him. Placing his hands on the counter, he needed to take a minute to breathe. He would not freak out, he lectured himself. Luc had survived much worse and when...no, if news of them got out and people made assumptions, there would be more trouble ahead.

They needed to be more vigilant. Grabbing his phone out of his pants, still on the floor, Bert called Mac.

"Hey, how's Uncle? He didn't want me to stay so I thought he might listen to you," Mac said in lieu of a greeting.

"I gave him a healing potion and put cream on the knife wounds. The shoulder one was poisoned, but I couldn't smell it until after we got him washed off." He didn't want Mac to feel bad about not catching it. He hadn't either.

"Shit. I didn't smell that at all. Healing potions will work for most poisonings, but not all. If you have a sample of his blood, he has a kit in the den. Desk drawer, lower right. You can test the blood to make sure the healing potion will work. Green means you're good. Black means get him to the hospital right away; it's something a healing potion won't help. Do you need me to come?"

Bert could hear the baby crying in the background and didn't want to pull Mac away from his family. "No, not yet. I'll test it and if it's something we can't treat at home, I'll call you back." He could hear murmurs in the background.

"Viv is sending over dinner. It's a casserole and fresh bread that will reheat well and you'll know it's safe. I'll just leave it in the kitchen. Call out if you need any help before I leave, or whenever," Mac told him before hanging up.

Bert had a feeling they were giving up their dinner, but he was grateful. He hadn't even thought about food, but Luc would need to replenish his energy. A minute later he felt a pop of energy downstairs and his phone buzzed.

Casserole in fridge with reheating instructions. Bread on counter. Call/text if you need anything. Give Uncle our love.

Grabbing the remains of Luc's clothes, he headed back into the den after peeking in on Luc. The hellhound was snoozing by his side and Luc's breathing looked better. Bert was hopeful that meant the healing potion was working, but he wanted to test to be certain. Pulling out the kit, he got it set up and squeezed blood out of the clothes since he didn't want to disturb Luc if he was actually resting. He let out a quick rush of air as it turned green almost immediately.

Cleaning up, he made his way back to the bed. Bert lay on the other side of Luc, placing a hand on his back, careful of his wings. He let the sounds of Luc's breathing draw him closer to sleep. Hopefully their next date would be better.

10

L uc woke slowly, not entirely sure what was going on. His mouth tasted horrible, he felt a little weak, and was very hot. His right arm was sweating. Opening his eyes, he realized Bal was on the bed and was drooling on his arm. Gross, but at least he didn't have only one appendage weirdly sweating. Realizing there was heat and pressure on his other side, Luc turned his head to find Bert sleeping next to him, a hand on his back.

He was still in his demon form, and Luc groaned as his muscles protested the switch back to human. The movement woke Bert.

"I need to go to work," Luc said, knowing by the thunderclouds gathering on Bert's face that they would be having their first real fight.

"You need to rest more. You're still healing. It wasn't just the blood loss and the wounds, you were poisoned. The healing potion took care of that, but your body is still recovering," Bert protested.

"I still need to go in. I can't show any weakness or it will encourage more of this behavior," Luc told him.

Bert was silent, but Luc could tell he was having an internal dialogue. "I'm coming with you then. Or call in Mac. You need someone you know will have your back no matter what. I'm not saying the Enforcers don't, but Mac and I are your family. We have even more to fight for when it comes to protecting you."

Luc bit the inside of his lip. There would be speculation as to why Bert was there. Luc thought about it, and he realized that he really only had one choice to make: hide their relationship for a little longer or let everyone know they were together. It wasn't much of a choice when he thought about it that way. "Okay."

"Okay, what?" Bert asked.

"You can come."

"Good. I need to port home to get new clothes. While I'm gone, you get ready and think about what you want me to call you. If I'm going to be there all day, we need to get this sorted out before we leave. Mac dropped off dinner last night, but we slept right through. We can have it for breakfast or dinner tonight."

"Dinner. I don't like dinner foods for breakfast. Margo usually has pastries in the office."

"Sounds good." Bert leaned in, gave him a gentle kiss on his lips and ported out.

Luc had been playing with ideas of what to call his mate, but none of them had stuck yet. He wanted to stay away from things like boss or captain, but he wanted to make sure it was respectful to Bert. He had thought angel, but considering half the Enforcers were angels, that would make it confusing in a mixed group. Bert didn't really have a long name that he could shorten to another word. Ber, maybe but said like bear? Sie, like sir but a strong I...no, too weird. Dom didn't really rhyme with anything good.

He got in the shower, eager to get the sweat off him. He knew he had gotten one the night before, but either purging the poison or sleeping between Bal and Bert had made him sweaty. What were some other things that he thought about a Dom. Cuffs, leather, whips, treb—like Bert spelled backwards. They all sounded stupid, he thought, getting out of the shower and picking out a new suit to wear. When he exited the closet, holding a pair of boots, his jaw dropped as he took in his mate. Oh. Hmm, that was all his, Luc thought smugly. Bert had trimmed his facial hair, leaving a nicely manicured scruff behind. He was wearing a light gray suit with a black tie. That was a gorgeous sight.

He wished they had more time so he could explore. "You're gorgeous," Luc told him.

"Thank you," Bert replied with a smile. "So are you. Did you come up with a word for me?"

"Not yet, mate. None of them sound right. Oh." Luc paused. "Can I use Mate? That sounds right and no one would think anything of it."

"I like it," Bert said, rewarding him with a kiss. "I was thinking of Love for you. It expresses my feelings, acts as a title, and also starts with the same letter of your name."

"I also like it," Luc said, smiling.

"Good. If I need to talk to you or want you to take a break, I'll say something like 'Love, there's a phone call for you,' which gives us the opportunity to take a break away from everyone."

"I may not be able to stop right away, it will need to be in between hearings," Luc explained.

"I understand. But I do expect you to acknowledge you heard me and take a break when that hearing is over before moving to the next one. I swear I won't overdo it, but I will look out for you first, everyone else comes after."

And didn't that send a tingle through him. "Yes, Mate."

"Hmm. I'll reward you tonight for being my good Love.

Let's go to work," Bert said, copping a feel of Luc's ass. He looked so good in a suit.

Luc laughed and ported to his office. He wanted to maintain his usual routine. Bert popped in seconds later, taking a seat across the desk from Luc. He turned the chair sideways so he could have easy access to whoever came through the door. Logically he knew Luc could take care of himself, but the lover and Dom in him wanted to take care of his sub. He had a feeling it had been a while since someone had taken care of Luc.

He knew his friend Mac loved his uncle, but he still viewed Luc as the adult in the relationship. He also knew Luc's parents had died quite a bit ago and he had never heard rumors of any lovers.

A knock on the door had Bert sitting taller in his seat, eyes on the door. He had his gun at the small of his back just in case.

"Oh, hello. Sir?" Luc's assistant looked confused.

"Good morning, Margo. How are you?"

"I'm good, sir. How are you feeling this morning? Do you want me to cancel the hearings for today?"

Bert saw her looking at him out of the corner of her eye.

"I'm much better. I'm ready to get back to work, but let's make sure we make those changes Steve suggested yesterday about always having at least two Enforcers in the room.

"Margo, I would like to introduce you to Bert. He'll be around here quite a bit. He's an Enforcer on the Arlysium side and also my mate."

"Congratulations! I am so happy for you! Oh, how exciting." Margo didn't quite squeal but it was close. She was absolutely bouncing on her toes. "It's nice to meet you, sir."

"Just Bert is fine." He smiled.

"Two coffees today? I stopped at the bakery and got the good donuts, if you're hungry."

"Yes please. Bert, how do you take your coffee?" Luc asked, willing himself not to blush that he didn't know something so simple.

"Black please, thank you."

They ate their donuts and drank their coffee before heading down to the hearing room. "I'm sorry you'll have to stand, there's only the one chair," Luc murmured to him, nodding to different people in the hallway. "Let me go in first," Luc told his mate. He knew Bert would want to go first, but it was important image-wise for him to appear strong and unafraid. Part of that was entering first.

Bert clenched his jaw to keep in the words and nodded. They were both learning how to adjust to each other, and he needed to work on his protective urges. He followed Luc inside, studying the crowd. People were watching Luc closely, not threateningly, but certainly appraisingly. Yeah, as much as he hated it, Luc had needed to show up today.

The chair, as Luc called it, was more of a throne. The wood was black in color and was intricately carved. As he got closer, Bert realized it was of flames and demons and angels. The center of the back and the seat were a deep red leather. The legs ended in clawed feet. At least it looked nicely padded. He hadn't noticed the finer details when he was stalking his mate from the back of the room.

Luc stood in front of his chair, Bert taking a stance slightly behind and to the right. There was a pop and four hellhounds spread out behind them, Bal taking lead and sitting next to Luc's chair. He was in full hellhound mode, having transformed to his larger shape, hellfire in his eyes, flames dancing along his fur. It seemed like even the dogs wanted to make a statement to those who would harm Luc.

Luc looked over the room, his face a mask of calm. "I'm sure you all heard about yesterday. Things like that will not be tolerated and will be met with lethal and brutal force."

Bert glanced over to see Bal baring his teeth at the crowd.

"Now, let's get the day started. First case, please," Luc told the Enforcer, who nodded back.

Luc took his seat, and the other hellhounds moved to line the back wall. Bert watched the crowd and his lover throughout the day. He didn't envy Luc this at all. While they both dealt with the evils of people, Bert had days where nothing happened, or it was all paperwork. He also had more comradery too, for as much as they tended to work alone. Luc sat alone day in and day out seeing the worst of the worst. He was the boss, so he didn't have the same outlet to vent about his day as Bert did. He had never really thought about it, but God probably had the same problem.

It was going pretty smoothly until it was time for the disputes. Good grief some people could whine. Holy shit, learn to communicate with each other and solve your own problems. He wondered if God had this problem with the angels. Luc dealt with a lot of different nonhumans, but it seemed to be mostly demons in these disputes. After the fourth one, he could tell Luc needed a break.

He pretended he was looking at his phone before leaning down to Luc's ear. "Love, there's a call for you."

Luc nodded, briefly touching his hand, all the while keeping his focus on the group in front of him. He finished advising the demons and stood.

"I have a quick matter to attend to. We'll reconvene in ten minutes," Luc stated before leading the way out, Bal following.

As soon as the door shut and they were alone, Luc dropped his mask, letting Bert see the exhaustion and discomfort. Bal leaned against Luc's leg, letting out a quiet whine. Luc petted Bal's head, leaning hard into Bert. Bert looked around, but when he didn't see any place to sit, he ported them to Luc's office, pulling Luc down to sit on his lap. It probably looked ridiculous as Luc was taller than he was, but it was the best way to wrap him in comfort. Luc scrunched down and tucked his head in against his neck, breathing in his scent.

"I can usually go much longer without a break, but today is harder. I'm tired and sore," Luc admitted.

"You're still recovering. Sit here for a bit, we'll grab a quick snack and a drink and hopefully the rest goes quickly."

Luc groaned. "Never say that. Then it always goes slowly or there's issues. Every time."

Bert snorted. "We'll see." He would enjoy holding his mate and hopefully they'd have a quick rest of the day and they could eat dinner together.

L uc looked up from the mound of paperwork sitting in front of him, rotating his neck in an attempt to get rid of the ache settling there. You'd think being in charge would mean he got out of it, but nope. That was a big fat oversized no. Margo did a lot to minimize the amount he had to do, but he still had several hours of work ahead of him. The hearings went long today and Bert had his own work, so Luc hadn't seen him since this morning.

His phone buzzed and he grabbed it, seeing it was from Bert.

Going to be late tonight. Don't wait up. Make sure you eat, Love.

Luc snorted. Bert had discovered his unfortunate habit of working until he was exhausted and falling asleep as soon as he got home. There had been plenty of nights where he had skipped dinner. Bert had not been amused and had told Luc to make sure he ate something every night. Since his partner was going to be out late, he might as well try to get through as much of this as he could, Luc reasoned to himself. He grabbed a handful of trail mix and absently chewed as he read through reports, approved time off, looked at a couple of resumes for people applying to become Enforcers, and filled out his own incident reports.

Each punishment and dispute hearing needed their own, as well as any time he spent in punishments acting as an Enforcer.

His predecessor had not felt the need to fill out reports or spend any time with his employees. It had caused a lot of resentment among his men. When Lucifer was appointed, he didn't want to make the same mistakes. Reports kept everyone more honest, there was a paper trail they could look at later if needed to know the why, how, or when things were done. Luc also didn't want his men to feel estranged from him, so he took the time to talk to them, to take an interest in their lives, to do the jobs they did on a daily basis. Morale had improved dramatically since he had taken over. That was something he was very proud of. He had a duty to the nonhumans and humans they protected by capturing and punishing the wrongdoers, but he also had a responsibility to his own people, both the demons and nondemons who worked for him.

Luc felt himself nodding off and forced his eyes open. It was almost midnight and he had been up since four this morning. He would finish this report and head home, he thought to himself, trying to focus on the words in front of him.

"Luc. Lucifer, wake up. Right now," an angry voice demanded.

Luc blinked, lifting his head up. Ow. That didn't feel good. He must have fallen asleep at his desk.

"Bert, are you done for the night?" Luc asked, still groggy.

"Yes. I went to your house and you weren't there. The sink and dishwasher are empty, nor do I see any takeout containers here."

Luc was really confused and not awake enough to

follow. Takeout containers? Was Bert hungry? Did he want Luc to have ordered food for him?

"I can see you're not understanding. Go home, Love. Think about it. After your punishment, we'll cuddle, eat, and go to bed," Bert commanded.

That was the first time Luc had heard the word Love in such a harsh tone. It was definitely the sound of his angry Dom. Oh shit, he was supposed to have eaten dinner and he clearly hadn't.

"I'm sorry. I meant to, I fell asleep working. It wasn't on purpose," Luc tried to apologize.

"You didn't make yourself a priority, even after I explicitly told you to eat dinner tonight. Go home and stand by the bed. When I give you an order, I expect you to follow it. When you don't, there will be consequences."

"Yes, Mate," Luc replied, feeling all kinds of things that he couldn't fully interpret at the moment. He felt disappointed in himself, devastated to hear that tone of voice from his Mate. His brain felt muddled by the lack of sleep. He couldn't even remember when his head had landed on his desk.

He ported home and stood by the bed waiting. And waiting. And waiting. And waiting. He shifted on his feet, his half chub from being near his mate waning as he stood there. Maybe Bert had to stop at the store? Or his house? He could see the minutes tick away on the bedside clock and still no Mate. He had said he'd be there, hadn't he? His exhausted brain suggested that maybe Bert had decided Luc wasn't worth the trouble to punish or that he was too new at this to satisfy Bert's needs; after all, he had hesitated for a year to even introduce himself to Luc. He felt his breathing speed up, hiccupping as he fought the slam of emotions running through him. It was fine, he told himself.

If Bert decided Luc was too much trouble to teach, he'd be fine on his own. He'd been alone a long time and he didn't need anyone besides his family. They loved him. He was enough for them.

He angrily brushed off a tear that escaped, telling himself to man up and stop sniveling. And yet he still stood there. This was stupid; he was exhausted and should just go to bed.

More than thirty minutes later he was still standing in place, his breathing heavy and ragged as he tried to control the tears that wanted out. He had a feeling that it was a losing battle. He stared at the floor, absently thinking he needed to cut his toenails soon. But it didn't matter because no one would ever see them. His neck ached from staring down at paperwork, sleeping on his desk, and now staring at the floor, but he couldn't bring himself to look up. He didn't want to see himself alone in the reflection of the window.

Warm hands wrapped around his body and his head flew up. When he saw his Mate standing behind him, the sobs ripped from his body. Bert moved to stand in front of him, keeping a hand touching him at all times.

"Tell me why you're crying," Bert demanded gently.

Luc shook his head, knowing he was ugly crying now, nose dripping and everything. How attractive.

"Tell me," Bert demanded, "or you're getting another punishment."

"You didn't come. I didn't follow the rules. I failed at a stupidly easy task. I'm too new at this and not what you need."

Bert stood in shock for a minute. That was not even close to what he thought or had wanted Luc to take away from this punishment. He had been thinking of it as more of a time-out, a chance to think about his choices, not for Luc to think he had abandoned him. Bert had forgotten how new to this Luc was. Bert had failed him, not the other way around. He should have talked it out more and explained better beforehand.

"Absolutely not," he said loudly and firmly, grabbing Luc's face and forcing him look at him. "You are not, have never been, and will never be, too much trouble. We're fated mates and I intend to love you forever. You're my Love, I'm your Mate. I am looking forward to trying things with you, it makes it all new again.

"I can make mistakes too, which I clearly did tonight. I should have explained the punishment better, told you it was a time-out so you could think about your choices so you could make better ones in the future. I apologize for that and will be clearer from now on.

"Now, I did tell you we would cuddle and eat afterward, Love, so let's go do that. I think a shower first though," Bert said, leading Luc to the bathroom. He was grateful Luc had an on-demand water heater so they didn't have to wait. Ushering his too quiet lover into the steam, Bert hurriedly got undressed and joined him. He gently washed Luc, dried him off, and helped him into sweatpants. He didn't think Luc would be awake long, so he left him in bed and ran down the stairs to heat up some leftovers.

Carrying the plates and bottles of water into the bedroom a few minutes later, he saw Luc was lying in bed, but his eyes were open watching the door.

"Sit up, Love. You need to eat something and then we can go to sleep."

Luc managed about half of his plate before he set it aside and snuggled into Bert's side. He put his own food on the nightstand, curling around Luc. As Luc's breathing settled and he fell asleep, Bert held him tight. They needed to set aside a big chunk of time so they could really explore their boundaries with each other and set firmer limits and expectations. He knew how to do this, he didn't know why he was failing now. They had been...not playing house, but not living the lifestyle with each other fully yet. It was like mini-scenes, similar to when he made Luc take a break at work, but they hadn't explored a full scene yet and they needed to.

They needed to do it soon so they could fully commit and say the mating bond. They had kept it to only hands and mouths because they had agreed that they didn't think they could stop from claiming each other during the heat of sex. The mate bond would have helped tonight though; Luc would have been able to feel Bert's love for him and the commitment he had toward him. He had thought they had moved past the delay of introducing himself to Luc, but clearly that was still in the back of Luc's brain if it was telling him that Bert had left him here tonight after deciding he was too much trouble or not enough. He imagined that Luc had also been told something similar in the past, either from previous relationships who didn't want the issues that dating the leader of Netherworld came with, or maybe even his parents. But someone had put that thought in Luc's brain for it to come up now. He was too confident in everything else for it to have come only from himself.

He needed a way to show Luc that he was committed to their relationship until they could finalize the mate bond. He wasn't budging on his stance that they fully trust each other first. It would only cause problems later if the trust wasn't the foundation of their mating. How could he—oh! Yes, that would work. Bert reached out and grabbed his phone, sending a text to another Enforcer. Their mate did amazing work and if they could rush it, he'd be able to grab it before breakfast in the morning. It wasn't a fix per se, but it should help reassure Luc when he had doubts. He grinned as he typed out exactly what he wanted.

L uc got dressed and walked downstairs. Bert was still here, although they hadn't talked much this morning. He was more than a little mortified at his behavior last night. Not only had he disappointed Bert, but then he had sobbed like a child when Bert hadn't come right away. He wouldn't blame Bert at all for not wanting to take this further.

He was quiet as he walked into the kitchen.

"Sit, Love. We need to talk," Bert said, placing a plate of eggs, toast, and a coffee in front of him.

Luc wasn't a relationship expert, but he had read a bunch of magazines when Mac was having trouble. Those words generally were not considered good.

"Get that look off your face. It's nothing bad," Bert told him, his lips quirking up a little. "I failed you last night." He waved a hand, cutting Luc off when he opened his mouth to protest. "No. I did. I've been in the lifestyle for years. I know better than to simply expect a newbie to know what is expected from a scene or punishment. I should have explained better, and I will do my best to do that in the future.

"I do think we need to take time to explore more of the lifestyle together, how we want it to be in our lives. Making you take breaks at work is a start, but I know that's not enough for me and I'm pretty sure it isn't enough for you, even if you don't know it yet. The mate bond would have helped you last night, but I still believe that we need to fully trust each other and agree to the Dom/sub relationship and the initial boundaries we set up before we take that step. Boundaries will change as we spend more time with each other, we may find something is a Green or something is a hard no, or you want more or less of my interference, but we need to have the groundwork more fully developed than we do now."

Luc nodded as Bert paused.

"I had two ideas that may help you know I'm in this, that I won't abandon you. One, I move in. It's soon, but if I move in and get rid of my apartment, then you'll know I'm always coming home to you. Two, I would like you to have this. It's a human custom to give rings, and while marriage is more of a human thing, I would like for you to wear this. You can see it every day and know you're mine and I'm yours," Bert said, holding out a ring. "I view it as similar to a collar, but something that will work with your position."

Luc reached out, taking the ring and examined it. It was a black metal band; the center had a thin inlaid band of black and white diamonds. It was much flashier than anything Luc would have picked out for himself.

"It's made with hellfire midnight diamonds for the black ones, and Arlysium starlight diamonds for the white ones. I thought it was a good visual representation of both of us," Bert explained.

Luc loved it for that. "Put it on me, Mate?" he asked. It felt right that Bert be the one to slide it on his hand. He felt more settled as it slid all the way on. "I'll cancel the hearings for this weekend. We can lock ourselves in the den so we won't be disturbed, unless you have work this weekend?"

"I don't, just paperwork, but that can wait. Have a good day at work today and I'll grab some things from my home that we can use to explore your checklist of yeses and maybes. I need to buy a couple of things before I come over tonight as well. Some things will need to wait until we stop by the club or have special equipment brought in or built for us."

"I'll throw a roast in the slow cooker for dinner with some potatoes and carrots," Luc offered. It was easy enough and it could cook on low all day. He had made it often when Mac was little.

"That sounds like a plan then. I'll see you tonight," Bert gave him a kiss, making sure he was breathless before he pulled away.

Luc couldn't stop his grin as he grabbed the slow cooker and roughly chopped some onions, carrots, and potatoes to cook with the roast. He was curious to see what things Bert brought back tonight. Clenching his hand shut so he could feel the ring, he ported to work eager to get the day started so he could finish.

Bert grabbed his leather pants, cuffs, and vest. He didn't want to completely overwhelm Luc, just overwhelm him enough. He grabbed a duffle bag and threw in a combination of some things he had at the house and some new items he bought today: lube, both warming and regular, a cock ring (he'd get Luc fitted for a cage later), a flogger, a paddle, blindfold, ropes, cuffs, a smaller whip, and a cane. Luc already had candles at his house if he wanted to try playing with different sensations, but he grabbed a feather and a specialty piece he had custom made years ago. It had soft leather on one side, hard bumps on one, spikes on another, and the last side was spelled to get either hot or cold with a word from him. It was great for sensory play. He grabbed a tube of cream in case they got into a heavy scene or even a harder spanking.

He thought Luc's ass would look amazing red after being spanked. Hopefully Luc enjoyed it. It was one of Bert's favorite things to do. And if he did it just right, it could turn into one of Luc's favorites as well. They needed to have a serious talk before anything happened though. Luc's reaction last night had been unexpected and Bert needed to make sure Luc was okay going forward and that he took the time to explain things better. Some of the time Luc wouldn't know what was going to happen in a scene and that was on purpose, but Bert could make sure Luc knew how it would begin, that there would be a scene, that no matter what Bert wouldn't leave him and they would talk and/or snuggle afterward.

Looking through his apartment one more time, he made a mental list of the things that he would want to take with him when he moved into Luc's. Maybe they could get that started this weekend. His motorcycle and clothes were the biggest ones. He was pretty minimalist when it came to keeping things through the years, so other than his favorite toys, he didn't have much he needed to keep. A few pictures of his family, some favorite books, but really that was it.

He ported directly into the den at Luc's. He never knew when someone might be in the house visiting or an Enforcer changing shifts or asking for advice, so he wanted to put the gear away first so no one else saw it or asked questions. Most of it fit in the bag, but the cane did not. Bert took the time to lay a few items out, both as a shock value, but also to show Luc the different types of things available. He placed his checklist next to Luc's on top of everything on the table. It would be where they started tonight.

"Bert? Are you hungry? The roast is ready," Luc said from the doorway. The couch blocked the view of the table where most of the things were laid out.

"I am," Bert replied. "I was just getting a few things ready for tonight. I think we'll have a talk first and then we can start our weekend of exploration." Bert followed Luc down the stairs, ignoring the way Luc kept glancing over his shoulder at the den.

"Mmm," he moaned around his first bite. "This is delicious, Love. Thank you." The roast was tender and moist, and the carrots were perfectly cooked, just done enough to not be crunchy but still firm. His always turned out mushy. He smashed the potatoes with the tines of his fork, topping them with butter.

"Thank you," Luc replied, his cheeks taking a slight pink hue. That was adorable. He wondered if he could find other ways to make Luc blush. He was such a ruggedly handsome man that the blush was out of character and Bert adored it.

Bert helped clean up, loading the dishwasher before taking Luc's hand and leading him upstairs to the den. Luc would have his phone in case of emergency calls, but otherwise they wouldn't be disturbed.

"First, I want you to go over your list and make sure it's still correct," Bert said, sitting Luc on the couch and handing him his list.

"I think it's still all the same. There are some things I

don't know what they are or have never tried them, so they might change," Luc said a minute later.

"Good. Now here's mine," Bert said, handing his to Luc. "I think we have a lot of things in common. One of my hard limits is humiliation and bodily fluid play. I'm fine with coming on you, but not anything else. I may call you my dirty little Love, or some other form of dirty talk during a scene or sex, but I am not into hardcore humiliation." He waited while Luc read through it, but he knew they were pretty well matched.

"Now, rules. We already established what works for your job, and I think it's been working pretty well. It's home we really need to focus on. My ideal would be for me to be in charge while we're at home, not completely like I expect you to ask permission to use the bathroom, but have it understood that I am in charge at all times. I would have the right to ask you to do something or stop something at any time and I would expect you to obey me unless something work related came up. If Mac and Viv are visiting, I understand that would be weird and we could go by work rules.

"For example, if you were doing the dishes, I could request that you do them naked. I could have you wear a plug while doing the laundry. I want control of your orgasms. No masturbating anymore. You get to come when I tell you. There will be rewards for good behavior and punishments for breaking the rules. I will be more explicit about punishments and explaining things from now on," Bert added.

"Can I get the rules written down?" Luc asked, biting his lip. He did well with lists and rules. His whole job was about rules.

Bert nodded, grabbing a pen and paper from Luc's desk.

"Rule one: Communication is big in this type of life-style. If something is bothering you, you have a worry, a concern, a question...you need to tell me right away. You need to use your safe words without fail. You will never be punished for using them. You will be punished for not coming to me with a worry.

"Rule two: Take care of yourself. You need to eat every day. I know work gets busy and you get caught up in things, but you need at least two full meals a day. Danishes don't count as an acceptable meal. We can add a mini fridge in your office and keep easy-to-eat things in there. Maybe protein drinks, yogurt, cheese, even leftovers to reheat. I think if we add an alarm to your phone that would help remind you.

"Rule three: Your job is to make me happy. My job is to make you happy. As long as we both strive to achieve that, I think we'll be on solid ground for everything else.

"Rule four: No orgasms unless I say so. No masturbating or playing with yourself, dick or ass, even if you don't orgasm. Cleaning yes; extensive cleaning as an excuse to fondle yourself, no.

"Rule five: I briefly mentioned this one this morning. Some people like collars. I don't see that as a good option for us. I do see your ring as a form of a collar. If you still agree with that, no taking your ring off for any reason unless I have told you it was okay. I understand some days you will be working in punishments and you may not want to get it covered in gunk, but you need to clear it with me beforehand."

Luc fingered the ring on his hand. "I agree. I like the idea of it marking me as yours." He got a quick kiss for his answer before Bert continued. The ring had been comforting to feel throughout the day.

"I don't see this as something that would come up with you, but I'm adding it anyway. Rule six: No piercings or tattoos without my permission. Rule seven: If I tell you to do something, I expect you to do it to the best of your ability. If it runs into something that turns out to be a hard no, use your safe word.

"Rule eight is for if we visit the club. It's common to address other Doms as Sir/Master or Madam/Mistress. However, that won't work without potentially harming your image as The Lucifer. If we would go to the club, the owner knows who you are and there would be a rule in place to either not address you expecting a common Sir response, or that you calling them Mister whatever their name is would act as the expected respectful response. Rule eight and a half: We do not play with others in the club. I do not share; I know it wouldn't be sexual with others, but I don't want anyone even seeing you naked or watching your pleasure. We can watch other scenes, but we will not be participating in group or share events. It works for some couples, but not for me.

"Rule nine: I will not interfere with your work unless necessary. For example, stepping in and asking you to take a break like we have been. I understand there will be late nights and emergencies, but I expect you to notify me of these, even if I'm on assignment. A simple text will work. I will also do my best to notify you if I will be late. Sometimes it's not possible if I'm in the middle of a chase, but I will let you know as soon as possible.

"Rule ten: Failure to follow the rules will result in a punishment. Those will change based on the circumstances. It could be a time-out; after last time, I think it would be best if I were present the whole time, but I would not talk to you during that time. Other ideas would be orgasm denial, spankings without a climax, things like that."

Bert didn't add his other rule about sexual monogamy. Once they had the mate bond in place, there was no cheating. And until then, Luc wasn't the type to cheat and neither was he.

"Any questions?" Bert asked, as he finished writing down the rules.

Luc shook his head. It all seemed pretty reasonable. The no orgasm thing might be challenging but something about Bert being in charge of his body like that made his cock twitch.

"What are your safe words?"

"Green, Yellow, and Red," Luc replied.

"Good. Now get naked and lie over my lap," Bert told him.

13

L uc stood at the command but paused when his hand landed on his pants button. Naked and over his lap. That shouldn't be hard to do, but when staring at Bert's lap, he had no idea how to actually do that.

"Is there a problem?" Bert asked.

"No," Luc replied slowly. "I'm not sure how to lie on your lap," he admitted.

"Clothes off and I'll help you."

Luc removed his clothes, even his socks, and stood there feeling a little awkward since Bert was still fully dressed, leaning against the back of the couch, legs slightly spread.

"Good, Love. Lie across my lap, make sure your dick is between my legs. Your torso and arms should be on one side of my legs, your legs on the other. Get as comfortable as you can. You can hold yourself up with your arms, or we can move back and have the couch support you."

Luc moved, trying to find a somewhat comfortable position. He felt very vulnerable with his ass essentially in the air and like he could fall off if he moved wrong. Bert laid a hand across his back, keeping him from sliding. His cock rubbed against Bert's jeans, the slight roughness of the fabric causing him to harden.

"We're going to start with spankings. You can orgasm if you need to."

Bert let his hand fly, not giving Luc much of a warning.

Luc let out a short shout as the first smack sounded, the crack filling the air in the room. He could definitely feel it. It wasn't quite what he thought it would be. The people he had heard talk about spankings seemed to really like it, but it hurt. He could still feel the lingering sting; that part wasn't bad, he rather liked it. It was the initial pain that startled him. Maybe what everyone had talked about was that lingering sensation?

"First one done. What do you think?" Bert asked.

"It stings," Luc said.

"It does hurt," Bert agreed. "Don't focus on the pain. I want you to focus on my hand, me putting my mark on you, focus on how it makes you feel. Don't focus on the pain itself, focus on the endorphins that come from it, try to lose yourself in the sensations. There is a way for you to make it work for you, I promise."

"Okay," Luc reluctantly replied. He didn't know how to do that, but he would try. As the next blow landed on his other cheek, he blew out a breath, letting the feeling flow through him instead of tensing. The next few seemed better, Bert alternating between his cheeks. The placement of the hits varied, some landing more on the sides of his ass, some on the rounded parts. He focused on that lovely stinging sensation and the feel of Bert's skin on his and finally started feeling the warmth flow through his body, his body relaxing on its own. When Bert paused, he arched his ass up, trying to ask for more. He wanted more, he wanted to get to the floaty-not-thinking feeling he'd heard about.

"More? Green?"

"Yes, Mate. More, please. I need…I don't know…more."

"I've got you," Bert promised.

Luc moaned as the next hit landed between his upper thigh and the bottom curve of his ass. That one stung more but it also made him fly higher, his cock dripping. He desperately wanted to rub against Bert's leg.

"Please," he begged.

Bert responded by letting his hand fly faster and harder, no pauses between the hits anymore. Luc got lost in the sensations, his brain effectively shutting off, a buzzing filling his body, pushing out all thoughts and worries. He felt nothing but his Mate and the endorphins flooding him. One last hard smack had his orgasm tearing out of him, taking him by surprise. He didn't even have the breath to moan. Bert gently laid a hand on his ass, his other hand holding him securely on his lap. Luc's head rolled to rest against the couch.

Bert took in his sub, loving how boneless he was. He'd never seen Luc this relaxed. Bert could feel the wetness soaking through his jeans and he was so pleased Luc had climaxed. He wasn't sure Luc was fully in subspace, but he was probably close. Bert let him lie there for a few more minutes before gently wrapping his arms around him to ease him down onto the couch, essentially switching places with him. He grabbed the cream, soothing the red skin as Luc rested. His own cock was throbbing, but he would wait.

"Mate?"

"Hey, Love. I'm so proud; you found a way to make it work for you." Bert knelt on the floor next to the couch, keeping a hand on Luc. He gently stroked Luc's back, easing him down from the high of his orgasm and spanking.

"Hmm," Luc murmured, lying there, enjoying the sensations running through him.

It took a few minutes before Luc turned to face him. "May I?" he asked, his hand hovering over Bert's belt.

Bert nodded, his skin rippling with excitement as Luc's fingers brushed over his skin. Luc drew him out, his hands exploring and gently touching. "In," Bert said, as he gently guided Luc's head to his cock, the tip already dripping. Luc wrapped an arm around Bert's legs, keeping those blue eyes on Bert's face as he inhaled his cock, lips stretched around the shaft. "Good. Take me deep and swallow, lots of tongue," Bert instructed. It didn't take long to feel his balls draw up tight from the wet heat surrounding his cock. Luc's mouth was magical, his tongue swirling patterns around his shaft as his head bobbed back and forth. Bert gripped Luc's hair, holding him in place as his release flooded Luc's mouth.

As he began to soften, he let go of Luc's hair and tapped his cheek to be released. "Thank you, Love." He stood, bending to pick Luc up and carried him to the bathroom, shuffling a bit as his pants fell around his ankles. A soak in the huge tub would help soothe Luc's body and give him an excuse to hold him longer.

Bert was stuck watching this piece-of-shit falling-down house when he really wanted to be home with Luc. The office had received a call this morning that there was a nonhuman stalking and ensnaring humans, bringing them here. They weren't sure what he was doing with them, but the humans weren't coming back home. He was watching the house where the caller had reported seeing him, but so far there wasn't any movement.

Taking out his phone, he sent a text to Luc to let him know he might be late. He wasn't going to make the rules and not do his best to follow them as well.

This may take a while. No movement, so I may be here all night. I'll text an update later if possible.

He smiled as his phone buzzed right away. *Be careful. If he's only being seen at night with no trace of the humans after, he may be a soul eater. They eat everything, body, hair, bones all in one big gulp. They can unhinge their jaws. It's honestly disgusting to see, even if they're only eating a cow or something not a person. They capture the soul as well.*

Huh. That was not something that Bert had come across before. *Not familiar with that one. How do I save the souls if that's the case?*

They're rare; haven't come across one in a long time. Saving the souls is where it gets tricky. It's best done if the soul eater is still alive. I can reach in and pull the souls out, setting them free. It can be done if they're dead, but the victims' souls get tethered to the soul eaters' and I have to grab his soul and work at detaching them. They get absorbed after a time and it can be a process to untangle all the souls. You would think it would be as easy, or easier, as when they were alive, but for some reason it's not.

Crap. Okay, that made his job potentially harder. *I'll see if I can't bring him in alive then. If I get him, I'll let you know.*

Call Mac if you need backup. He's not on any heavy cases. Luc texted.

Will do. Make sure you eat dinner, Bert reminded him.

Bert sat watching for hours with nothing happening. Suddenly a crack sounded in the air, and someone ported rather clumsily across the street. Shit there he was...only there were two of them. It looked like identical twins and they were dragging a poor human between them. The human looked drugged, stumbling to keep up, making flirty comments but the words were slurred. Yup they were ensnared. Two of them might be harder to take and look out for the human at the same time.

He started typing a quick text to Mac with the address but before he hit send, the man on the right dropped his jaw to the floor. Yeah, that was not right. How was that even possible? As a long tongue came out of the mouth to wrap around the ankle of the human, Bert left his hiding spot, dashing across the street hoping he would get there in time to stop them.

"Hey, asshole. That's not what's for dinner. Let them go by order of the Enforcers," Bert shouted as he ran closer.

He threw a knife at the tongue as he rushed across the

street. Black blood dripped to the ground as the knife found its target. As the soul eater released a scream and its victim, the other one roared, charging at Bert.

Bert leaned forward, crouching down as if he was going to tackle him. Instead, he grabbed another throwing knife, tossing it at the oncoming monster. This close, he could see all the teeth filling the creature's mouth as it opened wide. Rows and rows of teeth, hundreds, maybe thousands, all sharp and pointed. It reminded him of a shark's mouth, but even more terrifying. As his knife hit home at the shoulder, Bert spun, pulling out his phone to finish sending the text. He could use the help. These guys could literally swallow him whole.

He should have really kept his eyes on the first guy, Bert thought as he was suddenly looking up at the sky. He bounced to his feet, grabbing the now unconscious human and dragging them further away from the house. Maybe someone passing by would help them. At the very least he could get them out of the way of the fight. He grunted as a fist connected with his kidney, and he kind of tossed the human into some softish-looking bushes. He couldn't help either one of them if he was killed because his hands were full.

Bert spun, throwing his foot out in a kick, pushing one of the soul eaters away. The other was circling his back, he could feel the change in the air as they came closer. He waited until he thought the soul eater was within range and called out his wings, smashing them into the guy's face. He stumbled back and Bert quickly beat his wings, trying to get some air so he could get them both in front of him. One reached out, but he was just out of range. Bert turned, intending to fly into the building, away from human eyes on the street and where he could have a wall to his back, making it harder for them to get behind him. He'd barely made it past the doorframe when he was yanked down to the ground, landing hard with a grunt.

As he was dragged outside, he saw his phone on the floor. He stretched, fingertips glancing the edge, but he twisted and reached for all he was worth when he saw the huge open mouth in front of him. The stupid motherfucker had used his tongue to yank him down, Bert realized. Finally getting close enough to hit send, Bert slammed his finger down on the screen, hoping he hit the right spot as he was jerked past it, his head smacking into the doorframe.

Grunting, Bert twisted onto his back to be greeted with the sight of a second large drooling mouth open in a hideous smile. The man looked over Bert and licked his lips. He had never felt like such a piece of meat, Bert thought, disgusted, and not in the fun kind of way. Using all those hours in the gym and training to his advantage, he quickly curled into a sit-up, his fist flying to connect with the asshole's face.

As the one stumbled back, he felt a searing pain in his leg and looked down to find the other one didn't want to wait for a taste.

"Are you fucking kidding me right now?" he muttered, even as he kicked the head with his other foot. He twisted, trying to reach his other knife when suddenly the mouth on him went slack. Mac was there, choking out the soul eater who had bitten him.

"Don't kill him," Bert said. He got an incredulous look in return, but as soon as the guy passed out, Mac threw some cuffs on him. Bert could feel the magic and knew the guy wasn't going anywhere.

"You're going to have to chase him down," he said,

pointing to the other soul eater who was trying to run away.

"Can't kill this one either?" Mac sighed sadly.

"Nope."

Mac cursed under his breath and took off running. He was fast though and soon was dragging the other soul eater back by the feet, their wrists cuffed. If he wasn't such a murderous asshole, Bert would feel sorry for him as his head smacked along the bumpy sidewalk. He probably shouldn't have run where the sidewalk was being broken apart by tree roots, Bert thought vaguely.

"Thanks," Bert said. "I wasn't expecting two."

"What the fuck are they?" Mac asked, retrieving Bert's phone and handing it to him. Bert was busy ripping his shirt off to wrap around his leg.

"Soul eaters, I think. At least that's what Luc thought they were based on the description we got. Not sure why Base didn't include that possibility in their report. Would have been good to know what I was up against. Supposed to bring them to Luc so he can try to retrieve the souls they've taken." Bert sent his lover a quick text, letting him know there had been two and that he and Mac would be bringing them in shortly.

"So literal soul eaters then. Nasty. Are you okay to port there with cargo?" Mac asked in concern. He could see the blood from Bert's leg already soaking through the makeshift bandage.

"Yeah. Can you call in a healer who can give the human a quick exam?"

Mac nodded. "I know someone who will come. She'll drop them off at the human hospital if there's nothing magically wrong with them," Mac replied, already typing on his phone. A few minutes later a young woman arrived;

witch, if Bert had to guess. She started to go to Bert, but he waived her off.

"Check the human please and get them to a hospital if needed," Bert said.

"You need a hospital. Their mouths are full of awful bacteria," she replied.

"I need to get them to Netherworld first. Thanks for your help," he replied. He grabbed bitey-face and ported to Luc's hearing room. He knew Mac would follow.

Landing was a bit wobbly. Maybe he needed to tie the wrap tighter, it seemed to be bleeding a lot. Mac ported in next to him, close enough to stand shoulder to shoulder, inconspicuously giving Bert something to lean against without looking like he was leaning because he was weak. Luc was already standing there, concern on his face, but he locked it away, protecting both of them. To appear weak would be dangerous.

"Let's see what we have here," Luc murmured, coming closer. Bert slid a knife into his hand, not willing to let his Love be hurt by the creatures he brought in. And he said creatures because these were not people, they didn't care about others, they had crossed the line many times and had become the monsters humans thought they all were.

"You two have been busy. I'm not sure how you haven't been on the radar until now. Thirty souls between you. Greedy, greedy. Let's give them their freedom, shall we?" Luc's hand suddenly had his demon claws as he plunged it into the chest of bitey-face, causing the drooler to scream in rage and lunge at Luc. Mac grabbed him by his shoulder, holding a knife under his chin. If he tried that again, he'd ram the blade through his own skull.

Luc pulled his hand back out with a squelch, holding a

glowing pouch. He carefully cut it open, holding the pulsing lights gently as he examined it.

"Hey, God!" Luc suddenly shouted.

"What?" a disembodied voice replied grouchily.

"I need you here," Luc replied.

Bert made an effort to stand as straight as possible as his boss ported into the room. God glanced at his leg in concern but was quickly distracted by what Luc was holding.

"Soul eater? We haven't seen those in decades, maybe longer," God muttered.

Luc nodded, his face unhappy. That could be from the way Bert's leg was making a small puddle on his floor though. "These belong to you," he said, gently transferring the souls over to God's waiting hands. "I have one more to check." He plunged his hand into the other soul eater, squishing around in there for a bit before pulling out another pouch. Opening this one, he put the knife away, extracting two from the pile. "These are mine, the rest are yours," he told God, sliding the others into God's cupped hands.

"Thanks. Be well. Are we still on for game night?" God asked. When Luc nodded, he ported out, carrying the souls with him.

Luc looked at the two he had taken. "It seems like you at least got a couple of scum bags. It would have been better for you if you had only eaten the evil and left the others alone." Luc nodded over to a waiting Enforcer, handing him the two souls. "Level six," he instructed.

"This part would have gone much easier on you if you hadn't tried to eat my mate," he said with a downright scary grin, the flames in his eyes betraying his rage.

The two men screamed in agony as Luc plunged his hands back inside them, pulling out their intestines and...other things. That was kind of gross, Bert thought vaguely, as a spray of blood arced out and splattered him and Mac. He kind of lost track of time, his body still bleeding and weakening. He felt like he had a fever and his head was congested. Mac moved closer, letting Bert lean heavily against him. Finally, Luc plunged his hands inside the prisoners one last time. Looking up, he said, "Let go." Mac quickly yanked his hands off, forcing Bert to do the same. The smell of burning flesh filled the air as Luc called his hellfire and burned them from the inside out. As the souls tried to escape, Luc held up a hand, freezing them in place.

"You have killed, maimed, and taken the souls of those who did not belong to you. For that you are ended. You shall not be reborn," Luc declared, his voice deeper, throbbing with power. The flames in his eyes swelled, taking over the blue until only the black and flames of his demon remained. Closing his fist, the souls crumbled into dust, dropping to the floor, only to disappear in a blaze of fire.

That was hot, Bert thought as his mate came to stand in front of him, covered in blood, a streak of it across his cheek.

"Thank you, Mac, for helping. Go get a shower and head home. I'll call you later," Luc promised.

Mac looked at Bert, quirking an eyebrow up at his uncle.

Luc smiled, this time a normal love-filled one. "I've got it," he replied.

Mac nodded, patted them both on the back and ported out. Probably to the showers.

"Let's get you to the hospital," Luc murmured, coming over to wrap an arm around Bert's waist.

"I can wash it off at home and throw a healing cream on it," he protested.

"It's my job to look after you too," Luc pointed out. "Please, Mate."

Bert sighed, but if he expected Luc to take care of himself it was fair that he do the same. "Alright. Is there a local one?"

Luc simply grabbed him tighter and ported.

15

ert was ready to leave. It had been two hours since they had arrived. They had pumped him full of antibiotics on top of the healing potion and cream. The witch hadn't been exaggerating about the bacteria in a soul eater's mouth based on the way everyone had freaked out. There were a lot of puncture wounds, his lower leg looked a bit like a raw country fried steak when they cut his pant leg off, but he still thought it was all overkill. But Luc had asked him to get treated and he would honor that. He had been feeling really crappy, so it was probably best he came anyway.

What had him ready to rip out his IV and storm out the door was his Luc. Luc had ported them to the in-between realms hospital. He said it had the best doctors and the most resources. Considering it touched Netherworld, Arlysium, and Earth, it did have the best of all three. The longer they were there, the more agitated Luc got. It didn't have anything to do with Bert's leg, although he was clearly concerned about that as well.

No, it was something else. He studied his lover, looking past the work mask he had donned as soon as they had arrived. There was barely controlled panic in his eyes, his breathing was steadily speeding up and becoming a bit erratic. His heart was pounding. If he didn't know any better, Bert would think Luc was having a panic attack. But why would the ruler of Netherworld be panicking? He wasn't dying, no one was in danger. He had to be wrong.

As a light sweat broke out over Luc's skin, Bert grabbed his hand, noticing how clammy it was. Bert realized that something was very wrong with his mate.

"Luc, are you okay?" he asked quietly so no one could overhear.

"Yup. How are you?" came the almost dead-toned question. He had never heard Luc's voice so flat.

"I'm good. I'd be even better if you would look at me."

Luc's eyes darted to Bert's before scanning the room again. His breathing was ragged and uneven. Glancing at his IV bag, Bert realized that the nurses would be back soon. He needed a way to protect his mate quickly. He scrambled, trying to think of something that would help. Wait, Viv had panic attacks. Mac had mentioned an exercise that helped. What was it? It was a countdown or something. There was something about sour candy that helped too, but he didn't have any.

He forced his brain back on track, to focus on what Mac had told him months ago. It counted down from five. Grabbing Luc's hand he squeezed to get his attention. "Eyes on me, Mate. Now," he commanded, putting every bit of Dom in his voice.

As soon as Luc's eyes met his, he said, "Name five things you can see." As Luc muttered off items, Bert tapped them out on Luc's hand. "Four you can touch." Tap, tap, tap, tap. "Three you hear." Tap, tap, tap. "Two smells." He held in a grin at Luc's wrinkled nose. Tap, tap. "One taste," Bert said, pulling him down to kiss him. Tap.

Luc stared into Bert's eyes, not even blinking. "Good,

Love. Focus on me, focus on your Mate. I will not let anyone harm you. Yes? And you won't let anyone harm me," Bert said, giving Luc something else to focus on.

The exercise seemed to help, his breathing slowing down a little. Bert didn't remember seeing this before and wondered how common they were. How could he make this work without drawing attention to them? If they were in public, maybe he could use the taps as a signal. He'd have to practice with Luc at home. Squeeze for attention, taps to count down.

Minutes later, the doctor knocked on the door before coming inside. "It's looking all clear. Let's get you disconnected and you can go home. I'd like you to have one more healing potion, just to err on the side of caution, but I think everything looks good."

Luc's mask was firmly back in place, but he kept hold of Bert's hand as he stood stiffly next to him. Bert downed the healing potion quickly, signed some paperwork, and ported them home.

Where Luc immediately tried to hide. He fussed around the house, cleaning up, getting Bert a glass of water, having him sit on the couch and propping Bert's leg up. The skin had already healed, so the extra attention was unnecessary. Bert let it happen for a few minutes, but when it became clear that Luc wasn't going to stop, Bert grabbed his hand on the next pass.

"Luc, I'm fine. The house is fine. We'll heat up a pizza in a minute. Look at me please," Bert asked. Luc briefly met his gaze, shame in his eyes.

"Can you tell me what happened?" Bert asked gently.

The shadow of a patrolling Enforcer darkened the window. Bert stood, pulling Luc after him into the den and shut the door. No one else needed to hear. "You were fine at the hearing room. It wasn't until the hospital that something happened. Is it the hospital? Do they bother you?" He deliberately didn't use the word afraid; he was trying to get answers and he didn't want Luc to think for one second that he was making fun.

Luc shook his head. "No. I've been in plenty. Hospitals don't bother me."

"Was it me being injured?"

Another head shake. "I didn't like it, so please avoid it as much as possible, but it's part of the job."

When there were no other answers forthcoming, Bert took a minute to think. It was something his mate was ashamed of, something no one else knew, he would guess. He ran through everything he knew about Luc. His parents were dead, his brother and sister-in-law had been killed, he raised Mac, watched Mac get married here in Netherworld. He had gone to the same hospital to greet Mac's baby when he was born, which did make it seem like it wasn't the hospital.

Wait. Had he ever heard of Luc leaving before that? Many, many years ago, yes...but since his brother had been killed... No. Enforcers loved to gossip. He knew every time God went to Earth or Netherworld, had a dinner party, whatever. He never really heard that about Luc. It could be he was more private, but what if he didn't actually leave? God always came here, Luc never went to Arlysium. It wasn't because he wasn't allowed, so why did he never go there? And he noticed Luc was uncomfortable at the hospital waiting for the birth, if he remembered correctly.

Bert took hold of Luc's head, cupping it in his hands. "Luc. Are you agoraphobic?" Bert asked gently, forcing his eyes to meet his.

The flood of shame and self-hate and despair that filled

those beautiful eyes took his breath away. How was this possible?

"Not in the usual sense," Luc admitted quietly. "I can go anywhere in Netherworld. It's when I try to leave for Earth or Arlysium that I have problems."

This was a conversation that might take a while and Luc might need more of his Dom for this, so Bert pulled them down to the couch, sitting with his recently healed leg propped up on the couch, the other bent, foot on the floor. He positioned Luc in front of him, cradled between his legs, facing away from him. He thought that might make it easier for Luc to talk.

"When did this start?"

"After my brother and sister-in-law were killed. I was fine before then. I didn't love to travel, I liked being at home, but I could do it fine," Luc replied.

Bert knew they had been killed but he couldn't remember the particulars. "Can you tell me what happened? I only know they were killed."

He felt Luc's chest expand with the deep breath he drew in. He didn't mention the tremors that went with it.

"I was watching Mac while they took a short vacation. It was more of a long weekend. They had already visited parts of Netherworld and Arlysium and wanted to try Earth. They were porting to different cities and trying different foods, seeing the sights. We'd get little trinkets ported back home randomly, food or little toys for Mac, things like that. I'm still not sure what happened. This was back hundreds of years ago, and humans were even more superstitious and fearful then. They were muttering about evil demons, so either they saw them in demon form, a partial shift, or saw some magic that they couldn't explain. Whatever it was, they attacked. Eric and Olivia were outnumbered, but they were stronger. I don't know why they didn't defend themselves. They should have fought back, Eric especially. He'd made it through the wars and knew how to defend himself. I felt Eric's death in my soul and called one of my Enforcers to sit with Mac. I ported to him and—" Luc stopped.

"Couldn't you have interrogated their attackers to find out what happened?" Bert asked. As murderers, they would have gone to Luc's domain for punishment when they died.

Luc bowed his head, shaking it. "Eric was unrecognizable. They had mutilated his body, carving a cross on it. Like that would do anything," he scoffed. "And Olivia. They enjoyed themselves on her before they killed her. She had fought back, there was blood under her nails. Her clothing was shredded and there was a pile of blood pooling under her body," Luc said flatly, his voice void of any emotion.

Bert tightened his arms around Luc. What an awful thing to have seen and then he had to go home to tell Mac his parents were dead. Fuck.

"I went full demon and killed each and every one of them. I cut their tendons so they couldn't escape and I could take my time with each one of them. I tore strips of flesh from their bodies. I carved my name into their skin. I gave them the same torture that they inflicted on my poor sister-in-law. Hellfire-coated tails do not feel good, or so I gathered from their screams. I didn't make it quick. I made sure they felt every bit of pain they possibly could. They killed for no other reason than it was something they didn't understand and feared. They took my family from me.

"After I killed them, I grabbed their souls. I was going to get answers, I swear, but when I started looking...I only got glimpses of what could have been magic and them surrounding Eric and Olivia. I got feelings of smugness and lust, their joy in killing my family. I lost my temper and destroyed their souls. I needed to tell Mac something, so I made the best guess I could and said they saw his parents performing magic. It seemed like a logical answer based on what little I saw." Luc fell silent.

"What about having God talk to Eric or Olivia and ask them?" Bert asked when it seemed like nothing more was coming. Luc could have visited Arlysium to speak to them or God could have gotten the answers for him. Most people didn't have that option and he wasn't sure why Luc wouldn't have used it.

"I couldn't. I know it was a stupid response, but at first I was incredibly angry that they hadn't been more careful. It took me a very long time to lose that anger, and by then I had discovered that I couldn't leave Netherworld and asking God to do it seemed wrong. Not that he wouldn't, but I didn't want to put him in the middle. More time passed, I was raising Mac and trying to balance being there for him and work. They were dead, that wasn't changing, so I tried to put it all behind me. I just wanted them to have peace. There was no need to dredge it all up, I didn't think the answers mattered anymore."

Bert made sure to hold Luc tightly as he tried to process. Anyone would be angry their family had been murdered. There was a reason anger was one of the five steps of grief. He even understood the anger toward his brother and sister-in-law. It didn't make sense that the stronger nonhumans were killed by physically weaker humans. He'd seen it before though: someone could be hit from behind with a weapon or even a well-thrown rock and it dazes the person enough to be overcome, sometimes a loved one is threatened and the other person will allow themselves to be hurt or killed in an attempt to save them, and in the case of fated mates, when one dies, sometimes the other was so over-whelmed by the sudden loss of the bond that they're disoriented or lose the will to live. With Mac in the picture, Bert would bet it wasn't a loss of the will to live, but if one of them had died first, the other could have had a big enough shock to their system that they froze, giving the group of humans the opportunity to kill them.

It took a minute to reconcile the man he knew and loved, the man who raised Mac, with the man who was in the story. Torturing in forms of punishment yes, but using his tail to rape the men who had raped his sister-in-law... that did not match the loving and softer sides of the man he knew. Deep down, Bert also knew that Luc wouldn't have reached his position without having to do a few things to keep it. He'd never thought about it fully, about how much darkness there must be hidden deep in his mate or the lengths he was willing to go. Then again, Bert himself had supported Mac's torturing of the serial killer. Heck, he had even taken part.

He could say it was due to the circumstances or the trauma of what Luc had seen, but he'd also seen a different side of Luc tonight when he killed the soul eaters who had injured him. This was a pivotal point in their relationship, he realized. He could accept all of Luc or there was still time to walk away. They hadn't completed the mating bond yet.

Bert took a deep breath, the scent of his mate filling his nose. There was no way in this world or the next that he would ever walk away from this man again.

"I would ask that you not use your own body parts in future punishments," he said, trying to aim for a lighter tone. "Other than hands of course, or feet for kicking."

Luc snorted. "No. My tail got bleached and never used again. For anything."

Bert was startled at that bit of knowledge. Demon's tails were known to be very much a part of their sexuality, and that Luc had locked away that part of himself showed he was ashamed of how he had acted. That would be something Bert would try to work on later. Luc needed to love and accept all of himself.

"It was after that that you began having problems leaving Netherworld?" he asked instead.

Luc nodded. "No one knows, except God. He caught me during a meltdown trying to get to a meeting with him. I was late because I couldn't bring myself to port and he came to see what was taking so long. He comes here now. Oh, I forgot to tell you. We have a bimonthly game night here. It's next week."

Bert would address that later and see what he needed to do for game night. It would be weird hanging out with his boss, but it seemed like his mate and his boss were good friends, so he would need to get used to it.

"Do you think that we could look into ways to help you? I know how much you would like to be able to visit Mac and his family more. It would be great for you if one day you could do that."

"I tried on my own and you saw how well that worked. If you have ideas, I'm willing to try them, as long as you're with me."

"Always."

L uc was bored off his ass. He had already given up looking interested and was instead slouched down a little in the chair just enough that he was slightly reclined, legs crossed ankle over knee, arms draped on the armrests with his hands resting over the edge, head up but leaning against the back of the chair. The dispute hearings today were incredibly trivial. He'd already read both parties and they were both at fault.

He let them drone on as his brain wandered back to last night. He had been extremely relieved when blurting out the truth behind Eric's and Olivia's deaths hadn't pushed Bert away. Now he just needed to figure out how to seduce his partner into sex. Bert was clearly interested, and nothing so far had pushed him away.

Luc was also trying not to think about Bert being on another assignment. He knew logically the man was great at what he did and being injured was bound to happen sooner or later. Heck, even Mac had been injured multiple times and Luc had helped train him himself. He wondered if he could get them to partner up, although that usually wasn't how things ran in the Enforcers. Hmm...maybe he could get them both bonded to a hellhound and the dog could act as their partner. That wasn't a bad idea. Mac already had one for Viv; Luc could help add on another room to their house if needed for the dogs. He would have another litter coming in soon, maybe he could work it into a Christmas gift, although that seemed so far away. He could train the dogs and get their accreditation in order for when they were in the human world. It was something to think about anyway. He'd try to feel Bert out later.

How to seduce him though? It had been a long time since Luc had a bed partner, and never one that lived with him. Certainly, never one that was his Mate, both in the regular lowercase situation and in the uppercase lifestyle they now had. He didn't think Bert was the flower type or even love notes. Most of the stuff he had researched to help Mac didn't seem like a good fit. Bert did like sweets, so maybe chocolates would work. Luc drummed his fingers against his chair, thinking. Everyone in the magazines seemed to gush over gray sweatpants for some reason. He had a few pairs, so he could try wearing those when Bert got home. Maybe go shirtless too. Bert was generally in charge in the bedroom and Luc didn't want him to think he was pushing.

He was supposed to be honest at all times. Luc heaved out a sigh. How exactly did he bring that up though? *Excuse me, Mate. Would you please fuck and claim me?* Seemed a little much. He ran his thumb over the underside of his ring, reminding himself that Bert wanted this too. Luc forced himself to check in on the drivel in front of him. Holy shit, they were still arguing. Neighbor A didn't want to see Neighbor B walk around without a shirt on. Neighbor B hated when Neighbor A let their dog run between their yards peeing on everything. Neighbor B also had been walking around shirtless just to annoy his neighbor.

"Get a fence," Luc finally interrupted. "Either shut up

and deal with it or share the cost of putting a privacy fence between your yards. It stops you from seeing him without a shirt on, it stops your dog from going to the bathroom in other people's yards. Which is just rude, you should stop that anyway. Was this something you really needed me for? You couldn't have come to this conclusion on your own? You're both adults. Act like it." He got up and walked out. He was done for the day, his head pounding.

Bert was supposed to be back tomorrow, so Luc was going to go to the store, get steak, potatoes, and chocolate. He would do the laundry and make sure his sweatpants were clean and then try to seduce his lover into fucking him.

Bert rode his motorcycle down the road, loving that he was able to port it to Netherworld. Most people didn't have cars here since they could teleport, but since there were still streets, Bert had brought his. He wanted to take Luc for a ride soon and had bought an extra helmet. His assignment unfortunately was going long, but he had arranged for another Enforcer to take the shift tonight. He felt the strain when he was away from Luc for too long, although everyone said that would get better after they claimed each other.

He was earlier than expected at getting home; he was eager to see his Love. He parked the bike in front of the house. Walking in, he could smell baking potatoes, saw steaks waiting on the counter, and a metric shit-ton of chocolate scattered all over the table and the counters.

"What the…" Bert muttered to himself. He slowly spun, looking all over the kitchen. Did Luc buy out an entire chocolate store? Why?

"Luc? You home?" Bert called out.

"Yes! I'm here. I was in the shower," Luc shouted. Bert could hear his footsteps hurrying down the stairs. Hair still dripping wet, Bert watched as beads of water ran down that lovely bare chest. He followed one with his eyes until it disappeared into the band of gray sweatpants. Did Luc not have underwear on?

"You're early. I don't have dinner ready yet!" Luc told him, coming in for a kiss.

Bert slid his hands down to cup Luc's ass, confirming that no, Luc was not wearing underwear. Hmm, lucky him, he thought as his fingers kneaded the firm flesh. He grinned against Luc's lips as a moan vibrated in his lover's chest.

"May I ask what's with all the chocolate?" Bert asked, pulling his head back. He was fascinated by the blush that swept across Luc's face.

"I had a question for you and all the things I read didn't really fit us, but you do like chocolate and steak, and I had gray sweatpants. But then I didn't know which chocolate was your favorite, so I had to get all the kinds. There's white, milk, dark. All different percentages of dark really, plus all the fillings and toppings. I even got some candies that are covered in chocolate like the peanut butter cups."

Bert was amused by a babbling Luc and tried to figure how that all fit together. Chocolates and gray sweatpants—was Luc trying to seduce him?

"Mate. Stop," Bert interrupted. When Luc fell silent, Bert hooked a hand behind Luc's head, bringing their heads together. He placed one hand over Luc's heart, feeling it pounding away. "Ask your question." He watched as Luc's tongue darted out to wet his lips before speaking.

"Will you claim me?"

Bert chose not to verbally respond. He bent over, slinging Luc over his shoulder and ported to their bedroom. They had found out the hard way that Bert wasn't able to walk up the stairs carrying Luc without his feet or head hitting something, which was something he wanted to avoid tonight.

He took a few steps toward the bed, tossing Luc on it. "Stay there," Bert commanded. Bert grabbed a few things from his nightstand; the cuffs he had made for Luc, a blindfold, and the lube. "Scoot up a little, arms above your head. Make sure you're comfortable with them being there for a while." He watched as Luc moved into position, loving how with just a few words, he could see Luc relaxing. The cuffs were thick and sturdy but lined with a very soft leather. He didn't want to leave marks where they might show at work. They also had rings to attach chains that would clip to the bedframe. The chains were long enough that he could have Luc flip from his back to hands and knees, but not quite long enough that Luc could really sit up.

Bert let Luc get comfortable while taking off his own clothes. He straddled Luc's chest, brushing his dick against his skin, leaning over to attach the cuffs and chains to the bed and Luc's wrists. "Test those for me, make sure they're comfortable." He loved feeling Luc squirm beneath him. "Gorgeous," he complimented his mate.

Bert leaned down, kissing Luc, softly at first, gentle little barely-there kisses. As he felt Luc's cock harden completely, he bit down on Luc's lower lip, not hard enough to draw blood, but enough to make Luc gasp. Exploring and tasting his way down the hard body beneath him, Bert nibbled on Luc's neck, paying attention to the spot behind his ear that always lit him up, before reaching out to tease his nipples. Luc's were very sensitive and as soon as Bert brushed against them, they hardened into little peaks. He couldn't resist such a gift and he took one between his teeth, gently biting. Moving to the other one, he sucked the nub into his mouth, biting the entire area much harder. Luc moaned, his hips thrusting into the air. Bert moved lower, holding him down. Luc's hands rattled the chains, reaching for him.

"I'm not going anywhere, Love. Just playing and exploring," Bert told him.

He moved to lie between Luc's legs, which he had left unbound for now. He wanted to feel them wrapped around him, knowing that they were strong enough to break a man. The knowledge that Luc was strong enough to kill him but chose to submit was incredibly arousing. It was an honor he would never take for granted.

Bert slowly lowered the waistband of the sweatpants, just enough to allow the long thick shaft to escape. The foreskin was already pulled back, the head glistening with precum. Bert gently ran a single finger from the base of the shaft to the tip, where he flicked the head.

"Mate!" Luc shouted, his hips rising up and twisting, not sure if he wanted to get away or wanted more.

Bert held his hips down to the bed, taking Luc deep in his mouth and throat, swallowing around him. He kept his mouth tight, his tongue pressed firmly against Luc's cock, teasing it with long slow licks and fast head bobs. A few minutes later, he pressed one hand firmly on Luc's stomach to keep him still, moving the other hand to slide into the sweatpants to cup Luc's balls, his pointer finger and thumb curling to grip the base of the shaft. He felt Luc's sac tighten and he pulled off, blowing cold air across the tip. He wasn't ready for Luc to come quite yet.

Climbing off the bed, Bert reached back into the drawer and pulled out the simple leather cock ring. It snapped for easy removal, which they would need tonight. Closing it around Luc's shaft, he took in the sight of his lover lying there, chained to the bed, cock contained, chest heaving, pupils blown. Fates, he was lucky. Bert slid Luc's pants all the way off, jerking that pretty dick a few more times. Dropping a kiss on Luc's lips, he slid the blindfold over Luc's eyes.

"Use your words if you need them," Bert told him. They hadn't played with the blindfold yet, but he thought Luc would really enjoy it. He got a quick nod in return. As he moved around the bed, Luc's head swiveled, trying to follow the sound of him moving.

Bert grabbed both feet in his hands, massaging the arches, waiting until he felt the tense muscles relax. He ran his fingertips up one leg, gently pinching the head of Luc's cock before tracing down the other leg. Moving up the bed, he blew air across Luc's nipples, loving how tight they got.

"Turn your head, Love." Bert waited until Luc's head was fully facing him before he knelt on the bed next to him. Leaning over, he braced one hand on the bed to hold himself up, grabbing his dick and tapping it against Luc's lips. As his mouth opened, Bert slowly fed Luc his cock. "Swallow and long licks, please. Breathe when you can," he advised as he started thrusting down Luc's throat. He heard a few gags when he went deep, but Luc's tongue kept loving on him, so he wasn't worried. His mouth felt fantastic, warm, wet, just the right amount of pressure from Luc's tongue, his throat tight around his head. He enjoyed the feel of his mate for several minutes until the hot suction became too much and he pulled out, pinching the base of his own dick.

"Hands and knees," he ordered, watching as Luc's cock bobbed as he tried to get into position. The chains were now crossed but were still loose enough when Bert did a quick check. He took a minute to admire the rounded ass in front of him. Grinning to himself, he dove in without warning, holding the cheeks apart, his tongue finding Luc's tight hole.

Luc whimpered, pushing back into him. Bert licked until the opening softened, sliding his tongue inside. He licked and thrust until he felt Luc's legs tremble, grabbing the plug he had set aside earlier, wanting to keep Luc ready for him.

"What is," Luc began, breaking off on a moan as the plug slid all the way home.

"I found a nice plug for you," Bert replied, twisting it a little so it rubbed against his prostate.

"Uhn," Luc's voice strangled out.

Bert cupped Luc's sac, gently rubbing the balls between his fingers. He needed to see some angel wings on his man, he thought. Pulling back, he let his hand fly, the sound cracking through the air, leaving behind a nice handprint on Luc's cheek.

"Oh!" Luc gasped, hips arching into the sensation, searching for more.

Bert smacked the other cheek, loving his mark on his mate. "Hmm, I put some wings on you," he told Luc, placing his hands over the heated flesh, fingertips digging in a little.

"More, please," Luc begged.

Pressing a kiss to the small of Luc's back, Bert moved into a better position, letting his hand find its mark over and over again. When there was a nice even rosy hue, he leaned down to check on Luc.

"Good? Green?" he checked in.

"More, please. I need it harder, Mate," Luc sobbed, desperate for something but not knowing what. He was almost to that fuzzy place, and he wanted to get there so badly.

"I'm going to try something new, safe words please," Bert replied, walking to get the thin cane. They hadn't tried this yet, Luc had seemed nervous about it, but if he wanted harder, this would do it.

"Green, Yellow, Red. Please, please, plea—" the words broke off on a shout as the cane whistled through the air, finding its target, leaving a nice red line across both cheeks.

"Yes, more," Luc demanded, shoulders dropping to the bed, ass high in the air.

Bert stood behind him and laid down four more lines before ending with a fifth and final strike that came close to breaking skin, but stopped just shy of it. Dropping the cane, he moved to Luc's head, finding a smile on his lover's face, his body completely relaxed, other than the hard angry red cock. He dropped a kiss to Luc's forehead, moving to kneel behind him on the bed.

He gently slid the plug out and replaced it with his own shaft. He gritted his teeth at the tightness and heat of his lover's body and focused on slow steady thrusts. He ran a hand gently over Luc's back and ass, soothing the irritated skin. This was heaven. Playing with and loving on his sub. His body was coated in a fine layer of sweat by the time Luc roused enough to start meeting his thrusts.

"Ready, Love?" Bert asked between clenched teeth. He had been inside him for almost twenty minutes, and he was more than ready to come.

"Yes, please. Make me yours all the way," Luc demanded, a hand open and clenching for him.

Bert leaned over his back, holding himself up with one hand, his hips pounding into Luc's body. As his balls drew up, he tore himself away, gasping for breath. "Flip over." He wanted to see those blue eyes as he came.

Luc had barely settled before Bert grabbed his hips and impaled him on his dick again. Dropping down to lean over his lover, he kept his left wrist where Luc could grab it, using his other hand to rip off the blindfold and released one of Luc's wrists from the cuff. As Luc grabbed for him, he pressed his arm down into the mattress, holding him in place with his weight, his hips beating a hard, fast rhythm against Luc's body. As he felt his orgasm getting closer, he gasped out, "Now, Love."

Together they exchanged the words that would bind them together, forever. "You are my mate. I give to your keeping my body, heart, mind, and soul. I bind us together forever more." Luc surged up, chains clinking, his teeth locking onto Bert's chest. Bert turned his head, his teeth sinking into the tender skin between Luc's neck and shoulder, blood filling his mouth. As they both swallowed, Bert felt a burning in his wrist where Luc had grabbed him. He couldn't wait to see his mate mark. He had wanted his on Luc's wrist where everyone could see the marks whenever his shirtsleeves rode up. The caveman, or maybe the Dom, in him wanted everyone to know Luc was his and his only.

Feeling his orgasm rush through him, Bert looked down to admire the red angry bound cock of his lover. Ripping the cock ring off, he gripped the gorgeous shaft in front of him determined to bring his lover to orgasm. It only took two pumps of his hand before streams of cum pulsed out over Luc's stomach. Bert dropped to his elbows, keeping their bodies connected, resting against his mate until his cock softened. Pulling gently out of his lover, he reached up and released the other cuff, gently rubbing Luc's wrists.

"I love you," he told Luc.

"I love you too," Luc replied drowsily.

"Don't fall asleep yet, Love," Bert ordered, leaning over to grab one of the bottles of water he always kept next to the nightstand. "Drink this and then roll over so I can apply some lotion to your skin. You'll thank me tomorrow." He waited until the bottle was empty, used his shirt to wipe Luc clean before helping him roll over to his stomach. By the time Bert had finished smoothing the cream over the welts, Luc was softly snoring.

Bert climbed into bed next to his mate, holding him close, reveling in the bond he could feel forming between them.

Luc sat in his chair, grateful that there was adequate padding. Although the spanking and the caning had been exactly what he asked and hoped for, he was still a bit tender this morning. Bert had applied a soothing lotion last night, but Luc had said no to the healing cream this morning. He wanted to feel the proof of their mating night while Bert was gone again for his assignment. He could possibly be gone a few days this time. Luc couldn't wait until he heard the roar of the motorcycle coming down the street again.

Some of the kids on the street had seen it this morning and wanted to go for a ride. Bert mentioned he was going to order smaller helmets to have on hand so he could very slowly take them down the street. With their parents' permission of course.

"Sir, we're waiting on one more Enforcer before we begin," Greg told him. He liked to request time in the hearing room. He was a great Enforcer, but didn't really enjoy working in the punishment levels. He had been with the Enforcers for many years and they worked well together.

"Thank you, Greg. Who are we waiting for?" Luc asked.

"A new Enforcer, just got promoted. Keevhan, I believe his name is. I haven't worked with him before."

Luc wasn't familiar with him either. Which wasn't unheard of but was a little weird. He was normally introduced to new people when they made the rank of Enforcer, especially if they were employed through the Netherworld side of things.

"Do we know much about him?" Luc liked having a say on who was in the hearing room with him since things could get dicey. The Enforcers in the hearing room were on a rotation schedule. He didn't choose each person in here, but he did have a list that the scheduler usually used. While that list was pretty long, it still only contained experienced Enforcers who he was familiar with. He figured that having Enforcers in the hearing room who were skilled, quick, and able to handle a fight would be enough protection that he could give his personal guards time off while he was at work. The Enforcers who were in his personal guard were hand-picked by him. Their duties included patrolling his property and going with him when he had public-facing events, if he was going to be someplace questionable, or if there was an official meeting or work event. There was usually one or two in this building when he was here as well.

"No, sir," Greg replied. He hesitated, but moved closer to Luc, leaning over and dropping his voice. "I really don't like to gossip or be negative, sir. But I'm not comfortable with him being assigned to the hearing room. He's too new, most of us haven't heard anything about him or worked with him. Our job is to keep you safe, and the hearing room Enforcers have all trained or worked together so we can protect you to the best of our abilities. Having someone new that we have no experience with is asking for trouble.

"And I hate gossip, I really do. But I've been hearing that he got this job not through merit, but because someone slid him in above the other candidates."

Luc leaned back in his chair. He had known Greg for hundreds of years and he was right; Greg never spread gossip, at least not where Luc could hear. For him to actually say something meant that this was really bothering him. Paired with the fact that he had also never met this Keevhan, Luc was seeing red flags. It wouldn't be the first time a challenger had tried to sneak into an area where he was viewed as more vulnerable.

"Steve and Brandon?" Lucifer asked quietly.

"Same, sir."

Luc nodded. "Do we know who put him on the rotation?"

Greg shook his head. "I'm not the best with computers," he admitted. "I tried looking so I would have more to bring to you, but I couldn't come up with anything."

Luc grabbed his phone, calling his nephew. "Hey, I need you to check into something for me. I'll text you the details. Keep it quiet. Thanks."

"Thank you for letting me know," Luc told Greg. "If you ever feel concerned about something, don't hesitate to tell me. We've been together a long time and I want you to feel like you can come to me."

"Thank you, sir. Steve was having a friend of his snoop around to find out more. I don't like that scheduling could bypass all the normal protocols and add in someone so green. Steve, Brandon, and I will be maintaining the room today. We asked for Veek to be partnered with Keevhan to bring prisoners to the punishment levels, said it was part of the training for the hearing room."

"That's a great idea," Luc praised. "I have Mac looking

into it, and I'll see if Margo knows anything as well when I get back to my office. I think we should keep him on the schedule, but make sure he's paired with an experienced Enforcer we trust until we can learn who moved him up. I don't want to tip our hand and lose the opportunity to discover if we have additional problems. Please pass it on to Steve and Brandon when you get a chance with them alone," Luc added.

His gut was telling him that this was part of a bigger issue. He hadn't survived this long without listening to his instincts. Luc grabbed his phone again, sending a quick text to God. They usually heard different rumblings and sometimes when one side acted up so did the other, and he wanted to give him a heads-up.

There was a knock on the door, which had Luc raising an eyebrow at Greg. That was new.

Greg looked a little sheepish. "They knew I was working up to talk to you, so they said they would knock and wait to be let in, in case we were still talking."

Luc nodded. They really had talked about this amongst themselves. "Let's get started." He shifted in his seat, causing the remaining welts to send a flash of discomfort through him. Luc rubbed his ring, hiding his grin. He also reached down and made sure his dagger was still hidden in his chair. He probably needed to start carrying another weapon from now on until this all was resolved.

Greg moved to stand between Luc and the door, nodding at Steve to open the heavy wood doors. The doors swung open quietly, for all that they were immense. They had a solid steel core, surrounded by inches of thick hardwood. It would take a lot to get through them if they were bolted.

Luc quickly glanced at the prisoner. Ah, an assassin for

hire. Not a nice guy for sure, but certainly not someone who should have been brought before him. The judgment employees should have been able to handle this one. He'd ask Brandon who brought him to be tried.

He took a look at the new Enforcer. He honestly did not appear capable of the job. In general, Enforcers were larger, full of muscle and intimidating. His Bert was rather short for an Enforcer, although he was solidly built with plenty of muscles. That combined with his sheer presence, tattoos, and even the bald head, made him appear very intimidating.

This guy looked like he would run from a mouse. He wasn't intimidating anyone and looked like a feather could knock him over. Maybe he had hidden skills, Luc thought, chastising himself for making a judgment before really examining him. When he tried to look closer, he ran into a blank wall. What the fuck? He'd been able to read anyone since the day he earned this position. Anyone. Yet this new guy, he couldn't. Taking a deep breath disguised as a sigh, he realized Keevhan reeked of magic. They all did to a certain extent as it was so prevalent in their world, but this was too strong for that. It had a different scent than Keevhan's natural scent, so he would wager that he was spelled.

While Keevhan was busy gawking around the room, Luc made eye contact with Greg and Steve, giving them the signal that there could be trouble. They had come up with it years ago after a few altercations in the hearing room. Greg's face immediately turned into a scowl, thunderclouds passing over his face.

"I don't need to draw this out," Luc said, trying to cut any problems off before they began. "Level eight."

"Wait! What! You aren't going to try him, let him say he's sorry or anything?" Keevhan blurted out incredulously.

"Excuse me? Did you really just question The Lucifer?" Steve asked, his body going stiff with anger.

"Yeah. I did. So what? He didn't even talk to the guy," Keevhan said, his voice bordering on belligerent.

Luc saw his Enforcers take a step toward the new guy. He could feel a weird hum in the air and he rose from his chair, making sure the dagger was tucked in his belt before he stood.

"I don't need to. The power of this position lets me see into a person's soul. I know all the kills he's done, even those he committed just for fun before he decided to make a living out of it. I can see all the women he's raped, all the animals he's tortured. There is no remorse, no repentance in his soul. To give him mercy would condemn another to die. I will not have that," Luc stated. He stood close to the man, raising his voice to call in Veek and Brandon from the hallway. Once they had custody and were escorting the assassin out of the room, Luc turned his attention to the blank wall in front of him. Who appeared too stupid to realize he was in danger. Steve and Greg had moved to flank Keevhan, Luc facing him.

What most people didn't know was that if he tried hard enough, he could get past those pesky little blockers. It was literally in the job description that he passed judgment on any and all. To do that, he needed to see into their being, into their soul, see their lives. His eyes roamed over the man's body, seeking the source of the magic. It didn't read with the same energy as the rest of him, making it clear it wasn't his magic and also making it easier to follow.

Ouch. He'd participated in a little blood magic. That never ended well. Now the real question was if he had been made to participate, or if he had been willing. Hm. Gullible, but willing. What was the goal though…Luc needed to dig a little deeper and he left his body for a second, sending his consciousness to plunge into Keevhan.

"What's he doing? He's just standing there." Keevhan sounded very confused. Luc briefly registered that Greg had moved so that he was now standing in front of Luc slightly, better able to defend his body.

"My guess would be judging you," Steve said dryly, grabbing Keevhan's arm as he tried to run.

"He can't judge me! I don't consent to that. And I'm not dead; he has no control over me. Stop! I demand you stop!" The panicked voice kept rising. Dumbass. He didn't need to be dead for Luc to read him, and as an Enforcer, Luc definitely had control over him.

Hmm. He was not the brains behind this attempt to get insider information. It was a pretty poor plan as they hadn't trained him on how to blend and interact at all. Luc couldn't tell if it was a test to see if they could get in, or a blatant slap in the face that they could get this close to begin with. In Keevhan's memories, the leader always stood in the shadows, wore a hood, or obscured himself in some way. It was like he knew of Lucifer's powers and was finding ways around them.

That's okay, Luc thought. He would dig a little deeper and see what he could pull out. There had to be a phrase, a glimpse, a blemish on the skin showing somewhere. Keevhan never saw his face, but there had to be something. He saw the man in charge talk about leading them to greatness again, getting rid of Lucifer and putting a stop to this soft lazy way of life, promising his followers power and money and greatness. Luc sighed. Another power-hungry narcissist who wanted his job. Great.

"I said stop!" Keevhan was screeching now, making Luc's ears hurt even though he wasn't in his body. "What was it...expulsion...no...expedite...no, no. That's not it. Eviscerate?"

What was he going on about, Luc wondered. He knew his Enforcers were holding him, so he wasn't worried about physical harm to himself. There was something about the shadow man that was tickling his brain, something about him—

"Extirpate! Ha, that was it!" Keevhan shouted victoriously. Luc had a front-row seat to see a spell activate and he pulled himself out quickly. That was not going to end well.

"That was a kill switch," Luc said, adopting a conversational tone.

"He said it would stop you," Keevhan replied, still sounding smug.

"Oh, it will stop me from examining you right now," Luc agreed, "because it's a kill switch, for you. I can still grab your soul whenever I want to and have another look. However, it doesn't seem like you know much. This is just someone cleaning up after themselves, making sure you're not a loose end.

"Step back," he instructed his men, not wanting them to get caught in any backlash when the spell detonated.

"No, he promis—" Keevhan stopped talking, his mouth filling with bloody foam, his muscles spasming, his neck finally snapping on its own.

"Well, that's something," Luc murmured. "Let's get someone in here to clean this mess up. Keep your ears open. From what I could see, someone else was behind this, but he's being very careful not to let people know what he looks like. I don't think it's going to stop here. I believe there may be other incidents."

"Sir, maybe you should request scheduling to only assign certain people here. Until we get this figured out, I would feel better about having only people we can trust in here," Greg suggested.

"Who do you recommend?" Luc asked.

"Myself, Steve, Brandon, Veek, Scott, and Mal. If we need more, I have a few others, but between the six of us, we should have enough to rotate shifts."

"I agree, sir. I don't know what's going on, but we're not going to allow you to be injured on our watch. You've been the best leader we've had. We've had peace, and our families are thriving. You're fair but not a pushover, you can show compassion but can be vicious in defending your people. Your name strikes fear in other nonhumans, but your people love you," Steve spoke up.

Luc schooled his features, working hard on not letting a blush hit his skin. One would think he was too old to get flustered over a compliment, but he honestly had no idea his Enforcers felt so strongly. He cleared his throat before speaking. "Thank you. I don't say it enough, but I appreciate each and every one of you. Without you, none of this would be possible."

He watched as his men slapped an arm across their chest, bowing their heads to him.

This was bad, Bert thought. He watched as an incubus was brought into the shabby building he had been observing. They were clearly unconscious, their feet dragging as they were pulled by their arms. He was the third delivery of this kind in the last hour. He sent a quick message to Base, knowing that he would need backup, or at least help with cleanup. Cloaking himself, he snuck around the backside, using his wings to reach an open window on the third floor. He peeked inside, disgusted at what he saw.

The room itself was disturbing; a bare mattress on the floor, single light bulb hanging from the ceiling, chains and large metal cuffs attached to the wall, questionable stains splattered around the room. It smelled like old semen and blood. He held his fury back; killing the one or two that were here now wouldn't help stop this.

Keeping himself cloaked, he slowly turned the door handle, listening intently for any movement on the other side. When it remained quiet, he slipped out of the room and made his way down the hallway. The building was full of similar rooms, a few containing people chained to the wall or curled up on the mattresses. Some had clothes on, some were already naked, bruises marking their bodies. It looked like they had been here longer. He saw a vampire, his skin unhealthily pale. The man was skin and bones and had clearly not been fed for a long time. A gag was covering their mouth, keeping his teeth from biting anyone. It wasn't like any gag he'd seen before; it was clear so you could see his teeth. Everyone looked like they had been drugged.

As he moved his way to the second floor, he had to duck out of the way as the incubus was brought up the stairs. The men carrying him were nonhumans, which at least made his job a little easier in terms of paperwork, but not in terms of stopping them. He sent another text requesting backup to be on standby. He needed to locate the office to make sure documents weren't destroyed when it was raided.

Once they passed him, Bert quickly looked around the second floor. It was similar to the third, full of bare mattresses and signs of past abuse. He made his way down the stairs where the main floor looked nothing like the upper levels or the outside. It was designed like a high-end salon or club. There was a check-in desk, a waiting area, even a water cooler with lemon slices in it. The floors were polished, the walls painted a soft gray, plush couches and chairs were scattered about, soft jazz music playing. What the fuck? One wall was lined with glass shelves holding a variety of items. Based on what he'd seen so far, he would hazard a guess that this was a brothel using trafficked people as their merchandise. The shelves held sex toys, whips, even hammers and other things that should never be used in sex. He felt ill when he saw several items he himself had used in scenes.

Hearing raised voices, Bert made his way to the back of

the building, finding two people, a human and a nonhuman, arguing in what had to be the office.

"We need more variety," the human was saying.

"It's easy to grab humans, not so much for others like me," the one protested. "If you think it is, you go get some."

"People want to fuck something different and scary. Nonhumans want the humans for the novelty, they want to see how quickly they can break them. Humans want the thrill of having something that could kill them at their mercy so they can do whatever they want to them. We don't have enough to satisfy the clients right now and they're going to look elsewhere if we don't up our game."

"Look, we've got an incubus in tonight. Let him starve for a week and he'll do whatever we want. We won't have to even drug him as much as the others. I have a new drug coming in for the nonhumans. It's supposed to make them so horny that they'll do anything to feel relief; it chemically blocks everything else in their brain, ramping up their desperation. They'll feel like they'll die if they don't come. Of course, it also blocks them from orgasm, making them more and more willing to keep fucking. It'll make it more enjoyable for our clients when their purchase isn't just lying there drooling."

"What are we doing for the human ones?" the human asked.

How people could do this to each other, much less to others of their own kind, was something Bert would never understand.

"A modified version is coming for them too. The nonhuman version is too strong and would kill them. It will arrive before opening tonight and we can dose everyone before the clients show up. You need to stop worrying so much."

The human snorted. "Right."

Bert waited until they had both left the office, watching as they walked down the hallway. He quickly searched the computer, downloading its contents to his flash drive. As it worked, he rifled through the cabinets and drawers, taking pictures on his phone. They certainly liked to keep their records tidy. Nothing spelled out 'illegal,' but each invoice had a name attached to it, which would hopefully help the investigation grab more of the people involved. Trafficking needed to be stopped. End of story.

Bert watched out a window as a sleek black car pulled up, one of the owners running out to talk to the person in the car. He took pictures of the exchange. This had to be the drugs they had been discussing earlier.

He walked through the building one more time, sending images and locations of the victims to Base. He didn't want them injured when the other Enforcers arrived. He didn't expect the owners of this operation, or the 'clients,' to calmly let themselves be arrested.

When he heard multiple voices in the front room, he made his way there, keeping his phone recording. There were easily now twenty people of all different species in the waiting room. He sent out another update to work and also sent a text to Luc. He expected this to take a while, and he had promised to keep him updated.

His phone vibrated with the notification that the other Enforcers had arrived and were hidden outside waiting for his command. One of the men who had brought the incubus in, entered the room, tossing a syringe in the trash. No syringe canister here.

"Everyone is ready, boss," he said.

Shit. Goddamn mother fucker piece of shit. Bert had been hoping that he would stop them before they dosed the victims; he hadn't seen him when he was upstairs cataloging locations. He sent a request for medical to Base. Before he could put his phone away, he received the signal that a security dome had been enacted. He gave the sixty-second signal before uncloaking himself and stepping into the room.

"You're all under arrest by order of the Enforcers," he announced, holding his gun by his side.

He watched as the various men and women gathered looked around and laughed seeing only him.

"Kill him," the human boss ordered.

Well that went to crap fast, Bert thought as he brought his gun up to shoot at the advancing group. He wanted to keep as many as possible alive for questioning, although he could always have his lover grab their souls and question them later, he thought with a grin.

As a knife glanced over his bicep, the front door was shattered by the Enforcers storming in. He heard others entering from upstairs and the back door. Bert threw himself into the fray, firing away with one hand and slashing his knife with his other.

Bert stood in borrowed scrubs, his own clothes destroyed. They had been coated in blood and that shit never came out. He was checking on the victims they had pulled out tonight. A lot of souls had been sent to Netherworld for processing. They had managed to keep a few alive though and they were currently being questioned. He wouldn't feel good about going home until he laid eyes on all the victims and made sure they were getting the help they needed.

He was currently standing outside a room, watching as the unconscious man continued to hump the air. The doctor checking the man's vitals turned, seeing Bert. Stepping out of the room, the doctor gestured him further down the hallway.

"We've given them an antidote, but it takes time to work. We're keeping them all unconscious while the drug leaves their system, in an attempt to lessen the strain on their bodies. The vampire is getting blood through a feeding tube, humans are on IVs with fluids. The rest are being similarly treated based on their species. I'm glad you brought them here instead of a human hospital; we were able to magically scan for sexual trauma and disease since there were both human victims and abusers. We have therapists standing by for when they wake up.

"This kind of thing makes me sick. I hope you killed them all," the doctor said before clapping him on the back and walking away.

Bert checked in with the Enforcers who were stationed nearby. They wanted to make sure the victims were kept safe while they recovered. It appeared to be a single operation, but until they went through all the evidence in the office and confirmed there wasn't anyone higher up who could come after them, there would be guards nearby. He ported to work, finishing his paperwork, before heading home. He needed to hold his mate and forget that people were horrible for a minute.

Luc was stirring the chocolate pudding on the counter, wanting to have something sweet for when Bert came home. It could sit in the fridge until they were ready to eat it.

He felt the wards flex as someone ported in. Strong arms wrapped around his waist, and he smelled his mate under the scent of soap. He hurriedly ran the pudding through the strainer, scraping it into the waiting bowl and covering it with plastic wrap. He'd put it in the fridge in a minute. He could feel the tension in the arms holding him and he wanted to give him his full attention.

"Are you okay?" he asked, turning around to hold Bert tight.

Bert shook his head. "I need you tonight and I don't know if it will be gentle or not. I need to forget for a bit."

"Whatever you need, Mate. I've got you. I trust you." Luc knew Bert would never hurt him and with one word he could stop everything. He wanted to make his mate feel better and if this was what he wanted, then Luc would do his absolute best to give it to him.

Bert drew in a shuddering breath. "Go put that in the fridge. Thank you for making it. We'll eat it later," he said, releasing Luc, tapping him on the ass. He wanted to lose himself in the feel of his mate, erase the images from tonight, both from what he had seen and the recordings they had found in the office. The men who had frequented the brothel had used some of the same tools he did during scenes, but they had perverted it. There were no safe words, no care given to their partner. He was fine with anyone who chose to become a sex worker, but those people had had no choice. They had been kidnapped and drugged. What had been done to them was abuse, not anything remotely like the true practice of BDSM. But the visual still made him feel dirty. He wanted to erase it, to cleanse himself through his mate's love.

"Go upstairs, in the den please, Love. Wait in your position," Bert instructed.

Luc nodded, pressing a soft kiss to Bert's lips before shoving the bowl in the fridge and rushing up the stairs. Bert waited a minute, taking the time to calm himself as best he could. He opened the refrigerator and swiped a quick bite of the pudding, almost burning his tongue. That was going to be delicious when it was cold.

He slowly made his way up the stairs, his breath catching as he saw his mate kneeling on the plush rug that they had bought for just this purpose, completely naked, waiting. Bert walked by him, resting a hand on Luc's head for a second before going to his cabinet to pull out some toys and the bottle of lube. He debated on what to use; no blindfold tonight, he needed to be able to see Luc's blue eyes looking back at him. A plug and cock ring of course, giving them more time to play. A paddle maybe, or he could do a traditional spanking. They hadn't tried the nipple clamps or flogger yet, he thought, pulling those out.

Walking back to his lover, he saw Luc was already hard from the anticipation of what was going to happen. Bert wished they had a St. Andrew's cross in here. Luc would look incredible on it, but he didn't want to leave to go to the club right now, not with a naked sub waiting for him. Maybe next weekend.

"Color?"

"Green, Mate."

Bert nodded, running a hand over Luc's penis, earning himself a groan, precum leaking from the tip. He quickly snapped the cock ring in place.

"Up on the table, hands and knees, arch back for me."

He bit his lip as he watched Luc climb onto the coffee table, his gorgeous ass up in the air. He laid the lube and plug within reach, kneeling behind him. Blowing a breath across Luc's skin, he admired the shiver and the way his hole clenched. Bert dove in, licking and nibbling, tearing moans and whimpers from Luc. He loved getting his mate ready this way, Luc was so sensitive and responsive.

Releasing the cock ring for a minute, Bert said, "Shift for me." They hadn't had sex yet in their shifted forms, and Bert wanted access to all parts of his mate. He watched as the black wings and tail appeared, the horns curling down to his ears. His mate was gorgeous all tan skin, his eyes black in this form, the wings covered in demon markings and tipped in sharp points. He was lethal and all Bert's.

He was glad he had bought a nonhuman cock ring, he thought, snapping it around Luc's shaft. It had several snaps, allowing for the change in shifted size. Lubing a few fingers, he plunged them deep in his mate, wanting Luc to feel the sting. With an evil grin, he pressed against Luc's prostate at the same time as his other hand rubbed the base of Luc's tail. It had been so much fun teaching Luc to embrace and enjoy tail play again. He only stroked for a minute or so, until he felt the tremor in Luc's legs, knowing it would be overstimulating soon. Running a hand over Luc's back, he traced over the area where his wings sprouted. The texture here was such an odd mix of human skin and the leathery feel of the wings, the bones protruding a bit, prominent enough to feel.

"Arms crossed on the table, head lying on your arms, Love." Bert leaned over, gently biting an ass cheek before sliding the plug inside his mate. He tapped the base, knowing it would nudge Luc's prostate.

"Mate, please," Luc gasped.

"Are you ready?"

"Yes."

Bert knelt next to Luc's head, his hands finding the little nubs of his nipples, pinching them and getting them ready. Once he had Luc twitching and gasping, Bert attached the clamps, tightening them enough to cause a little pinch. Grabbing the flogger, he gave a practice swing as he moved to stand behind his partner. He hadn't played with this in quite a while. It wouldn't hurt much, but it would warm him up. Keeping an eye on Luc's body language, Bert let his arm go, the leather connecting with Luc's skin, just barely kissing it.

"Oh," Luc sighed. He could do better than that. Bert let it fly a little harder, but it still didn't seem enough. Looking at his tools, he grabbed a paddle stick. It didn't have the softer padding his round ones did. This one should have more of a sting. He gave a test tap. "Un! Yes, that," Luc said, his body moving to seek out more.

Bert alternated cheeks, tapping the back of the legs as well, watching as the red color appeared. Lovely. Luc's body swayed with the strikes, his eyes becoming unfocused as he lost himself in the sensations. Bert gave one final strike, tossing the paddle stick to the side. He needed to feel surrounded by his mate. He slicked up his fingers, sliding them into his own hole, quickly stretching himself.

"I need you in me, Love. I need to feel you everywhere," Bert demanded, grabbing Luc's tail and slicking it up.

Holding the red, heated cheeks apart, he watched as his cock sank deep into Luc's body, stopping and holding still when he was fully seated, letting Luc adjust. His own wings flew open, feathers brushing against Luc's skin in a caress. He felt the tail slide against his skin, loving on him before sliding into his body. Bert hissed as he struggled to adjust; the stretch was intense. It had been years since he had allowed anything in his ass. The tip of Luc's tail was a little wider than the rest of it, making it a jolt when it first entered him. Luc stopped, pulling back a little at Bert's noise. "Keep going, Love. I'm fine."

He could feel the slow progress of Luc's tail and as his body finally relaxed, he began a steady tempo with his own hips. His arousal ramped up as he listened to Luc's sounds, the heat of the channel clenching around his dick, the smell of their sweat. He gasped as Luc curled his tail, the tip rubbing directly over his prostate. Bert's balls pulled up tight as lightning speared through him. He began pounding into Luc, no finesse, no rhythm, just pure lust and need. Luc's body was incredibly tight and hot around him, his tail playing with his prostate perfectly. Luc's wings spread out, helping him balance and push back into Bert, his own desperation coming through their link. It was creating a heady feedback loop.

"Mate...please...I," Luc broke off on a groan as Bert let a hand fly and a crack filled the room. "Yes," he moaned.

Bert's body was covered in sweat, his balls aching to release, but he clenched his teeth, alternating smacks to Luc's cheeks. He watched as the already rosy color deepened. Luc keened, the sound low and deep, his body shuddering in a dry orgasm. That. That was what he needed. To know he was the one who made Luc fly.

Luc's body clenched tightly around his dick and he knew he wouldn't last much longer. "Come when you can," he ordered as he ripped the cock ring off. His wings lifted him off the ground, Luc's beating to keep them together. His fingers gripped Luc's hips almost brutally, he would probably have bruises tonight. He fisted a handful of Luc's long hair, tugging him back so that his back rested against Bert's chest. Gripping a shoulder, he used Luc's body to help stabilize himself before his hips drilled him deep into Luc's body, absolutely destroying his hole. The shuddering breaths and moans encouraged him to go even harder, but Luc wasn't passive either, his tail thrusting in time. When he looked down and saw his mate mark on Luc's wrist, he was overcome with the urge to mark him again. Bert bit down on Luc's shoulder drawing blood, his body exploding as he drew his mate's essence into himself. He fought to keep his eyes open, watching as Luc came hands-free.

Luc's body drooped as soon as his orgasm finished. Bert held him tightly and slowly flew the few feet to the couch, laying Luc on his stomach on the soft fabric, their bodies still connected.

"Alright, Love. Let go so I can take care of you," Bert told him. Luc had a stranglehold on his arm and his tail was still inside him.

Luc whined, but gently pulled out. Bert winced as the tip stretched his hole. Maybe they both would need some cream tonight. Grabbing a warm washcloth and the healing cream, he was a little ashamed to see the proof of just how rough he had been. Luc's body had marks scattered all over it, his shoulder still sluggishly bleeding.

"Don't," Luc said harshly. Bert's eyes flew up, startled to see that Luc had turned his head to watch him, anger and flames in his eyes.

"What?"

"Don't. Don't look like that."

"I was rougher than I wanted, Love. I hurt you," Bert explained.

"I wanted it. I liked it. I came multiple times. I could have safe-worded and I didn't. You hurt me just enough. I don't know what you saw tonight, but I can guess. We are not them. What we do together is nothing like what they do. You can break skin, you can leave bruises, you can terrorize my hole. But it's all done out of love. And from a place of consent. You will not take this from me when I just found it. Got it?" Luc demanded.

"Yes." Bert leaned down, giving him a gentle kiss as an apology. "I love you."

"Good. I love you too. And I really need you to, um. Can you put some cream... Well, I wasn't joking about my ass." Luc added, his face red.

"Let me see," Bert told him. He winced as he saw how red it was when Luc spread his legs. He really did go hard. Thank the Fates for healing cream. He slipped a bit on himself as well. Sliding his arms under Luc's body, he lifted him and carried him to their bedroom. He laid him on the bed, sliding in after him, pulling the covers over them. They'd go eat the pudding in a little bit. Maybe off each other.

Luc hid his wince as he got up from the bed. He wouldn't have changed anything about last night, although he was stiff and a bit sore this morning. Nothing a steamy shower wouldn't fix. Bert had finally fallen asleep after he had sated himself on Luc three more times. Not that Luc was complaining, he had come at least twice that much. But now he needed to go into work. He dressed in another suit, putting on his favorite shit-kicker boots, and pressed a kiss to Bert's forehead.

"I need to go to work, Mate. Love you," he murmured.

"Love you too," Bert said before rolling over and burying his head in Luc's pillow. Bert always stole his pillow as soon as he was out of bed. He claimed it smelled better than his.

Walking into his kitchen, he found his favorite nephew eating a donut, a box open on the kitchen table and to-go coffees as well.

"Hello, nephew," Luc said, giving him a hug. He breathed in the familiar smell of family.

"Hi, Uncle. I wanted to see how Bert was this morning. I heard about the case yesterday. And to update you on the other situation you asked me to look into."

"He's sleeping now. We didn't get to talk much," he admitted.

"It was bad. Human and nonhuman trafficking, using drugs to keep them under control, but not even drugs like you'd think. These ones made them painfully aroused with no hope of orgasm, causing them to eventually be willing to do anything," Mac told him. "They had a variety of...tools available for their clients to use on the victims. I saw some of the reports and it was disturbing."

"Shit. No wonder he was upset," Luc said, grabbing a donut and a coffee. He had gotten over the queasiness of eating when discussing awful things many, many years ago. He made a note to ask Bert if he had learned everything he needed to stop the trafficking. He was more than willing to interrogate any souls; after all, what good was the ability to read everything about a person and not use it to stop something so horrendous.

"I'm still looking into the other thing, and it's been frustrating. I normally have a lot more answers at this point in an investigation. He covers his tracks extremely well. There was an employee in scheduling, not someone who should have been accessing the schedule as they weren't that high in position, who made the changes. People always forget that even if they log on using someone else's identification, our system logs biometrics. They've been suspiciously out, called in sick. I'm going to check out their house and see if I can't track them down. If there was one, there might be more," Mac warned. "As for your masked man, no leads yet to his real identity."

"I'm being careful. We've already arranged the Enforcers in the hearing room. It doesn't matter if they try to change the schedule again. The Enforcers have worked out their own schedule."

"Be safe. Love you," Mac said, bumping his shoulder against Luc's.

"I love you too. Watch your back as well," Luc cautioned. Mac nodded and ported out.

Luc sighed, finishing his donut. He brushed off any crumbs and ported to his office.

"Good morning, sir!" Margo called out cheerfully from her desk.

"Morning, Margo," he replied. "How was your day off yesterday?"

"Wonderful. I have new pictures to show you," she said, coming into the office with his coffee. "Thank you again for the hellhound. The grandkids adore him."

"I didn't like you being home alone," he replied. Margo's mate had died a few years ago, and while she was close to her family, she was still home alone. She had grown to be a friend of sorts after all these years and he felt better knowing one of his pups was looking after her. He was from the same litter as Faolán. "I'm glad the kids are enjoying him though. It will keep him busy."

Margo laughed, pulling out her phone. She pulled up a video, putting it in front of him. "Look," she said.

Luc had to laugh at the pup and the kids running around the yard. He got dizzy just watching how many times they threw the ball for him. "Did they all sleep very well?"

"Passed out as soon as they got inside," Margo said, a bit smugly. He knew she had trouble getting the little ones to sleep sometimes. They wanted to just keep going and going and going. "Greg stopped by already and stated that he, Veek, and Mal are on deck today. Scott is taking a turn in the hallway, as it's Brandon's day off."

She leaned down, dropping her voice to a murmur. "I've

searched all the cameras. I haven't found any trace of Keevhan meeting with anyone strange. No sign of someone hiding their face from the camera. Either someone deleted the footage, or they didn't meet near here. I checked the outside cameras as well. Mac gave me the name of the person in the scheduling department. I pulled up their personnel file, so I know what they look like. I'm going to run a facial scan for them. I'll let you know what I find."

"Thank you," he replied. "You may want to have your pup meet you here before you leave for the day if you're walking home, or he can stay in the office if he wouldn't be bored." Margo teleported a lot, but some days if she had been at her desk all day, she preferred to walk home to stretch her legs.

"I will. He's still pretty active, so I'm not sure how well he'll do sitting here," she fretted.

"Think about it. You can bring his bowls, toys, bed. Take him on walks with you around the building or at your lunch. It's up to you. I just wanted you to have that choice," Luc said. He didn't want to push it if she wasn't interested, but the pup would be better behaved simply because he was here as well.

"Thank you, sir. I'll have him meet me here for now, if I'm walking home. I'll think about the other," Margo said.

Luc just nodded. "Alright. I guess I better get this day started," he said, finishing the last of his coffee. "Perfect as always," he told her.

Reaching his hearing room, he sat down in his chair, thinking again about ordering another one so Bert had somewhere to sit. He was sure some people would throw a fit over it, as Bert was an angel, but Luc didn't give a shit what they thought. If he wanted his mate to sit by him, he would sit by him. It seemed dumb to have Bert stand there.

He wanted it to be different though, not the red of his. That might be pushing it too far, and it didn't fit Bert at all. Maybe in white. Have a black wood like his, but the seat upholstered in a white. Would the red and white look too corny? Like a Valentine's Day thing? Although the black might offset that. A cream color might work as well.

A loud resounding knock sounded at the door, indicating that his Enforcers were about to bring in a soul for judgment.

"Sir?" Greg asked, making sure he was ready.

"Go ahead."

Veek moved from his position to open the doors. It looked like a full docket today from what he had seen of the files this morning. He really only glanced at them though; the souls would tell him everything he needed, although he normally liked to have a little background so he didn't risk showing any emotion when they came in. He had years to develop his bland face, but every so often something still shocked him.

Luc settled into his position, legs crossed, right ankle resting over his left knee, his arms casually resting on the armrests. His dagger was in a holster against his back, his gun tucked into the cushions. It was spelled to only fire when he was holding it. He had made that mistake when he had been younger; it was never fun being shot, but it was especially mortifying when it was with your own gun.

Wow, they were starting the day off with a doozy. Child predator who had been active for years until a victim's father had killed him. Good for him. He sent a text to Margo to make sure the father had good legal counsel and wouldn't see any jail time. He had probably saved countless lives. This predator tended to kill his victims when he was done. The father had had the foresight to put a tracking chip inside the child's pocket when he heard of a couple of local kids going missing and had managed to find them before their child was killed. Luc also sent a follow-up text to have one of their therapists reach out to offer free sessions. They always said it was through a state or federal program and had created a fake company with a website and reviews to make it look legitimate so people would take advantage of the offer.

He viewed it all as part of keeping the balance. There was no reason to allow suffering to continue. God had fully supported the program and had offered to staff some therapists as well, that way they could make sure someone was always available for victims or their families.

The man in front of him refused to talk, but he didn't seem to realize that wouldn't matter in front of Lucifer. This man's sins went way back, some to when he was even a child himself. Some souls were just born dark and there was no redemption for them. He had no idea why. Earth-based religions would say he caused it somehow or he corrupted them in some way, but he and his demons had no control over the good or evil in someone's soul. Original sin was a myth. Lucifer and his Enforcers kept the balance by punishing those who did wrong, but other than that, they didn't have a direct influence on humans. They didn't compel, bribe, or seduce anyone to do evil. Of course there were bad ones in all races, so some demon somewhere probably gave them all a bad name. God had the same limitations he did; they judged, punished or rewarded, and did their best to set a good example for their people.

"I don't need you to talk to know what kind of person you are," Luc said, keeping his tone deceptively neutral, almost conversational. "I can see straight into your soul, everything good or bad you've done. I can see what you did to your neighbor. I know how your cat died. I know your parents were too scared of you to say anything as you got bigger and older and threatened them. I know one day you came home and they were gone. They took a coward's way out in my opinion and ran from you, instead of alerting the authorities to their concerns. But it was still all your choices, all your twisted desires that led you here.

"Level twelve," Luc said. "I would recommend Lilith for this one."

The man scoffed. "I'm not afraid of some girl."

Luc grinned. "You should be." Lil was fierce about protecting children and took a lot of delight in punishing those who harmed them. She might look small in human form, but she had the strength of at least a dozen human men.

Veek grinned in return, grabbing the man's arm and dragging him from the room. Lil had quite the reputation among the employees.

As Veek took the prisoner down to punishments, Mal moved to be closer to the door, Greg moving to be halfway between Luc and the entrance. Scott waited a few minutes before knocking to announce the next hearing. Mal took hold of the prisoner, walked him to meet Greg, who brought the woman the rest of the way to Luc, while Mal moved back to the door. The new process took a bit more time, but Luc had to admit it would be harder for a prisoner to cause issues this way.

Before they reached him, Luc felt a pop in the air and found Bal sitting beside him. Doing a quick scan of his hellhound, he didn't think anything was wrong but wanted to check.

'*Everything alright?*' he asked.

He got a bored feeling in return. He wondered if Bert

was still sleeping or if he had gone into the office. Normally Bal would bug Bert to play with him if Luc wasn't there. He rested a hand on Bal's head, his fingers hidden behind the large ears, allowing him to secretly rub Bal's favorite spot while he focused on the woman in front of him. She seemed to have an accomplice who was still running around on Earth. That had to irk her quite a bit. She was a bit of a narcissist.

"Do we have anyone currently in Illinois?" Luc asked. There was no reason to let the man continue.

"I believe we have someone close to there," Greg replied.

"Great. Ask them to retrieve one Simon Doe." He grabbed an image of him out of the woman's mind, willing it into existence as a photograph. "Send this to them please and have them bring him straight here."

Greg took the photograph, texting it to the other Enforcer. They waited, all of them quiet, although the woman began squirming the longer the silence stretched. Luc already knew her crimes and he wasn't interested in talking to her more than needed.

"Ah, thank you, Az. I appreciate you taking the time to find him," Luc said as an Enforcer ported in dragging a man with him.

"He wasn't exactly hard to find," Az replied dryly. "He was practically broadcasting his excitement over a new scheme of his."

"I am grateful nonetheless," Luc said. Az nodded, bowing his head before porting out.

"Now that I have you both here, let's get this hearing started."

21

Luc gave Dec one last hug and a kiss, inhaling that baby smell. Why did babies smell so good? Other than diaper changes, those were gut-punching, vomit-worthy olfactory offenses.

"Thank you for coming to dinner," he told Viv, giving her a hug as well.

"Anytime. We love seeing you," she replied, kissing his cheek. She had never been afraid of him and it was wonderful. "I left an extra batch of cookies in the kitchen to share with Bert when he gets home. If he ends up being gone more than a day or two, they'll keep in the fridge or in the freezer.

"I'll try to leave some for him." Luc grinned.

Viv just laughed, hugging him one more time.

Mac thumped him on the back. "Love you, Uncle. I might pop into your office in the next couple of days. I'm still hunting down a few leads and I'm hoping I get some results soon."

"You can stop in anytime, you know that. You're a good boy, Faolán," he said, sneaking the hellhound an extra biscuit.

He waved goodbye to his family as they ported out.

He puttered around his house, watching some videos

on his phone, reading for a little bit but not even the new mystery book could keep his attention long. He played with the rest of his pack, training the puppies for an hour or so. He felt restless. The house was too quiet. He could hear the guards outside occasionally, the hellhounds in the back-yard, the occasional bird or the wind. Maybe some music would help. He pulled up his favorite playlist, making sure the bass was turned up. The thump of the music usually helped relax him, but even that failed tonight.

Luc had no idea what was wrong with him. He had spent countless nights alone, or for quite a few years, with Mac sleeping in the other bedroom. How had he become so used to Bert being here in such a short amount of time? He tried going to sleep and when that didn't work, a hot bath with calming oils. Nope. Nothing.

Finally, about one in the morning, he gave up, throwing on some gym shoes. He'd go for a run. Bert wasn't sure if he would be back tonight and had warned him that he would be pretty silent with this case, so Luc didn't bother sending a text message. He didn't want to interfere with Bert's job, just like he didn't want Bert to interfere with his.

"You stay here," he told Bal, when he raised his head from the floor. He had been watching Luc pace back and forth in the room.

He got a disgruntled woof in response. Luc knew Bal would probably love a run, but he wanted to be completely by himself while he tried to work himself to a state where he could sleep. He was grumpy and wanted to be alone.

Luc nodded to Alan, one of his personal guards as he left the house.

"I'm going for a quick run. I won't be long, just need to clear my head," Luc said.

"Let me grab someone to go with you, sir," Alan said.

Luc shook his head. "Don't bother anyone. I won't be long and I need to be by myself."

"Sir," Alan began.

"It'll be fine. I should stay within shouting distance of someone," Luc said.

"Yes, sir," Alan said, resignation in his voice. It wasn't often Luc put his foot down and disregarded his guards' advice, but he was out of sorts and didn't want to keep the mask on while someone ran with him. Some little part of his brain reminded him that Bert would want someone with him, but Luc smashed it down. He had taken care of himself for thousands of years and tonight would be no different. It would be fine.

An hour later, sweat dripped down his body. He may have lied about staying within shouting distance. He had started local but ported to the ocean, specifically to his favorite beach. He took a minute to breathe, taking in the black sands and the large full green moon. The water looked black tonight, but he knew in the daytime it would be a deep vibrant red. He could see the predators in the ocean, hunting for their dinners. Although he didn't have the same affinity for them as he did his hellhounds, he still was able to communicate with them a little. He sent them an apology, knowing he hadn't been here in years. He used his magic to port some steaks from his fridge to drop them in the water. He watched as they swarmed, their gigantic bodies churning the water. Thomas's fear of the small fish at most Netherworld beaches popped in his head and he had to chuckle. They were odd-looking, but harmless to human-sized beings.

These creatures though, they weren't found at the popular beaches where people went swimming. No, they were only at a few places and most people avoided those areas. Their sheer size was terrifying, not to mention what they looked like. They resembled a mixture of a shark the size of a megalodon, their matte black bodies were speckled with fluorescent stripes, with the hunting filaments and freaky face of an angler fish, and the ability to extend their jaw to capture prey. Their mouths were massive and had several rows of needle-thin teeth like the angler fish, but behind those were rows of larger traditional shark-like teeth.

He got a feeling of contentment back from the creatures. He breathed in the salty air, listing to the soothing sound of the ocean and finally felt his brain calm a bit. Here there was no one who was watching or judging or wanting something from him. The feeling of the sand beneath his feet drew his attention and he bent down, grabbing a handful. As it flowed through his fingers, he called forth his hellfire, letting it play along his skin. He used to make little sculptures when he was younger, long before he had this position. It had been many years since he had attempted to create something. It required focus to keep the flames at the right level and to manipulate the material he was using, and his job had just seemed to have taken over all of his life, excluding the parts where he raised Mac. He wondered if he still had the skills to make anything.

Maybe something for Bert. Viv seemed to like it when Mac brought her flowers, and D did the same for Thomas. Luc liked them well enough, but he wasn't sure if Bert was the flower type. It would be easy enough to make a donut, he thought with a laugh. No. Oh! A motorcycle. Bert loved his bike; Luc only hoped he could remember what it looked like enough to try to recreate it. He knelt in the sand, tracing out a design.

Luc tilted his head, trying to figure out how he would

make it work. Digging out a bowl in the sand, he called back his hellfire, letting it flow down into the divot. As the surrounding sand began to melt, he stirred it with his finger, making sure it was all the same consistency. Pulling a little bit of the melted sand out with his hand, he partially shifted. Using the longer and pointed ends of his claws, he created little details as the glass began to cool. Alright, one wheel done.

He had no idea how much time had passed, but he finally sat back with a groan, his back popping from being hunched over for so long in an awkward position. He quickly attached the muffler and blew on the glass to help it cool. Oops, that wheel was a little flat from where he held it. Luc gently reheated the glass, reshaping the wheel to be round. He held it by a small piece that had been already set while the rest cooled. Not too bad for his first one after hundreds of years, he thought happily.

As the air shifted around him, he opened a small portal and sent the glass motorcycle home. Hopefully it landed on his bed safely. Popping up from the sand, he looked around. He probably should have stuck closer to home, he thought wryly as he took in the group now surrounding him.

Luc kept his partially shifted form. The claws would help in a fight. "Can I help you gentlemen and lady?" Six against one. He had this.

"Our boss wants you to step down," the biggest one said. It was interesting that it was a mix of nonhumans.

"No thank you," Luc replied cheerfully, bouncing on his feet, getting his legs stretched out a little after being crunched from working on the glass. He eased his shoes off, wanting to be able to grip into the sand with his toes if needed.

"You've had this job for too long. Our people are getting

soft, no one wars anymore. The humans don't fear us, most don't know we exist. The strongest should be in charge, not some bitch appointed by the Fates or whatever," the women stated.

Some bitch, huh? He wondered if this was because he was mated to Bert and what they had feared would happen was beginning or if it was a coincidental choice of words. The Fates would be pissed to hear their decision being challenged and this group was lucky they weren't here right now. They weren't the most forgiving.

"War doesn't help anyone. Children die, even the strong die. It separates us, making us unsure who we can trust. Peace allows us to thrive," Luc protested softly. He knew it would fall on deaf ears, but he wanted to give it a shot.

The sand behind him shifted, warning him that at least one behind him had moved. Luc took to his wings, propelling himself straight up into the sky to avoid an attack. There were shouts of surprise below him; they probably had never seen anyone shift that quickly. There was a reason he had been picked for this job and that was one of the factors.

He landed, making sure to keep the water to his back. He never had a problem with the predators in the water, they had come to an unspoken agreement many years ago when he had been a child and had come to this beach to be alone. In fact, they may help him if any of these idiots were stupid enough to go into the water. This wasn't the typical beach many nonhumans went to on vacation; the predators here made it inhospitable, and he would bet most of the people here were ignorant on how dangerous they were. He had never seen another person here in all the times he had come, and he wasn't quite sure how they had found it.

The big guy shifted first. Of course he was an ogre. Why

not? Luc was still confident he would win, but this would probably hurt. He sighed as the rest took their other forms; a scorpion shifter, a hydra, a regular vampire, some other type of shifter. Luc tilted his head, trying to figure out exactly what they were. It wasn't one he had seen before, maybe a hybrid of some sort? And the last was what the humans called a Medusa, or a gorgon, to round it out. They didn't turn you to stone, but did have the power to paralyze you if you met their gaze. Strangely enough, it was only the females that had that ability. Good thing he had restocked the healing potions after the last incident.

"If you don't step down, you'll be killed," the vampire stated, pulling out a large hunting knife.

Luc scoffed. "I doubt it."

Luc ported to the backyard, not wanting the Enforcers to see him like this and get upset. They usually patrolled the front and sides of the yard, leaving the backyard to the hellhounds. He stopped by the kennels to check on the pups, noticing Bal was sleeping with the pack.

A low growl filled the air as Bal scented him.

"Easy. I'm fine," Luc reassured his hellhound.

He got a feeling of disbelief and...betrayal? No, not quite right. Disappointment maybe.

"I promise you will go with me from now on," Luc said. "I should know better by now, huh?" He sat on the ground, holding in the groan, allowing Bal to lick over some of his wounds. Their saliva had a healing property to it, although Luc would still need a healing potion. He had torn the sleeve off his shirt to make a tourniquet for the leg where the scorpion shifter had gotten him. It hadn't spread too far yet and he wouldn't allow Bal to come in contact with any poisoned blood. "I'm sorry for not taking you."

Bal stared him in the face, clearly making his views known. He grumbled, letting Luc know that next time he was coming whether Luc wanted him to or not.

"You're a good pup. Thank you for helping. I'm going inside to grab a shower," Luc pressed his forehead against Bal's. "Sleep tight."

He limped across the yard, feeling the poison travelling up his leg. That burned like a bitch. Luc clenched his teeth to keep in any sound as he climbed the porch stairs. That was not fun, he thought, leaning heavily against the railing. He opened the door, dragging himself to the kitchen. He could use some water.

"What the fuck happened?" an angry voice demanded.

Luc slowly turned from the fridge, a bottle of water halfway to his mouth. Mentally shrugging, he chugged the water. He was already going to be in trouble, might was well get the hydration he desperately needed first.

"I was attacked," he replied calmly as he tossed the bottle in the recycling bin.

"Where?"

"My beach."

"Who—"

"A bunch of different nonhumans, claiming they had a boss who wanted me out of power. No angels or demons with this group though."

"How ma—"

"Six," Luc interrupted. He saw Bert's nostrils flare, knowing he was pissing off his partner with his short answers and interrupting, but he could feel the poison working through his system and wanted to get the interrogation over with so he could get a healing potion.

"And you were by yourself for some reason?" Bert asked, his voice strangely calm now.

"Yes."

Bert just nodded. Luc wasn't sure how to process that response. "What happened to the ones who attacked you?"

"Dead. I killed five. Their ashes are floating away by now. The sixth one, the monster in the ocean actually grabbed him as he tried to attack my back. He's deep in the belly of the creature."

"How badly are you hurt?" Bert asked, still in the calm voice.

"I need a healing potion. The scorpion got me at the end," Luc admitted, his body finally disobeying his command to stand straight as his leg trembled, making him sway a bit.

Bert cursed, grabbed him and ported to the den. "Drink this," he demanded shoving two bottles at Luc.

"One is good enough," he protested.

"Both. I need you fully healed for tomorrow."

Luc obediently drank. Bert pulled him into the bathroom, getting the shower started.

Half an hour later, Luc was clean, in a pair of soft pants, and was being held in bed by his lover. As he fell asleep, he wondered why Bert needed him to be fully healed for tomorrow.

L uc woke slowly, noticing that Bert's spot was empty. There wasn't a note, so he was probably downstairs. Luc forced himself to be an adult and got out of bed to find his partner. Bert was at the kitchen table, eating bacon and drinking coffee, Bal at his feet waiting for a bite. The glass motorcycle was sitting in the middle of the table.

"Morning," Luc said, grabbing a cup of coffee for himself before sitting.

"Morning. I found this on our bed and meant to ask you about it, but I was distracted by you coming home injured," Bert replied, a hint of something in his voice. Luc wasn't quite sure what that tone was.

"It was for you," Luc replied, looking down into his cup. He was second-guessing himself now.

"It looks like my bike, even has the ding on the muffler. Where did you get it?"

"I made it. At the beach using the sand and my hellfire. I used to make little things all the time when I was younger," Luc replied. At least when his father wasn't watching. Crafts were not a useful skill.

Bert nodded. "It's lovely. Thank you. Do you always use sand?"

"No. Sand, metal, things that can withstand the heat."

"Wood?"

Luc shook his head. "I tend to set wood on fire, no matter how careful I am."

"Were you careful last night?"

He really should have seen that coming. "I wasn't not careful," Luc protested. Although he did tend to get sucked into a project when he was creating a sculpture and wasn't the best at keeping track of his surroundings. He had thought he would be safe enough at his beach.

"You didn't bring Bal or any of your Enforcers. You knew there was a chance someone was coming after you and you didn't take any precautions."

"I couldn't settle down. The house was too quiet."

"So turn on the TV or the radio," Bert answered.

"Not that kind of quiet," Luc muttered.

"Not that kind of—oh. Did you need me and you didn't reach out?"

"It was just quiet without you here and I didn't want to interrupt your work."

"Uh huh. Do you know what's wrong with what you did?"

Luc stared at him. He was a grown-assed adult who had kept himself alive for thousands of years. He was smart enough to keep the comment to himself, but he was beginning to feel like a scolded child.

"No?" Bert asked, continuing without waiting for an answer. "You didn't take care of yourself. I promised I wouldn't interfere with your job, but this was outside of work. From now on, you have Bal or an Enforcer with you. Just because you can handle yourself, doesn't mean you should make it easy for them to get to you.

"Go get dressed in comfortable clothes. I already made

arrangements. It's time we go to the club. Today we're going to work on making you understand that you're mine. Mine to love, mine to take care of. You didn't take care of what was mine last night and now you're going to be punished." Bert placed a half-face mask on the table. It looked like a beanie hat but covered down to his nose. There were cut-outs for his ears. "Put that on when you come back down."

Luc paused for a minute trying to judge just how mad Bert was.

"Go, Love," Bert demanded.

Luc's cock twitched at the firm tone even as he replied, "Yes, Mate."

When he came back down, dressed in a pair of gray sweatpants, his gym shoes, and a tight black t-shirt, he stopped in his tracks at the sight of his Bert. Dressed in tight leather pants, motorcycle boots, and a black t-shirt, Bert looked good enough to eat.

"Come, Love. Charles has cleared the club for us. Time for your punishment."

Bert watched Luc's face as he looked around. Luc seemed a little overwhelmed by the space. The club's main room was set up like a lounge, with a bar, couches, and booths lining the walls. There was a dance floor toward one side of the room. Hallways on either side of the back wall led to different rooms. Those rooms were either for scenes, events, or classes the club offered. Changing rooms were toward the front, past the check-in desk. There were clear indicators for what kind of club it was, including a large Saint Andrew's cross by the dance floor, and floor pillows scattered about the room for subs to use if needed when they were kneeling.

Bert had never been in here when it was empty. The atmosphere was completely different, it was crazy how still it felt. He couldn't wait until he could bring Luc when there were other people here, if they ever got to that point. Charles met them at the door, his mate by his side. He gestured them inside, leading them to his office.

"The new wards are in place. Only Sky and I are here right now. Your privacy has already been blood sworn by the two of us, if you wanted to remove the mask. I put you in the Blue Dungeon room and made sure it was fully stocked. Please feel free to check out the other rooms so Luc might be more comfortable here. Bert, Sky offered to answer any questions your mate might have about being a sub, subspace, anything like that."

"Thank you. Maybe afterward or potentially he could call or text depending on how the night goes," Bert replied.

Charles nodded. "You know where everything is. We'll be here if you need anything."

Luc stayed quiet, remembering what Bert had told him about addressing other Doms in the club.

"We both appreciate this," Bert replied before leading Luc from the office.

Luc knew he was a bit wide-eyed as they walked down a hallway and Bert pointed out different rooms. Some were themed: he saw a classroom, a horse stable, one looked like a doctor's examination room, another like a normal office except for the toys lining the wall. There was even a room with a small pool. A larger-sized room was decorated to look like a nursery school or daycare. He remembered reading about littles. It looked like a fun space if you age regressed.

They finally stopped in front of a door. Bert paused before opening.

"Color?"

"Green, Mate." Luc was a bit nervous what his punishment would be, but his dick had been steadily getting harder as they saw the different rooms.

Opening the door, the room was painted in a dark blue with a dark gray floor. He couldn't tell if it was concrete or a tile in the dimmer lighting. There was a large bed straight ahead, a mirror on the ceiling. There was a spanking bench, some chains attached to the wall, a cabinet in a dark gray metal with silver accent pieces.

"Undress and stand in the middle of the room. I'm not going to tell you everything that is going to happen tonight. Use your safe words if needed. You will not be allowed to come until I tell you," Bert said, moving toward the cabinet.

Luc whimpered. Bert was amazing at edging him and had gone hours before finally allowing him to come. He rushed to follow directions, stripping all the way down and folding his clothes before placing them on a side chair. He moved to stand in the middle of the room, his cock already hard and leaking. The tone of Bert's voice, the atmosphere, and the fact that he hadn't come in days made him wonder just how he could keep from coming too soon.

Bert had his back to him, but Luc could see him laying several things out along a side table. He could see a plug, a paddle, and a bag of some sort. Oh, and nipple clamps, although those looked a lot more vicious than the ones they used at home.

"I see you might need some help listening," Bert said when he turned and saw the precum glistening on Luc's dick. He already had a cock ring in hand. "Hands behind your back."

Luc stood, hands clasped behind him. He clenched his teeth, nails digging into the palms of his hands with the effort to not come or reach out and touch as Bert's hot mouth closed around him. It didn't last long, Bert pulling back after a few deep sucks, his tongue flicking the tip of Luc's head to collect the remaining drops of precum. Luc whimpered, looking down to see his dick already snug in the cock ring. Desire rode him hard, but at least now he wouldn't be able to climax.

"We're going to try something new tonight. Go to the bench, get in a comfortable position you can maintain for a while," Bert told him, giving his dick one last stroke.

Luc walked over slowly, looking at it. They hadn't used one at home, making use of the bed and the coffee table in the den. This one had two padded areas, at different heights. Maybe kneeling with something against his chest for support, if it was going to take some time? He knew he would eventually get tired if he had to stand or support himself as he bent over, but this had a built-in support. He settled in, testing it out. Bert let him lie there for a minute before speaking.

"Are you comfortable?"

"Yes, Mate."

"Good."

Luc suddenly lost his sight as a blindfold covered his eyes.

"Grab the handles, please."

As soon as Luc grabbed hold, Bert let his hand loose, and Luc heard the crack before the pain of the smack registered. He smothered his shout.

"No. Let out all the noises. I own those noises and I want to hear them all. Your job is to please me, right?"

"Yes, Mate."

"Your job is to keep yourself safe for me and you failed. You didn't take the precautions you should have. Your punishment is to remind you that your goal is to make me happy, my job is to make you happy, to support you. To make me happy, you need to keep yourself safe, that means eating, taking care of yourself, keeping your guards close when there have been signs of threats against you."

After each sentence, Bert laid another spank to Luc's ass. There was a pause and Luc tilted his head, trying to hear where Bert was. The whistling sound of the cane was his first clue as a line of fire was laid across his skin. Five more followed, the last across the top of his thighs. He moaned as the sting spread through his body transforming from pain into pleasure. His cock throbbed with the need to come.

"Not yet, Love. I'm nowhere near done with you."

Luc felt cool slick fingers probe against his ass. He pushed out, seeking Bert's touch. Bert slowly stretched him before slamming his cock deep into Luc's body. He moaned, loving how suddenly full he was. Bert gripped his hips tightly, absolutely using his body for his own pleasure. Every time Bert's hips made contact with his ass, the stripes from the cane stung, sending pulses of pleasure down to his dick. Luc's nerve endings sang as Bert's cock rubbed against his prostate. He could stay here for hours, he thought. A flood of heat filled him, and Luc's cock twitched feeling his mate's climax, but the ring kept his own orgasm at bay.

"Now I can play with you longer," Bert said, pulling out of his body. Luc felt a plug slide in, keeping Bert's cum inside him. Bert helped him stand and guided him across the room, blindfold still in place. "Sit on the bed and then lie down on your back, no touching yourself or me. You can grab the headboard if you need to hold something."

Bert's hand circled his cock lightly stroking, keeping his arousal high, as his mouth found Luc's nipples, teasing them into hard points. Luc gasped as he felt cool air blown across his skin, sending shivers through him. Sharp points of nipple clamps closed around him, tightening as Bert closed the screws. Luc moaned, whimpering a little at the overwhelming sensations. The clamps were painful, but his body seemed to like it, his balls drawing up tight.

He writhed on the bed as the sensations of his cock being stroked warred with the dulling of the cock ring, the sharp sting of the nipple clamps, and the welts on his ass rubbing against the sheets. His ass was full, his skin on fire. His Mate let him bask in the sensations for a minute or two before the hand left his shaft. Luc whined, his hips chasing, wanting the pleasure back.

"Not yet, Love. I have something new for you. Now you need to hold perfectly still for me."

Luc strained to listen, the sound of his own breaths and heartbeat filling his ears. Bert closed his hand around Luc's shaft, holding it firmly. Not moving, just holding. Luc tensed as he felt something metal touch the tip of his cock, sliding into his slit. His hips tried to move away, but a smack to his hip stopped him.

"Stay still," his Mate ordered, grabbing his cock again.

Luc panted as he felt the metal slide into his dick. Into. His. Dick. He clenched his teeth, biting back the urge to move, not sure if he liked the feeling. Bert slowly slid the rod out and back in. It never fully left his body, continuously stretching the one opening that he had been positive was exit only. Sounding, his brain randomly provided the word for it as he scrambled to make sense of what he was feeling. The fullness in his cock, the fullness in his ass, the pain fading to numbness in his nipples. It was all getting to be too much.

He screamed as the plug began vibrating, matching the rhythm to the thrusts in his shaft.

"Please, Mate. Please. Please," he begged. "Please let me come." Bert had gently moved his shaft, and the sound slid deeper, hitting something new, ramping his pleasure up.

"Who do you belong to?"

Luc struggled to get the words out. The sound combined with the plug was somehow doing something incredible to his prostate and he gasped for air, words lost to him. Bert pulled the sound back a little and Luc was able to mumble out, "You, Mate. You. Always."

"Yes, me. Always me, always you. What is your job?"

"Make you happy," Luc gasped, his hips following the sounding rod.

Bert tapped the rod, sending sparks through Luc's body. "How?"

"Keeping myself safe," Luc said, his body now coated in a sheen of sweat. He was gasping for breath like he had run for hours, every nerve ending alive with sensation. It felt like his whole body was buzzing.

"Good, Love. I'm going to let you come now," Bert said.

Luc felt the bed dip as Bert climbed onto the bed. He groaned as he felt the loss of the plug and the sound, his body now empty, and he clenched the headboard, trying to keep from reaching out. Bert's cock slid into him, Luc sighing in relief as he was filled back up. Luc wrapped his legs around Bert's waist keeping him deep inside him. Bert's hips started slowly thrusting, slow even movements, his width and length dragging against the inside of Luc's channel. At this point, his body was so sensitive it wouldn't take much for Luc to explode.

"Please, more," Luc begged.

Bert slammed into him, finally letting Luc get the pounding he needed. Luc felt the heat of his lover's body come closer, Bert's breath ghosting across his face. "Ready, Love?"

"Yes!"

Luc screamed as the nipple clamps were removed and the pain flooded his body, Bert pounded into his ass for another minute before releasing the cock ring. Three strokes of his shaft and Luc's orgasm exploded out of him, his body flying, his mind floating on a sea of cloudy pleasure. He lost himself in the feeling of his brain finally completely shutting off. All he felt was warm and safe, surrounded and filled by his mate.

Luc blinked slowly, feeling sensation come back into his body. His eyes began to focus and he could make out the room. The blindfold had been removed and he was cradled in Bert's arms.

"Here, Love, drink," Bert said, holding a water bottle to his lips. Luc drank, finishing the bottle quickly. He was so thirsty. Another bottle appeared and he drank half of that one.

"How do you feel?" his lover asked.

"Good. A little sore. Buzzy."

"Buzzy?"

"Hmhm," Luc nodded, rubbing his head against Bert's chest. "Tingly all over. Thank you," he said.

"It's my pleasure and my honor, Love. I'll hold you for as long as you need, then I want to apply a cream to your skin. Charles and Sky have a light dinner waiting for us whenever you are ready. Sky's eager to make a new friend.

Everyone here is scared to be friends with the sub of the Dom who owns the club."

"I could use a friend. I have the same problem," Luc admitted.

"I know, Love. People see your job and not you. But I've known Sky for years and I think you can become very good friends."

Luc nodded, drifting off to float for a little while longer. His body throbbing with pleasure and a little pain, reminding him that he had someone who loved him.

Luc woke, his body still a little tender from the night before. They'd had a lovely dinner with Charles and Sky. It was nice to have someone else to talk to; the others Luc knew in the lifestyle were Doms. From what Luc could see, he and Sky would get along well. He was strangely eager to make a new friend. It had been years.

When they got home, Bert had drawn him a bath, which led to another round of sex. More of the traditional style of intimacy, but still lovely orgasm-producing sex. He reached out, his hand not finding anything but air and sheets.

Frowning, Luc rolled over to look at Bert's side. There was a wooden rose on the pillow with a note. Luc grabbed the rose, admiring the little realistic touches. It was clearly handmade, but very well done. Looking down at the note, he read.

I'm in the den, Love.

Luc stretched, feeling the pull in his muscles, before going to the bathroom to pee and brush his teeth. He wanted a kiss and didn't want Bert to have to deal with his horrendous morning breath. He grabbed the rose from the bed, walking down the hall to the den.

As he entered the room, he took a minute to admire the

back of his mate. Bert was sitting on the couch, legs crossed, ankle over his knee. He looked relaxed, so Luc didn't think there was any leftover anger from yesterday. He understood where Bert was coming from and it was a place of love and worry, but Luc really hadn't thought it was a big deal for him to go off on his own. He had done it before. Of course, he would admit that if it was reversed, he would be angry that Bert had chosen not to have support close by if there was a threat.

"There's nothing worth sighing that deeply over," Bert said, turning in his seat to look at him.

Luc hadn't been aware he had sighed out loud. He walked over, sitting next to his mate, leaning against him. It was something he had become adept at doing, finding a way to rest against his shorter mate but still feeling like he was being cared for.

"Thank you for the rose. I love it," Luc said, still holding it.

"I'm glad. Sometimes stakeouts take forever, and a knife and wood are easy enough to carry around or find so I started carving years ago. I had a hard time sleeping last night and wanted to make you something to say thank you for the motorcycle."

"I was worn out. How were you not able to sleep?" Luc asked incredulously. Seriously, he had fallen asleep before Bert had even cleaned him up after their final round.

"My brain wouldn't turn off. I was worried about it being too much thrown at you at once last night."

Luc sat up, looking Bert right in the eyes. "No. Last night was perfect. I don't know that I would want to do sounding often...it was intense. Not bad, but intense. In a different way than the spanking or plugs or the other things we've done. Maybe that's a good one for punishments," he said wryly.

Bert laughed, pressing a kiss to his forehead. He was already making plans to order a stopper version for their next 'punishment.' The base wrapped underneath the head and a small plug sat an inch or so into the shaft. It would drive Luc nuts, but it may not be quite as intense as the longer sound. "Noted. I had a plan for today, but that was before last night. Now, I don't know if it's a good idea."

"What is it?"

"I want us to try working on your agoraphobia," Bert said gently.

Luc shook his head. Nope, he was good staying in Netherworld. He knew he had said yes earlier, but he had secretly hoped that Bert had forgotten about it the longer it went without being brought up again. Bert laid a hand on his knee.

"Love, look at me," Bert ordered, still gentle but with a thread of steel in his voice. As soon as Luc looked at him, Bert softly grasped the back of his head, fingers wrapped in his hair.

"One, I need you to be able to get to places safely or to save yourself. What if you were injured but couldn't make yourself port to the hospital between the realms? It's the best one available, but you might freeze when trying to leave Netherworld.

"Two, I know you want to go to Mac's Earth home and visit. You enjoy being with your family. Three, what if Mac or I were injured and needed help somewhere not in Netherworld? D would help, and although I believe Viv and Thomas would do anything they could, they're still human. You're the only other one we both fully trust to call." Bert knew he was laying it on a bit thick, but he truly believed it was a safety issue for his mate. Luc kept healing potions in his den so that he wouldn't have to port to the hospital. What if he was alone and couldn't get to the potions or passed out before he drank enough?

"I've gone to Mac's house to double-check the wards and to the hospital when the baby was born," Luc protested.

"And you were a mess. I want to give this to you, Love. Please? We'll work up to it, it won't be long stretches at first, probably seconds at a time."

Luc took a deep breath, holding it before letting it out slowly. He closed his eyes, focusing on the breathing in and out at a steady rhythm. Even the thought of leaving caused his heart to race.

"Just a few seconds? And you'll be there?"

"Always," Bert vowed.

Bal whined, coming over to lick his fingers. Luc buried his fingers in Bal's fur, letting the scent of his mate and the feel of his hound ground him. He nodded his head once. He gasped as he felt Bert port them away; he hadn't thought he meant right now. His breathing became choppy, his heart racing, his eyes firmly closed. If he didn't open them, he was still in Netherworld.

"Love. Open your eyes. Just for a minute," Bert said. Bal was leaning hard against his leg, and he could hear a whooshing type of sound. Water or wind, maybe. It smelled salty.

He didn't want to open his damn eyes. Bert moved to stand behind him, arms wrapped around him. Luc frowned as Bert took hold of his hand, pulling his pointer finger out from his right hand, moving it to touch his left hand. What was...oh. His ring. Bert's promise that he was always with him and would care for him. He gripped the ring tight, leaning back into his Mate, and opened his eyes to see a glorious sunrise.

"Not all the outside world is horrible. There's beauty everywhere. Plus, weren't you just attacked and poisoned at home? What happened to your brother and his mate was horrible and should never have happened, but it could have happened anywhere. Hate, rage, and evil exist everywhere. You know this. But so does love, beauty, and happiness," Bert said, tightening his arms around him before porting them home.

Luc felt his heart slow down as he realized he was back in his bedroom.

"Good, Love. I'm proud of you for going," Bert praised. "You get a reward for that," he added as he dropped to his knees. The adrenaline from the fear was warring with the sight of Bert's mouth in front of his groin. Luc's body was a bit confused; he still had the remnants of fear running through him, but the sight of his mate on his knees, hands pulling down Luc's pants, would always turn him on.

He gasped as Bert blew cool air across Luc's balls, causing them to tighten. Bert ran his tongue from his taint, up over the sac, all the way to the tip of Luc's penis where he swallowed him whole. No gagging, nothing but tight deep suction. The wet heat and the swirling tongue made Luc's cock fully hard in seconds. Bert's hand cupped Luc's testicles, lightly running his fingers over them, almost in a downward V pattern, starting wide at the top near the shaft, fingers gently pulling down to meet at the bottom of his sac. His tongue was always moving, stroking back and forth in long licks as his head bobbed up and down. Pulling off, he sucked his own fingers into his mouth, coating them in saliva.

He pushed against the inside of Luc's legs, urging him

to spread. Bert tapped the entrance to Luc's body, taking his shaft deep into his mouth. As his cock was engulfed by wet heat, a finger slid inside him. Luc's hole clenched, trying to draw it in deeper. Bert slowly thrust a few times before adding in another finger.

As he stretched Luc's body, he moved his hand faster and faster, feeling the telltale signs that Luc's orgasm was getting closer. A third finger joined in, and he could feel the glide of fingers across his prostate, sending little lightning bolts down to his balls.

"Oh, gods. Almost here," Luc moaned, gripping Bert's shoulders for support as his knees wobbled from the pleasure. Bert crooked his finger, pressing on Luc's prostate.

Luc moaned, his body tensing as his orgasm filled Bert's mouth. He watched as his mate stood, tucking him back into his pants.

"Good, Love."

Luc stood in the alleyway not sure he was going to make it the full fifteen minutes. They had been working on increasing his time away from Netherworld, but there were so many people nearby and it was making him nervous. He glanced at the timer, clenching his teeth to make it to the end.

"Hmm, good job, Love," Bert praised. "Now hold the wall."

Luc turned, bracing his hands on the wall, but he was a bit confused as to why—he quickly swallowed his shout as Bert suddenly yanked his pants down and spread his cheeks, tongue finding his rim, his body softening and opening under the licks and gentle pressure. Bert's tongue pierced his body, thrusting a few times until Luc was biting his bottom lip to keep his cries in. Bert bit an ass cheek as he slid in his fingers, stretching Luc's hole even further. Luc pushed his body back seeking more of the pleasure as it suddenly disappeared. Turning his head, Luc saw his mate spitting into his hand, smearing it around his cock. Luc bit his fist, keeping his moans quiet as Bert slid his thick cock into him. It wasn't a drawn-out lovemaking, but a quick and dirty behind the building.

Bert's hand reached around, grabbing Luc's dick, stroking. "Come for me, Love, take your reward for being so good," Bert growled in his ear. Bert shifted his stance just a tiny bit, slamming hard on the next thrust and nailing Luc's prostate. His climax rushed through him, his release coating the ground in front of him. His head dropped to rest against the wall as he felt the heat of Bert's cum. Bert's arms wrapped around him as he ported them home.

They landed in the shower, Bert's dick still deep in his body, his pants around his ankles. Bert quickly stripped them both, turning the hot water on. As he washed his hair, Luc vaguely thought about protesting that he wasn't one of Pavlov's dogs and that he wouldn't simply start associating orgasms with leaving Netherworld. At the back of his brain, however, he was also aware that toward the end of the timer, his dick had started twitching knowing what was coming, despite the fear he may have had.

He'd give it to his mate. He certainly was finding a way to make Luc want to leave Netherworld.

24

Bert cursed under his breath, hanging up his phone. He was needed on a case, but Luc was still at work. He had promised that he wouldn't interfere with Luc's job, so he refrained from porting in to grab a kiss goodbye. Instead, he sent Luc a text with some details about the job. He would be late tonight, possibly even gone until tomorrow depending on how this played out. He had carved a new flower for Luc a few days ago for just this type of thing. He wanted to leave something for his mate to find that would let him remember Bert was thinking of him. He had given Luc his ring, but it seemed like he may need more reminders when he was home alone. He had a few other carvings stashed away for later. He would fill the whole house if needed. While Luc slept or was at work, Bert had begun playing with different stains in an attempt to give him some colorful additions as well. There were some drying in the one bedroom that had been designated as his office. He had also ordered in a few wood blocks that were naturally colorful. There was a deep purple one he was eager to try.

He had never thought of having an official home office before, he had previously just worked at his kitchen table. When he first moved in, Luc had cleared out a bedroom that had been used as a catch-all in terms of storage and had him order furniture he liked. It was nice having a home office; he didn't have to go into the work one as often. That place was so stifling with its rows of cubicles. He completely agreed with Mac that they weren't meant to be stuck inside.

Grabbing a quick shower, he threw together a go-bag with extra battery packs for his phone, some snacks and water, a first aid kit, phone charger, deodorant, toothbrush and toothpaste, and a change of clothes. He normally packed shorts and a t-shirt or gym pants, something that was smaller and fit in a backpack. It sucked in the winter, but it was better than standing around in bloodied or ripped clothes.

Placing the flower on Luc's pillow, Bert paused. Should he leave a note? He didn't want to treat Luc like a child. He was the ruler of Netherworld for fuck's sake, but his sub clearly didn't always take care of himself. Letting out a sigh, he gave in and grabbed a piece of paper from his notebook.

Love, I need to go on a case. Hopefully back tomorrow. I'll let you know if that changes. Keep yourself safe and make sure you eat. I expect my Love to take care of himself for me. I love you. B

Bert tucked the note under the flower and gave Bal a scratch behind his ear.

"Watch after him for me, Bal. You're a good boy," he praised the hellhound.

Luc pressed a kiss to Bert's head, tucking the blankets in around him. He had been gone a week this time hunting down a serial killer. This one had been human; he had evaded the human authorities for years and a fellow nonhuman in law enforcement had asked the Enforcers to step in. The man had been extremely skillful at hiding and evading even the Enforcers, who by all rights had better senses than a human. They had finally tracked him down last night, but the processing had taken a while as he had been very combative from what Luc heard. He placed the glass hellhound on the nightstand next to Bert's side of the bed. He still found the house too quiet when Bert was gone, but he had discovered that losing himself in the creation of something helped pass the time. He had a stash of sand and metal delivered while Bert had been gone and had been experimenting with different designs.

He really wanted to find a way to combine glass and metal into one sculpture. He could see it in his mind, and had it completely planned out, but so far the experiments had failed to come together the way he wanted them to. So, instead he had made a hellhound, one that looked a lot like Bal.

Looking down at his watch, he realized he was running later than he had expected to be.

"Crap," he muttered. "You stay here today, Bal, and watch over Bert." He pressed a kiss to his hound's head too, ignoring it when he crawled into bed where Luc's spot was. He was following directions; he was porting directly to his office where he had Enforcers throughout the building so he would have guards around him. He still didn't want to make someone follow him around, it seemed unnecessary, and it also had the potential to make him look weak. Which was something he couldn't afford.

He arrived in his office to find an almond croissant and a coffee sitting on his desk. He walked out to Margo's desk;

she wasn't there, but her lights were on so she must have stepped out. There was a man leaving, dressed in coveralls and hat pulled down low.

"Can I help you with anything?" Luc asked.

"Just fixing the printer. It jammed again. Should be good to go," the man replied, never turning around, continuing to walk out of the office. "Have a good day now."

Luc watched as he walked out. Something about him seemed familiar, but he wasn't one of the regular maintenance techs on their floor. His brain was shouting that the man was known to them, but Luc couldn't place him. He'd ask Margo when she came back.

He sat at his desk, grabbing the files for today's cases to review. Heaving a sigh, he wondered if God ever got bored from seeing the same type of crap come across his desk. He'd have to ask him during the next game night. He couldn't remember if they were supposed to be having video or card games. They had a schedule, but he never paid that much attention to it. He just kept both on hand.

As he started reading, he absently reached out and grabbed the almond croissant. He enjoyed them, but they weren't something Margo usually picked up. It must be his lucky day. He took a large bite, knowing he didn't have a lot of time before the hearings needed to start. He chewed, knowing he probably had chipmunk cheeks with how much he had in his mouth. As he swallowed, his nose wrinkled at the aftertaste. It was more bitter than he would have expected. Usually there was a sweeter marzipan filling to these types of croissants. Maybe they had burned some of the almonds. He grabbed his coffee to wash the taste out. He swished the hot coffee around his mouth and swallowed before taking another large gulp. Ug. The bitter taste lingered, making even his coffee taste off. He needed to let

Margo know not to go to whatever bakery those came from again.

He finished making notes on the file in his hand and grabbed the next one when his left eye began tearing. Wiping it, he forced himself to concentrate on the files even though a low-grade headache was forming and his stupid eye wouldn't stop watering. He tried another sip of coffee before setting it aside. It wasn't just the pastry making it seem off, that was not good coffee. He tried to take a deep breath to calm his body down, but he felt like he couldn't get a full breath.

Hearing Margo come back into the office, he moved his chair back so he could ask her about the coffee.

"Sir! Are you alright?" Margo asked, hurrying over to meet him as he stood, his body swaying.

"Where did you get the coffee and the Danish today? They tasted a little off," Luc asked, propping himself up by leaning against his desk. Something wasn't right.

"Sir, I didn't stop at the bakery today. I wasn't sure when you were going to be in, so I haven't made the coffee yet."

"Call Bert. I think I've been poisoned. Again."

"Sir!" Margo's scared shout was the last thing he heard as he crashed to the floor.

Bert woke to his phone ringing incessantly. Bal suddenly jumped up, grabbing Bert's arm in his mouth and dragging him across the bed. Bert grabbed his phone, trying to get his arm free.

"Bal, stop it. Let go. Hello?" he asked as he answered.

"Bert. Get here now. I think Lucifer has been poisoned," Margo's scared voice sounded on the other end.

"Coming." Bert hung up the phone, noticing that Bal had let go. He ran to the den, grabbing their supply of healing potions. Bal had followed him, nose pressing to the back of his leg, urging him to go faster. "You sensed something, didn't you?" He made sure to tuck his weapon in the waistband of his pants before placing a hand on Bal and porting them to Luc's office. He saw that Margo had closed and locked the door, placing her coat under Luc's head. He was prone on the ground, his breathing sounding labored.

"What happened?" he asked as he dropped next to his mate. Tilting Luc's head back, he slowly dribbled the healing potion down his throat.

"I got called away. Someone had a scheduling question, but it was on the other side of the building. When I arrived, no one was there. I thought maybe I got the time or place mixed up, but I checked my texts, and I was right where it said to meet. I waited a few minutes and then gave up and headed back. Mr. Lucifer was already in his office. He was having trouble standing. He asked me about the coffee and Danish, but I hadn't brought any in this morning. I wasn't sure if he would be in late today since you just finished your assignment and got home," she replied, twisting her hands anxiously.

"Call Mac, please. Ask him to come straight here. Thank you for locking the door," Bert said. Bal stood guard at the door, but he kept looking over at Luc.

A minute later Mac ported in. "Are you fucking serious? What the fuck happened?"

"Can you check the pastry and the coffee? Don't eat them, they're probably poisoned."

Mac cursed but made his way around them to the desk where they still sat. Picking up the Danish first, he took a deep sniff and then repeated it with the coffee.

"Almonds."

"It is an almond croissant," Bert pointed out, finishing the first bottle and pulling out another.

"Yeah, but the coffee isn't. It's got a slight bitterness to it that shouldn't be in a pastry. My guess would be cyanide, and based on how quickly Uncle fell, a large dose of it too. How many potions do you have?"

Bert did some mental calculations from what he remembered from his training. "I should have enough. He has some here as well, but I wanted to use ones I knew were safe."

"Margo, has anyone been hanging around who normally isn't here?" Mac asked. Bert was concentrating on not choking his mate with the liquid but going as quickly as he could. The sooner he dosed Luc, the better.

"Not that I noticed. I've been more vigilant about people getting close to Mr. Lucifer since the attack in the hearing room. He told me that you all suspected there might be someone trying to work against him, so I've been very careful about who I allow near him," Margo replied adamantly.

"Tell Mac about your text message," Bert told her.

She pulled out her phone, showing it to Mac. "I had a meeting request, but no one showed up."

Mac logged onto Luc's computer, typing away. "It's not one of ours. There's no record of this number in the system. Burner phone maybe? I'll see what I can track down. I have a hacker that I trust. I'll pass on the number and see if she can find anything. My guess is that someone lured Margo away so they could get access to Uncle's office."

"It's my fault Lucifer was poisoned," Margo cried, tears falling from her eyes. Bert could tell she was honestly distressed at the thought. He looked at Mac and saw the same feelings reflected in his eyes.

"No," Bert said firmly. "It's most definitely not your fault. You didn't poison him and you called for help right away."

He quickly pulled away the bottle as Luc started coughing. When he saw Luc's eyelashes flutter, he moved to sit behind him, pulling him up to rest against his chest. "Easy, Love. Take a breath." He waited until Luc got his coughing under control before holding the rest of the healing potion to his lips. "Drink." Bert waited until Luc drank a couple more before asking him any questions.

"How do you feel now? Do you need another one?"

Luc shook his head. "I think that should be good. I really hate being poisoned."

"I'm so sorry, sir. I shouldn't have left my desk," Margo tried apologizing.

"It's not your fault. You are allowed and are expected to leave your desk as needed," Luc replied, his voice sounding a little hoarse.

"We think Margo was lured away on purpose so someone could have access to you," Mac said.

"There was a maintenance guy here, said he was fixing the printer, that it jammed again," Luc replied, taking a sip of the water Margo handed him.

Margo shook her head. "The printer was fine. I never called a repair person."

"What did he look like?" Bert asked.

Luc shrugged. "Coveralls, average height. He had a hat on, pulled down low. He wouldn't look at me when I was talking to him, just kept walking out. I never really saw his face. There was something familiar about him, but I can't place him, just the feeling that I know him."

Bal whined, still protecting the entrance, but wanting to see Luc.

"Come here," Luc said. Bal darted over, curling over Luc's lap. He was honestly much too large to be a lap dog, but he clearly needed to be reassured. Luc often forgot just how young he was. "Hush, pup. I'm fine."

"I'm going to go see what I can find. I'd really appreciate it if you just invited us to dinner, Uncle. You don't have to go to such extremes to see us," Mac joked. He bent down to give his uncle a hug, squeezing tight.

"Yeah, yeah," Luc replied, hugging back as hard as he could. "Why don't you all come over this weekend? We'll grill out. Faolán can play with the others and I'll get a chance to spoil my great-nephew."

"Sounds good. Let Viv know what we can bring. You know she'll want to contribute something," Mac said before porting out.

Luc nodded. "Help me up, please, Mate." He still felt a little shaky. "Margo, can you run to your bakery and get an almond croissant and a new cup of coffee?"

"Of course, but may I ask why?" Margo questioned.

"We're going to keep them guessing. There's no reason anyone should know that the poisoned items affected me. I plan on bringing them into the hearing room and munching away as the day goes on. If they have any other spies in the building, I'm sure it will get back to them and they'll be wondering if it worked at all, if they made a mistake. I don't want them thinking they won even a little bit."

Or they would double or triple the poison next time, Bert thought privately. He wouldn't contradict his mate in public, but he would make sure to tell him later not to eat things left out or given to him by someone he didn't fully trust.

Margo nodded, porting out.

"Love. You know that may just incite them to be more daring," Bert cautioned quietly.

"I know, but if they know they injured me for even a short time, it would do the same thing, maybe even more so."

"Is there a reason you didn't bring Bal with you?" Bert asked, keeping his voice calm. He wasn't sure if Bal would have been able to scent the poison or not, but it was worth a shot.

"I was going straight to work, where there are Enforcers throughout the building. He's still a pup. He's been trained, and we're bonded, but he's still young. I usually don't have them with me until they're a year older. It's not fair to ask a pup to stay still all day long. If I was going somewhere without an Enforcer presence, I would have brought him," Luc promised.

Bert sighed but nodded. "I think we might need to think about office security. I don't like that someone was able to slip in here and then leave poisoned items behind. Neither of those should have happened."

"I think we can put a spell on the office to record what goes on. I'll need to be able to turn it off for private matters, but maybe it can work while I'm not in the office or be activated with a certain word. That way if it's an emergency, I can activate it quickly," Luc suggested.

"I like that idea. At least we would be able to review it and try to catch whoever was trying to sneak in. The office should also be locked if you or Margo aren't here."

"I'm going to bring Spot with me when I come into the

office from now on," Margo added as she ported in with her hound. "He can guard the office when I have to leave. No one is going to want to mess with a hellhound. He'll get enough exercise when I take him out for lunch or when the grandkids come over after school."

Bert thought it was hilarious that she had a hellhound named Spot. But he supposed that's what happened when you let kids name him.

"I guess it's time to start the day," Luc said, his voice clearly unhappy about it.

"How about I walk you down?" Bert suggested. He did want to spend more time with Luc, but he also wanted to be close by in case there were still effects from the poison. He watched as Bal nudged Luc's hand, clearly not ready to leave him either.

"Alright, Bal. You can stay today, but port home if you get too bored." Bored hellhounds were never a good thing. "And yes, I would like that. Although I would recommend putting some clothes on first or I'll be distracted all day," Luc said, pressing a kiss to Bert's cheek.

Bert looked down at himself. He had completely forgotten that he only had gym shorts on. He hadn't taken the time to even grab his shoes. "Give me a minute, Love. I'll be right back." He ported home and hurriedly threw on some deodorant, brushed his teeth, and got dressed in jeans, a t-shirt, and his boots. He wouldn't stay in the hearing room for long, even though he wanted to, so he didn't dress nicer. In less than ten minutes, he was back in Luc's office.

"Thank you, Margo. I'll throw a quick spell around the office and we'll lock the door when we're both out. Make sure you take a long lunch today," Luc said as they got ready to leave.

Luc grabbed the coffee and the Danish. He walked slowly, his muscles still sore. Didn't matter what kind of poison it was, it always left his body aching for at least a day. Bert stayed next to him as they walked down the hallway, Bal following. Luc could hear him walking, which meant that Bal had partially shifted. Hellhounds had the unique ability to draw their claws back so they could move quietly. Bal wanted to be heard.

He forced himself to take a bite of the Danish, this one tasted much better, sweeter like it was supposed to. He hoped this didn't ruin one of his favorite treats for him. He slowly ate it, making sure to take drinks of coffee in between. Bert opened the door, letting him go through first, then Bal, Bert taking up the rear.

Luc settled into his chair, Bal sitting next to him on the left. "Have a good day, Love. I'll see you at home," Bert said, raising Luc's left hand to kiss, pressing his lips right above the ring. Luc knew it was his way of reminding him that Bert was here for him. Luc set his coffee down on the arm, using his now free hand to pull Bert down for a deeper kiss. Letting go, he also made sure all his weapons were in reach.

"I'll call or send Bal if I need anything," he promised softly.

Bert nodded, giving him one last look before porting out. Luc knew how much that would have strained Bert to leave him right after being poisoned, but he was trying to keep his promise not to interfere with Luc's work. Luc would make it up to him tonight.

"Are you ready?" Bert asked.

Luc took a deep breath, ignoring how it was a little shaky, before nodding.

"You can do this," Bert encouraged him.

Maybe. They had been working up to it. They were invited over to dinner at Mac's and he wanted to go. It was a safe place, he repeated to himself. Two hours, that was all he had to do. He grabbed the gift bag, toys for the baby and the hound, a bottle of wine for the dinner. Mac had assured him that dinner would be ready as soon as he arrived, so it wouldn't be drawn out. At this point, the whole family knew what he was going through. Mac had been horrified that he hadn't caught on sooner; Luc was just grateful that he had hidden it so well.

He grabbed Bert's hand and ported them to the front porch. The door opened before he could even knock or ring the bell. Mac had a weird look on his face. He came outside and shut the door.

"Uncle. I hate to do this to you. Thomas' parents dropped in on their way home from the airport and they haven't left yet. We didn't know they were coming. Do you want to reschedule, or we can bring the dinner to your house later?" Mac asked.

Bert could tell Mac was really upset. He had been supportive of Luc as he worked on expanding the time he could be away from Netherworld, even going someplace before they arrived so Luc would have a familiar face. Bert had heard stories about Thomas' parents and knew they were very nice people; he privately thought it would be okay to have dinner with them, but he would leave it up to Luc.

"Is dinner ready already?" Luc asked. Bert could see him fidgeting with his ring.

"Yes," Mac replied.

Luc nodded, taking a deep breath. "I would like to officially meet them, if that's okay. I've heard so much about them and they're probably wondering why they've never met me. Maybe we can make up an excuse for why we don't stay the whole night."

"Set an alarm on your phone for two hours," Mac recommended. "That way you act like it's ringing and say it's a work matter. Gives you a reason if you need to leave."

Luc nodded and pulled out his phone. Bert was grateful Mac had given him an easy out, but he was hopeful Luc wouldn't need it.

Walking into the house, Faolán rushed over to Luc, voice rumbling telling Luc all about it. Bert loved seeing the connection Luc had to all the hellhounds.

"I'm so glad you came," Viv said as she came over to give them both a hug. "What do you want to drink? Sit down and we'll bring out dinner."

As Bert sat, Thomas introduced them to his parents. They had a nice vibe about them. These were good people.

"It's so nice to meet you both. We've heard such wonderful things from Viv and Thomas. What is it you do?" Thomas' mom asked.

"Management," Luc replied.

"Government," Bert said at the same time.

Mac laughed. "They're both in similar jobs as mine. Uncle's in the same division I am, but he's the one in charge of everything," Mac explained, smoothing over the jumble. It was technically true after all.

"Oh! No wonder you're so busy all the time. Thank you for everything you do to keep us safe," she said sincerely. Luc really needed to ask his nephew exactly what he had told them they did for work so he wouldn't flub something up later.

Luc felt himself relax and start to enjoy the evening as the night wore on. They were very easy to talk to, and Luc could tell how much they loved all the people in the room, including D and Mac. His phone buzzed, letting him know his two-hour timer was up.

"Would you excuse us for a moment? That's work," Bert asked, pulling out Luc's chair.

"Of course!"

Bert led Luc down the hallway to the guest bathroom on Viv's side. He shut the door and yanked Luc's pants down.

"You've done such a good job tonight. I think you can make it a little longer, don't you?" he asked as he wrapped a hand around Luc's cock, slowly sliding his hand up and down until he was fully hard. "If you can stay a little more, we'll have some tail play tonight. You can fill me as I stuff you full of my cock. How does that sound, Love?" He loved how Luc's eyes were blown, his breaths coming faster, the precum dripping steadily.

"Please," Luc whispered hoarsely.

"Please what?"

"Make me come," he begged. "I can stay a little bit

longer. Want you..." He broke off on a moan as Bert dropped to his knees and deep throated his cock.

Bert looked up, watching as Luc bit his fist to keep his sounds muffled. He couldn't wait until they were home and he could fill the room with the sounds of his lover. He loved on the underside of Luc's shaft, his tongue swirling and licking. Cupping Luc's balls with one hand, he slowly stroked his fingertips across the surface. He pulled back once, catching Luc's eyes with his own.

"I'm proud of you. I love you." Bert sucked on his own finger, spitting to make sure it was wet before sucking down Luc's shaft again. He took him deep, the smell and taste of his mate surrounding him. He slid his finger between Luc's cheeks, tapping the hole when Luc spread his legs as wide as he could with his pants still on. Bert thrust deep, searching for the magic spot, swallowing and tightening his throat around the hot length in his mouth. As the muscles in Luc's thighs tightened, he knew he found it and pressed his fingers, rubbing. Seconds later, Luc was coming down his throat. Bert swallowed before he stood, grabbing Luc's head and pulling him down for a kiss, sharing the salty slightly bitter taste with him.

He washed his hands and rinsed out his mouth. He hated washing the smell of his mate off, but he also didn't want to take the chance of Thomas' parents knowing what they had just done. Luc was still standing there, a little dazed. Bert smiled, standing up on his tiptoes to press a kiss to Luc's forehead. He pulled Luc's pants up, carefully zipping them shut, closing the button and then the belt. "I'm going to go let them know we can stay for a little longer, Love. Take your time."

Luc dragged Bert into their bedroom. He had been good all night and he wanted his reward. He had managed to stay two additional hours after dinner, which was a record for him. But Thomas' parents were everything Mac claimed they were, and he had a feeling that he and Bert had been adopted in as well. If all people were that nice, the world would be a much better place.

But now he wanted his tail in Bert's ass and Bert's thick dick stretching his.

"In a hurry, Love?" Bert asked, laughter in his voice.

"Yes. I was good. I want what you promised," Luc said as he began stripping down. Standing near the edge of the bed, he bent down to untie his shoes. A sharp smack had him gasping.

"I'm still in charge, Love. Be good, or I'll restrain you and you won't get what you want," Bert warned.

"Yes, Mate," Luc said, waiting.

"Strip and let me see your demon form," Bert ordered. He loved seeing Luc's shifted form. He stood still, admiring for a minute before walking closer and lightly touching yards of delightful skin in front of him. Luc's demon was just as gorgeous as his human-like side. They had played while shifted before, but only one other time with Luc's tail penetrating him. Bert normally wasn't one for ass play, but tonight he wanted to feel his mate inside him at the same time he was inside his mate. He didn't know why, but he was craving the extra connection, something he had never really wanted with someone else. He traced a few of the demon markings with his tongue, his hand finding the heavy cock already hard for him.

Bert stayed away from Luc's tail, knowing just how sensitive the base was. He would leave that until he wanted Luc to come. He stayed in his human form, loving the size difference. He didn't know what it was, but he never felt more powerful than when Luc submitted to him like this. Luc was always taller than he was, but it was extreme now.

"Bend over the bed," he said, gently pushing between Luc's wings. His mate rested his arms on the bed, his head lying on top, his ass pushed out, waiting for him. Fates, he was lucky. He quickly stripped down, pulling the lube off the nightstand. Squatting down behind his mate, Bert followed a trail of demon markings with his tongue, leading him toward the furled hole. He spread Luc's cheeks, blowing a breath across the skin, loving the shiver that moved through his lover. Luc stayed still otherwise, and Bert rewarded him with licks and kisses.

As the skin grew wet and the hole loosened, Bert slid a finger inside his mate, slowly stretching him. He kept it light and avoided his prostate, knowing Luc would be getting more and more desperate.

"Ready for me, Love?" he asked.

Luc nodded, arching and giving his ass a little wiggle. Bert lubed himself, using just enough to not hurt, but knowing it would still sting in the best of ways when he slammed in. Grabbing Luc's hips, he thrust hard, sliding all the way into his mate's body. Luc made a sound, a combination of a groan and whimper.

"Color?" Bert gritted out, clenching his teeth in an effort not to come or thrust yet. Luc was so tight and warm around him.

"Green, so Green. Please. Perfect. Need you," Luc panted out.

Bert squeezed him tighter, leaving bruises that would probably fade by the time they were done. He let his control go, his hips pounding into Luc's body, the sound of skin hitting skin filling the air. As he got closer to his own orgasm, he grabbed Luc's tail, lubing the end.

"Now, Love. I need you in me. I want to come deep inside your body while you're deep inside mine," Bert said, widening his own stance to welcome his mate.

He clenched his teeth, bearing down as he tried to loosen for Luc's tail. The stretch was incredible. He must have made a noise or gripped Luc tighter because he paused. "No, keep going." He waited, thrusting his hips in tiny increments to stop his own dick from softening from the discomfort. Soon enough, Luc was deep enough to reach his prostate, curling his tail up to press against it, the double arrow tip design of the end rubbing back and forth. Shit. That felt so good. One would move off, there would be a slight respite, and then the other ridge would glide against him.

He couldn't hold back any longer, he gripped Luc tightly, slamming his dick home over and over, losing himself in the feel of his mate. Luc's tail moved with him, always keeping pressure over his prostate. Bert felt his orgasm cresting and he moved a hand to grip the base of Luc's tail, rubbing it much like he would Luc's sack.

"Please please please," Luc chanted.

Giving the tail one last firm squeeze, Bert grabbed Luc's cock, loving the different textures of the demon form. If he loved to bottom, it would be the perfect dick with its bumps and ridges, he thought. He stroked Luc faster, pressing his thumb against the slit. As his orgasm rushed through him, Bert leaned forward.

"Come for me, Love," he ordered, biting down into Luc's flesh, drawing a bit of blood. He felt the hot liquid of Luc's orgasm spread over his hand, ass becoming a vise on Bert's cock. Bert leaned against Luc's back, enjoying the pleasure sweeping through both of them. After Luc gently removed his tail, Bert pulled free of his mate's body. He kept one hand on Luc's back to keep him in place. He watched as his cum began to leak out of Luc's hole, sliding down his cheek, down his leg. A surge of possessiveness flooded him at the sight and Bert knelt down to lap it up. Once his mate was clean from behind, he urged him to flip over and gently licked his shaft clean as well. He tucked his mate in under the covers before going into the bathroom to wipe himself down. As great as the prostate play had been, he absolutely hated the feeling of lube on his ass.

L uc drummed his fingers against the arm of his chair. Today's punishment hearings had been tedious and the afternoon disputes were ridiculous. He felt like he was a babysitter to a bunch of toddlers who didn't want to share their toys. They were grown-ass adults who couldn't handle their own shit. He wondered, not for the first time, if he should stop holding these and let them sort their own crap or appoint someone he trusted. Now probably wasn't a good time to appoint someone since there were traitors somewhere in his organization.

He had started the dispute hearings as a way to connect to his new constituents and also as a way to minimize the in-fighting. When he and God first took over, it had been a large uphill battle to make the two sides come together for a common cause. He'd thought most of them had understood it by now, but apparently someone still wanted to go back to the old ways. The old ways left many of them dead, always looking over their shoulders for enemies, and their birth rates had been abysmally low. If it had kept going, there was a good chance that their species would have eventually died off.

At this point though, they should be able to handle their own problems. It had been long enough for them to figure out how to deal with each other without fighting. He wanted to spend more time with his mate and their crazy schedules sometimes made that difficult. Maybe slowly weaning the disputes back for only the most critical ones would be a good start. He needed to brainstorm about who could take over if it seemed like the dispute hearings were really still needed.

Bert was out late tonight as another case had come up. The Enforcers were sent all over, their groups in charge of keeping the balance and the peace for all three realms of Earth, Arlysium, and Netherworld. There was always someone stationed at the inter-realm hospital as well. It seemed like there had been an uptick in cases needing Enforcers lately and he had to wonder if it had to do with the attacks on him. God said other than the Enforcers, it had been quiet on his end, which only confirmed that it was a directed attack on him.

Luc had some people looking into it and God had ones on his side as well. It felt good that his friend had his back. Sighing, he brought his attention back to the case in front of him.

"I really don't see why you felt the need to bring this to me. Again. You're both adults, you both agreed to the terms of the contract agreeing to split the costs. The builder has already completed the fence. Just because you changed your mind at the end does not mean that you can withhold payment. You must honor the contract. Pay the builder or face my consequences. There was plenty of time for you to change or back out before it was finished," Luc interrupted, done with the complaining. There was documentation that both sides had signed off on the style and color, and now the one party didn't like how it looked completed. He personally thought the pictures looked amazing. The builder had done a great job.

"Case closed. Pay your part," Luc ordered before standing up. He gave his guards a nod and left the hearing room. He felt antsy, not quite settled. He wasn't sure if it was because Bert was gone or just the long day. Something was up though and even his demon side was taking notice.

He entered his office, loving the feel of the new wards closing around him and allowing him to relax.

"Sir?" Margo asked, looking up from her desk, her hellhound watching the door closely.

"Just a long day," he replied. "I think I'm going to take a walk through the punishment levels. It's been a bit since I've been down there." Maybe he could work out this feeling while he was there.

"I brought in a sandwich for you in case you were working late," she said. "It's in the fridge in your office."

Luc smiled. Ever since the poisoned coffee, she had been vigilant about what was allowed in the office, even with the wards. She often brought in food for him instead of getting it out. He also wondered if she had overheard his mate talking about the rule for him eating, because there always seemed to be an "acceptable" meal ready, even if it was a simple sandwich and some fruit. If she had, he could only think that she knew about their dynamic and had accepted it. Otherwise, why would she go to the effort?

"Thank you, Margo. I appreciate that. I'll eat and then I'll head down."

"Yes sir. I'll get a fresh pot of coffee going. I think I'm going to catch up on paperwork as well."

Luc looked at her closely, but only nodded. He thought she still felt guilty about allowing poisoned coffee in on her watch. Of course, she hadn't even been in the office when it was delivered, but she wouldn't hear otherwise. He had noticed she made a point of being at work for as long as he was if Bert was out of town or late. She was fierce in her protection of him, and he adored her. It was another reason to cut his days shorter; he wanted her to feel like she had a fulfilling life outside of work, especially with the grandkids.

He made sure to take the time to fully enjoy the sandwich, especially since she had made his favorite. There was a bag of salt and vinegar chips and a crisp apple as well. It certainly made his stomach happy. He cleaned up his desk, washing before he took the suit coat off and rolled up his sleeves. Luc debated on the gun but left it in his desk drawer. He kept the ankle knife and added another to his belt. It blended well; it was small by design but expanded to almost sword size when open. Magic was a wonderful thing.

Luc nodded to his Enforcers as he left his office and began walking down the hallway.

"Sir?" Alan asked as he kept pace. After a threatening letter had been found outside the building, at least one of his personal guards had stationed themselves by his office. Luc had never asked them to be there, and he felt awful for thinking about asking them to stop. They were doing their job and he respected that.

"Heading to the punishments for a while," Luc responded.

"Yes, sir," Alan replied.

"You can take a break for a bit or head home," Luc pointed out, trying to do so nicely. It wasn't Alan's fault that he felt constricted with his movements, even more so when Bert was gone for some reason.

"Yes, sir. I'll stay near the entrance. Just in case," Alan replied calmly.

Luc held in the sigh. He was starting to feel like he was being babysat. Bert would probably tell him to see it as a sign that they cared about him. In the end he nodded once and told Alan thank you. He really needed to work some of this aggression out or he was likely to snap at someone who didn't deserve it. He worked hard to be a good boss and his Enforcers certainly didn't deserve him losing his shit for no good reason with them.

He had initially thought he would walk around and talk to his men, maybe take part in something small, but he changed his plans and traveled further down the levels, reaching the more severe cases. Luc could feel himself transforming into The Lucifer. He saw himself as Luc, and his job as The Lucifer when it came to the dirty work. The Lucifer meted out punishments, often quite severely. He fought against his enemies so brutally that no one had dared to rise against him in hundreds of years. There was a reason people said his name in fear.

As he slowly traveled the hallway, soaking in the energy, he let his senses seek out the one who would be his therapy for today. Each body or soul who belonged here had their own space, their own ongoing punishment. It was never ending, most of it magic-based. Those that worked on the punishment floors rotated, switching between the more violent and torturesque punishments to the easier ones. He knew it was a demanding job and wanted to make sure his people didn't burn out or get too jaded. Looking back, he saw Alan positioned in a ready stance near the exit door. Nothing called out to him, and he walked far enough that he couldn't see Alan any longer. Turning the corner, the hair on his arms stood up. Something was wrong here, someone was out when they shouldn't be. Dammit. There went his plans for a relaxing night. He forced himself to keep walking, bringing his demon side just under the surface, not enough to show, but enough to help enhance his senses.

Hmm. He knew this one...ah. The assassin from earlier with the traitor Keevhan. He probably should have realized he was a plant when they knew Keevhan was dirty. Too late now. Not that it mattered much. Somebody still would have needed to let him out of his cell. He felt the shadows move behind him.

"I know you're there," Luc said calmly, keeping his tone conversational.

"Pity. I could have made this quick," a voice said from the dark.

A Shadow maybe, Luc thought. No, the assassin wasn't mated but had a physical form. He couldn't remember what kind of nonhuman the assassin had been, although there were several species who could hide in the shadows.

"I won't give you that privilege," Luc replied, smiling. He found a smile normally threw them off guard.

"It's hard to fight what you can't see," the man taunted, a knife finding its way across Luc's back.

He kept his face still, not showing any pain or emotion. That one might need to be looked at later. Luc shifted his hands, letting his claws come. He could still grab his knife with them, but they were a weapon themselves. The man would physically die for this, no doubt, but if he played it right maybe he would be able to get some information from him first. He seemed like one who liked to brag.

Luc spun, his hands flung out, finding their target as he sliced through the other man's arm, blood dripping to the floor, giving away his position. He heard a muttered curse and smiled.

He kept track of the other man, who was circling him, debating on what to do next.

"How did you get out?" Luc asked.

A mocking laugh sounded in front of him. "Magic of course."

That seemed like an honest answer. There was more to it, but it wasn't setting off his senses as a lie. He supposed it was possible that there had somehow been a spell snuck in with him. It was more likely that someone had brought it in later. He needed to go over the security footage. He didn't have the luxury of taking the time to do a reading right now.

He waited until the man was behind him again before he spun, sending out a roundhouse kick, connecting with the man's torso, kicking him back into the wall.

"Who sent you?" Luc asked.

"Myself," the man replied.

"Hmm. No, I don't believe so. This is a coordinated attack, planned way in advance. You're smart, but not that smart. You like the money, but you don't actually have a lot of ambition. People come to you, you don't go looking for work. No, this type of thing is beyond your scope," Luc taunted.

He ducked, but not quite quick enough and felt blood well from his ear as the knife flew past his head. Luc made himself focus. The assassin had skills, he admitted. Keeping the grin on his face, he fought back. Not to his real ability, just enough to keep from getting truly hurt and letting the assassin think he had an actual chance of winning.

"Why are you here?"

"Eh, the pay was good. I don't give a shit who's in charge. Plus, he said he would let us have more freedom if he took over. None of this having to behave bullshit. The humans should fear us. We used to be the stuff of their nightmares and most have forgotten us. We're a fairy tale."

"It's best for everyone," Luc grunted, taking a kick to the stomach. As he lost control over his breath for a second, there was a disturbance to the air and Bal ported in, rushing toward the man.

"No, pup. He's mine," Luc said gently, dodging another knife flying at him.

Bal stood back, but let loose a howl, calling for help. Alan came rushing down the hallway, full demon, sword drawn. Luc waved them both back, staying him with a hand. He should just finish this. Margo was upstairs and he knew she wouldn't leave until he did. He apparently wasn't going to get what he wanted tonight, but maybe he could get something else. He heaved a sigh. No more playtime.

"Did you know that I was picked for this position for a reason?" Luc asked.

The other man laughed. "I don't care."

"You should," Luc replied. That was the only warning he gave before reaching out and grabbing the shadow in front of him. "Not only can I read your being, which helps me know where you are, but my family line has a few special traits," Luc told him, holding on to the mist with one hand. He felt the man's shock that Luc was able to touch him. Which was understandable, most wouldn't be able to. Calling his hellfire, he let it flow down his arm, down to his hand. He gripped the man tighter as he fought to get away. "My hellfire works on *everyone*," he said.

Luc listened to the man's screams as his skin slowly burned away. He kept hold, feeding the fire, sending it to coat the entire body in front of him. Luc focused on the man's mind, blocking out the scent of burning flesh. He dove in deep and quick, not bothering to do it gently. He tore through memories, searching for anything that might help. Son of a bitch. The asshole didn't know anything. He was contacted on a burner phone, everything done over messages. He had a faint glimpse of a man in a maintenance outfit slipping him a potion in the prison. Nothing terribly new. Luc made a mental note to see if any cameras down here caught anything. They needed to inspect the maintenance department for missing uniforms and disgruntled workers.

The man's screams suddenly cut off, bringing Luc's attention back in front of him. He was completely engulfed, burning so bright that even Alan could see him now too. He was like a torch lighting up the hallway. This level would need some additional airing out, Luc thought, watching as the body crumbled to ash in front of him.

Dusting off his hands, he turned to Alan. "We have a problem in maintenance."

Bert was at a bit of a loss. He desperately needed to help his lover, but his hands were tied for helping in public. He had gone to his boss, but God already had people on it. God was pissed. Luc was his friend and they had been keeping the peace between their people, and Earth for that matter, for over a thousand years. Two thousand years? After a while it all ran together, but it had been a really long time.

He was pacing in the office, getting lots of looks. He had been scouring the security footage again. No matter how many times he watched it, he couldn't find anything different. The man clearly knew where the cameras were and skillfully avoided showing his face. Luc was positive it was the same man that had been in his office before the poisoning. He also didn't match anyone on staff, thank goodness.

"Get your ass in here," God yelled at him from his office.

Bert sighed but went. He sat down heavily as his boss shut the door. Snapping his fingers, God activated the silencing spell.

"He's a grown-assed man that can take care of himself. The fucktard will make a mistake sooner or later and we'll get him. I'm not working with someone else, and the Fates themselves appointed Luc."

"I know he can take care of himself. I've seen it. Heard the stories. His reputation is terrifying, especially if you don't know he's secretly a softy. But he's still my sub. I need to do something to help him," Bert replied. He knew God understood. The man spent almost as much time in the club as he had.

"I know it must be driving you nuts, but you pacing in here isn't helping anyone," God pointed out dryly.

"Yeah, I know. But it's better than at home. I promised I wouldn't interfere with his work."

"Which is good. He's incredibly capable. However, you're still his Dom. You can help him in other ways. How long has it been since you've had a good scene? Take him to the club. I had a room reserved for tonight, but I don't need it. You guys should go."

"Are you sure?" Bert asked. It was a generous offer, especially since he didn't think God had gone in a while.

"Yup. Go. Have fun, relax. Make it hard for him to sit down or walk with a limp, something I can tease him about tomorrow at game night," God replied, grinning. There was an evil little glint in his eye.

Bert shook his head. Doms were all the same.

"Thanks. I will. What's tomorrow?" he asked.

"I think we're on video games. I bought a few new ones to try out."

"Awesome. I'll make the pimento cheese dip you like," Bert promised. In fact, he could throw it together tonight before they left so it had enough time to have the flavors really come together.

"Hmm. I love that dip," God replied. Bert wondered if he knew he had licked his lips.

"Alright. I'm going. Gotta grab my sub and drag him away," Bert joked, standing to shake his boss's hand. In their home, they exchanged hugs but kept it more professional at the office.

"You're good for him," God told him seriously. "I had a suspicion he might have sub tendencies, but there was no way I could step into that role for him. We get too much attention when we're together and there would be no hiding it. Plus, he's like my brother. He's my family, I'd do anything for him. I'm grateful you turned out to be his mate."

Bert gave a single nod. "It's my honor."

"Dress in your leather pants and a black t-shirt, Love," Bert called out as he entered their home.

Luc poked his head out from the den's doorway at the top of the stairs. "Are we going somewhere?"

"Yup. To the club," Bert replied. "God isn't using his reserved room tonight and gave it to us."

"But there won't be time to close the club, there'll be people there," Luc replied. Bert could hear the nerves in his voice, although he didn't think anyone else would have.

"True. But I brought you this," he said, pulling out the bag behind his back.

Luc pulled the contents out, looking at the full mask. This one went all around his head, hiding even his hair. It would be hard to tell who was behind it. He looked up at Bert.

"For getting into and around the club. We'll take it off once we get to the room. Charles said he'd up additional protections on the room before we get there. If you were interested, he and Sky invited us to dinner in their apartment when we're done. It's above the club, but he has amazing wards on it. No one will know you're there."

Bert waited, knowing God was right and that this was what they needed, but he also wouldn't force Luc to go. They could do a scene at home as well, although they were more likely to be interrupted.

"We'll go straight to the room? And then to the apartment if we stay?" Luc asked.

"Yes," Bert replied.

It took a minute, but Luc gave a single nod of agreement.

"Good. Go get dressed. Black boots too. Then bring me my leather pants, vest, your cuffs and mask," Bert ordered. He watched as Luc left to do as he asked before gathering a few items he wanted to bring with them. He grabbed a small bag, tossing in his preferred lube, Luc's cock ring and nipple clamps, his favorite flogger. The room would have supplies, but he wanted to bring some of their own things so Luc had something familiar.

Luc came back into the room, looking delicious. He wasn't quite dressed as a sub, although the cuffs would certainly hint at it. He wanted Luc to be comfortable and also blend in easily. With his height and mannerisms, people would automatically think Dom. Bert watched, biting the inside of his cheek to keep his dick in check as Luc began undressing him and helping him into his leathers. Bert played with Luc's hair as he knelt in front of him, lacing up Bert's biker boots.

"Thank you, Love. Wrists please," Bert said, grabbing the cuffs. He gently placed the medium weighted cuffs on Luc, making sure they weren't too tight. They had found that Luc liked the feel of them. Bert was having some made that Luc could wear under his dress shirts and suit coats at work. It was a balance to find the right design so they would blend in but still give Luc emotional support when he wasn't there. Bert stood behind him when he was done. "Ready for the mask? It might feel very weird. If it doesn't work for you, we'll use the other one. I just thought this one would provide more coverage and might help you relax since it won't come off easily."

"I'm ready," Luc replied, taking in a deep breath.

Bert carefully slid it over Luc's head, keeping a finger between his hair and the zipper so it wouldn't get snagged. Walking to the front, he checked the fit. Seeing his lover in the full mask, only openings for his eyes, nose, and mouth had Bert's dick hardening. There were holes cut out so he could hear, but even his ears were tucked inside the leather.

"Gods, Love. You make me so hard," he said, pulling Luc's hand to press against his cock.

Luc laughed, gently rubbing. "It's not my favorite, but I can handle it for a short time," he said.

Bert nodded, twining his fingers together with Luc's. "Let's go then." He ported them to the club, landing in the lobby. The receptionist knew they were coming and waved them through in front of the lines. Bert could hear the club-like sounds coming from the main room, music and voices creating a din of noise. As they walked through the club, he kept his hands to himself, trying not to let on who was with him. He led Luc to their room, swiping his hand across the sensor to open the door.

As they entered, Luc's eyes grew even wider. Bert kept his laughter inside, but he was sure Luc was still picking up on it. He had forgotten that God usually went for this room. It was more hardcore looking than the other room they had been in. Luc looked a little shellshocked.

"You okay, Love?" Bert asked.

Luc nodded, flabbergasted. He had known God was a Dom. It had come up before, but they never went into specifics. He didn't think he needed to know quite this much about his old friend. He looked around the room hoping that Bert was not planning on using half of what was in here. Was that a…? Wow. Okay. He needed to never be here the same night God was. Some things he didn't need to take up free rent in his brain for the next thousand years or so.

Bert let him have another minute, while he laid out the things that he had brought, as well as collecting a few items from around the room.

"Strip and kneel by the bench please," Bert ordered.

Luc took his clothes off, folding and placing them on the dresser. He moved to kneel next to the spanking bench, making sure he was comfortable. If he was kneeling, it usually meant a longer session. Bert gently removed the mask, but quickly slid a blindfold over Luc's eyes. He strained to hear where Bert was moving around the room.

"Lay over the bench, arms out. Make sure it's comfortable; you may be here a while."

He laid his torso over the bench, arms in front of him. He heard Bert walking around, his footsteps coming to a stop in front of him. He felt his Mate's hands gently move his arms, clicking his wrist cuffs to the bench.

"Test that and see how you feel," Bert said.

"Green, Mate," Luc replied after taking stock of his body and making sure nothing was straining or tingling. His arms were down and out to the side a little, but it wasn't really pulling on his shoulders.

"Good. I have something new to try. Spread your legs for me. Make sure you're comfortable enough."

Luc tried to listen for clues, but he couldn't tell what his lover was up to. He spread his legs, keeping his balance.

"I'm going to move you where I want you to go. It may be a little uncomfortable, but it shouldn't be painful. What are your words?"

"Yellow to pause, Red to stop," Luc said.

"Good," Bert replied, running a hand down Luc's back, teasing his cock before letting go. Luc felt a boot gently kick his legs further apart. There was something naughty, almost forbidden feeling with Bert being fully clothed and him completely naked. His legs were spread wider, his hips twinging a bit. He squirmed a little, but didn't move.

"There?" Bert asked.

"It's pulling a bit, but not painful," Luc told him.

"Hmm," Bert replied simply. Luc startled as he felt cuffs close around his ankles. He heard a gentle clang of metal next as Bert fiddled with the cuffs.

"You look amazing. My perfect Love," Bert praised.

Luc lay over the bench, wondering what was going to happen when something cold suddenly touched his hole. He clenched his cheeks tight, trying to close his legs to keep the sensation out, only to find he couldn't.

"Ah, no. You have a spreader bar, Love. Tonight you're going to give up all control to me. I want you to really let go. You've been under so much stress at work. I made a promise not to interfere there, but here you're all mine to do with as I will. Use your safe words if you need them, I'm always listening," Bert told him.

Luc waited, listening for some clue to give him a hint of what was going to happen. The barest touch drifted down his back, more of a tickle than anything. He gasped as it slid between his cheeks to swirl around his balls. He wasn't sure if he liked it or made him want to itch to get rid of the sensation. It circled his cock, sliding up his stomach to tease his nipples into hard peaks. Luc relaxed into the sensation but let out a short shout as clamps were applied to both nipples at the same time. They must have been the clip kind not the screw kind. Oh, that stung. He heard a little jostle and the tug of a chain between them.

He was so focused on the pain in his nipples that he didn't hear the flogger until it landed on his skin with a thwack. Luc let his body sink into the bench as the flogger worked its way up his back, finally caressing both shoulders. His skin was feeling warmer, his cock hard, precum gathering at the tip.

"Hmmm, nice," Bert said, his voice husky. Luc gasped as his cock was suddenly engulfed in Bert's warm wet mouth. A few more strokes and he would come...he groaned as he felt the cock ring snap into place.

"Not yet, Love. We have all night," Bert promised.

Luc waited, head tilted and ears listening. Bert was so silent on his feet that he couldn't pick up his movements. He heard a whistle in the air and a line of fire lit across his ass. Oh gods, the cane. Luc loved the deep harsh sting it gave him. It got him out of his head faster than anything else. Bert usually didn't do too many strikes with it though. Luc arched back as much as he could, asking for another. Six more lines were laid down on his body, from the back of his thighs all the way up to the rounded part of his ass.

Yes, that was what he needed. Luc felt the lovely fog start to fill his head, and he wanted so desperately to get to the place where nothing touched him, where he could let all of the stress go away. Wet fingers circled his hole and he moaned, seeking more. He wanted to be filled, needed to feel Bert's cock inside him. He wanted to come, to feel the rush of endorphins that left him feeling boneless and relaxed.

He felt Bert's hand rest on the small of his back, holding him still. Soon Bert's dick was spreading him wide, the head barely penetrating his body, but the heat and stretch of it made Luc gasp. He tried to push back to get more of it, but Bert smacked his hip and pulled all the way out.

"No, Love. I'm in charge. You'll get what I give you, when I want to give it to you. Be a good boy and let me use your body."

Luc dropped his head, forcing his body to relax. Bert would take care of him. He moaned as the hot length slammed fully into him, the suddenness of it stealing his breath as his body fought to adjust. Bert's hips pounded into him, never pausing, the sound of their flesh smacking against each other filling the room.

Bert leaned over his back, whispering how good he felt, how much he loved him. His hips never stopped, slamming into Luc's body over and over again. His ass was hot from the flogging and caning. Bert's skin rubbed against it, causing the pain to flare again, merging with pleasure as Bert changed angles and hit his prostate dead on. Luc shouted, encouraging Bert to do it over and over again.

Luc gasped as the chain between his nipple clamps was tugged, causing pain to shoot through him again. He moaned as the sharp sensation faded, the lingering tingle leading straight to his balls. He was going out of his mind, he wanted to come so badly; his cock incredibly hard, the precum leaking steadily, but the damn cock ring stopped his rising orgasm over and over.

"Please, Mate," Luc begged.

"Not yet," Bert replied.

Bert kept a steady punishing rhythm, Luc whimpering, unable to move as his Mate used him for his own pleasure.

"Good. Focus on me, how much you're pleasing me. You're doing so well," Bert praised him. There was a stream of other words, but Luc lost track of what his lover was saying as a hand came over his cheeks, gripping the fresh welts. Luc groaned, the pain sinking deeper, right to his balls.

"Five more," Bert said.

Five more what?

Luc screamed as a hand landed over the stripes with a smack. The other side received the same treatment, and then Bert rotated back. The last one landed across the tip of his dick. Luc lost control of himself, his mind floating away, that heady buzzy feeling surrounding him, filling him, taking him away. He collapsed fully on the bench, trusting his Mate to have him.

He never noticed when Bert's orgasm filled him, the heat running down his legs, or when Bert snapped the cock ring off and his own orgasm tore out of him. His body and mind floated, no worries, no cares, only the feel of his Mate surrounding him.

Bert grinned as God came in the door, bright and early. Bastard wanted to see if Luc was limping.

"Good night?" God asked, smiling evilly.

"Very good night," Bert confirmed. "He flew so high. Isn't it a little early for game night?" he asked dryly.

God shrugged unrepentantly. "Luc! I have new games.

Stop being lazy and get down here. I brought donuts!" he shouted.

"It's too fucking early for game night," Luc grumbled, coming down the stairs. "It's called game *night*, not game breakfast."

"Don't be a grouch. I got your favorites. And coffee," God bribed him.

"Coffee?" Luc asked, bleary-eyed. Bert had worn him out multiple times last night. They'd had a late snack with Charles and Sky and then Bert claimed him twice more until late this morning. He had been planning on sleeping in until he heard his old friend's booming voice downstairs.

"Coffee," God confirmed, holding out a cup for him.

"Fine," Luc said grudgingly. "What games did you bring?"

"Some zombie ones. Got a new one; it looked okay and we haven't played it yet. It has a multi-player option so all three of us can play."

Luc sighed but took the games, gingerly bending over to turn everything on and insert the disc.

He caught God giving Bert an approving smile when he turned around. He had forgotten he only had on his old soft sweatpants that slid down easily. He had thrown them on last night because they were so loose and soft. Clearly the remaining welts were on display when he had bent over. Fucking Doms.

"Are we doing this or what?" he asked, making grabby hands for the donuts.

Bert laughed at him, handing over a donut and a napkin. Luc settled into the couch, grateful it was cushy, but incredibly happy to be sharing this downtime with his lover and best friend.

"By the way. We need to never be at the club at the

same time," Luc told his friend. "If that room is what you like, I will never have enough bleach to get anything I see out of my head," he said teasingly. But also, it was the truth. He loved him, but he never wanted to see his oldest friend during a scene.

"No, I understand that. I can appreciate your lines, but I don't ever want to see you in a scene either." God shuddered. It'd be like seeing your brother. That definitely did not do it for him.

Luc laughed as his friend plopped down on the couch next to him, his lover on the other side. He settled in, learning the different controls for this game. It'd be fun to see who won.

Luc left his suit in his office, changing into a pair of black dress pants and a black shirt after eating a quick sandwich. It was still dressy enough for his position, but he wouldn't ruin yet another suit. He was going down to the punishment levels to do some work. It had been too long since he had been down there, and he had a bunch of anger over the situation he needed to work out anyway. He'd been shoving it down for months now, trying to keep an upbeat appearance for everyone else, but he knew he would blow soon if he didn't work some of it out.

Bert was on an assignment, so he had all night to get himself in a better mood. He called Bal to him, ensuring he was following his Mate's rules. There had clearly been someone inside his organization who was sneaking in the hooded man and his lackies. They had found evidence of schedules being tampered with and some security cameras had been removed, not to mention hours of camera footage being deleted. Luc had placed a few more recorder spells in important locations so that if the cameras went missing again, they would at least have a backup option.

It had been extremely frustrating that they hadn't found the main instigator yet, but they would. Hopefully soon. He was sick of always being on guard and not knowing who he could trust. Not to mention poor Margo was staying later than she should and he suspected getting to the office a lot earlier to make sure it was safe, even with the wards they put in place. No matter what time he arrived in the morning, she was already there. He had sent her home today though; he had plenty of Enforcers around as well as Bal.

He supposed the wards were one good thing to come out of this. He had never thought someone would come after his staff to get to him, it had never happened in the past. To be fair, they hadn't come after his employees yet either, but at least this way, Luc knew Margo was protected. She had been with him for years and she was like a de-facto mother or grandmother at this point; she fed him, encouraged him, looked out for him. He adored her and would be devastated if something happened to her because of him.

Alan met him at the door to the punishment levels. Luc sighed. Alan had been staying closer since the attack in the levels last time.

"Sir," he said, following Luc through the hallway. "Punishments today?"

Luc nodded. "It's been a bit since I've been down there."

Alan nodded. "I'll keep watch, sir."

"Thank you." He knew Alan was simply doing his job and was grateful he seemed to care about Luc's well-being, but he also missed the days where he could wander around by himself. He wondered if his guards viewed him as having gotten soft since it had been hundreds of years since he was challenged or if they guarded him for another reason.

Luc knew exactly who he wanted to visit today. One of the bastards that had attacked his niece last year. Most of them had been souls when they came to him, Mac and his people having killed them when they finally found Viv. Not that it mattered what form someone was in; souls could be punished just as much as the physical bodies that were here. Once the physical part died, the souls were still contained in their cell, their punishment continuing. Luc could also give the soul a corporeal form in short durations for different aspects of their punishments. It wasn't necessary, but sometimes it was useful for jarring them out of their complacent state. They routinely changed guards and punishers to keep the prisoners on edge. Even torture could become common place and tedious, both for the Enforcers and the prisoners. The mind or body could adapt and get used to horrible things, so change was necessary.

Today, Luc felt like having something physical to beat against, so he gave the man a physical form as he entered the room. Alan shut the door behind him, standing guard on the outside with Bal.

"Hello again, Donald. It's been a while. I can see you still feel no remorse for the things you've done, including taking part in the torture and attempted rape of my niece. From what I can see, I honestly don't think you have it in you to feel remorse. I think you're missing the moral compass needed to be a decent person. I personally don't give a shit if you ever leave here," Luc said, tracking the man's movements. They always tried to fight when they got a physical form, never thinking that he could just as easily take it away. He wouldn't today, he was looking forward to a good fight. He hated people who thought they could violate someone else's rights, and he really hated people who fucked with his family.

It didn't take long, the man lunging forward to throw a punch with his right arm. It was sloppy at best, broadcasted way in advance giving Luc plenty of time to dodge it, throwing up an arm to deflect. Lifting up on the ball of his foot, Luc spun, throwing his other leg out in a kick, shoving the other man back. He grinned as Donald crashed into the wall. Luc waited, letting the man make the next move.

Donald lowered his head, charging, trying to knock Luc off balance, his weight carrying them into the opposite wall. Luc let the momentum carry them back, giving Donald a brief moment of feeling like he was getting ahead. He felt his head knock into the concrete which pissed him off a bit. He didn't want to have too many marks that he would need to explain. Wrapping his hands around the other man's neck and shoulders, he pulled down with all his strength, raising his knee to connect with the man's face. Luc smiled as he heard the crunch of bone and knew he had broken the bastard's nose.

The other man dropped to the ground, but he tried to pull Luc's legs out from under him. Luc jumped into the air, landing a few feet away. He waited for the man to get back to his feet as he walked away. A burst of air warned Luc that the other man was moving. As he felt the arm reaching for him, he turned slightly, grabbing the man's arm and pulling it up and over his shoulder. Using the other man's momentum, he bent his torso, catapulting the man over his body. As Donald hit the floor with a satisfying thud, Luc released his wrist.

This wasn't as satisfying as he thought it would be. The man had clearly only preyed on those weaker than him and had no real fighting skills. He wasn't even really trying to fight the man. Maybe God would spar with him, he thought. Although the last time they had done that, they had destroyed a small building. Granted it was on his land, so it didn't matter as much, but he'd have to think of where they could go. They wouldn't want an audience. The last thing he needed was to have his enemy observe his fighting techniques. If it came to a challenge, he didn't want to give his opponent any easy wins.

He was lost in his thoughts and didn't recognize that the other man had been moving until he felt the fists connecting to his kidneys. Luc sighed. Grabbing the man's arm, he pinned it against his body before spinning around to face him. His other hand shot out, grabbing Donald by the throat, holding him immobile. Luc stared into his eyes, letting all of his rage, all of the darkness inside of him flow out. He could tell when the other man finally realized just who he was really up against as he started to struggle. Luc had been playing with him until now, but he was done with that. Grinning, he shoved the man back, giving him the illusion of freedom.

"I hope you're ready for the next part. I think you'll find it won't be as easy," Luc warned him. After letting the mask drop, his rage wouldn't be contained any longer and Luc stopped holding back.

He sped forward, his fists finding their mark over and over, faster than the other man could track or defend against. Donald tried to fight back, but his hits and kicks were easily blocked, so weak comparatively that Luc didn't pay attention to them if they landed on his body. When the man was finally lying in a fetal position, arms raised to protect his head, bruises and cuts scattered across his body, Luc paused. Panting slightly, he started to compose himself. He felt marginally calmer than when he entered and he desperately needed a shower at this point, the feel of small cuts and bruises and the sensation of blood splattered over his skin finally making themselves known. One of the things he absolutely hated was the feel of blood cooling and coagulating on his skin.

Luc straddled the other man, flipping him over onto his back. "It's been fun, Donald, but it's time to go." He called his demon's claws out, tilting the man's head back before raking them across his throat. Luc stepped back from the arterial spray, watching patiently as the man's physical body died once again.

He didn't say another word to the soul now floating over the body; he simply made the physical form disappear and walked out of the room. As the door closed behind him, the magic activated to make the blood disappear. That was one of the first things he had installed when he had taken over. There was no reason to leave a mess for someone to clean up and he had wanted to make the lives of his employees easier. Now all they had to do after a punishment was to leave the room. The simple act of them crossing the threshold activated the magic. Of course, you needed to be keyed to the spell for it to work; if a prisoner escaped and caused injury, the evidence wouldn't disappear since the Enforcer didn't activate it.

He gave Alan a nod and made his way back to the showers. He hoped he still had a change of clothes stored there. He wasn't sure if he had replaced them after the last time.

L uc was furious, all the calm he had found earlier vanished with one simple picture. He had taken his time in the shower, his muscles winding down, Bal waiting outside. He had dressed and headed back to his office to find a picture of Margo taped to the door. It had been of her outside her home. Whoever had left it had clearly known not to try to enter the office when it was locked. He wanted to find whoever the fucker was behind this. His people were off limits, something that should have been made clear when Mac punished the serial killer who had targeted Viv. Of course, they had mentioned the Enforcers' families, but not the staff. He'd make sure that wasn't under question ever again. Only cowards targeted those weaker than them.

He was currently scouring through the video footage to find the asshole who needed to die. A shadow showed on the screen and Luc leaned closer, squinting to get a better look. He enlarged the image, using the software to clean up the face a bit. Gotcha, he thought smugly. He had no doubt that this was just another lackey, but he'd use him to make a statement of his own. It was time for people to remember just who he was and why he was in his position.

Grabbing his phone, he called Margo. "Margo? I need

you to listen and not argue. Port to your daughter's house with Spot for a few days. I'm sending an Enforcer to watch over their house while I put protections on yours. Whoever is coming after me left a picture of your home taped to the office door. No more walking home, please. I need you safe. You can take the next few days off as well."

"I will do no such thing!" she replied indignantly. "I'll go visit my daughter, but I will be coming into work tomorrow. Some butthead isn't going to keep me from my job. Can Veek watch over the house? He's nice to look at," she asked, humor coating her tone.

"Sure," Luc replied with a smile. "I may be out tomorrow. I have hunting to do. When I get back, I need the stage to be ready and the broadcast set up."

"Making another statement, sir?"

"Yes," Luc said simply.

"Good. I'll be there for that. No one gets to threaten me. My grandbabies come to my house. They should know better than to go after an old woman."

Luc laughed. "Old woman my ass. You could probably outwork me. I know I don't say it enough, but I'm grateful for the day you came to work for me. I don't know what I'd do without you."

"Pshaw," Margo scoffed. "You'd be fine, but I don't plan on you ever having to do this alone. You're an amazing boss. I'm going to go give Sarah a call and let her know what's going on and pack a bag. Go give him hell."

Luc shook his head as she hung up on him. He called Veek to let him know his new assignment and sent another one of his hellhounds to watch over the grandkids. She could follow them to school and keep them safe. She was a great protector. He sent Margo a text letting her know of the added protection.

Now for the hard part. Calling Bert.

He waited for the phone to ring, but after a minute it went to voicemail. He hadn't expected Bert to be able to answer, but he was making sure he was following his Dom's rules.

"Hey, Mate. I'm going hunting. Someone decided to target Margo. I should have them tonight or tomorrow morning. I'm planning on having an event on the stage when I get them. Margo is moving someplace safe for a few days with extra guards. I'll bring Bal with me and have Alan on standby. I'll let you know once I get him. Love you." Luc hung up before paging Alan.

There was a puff of air as Alan landed in the office. "Sir?"

"I'm going hunting. I wanted to give you a heads-up. Someone decided to set their eyes on Margo as a way to get to me and that is unacceptable," Luc said, tossing the picture on the desk so Alan could see it. He watched as the Enforcer's eyes filled with flames, his jaw clenching.

"Only a coward would," Alan started to say, but shook his head instead. They all knew the man behind this didn't have the courage to face Luc yet.

"I know. She's safe for now. I found the man on the security cameras and I'm going to go pay him a little visit. I'd like for the stage to be ready for when I get back."

"I'll ask Garon to set it up. I would like to go with you, sir. I know you can handle this yourself, but Margo is like a mom to all of us who work in the office or close to you. This isn't right," Alan replied.

Luc paused for a minute before nodding his consent. There was no reason to get in a pissing contest with his Enforcers over this and he didn't want them to feel left out. "Let me gear up and we can go. Here's our target," Luc said, turning the screen around. He had already sent a copy to Margo and Veek so they would know who to look out for.

Opening the closet door, Luc pulled out his favorite gear. His expanding knife, a couple of guns, a pair of spelled cuffs, and a vial of healing potion just in case. He tossed one to Alan as well. They were in unbreakable bottles so they would be safe in a fight. Luc pulled his hair back into a braid, twisting it into a bun. No reason to give someone something to grab on to. Sliding his dress shirt off, he changed into a leather shirt. It had a chainmail-like weave to the inside, giving him additional protection without being obvious. He wanted to minimize the chances of being injured as best he could. There was no reason to annoy his Mate.

Turning around, he saw Alan had also grabbed his own weapons, a Kevlar vest now covering his chest. Luc bent down, attaching what looked like a harness to Bal. If something came at the hellhound, the harness would expand to create armor, keeping his vital organs safe.

"Ready?" Luc asked. Alan nodded and they were off.

As Luc landed outside a run-down house, he motioned Alan to circle around to the back. Bal stayed with Luc. Luc opened his senses and could tell the man was cowering in the basement. Well, this was going to be easier than he had expected. His soul was not a pleasant one, but not the worst he had ever seen. He was a bit of a coward at heart, only picking on those that he knew he could win against. Honestly, unless the man had weapons or something, Margo could probably take him in a fight. It didn't matter though. He had chosen this path, and Luc would make sure that others would think twice before coming after those he cared about.

Luc ported into the basement, watching as the man

pissed himself. He immobilized the man with a wave of his hand. He didn't want to risk him activating a kill-switch spell like the others. "Unfortunately for you, I care about those I work with. Margo is the sweetest woman, and she has lots of people who care about her. You really should never have come after my employee. While your soul is gray, not completely black yet, you will unfortunately be used to make a statement. Sorry not sorry." Luc ported them both outside, a bit disappointed that there wasn't more of a fight.

"Alan, I have him," he said in a normal tone, knowing he would be heard. As Alan joined him, his skin crawled with the sensation of being watched. He carefully turned his head in all directions, letting his demon side come to the surface. He couldn't pinpoint where it was coming from, and he didn't see anyone close by. He motioned to Alan to be cautious, but when nothing happened, he nodded once and ported out. Landing on his stage, he saw it had been readied in the short time they had been gone. The stage was only used for broadcasts to his people, or in cases like this, for public executions and punishments. Today would be both.

He saw Margo standing with Garon, her son-in-law also standing close by. Mac and D ported in minutes later.

"Uncle," Mac said in greeting. "I know you don't need any help, but I wanted to be here to show support."

"Ditto," a familiar voice said. Luc grinned as he turned and saw God standing there.

"Are you going to be able to handle it?" he teased quietly.

He got a full-on annoyed Dom stare in return. Luc shrugged, not repentant at all.

"I'll handle the broadcast," God said, patting his shoulder before moving away.

Luc stripped off his leather shirt, grabbing a t-shirt Mac handed him. He typed a quick message to Bert before handing his phone to Mac as well.

"Sir. I know you told me to stay safe at Sarah's, but I'm going to watch. Veek brought me here, but he's with the grandkids just in case. I'll stay close to Garon and Mark," Margo promised.

Luc nodded, touching her shoulder and sending a protective spell over her. "It's going to get messy," he warned.

Margo nodded before stepping back to the outskirts with her guards.

God moved up beside him holding the remote for the broadcast system. "Ready?" he checked before clicking the button to go live.

"Hello, my fellow nonhumans. While I hope you're all having a good day, this unfortunately isn't a pleasant broadcast. Please send all children out of the area. This is not appropriate for them," Luc said. There was a spell to keep children from seeing and hearing the more graphic broadcasts, but it never hurt to be extra cautious. He waited a minute before continuing. "Someone thought it would be a good idea to threaten my employees as a way to get to me. Only a coward would attack those weaker than them. Only a coward would go after family, friends, or employees instead of their real target.

"I thought this was made clear when someone went after an Enforcer's mate. Sadly, somebody didn't get that memo and decided to threaten my administrative assistant, Margo. For those of you who know Margo, you know what an absolute treasure and wonderful person she is. This type of behavior will not be tolerated. I found the man who was sent after her, and while he is not the brains behind the plan, he still willingly took part. Anyone who goes after an Enforcer's family or friends, after God's or my family, friends, or employees, instead of who they are really targeting, will be dealt with harshly."

"Our sides have had peace for years. Our numbers are growing. We will not tolerate a threat to that peace," God added. He clasped Luc's shoulder, moving back behind the camera.

Luc snapped his fingers, popping the prisoner onto the stage. He allowed him movement and speech again but had added his own blocker spell. If he had a kill switch inside him, Luc's magic was now blocking it. He wanted everyone who was part of this threat to hear the man's screams. Luc took a deep breath and locked down his senses and emotions, burying them down deep so he could do what was needed.

Bert ported into the back of the room. He received Luc's voicemail and text and had rushed through the last of his case and handed it off to another Enforcer for processing and ported to the stage room. He stayed toward the back so he wouldn't distract Luc. He couldn't believe someone had been stupid enough to threaten Margo. Although it wasn't an obvious threat, it had been clear that they had been saying they knew where she lived and could get close to her. Plus, Luc would have read the man before going through with this.

It had already started by the time he got there, a puddle of blood beneath the man's feet indicating this had been going on for a while. Luc was dressed in dark pants and a black t-shirt, his demon and mate markings showing. His muscles bunched as he let his whip fly, striking the man and pulling a strip of skin with it. Bert looked closer and saw it wasn't like any whip he had seen before. The bulk of the whip was made with a length of chain, the handle a black metal. The end piece, the cracker, was a thinner wire. The entire piece looked rugged and sexy as hell. It was also loud and extremely painful based on the cries.

As Luc took a breath and repositioned, the man tried to crawl away. Bert watched in awe as Luc flung out his whip, capturing the man around the ankle and dragging him back. Luc stepped on the man's leg, keeping in place as he handed off his whip. Bending down, Luc hoisted the man in the air, using his strength and maybe a bit of magic to hold the man in the air with one hand around his throat. Bert winced as the other plunged into the man's stomach. Screams filled the air as Luc slowly dragged his hand up the man's chest, his razor-sharp claws splitting the flesh, leaving a large wound with flaps of skin hanging to either side like a demented envelope.

He looked closely at his mate, seeing the rage there but also the distance that Luc used to protect himself from these types of scenes. He knew right then it was about to get much uglier. Thank gods they couldn't get blood-borne diseases, he thought absently. Luc was already splattered with the other man's and if it went the way Bert suspected, he was about to get coated in it.

Luc easily held the squirming man with his left hand. His free hand grabbed one flap of the man's skin, ripping it completely off. A hoarse scream sounded, gaining volume as Luc did the same to the other side. The muscles covering the man's rib cage were now completely exposed. Bert watched as Luc thrust his fingers in between the ribs, closing his hand to grip tight. He moved his other hand to do the same to the opposite side of the rib cage before pulling. Bert winced as a grinding, cracking sound filled the air; he noticed many others covering their ears. The screams were one thing, but that sound was horrifying. The man's screams cut off, small whimpers escaping him, his chest now deformed looking.

"No one fucks with my family," Bert read from Luc's lips. It was said too quietly for him to hear, but he knew exactly what his lover was saying. Luc wiggled his fingers free, once again grabbing the man by the throat. Bert was grateful that it was the one wearing Bert's ring, as the other plunged back into the man's body. He watched as Luc disemboweled him slowly, pulling the intestines up into the air ensuring the prisoner saw what was happening to him. The air was filled with squelches and the sound of blood dripping. At one point the man passed out, but Luc snapped his fingers making him conscious again.

Once all of the intestines were pooled on the floor, Luc studied the chest in front of him, using his claws as a surgical knife to carefully peel back layers of muscle and fat. Luc nudged the mangled rib cage out of the way, forming a window into the man's chest. A few more careful dissections and the lungs and heart were on full display. Bert didn't think he had ever really seen an open chest like this before and it was as fascinating as it was disturbing. The heart sat toward the middle, but the lungs slightly overlapped it. He could see the lungs filling with air, the heart beating.

His mate traced a nail down one lung, causing the man

to buck in his grip. Luc smiled at him as he grasped the lung, yanking it out of his chest, flinging blood across the room. The room was filled with a gurgling sound as the prisoner desperately gasped for breath. Luc's claws gently circled the heart. He stared straight into the eyes of the prisoner as he closed his fist, slowly crushing the heart, a squelching sound the only thing to be heard. Blood bubbled out from the man's lips, his eyes dulling as the life left him. Luc dropped the body to the ground, letting everyone take in the mangled mess. Stepping around it, he stood at the front of the room. God moved to stand beside him.

"Our people are off limits. You have a problem with us, you come to us. You leave families, friends, and employees alone. Or the next one will be worse," Luc threatened. His voice was calm, which made the whole thing even more terrifying. God nodded before cutting the broadcast feed.

Bert made his way to the front of the room. "You made such a mess," he heard God complain. Luc laughed, calling his hellfire to destroy the body and the blood on the ground. He captured the soul, handing it to another Enforcer. "Level five. Thank you."

"Mate! I thought you were still working," Luc said when he saw him. He could tell Luc needed reassurances, but this wasn't the place. Too many ears.

"I wanted to see you in action," he replied simply. He grabbed Luc's ring hand, wiping a spot free of blood before raising it to his lips to kiss by the ring.

"Margo, go home. I'm keeping Veek assigned to you for a bit to make sure there's no backlash. Alan, thank you for your assistance. Everyone, please head home. Thank you for your help tonight," Luc added, looking around the room. He headed over to D and Mac, Bert following him. "I'm going to spend some time with my mate. Thank you for coming.

I'll see you later," he said. Mac handed Bert Luc's shirt and phone, giving them both a nod before porting home.

Luc waited to make sure everyone headed home, gave the stage a last look to make sure he didn't miss anything. When it looked good enough, he grabbed Bert's hand and ported them to the showers. He stripped in the middle of the room, dropping his clothes down the chute. Climbing into the shower, he started the process of getting clean. As he scrubbed his nails and horns, he felt a draft of air as Bert climbed in with him.

"I sent your phone and shirt home so we wouldn't forget them," Bert said as he grabbed the loofa and helped rinse Luc off, making sure all of the bits of gore were washed down the drain. The showers on the punishment levels were made to handle the larger sometimes chunkier runoffs. He grimaced as he plucked off a piece of skin that was hanging off a horn. It took a few washings to get the pieces off, but once Luc was clean enough, Bert ported them home and finished washing him there. Luc's shower could handle any blood that was left and Bert wanted to get Luc into the privacy of their own home as quickly as possible.

"Thank you for taking extra precautions, Love," Bert said as he massaged shampoo into Luc's hair.

"Hmm, that feels good," Luc said, his eyes closing. "I was so angry when I saw the picture of Margo. We knew he was cowardly with sending other people, but this was crossing a line."

"I'm glad you found him; I think that was a pretty strong message to send. I loved seeing you work," Bert said. Luc's eyes were still closed, head tilted back to rinse the suds away. Dropping to his knees, he grinned around Luc's cock at the surprised shout that filled the shower. He took

Luc in deep, tongue laving long strokes across the shaft, wanting to reward his lover for listening to the rules. "Hmm, just like that," Luc panted. As he released down Bert's throat, Bert grabbed his hips, porting them to the den. Bending Luc over the table, Bert spit on his hand, coating his dick before slamming it home. As Luc's body clenched around his, he only hoped that they could find the asshole behind all of this soon. Before he caused any more damage.

L uc watched as Margo ported home with Spot. He had placed protective wards all over her property and added additional ones to the office. She had insisted on coming back to work the next day, even bringing him homemade cookies as a thank-you for helping keep her safe.

He wanted to argue that she wouldn't have been in danger if it weren't for him, but he knew it was a losing battle and kept his mouth shut and simply thanked her for the sugary goodness. It had been quiet, almost too quiet for his liking. Even hearings were subdued at the moment. He hoped it was because of the message he sent and not because something new was brewing. Unfortunately, he thought it was probably the latter.

After the previous attacks and the implied threat to Margo, Luc was watching, looking for anything that stood out or was different. It was exhausting. Bert was worried but was trying not to show it. They both knew that Luc's public display would probably ramp up the instigator. He had been publicly called out as a coward and would more than likely respond in some way. They just weren't sure what direction the crazy would take. Mac and D were keeping a close eye on Viv and Thomas, although Luc couldn't see the masked man going after someone on Earth. God had heard nothing back from his investigators either.

Luc had asked Veek to stay as Margo's guard, until the leader was caught. The fact that it was a man was about the only thing that they did know for sure. It had been frustrating. Every precaution set in place to help them were being thwarted. Like the cameras, the man seemed to know where each and every one was. Even the hidden ones. Any lackey or minion they came across had limited knowledge as well; most were contacted over a burner phone or never saw the man's face; it was always in the shadows or covered in a mask.

Bert was working on a case, even though he had wanted to stay home. Luc knew Bert would go stir-crazy with nothing to do and had encouraged him to go to work. He could always call him if he needed him, he reasoned. Bert reluctantly agreed, although he was making it a point to come home every night and have someone else take the nightshift as needed.

"Sir, we received a page for you to come down to the scheduling department. I'm not sure what this is about. Should I call them and see if it can be something that can be taken care of up here?" Alan asked.

"No, that's alright. It's probably because Margo is gone for the day. I could use a walk. We'll take care of this and then head home. I know you want to get home to your family," Luc said, standing up and stretching. He thought he might take Bal for a run tonight. He had sent Bal home earlier, knowing he was getting bored. He had kept several of his Enforcers close by as compensation.

Alan nodded, following him out of the office. Luc touched his ring as he walked, eager to see Bert if he made it home tonight. He wondered if they could sneak in a visit to the club. He thought they both needed the release and although the den had some new features, it still didn't have the space to have all the fun toys. Luc was curious about the Saint Andrew's cross but knew it would have to wait until they could go when the club was closed. There were a few smaller ones in the private rooms, but he wanted to experience the large one in the main room.

"Sir, I don't like this," Alan said suddenly, looking around. "I'm calling in a few more guards."

As three other Enforcers popped in, Luc felt the hair on the back of his neck stand up. "Someone's here," he said quietly. "We need to get out of here, this hallway is horrible defense-wise, we're sitting ducks." He pulled his knife out from the small of his back, holding it down by his side. He tried porting out but something was blocking him. He could have forced his way through, but knew his men would be left behind. They would have no way to get out and he wasn't about to leave them.

"Sir, someone threw a containment spell," Alan said, his face frustrated as he tried to port.

"I know. We're going to have to make a stand," Luc said grimly. He pulled out his phone, typing a quick message to Bert. Maybe he would be able to reach them in time and bring help. He also sent a call out to Bal. The hellhounds should be able to help balance the fight and track down where the person or people were.

Luc grabbed his gun, switching hands so that it was in his dominant hand. He shot better with his right, and he could still defend well enough with his knife if they got close. His Enforcers closed ranks, keeping him in the middle, their own weapons drawn.

His eyes roamed all over the hallway as he slowly turned in a circle. He heard high-pitched whistling sounds screaming through the air and his men grunted as something struck them all at once.

"Sir, go…" Alan tried to say, but his voice was slurred as he dropped to the floor, followed by the rest of his Enforcers. Luc hoped it wasn't a poison. He didn't want his men to die.

He readied himself for an attack, refusing to leave his vulnerable men behind. The man behind this clearly didn't have a problem attacking those who were defenseless. A masked man ported into the hallway, not saying a word. Luc gripped his weapons, muscles prepared to launch himself at the man, but several sharp whistles sounded, and something struck the back of Luc's neck, his arm, and chest. Son of a bitch. He quickly yanked them out, but he was already weakening. Luc forced himself to stay upright, shooting down the hallway but when his bullets seemed to miss, he threw his knife.

He blinked, finding the man standing right next to him as he plunged another needle into Luc's body. As he fell, he only hoped that Bert got his message so medical could help his Enforcers. He tried to send feelings of love to Bert, wanting the last thing he did to be something of love for his Mate.

Bert stared in disbelief at the four Enforcers lying on the ground. His mate was nowhere to be found, but there were darts lying on the floor smelling of his mate and chemicals, as well as bullet shells and Luc's knife protruding from the wall, his phone kicked off to the side, smashed.

"Mac, get here now. Bring D and anyone else you trust with your life. Luc's gone."

He hung up before Mac could ask any questions. Bert opened his senses, trying to feel his mate, only to be met with a blank wall. Either Luc was blocking him, or he was spelled. It only took seconds until he felt the air pressure change with the number of bodies porting in. D, Mac, their friends Gina and Liam who worked as cops in the human world, God, and Margo.

Medical soon followed, grabbing the darts and the Enforcers. "I want to know anything you find out," Bert demanded. "What was in those darts, anything they remember when they wake up. None of this is to be spoken of." He got nods of confirmation before they all ported out. He noticed God flinging magic at the medical team before they left, probably a silencing spell.

Margo stepped forward with Spot. "I'm going to the office to see what I can find on the cameras." She had tears in her eyes, but she was keeping them from falling.

"Wait a minute," Bert demanded. "She needs a guard," he said looking at God.

"Call in Charles," God suggested.

Bert nodded, pulling out his phone and quickly dialing. "Charles. I need you to port to the scheduling department hallway of Netherworld. Tell Sky where you're going, but no one else."

A minute later, the other man was there, completely geared up. Bert raised an eyebrow, although he was also relieved. "If you're calling me that urgently, I knew it had to be bad and I wanted to be ready," Charles explained.

"Luc's been taken. His Enforcers were all drugged. It looks like he fired his weapon, but there's no blood anywhere. Luc doesn't miss, so I'm guessing he was also drugged. Medical is taking care of the men and testing what the drug is. This group here are the only ones I fully trust right now. I need you to protect Margo as she goes through the footage. Can you and Sky see if you hear anything through the club or your connections?"

"Of course. Are you going to be here or are you going hunting?"

"Hunting. Everyone split up, check with any sources or informants you have, see if there's been any talk lately. Check the usual places and the usual suspects. Anyone who was on our list of suspects should be interviewed thoroughly. Make sure you have healing potions available, if you don't stop by Luc's office and Margo can give you some. Keep phones on and keep us all informed with your progress. Keep it as vague as possible. We don't know if someone is listening in."

Everyone nodded, pulling out their weapons.

"May the Fates be with you," Charles said before running down the hallway with Margo.

"We'll find him," Mac vowed before porting out.

Where are you, Love? Bert thought, trying to find a trail, but sensing nothing. God clasped his shoulder before porting out. They had to find him.

31

Bert wanted to kill someone. They finally had a lead to an underground sex club. He was terrified to think of why they were holding his mate there. Mac was growling behind him, D, Liam, and Gina providing backup. They were the ones he trusted with his life, and more importantly Luc's.

If needed, he could call Charles. Right now, Charles and Sky were probably getting ready to leave Luc's house. They'd agreed to create a diversion and an alibi for Luc and Bert. A few hours ago, they'd had a public conversation with the receptionist at the club saying that they were having dinner at Luc's home, if she needed to get ahold of them later. Bert had given them a key so they could get in. It would put doubts into anyone's head about Luc's where-abouts. God was also sitting out, as he would draw too much attention. He was pissed about it too. He was collecting all the healing potions and creams that he could find and was waiting for word.

Gina threw a containment spell over the club. No one would get away from them tonight, not before they questioned and possibly eliminated them.

"Thank you all for coming with me," Bert said, taking a deep breath.

"We're family," D said, clasping him on the shoulder.

Bert nodded, glad he wasn't doing this alone. "Everyone ready?"

The sounds of weapons being drawn filled the air as everyone nodded. They didn't have much of a plan other than to find Luc and kill whoever needed killing. Gina enacted a concealment spell on her and Liam since they were here off duty, D and Mac blended with the shadows, and Bert concealed himself as well. They slid through the front door, spreading out about ten feet apart, close enough to see a signal, but far enough away that they covered ground quickly.

Bert looked around as they moved through the room. His nose wrinkled at the overwhelming smell of pheromones and bodily fluids. The lighting was dim, more due to burned out and missing light bulbs than for atmosphere. The floor was littered with used toys, empty lube bottles, and other paraphernalia. He was grateful he had worn his sturdy thick-soled boots, especially since they wanted to stick to the floor with every step. People were passing around drugs and anyone who was eager for sex had their pick of partners. He took note of a group jerking off to a snuff film; he needed to investigate that later. Everyone here registered as a dark soul to his senses.

As they reached the middle of the room, he finally caught Luc's scent. He couldn't pinpoint where it was coming from. He turned to signal to Mac, but Mac had clearly caught it too; his eyes were pure flames as he shifted to his demon form in rage.

"I smell blood," he said, his voice hard and cold when he met up with Bert.

"Can you follow it?"

Mac nodded, and Bert followed, eyes constantly searching, Liam and Gina still flanking them.

"Bert—" Mac broke off. They saw a wall with a hole cut out, a line of men at it, a sloppily hung sign pronouncing it the glory hole.

Bert took a deep breath, his wings shooting out as he realized exactly where they were holding his mate. "Kill them all. Keep the club owner alive for questioning," he ordered, his voice flat. As he saw a man walk up to the hole, pulling his pants open, Bert ran forward, his wings pushing him through the crowd, sword swinging down and cutting off the appendage before it could get close. Bert shoved the severed dick down the man's throat, cutting off his screams.

"Get Uncle. I'll handle these," Mac said, a demented smile taking over his face as he stepped out of the shadows and rushed the crowd. Gina quickly uttered a silencing spell, covering their actions from anyone not paying attention. As the blood started flowing, Bert searched for a door to get to his mate.

Grabbing a server, he held his gun to his head. "Get me inside this room. Now."

"But, we're not—" the man stammered.

"Unless you want your brains on this wall, I don't give a shit what you're supposed to do. You took my mate."

The man's eyes went wide with fear and he fumbled with a keycard, leading Bert to another hallway. Bert followed behind him, keeping a hand on his shoulder to keep him from running away. The server pressed his card to the door, unlocking it. As he opened his mouth to yell a warning, Bert drew his knife across the man's throat to shut him up.

Entering the room, his heart stopped. Literally it

stopped for a few beats. The smell of cum and blood was overwhelming in the closed space. It was dark, dimly lit but he could see his mate, his lover, his best friend and partner, the leader of Netherworld tied over a pummel, his ass against the wall directly where the hole was. There was a man standing with his back to Bert, his dick out, slowly stroking it while hovering over Luc's body.

"It's not your turn yet. I still have ten minutes," the man grunted, stroking his dick faster but never turning around. Bert quietly moved forward, shoving his sword through the man's spine. As he dropped to his knees, Bert grabbed hold of his head, twisting to break his neck.

"Oh Fates," he whispered, stepping over the body. "Luc. What did they do to you?"

He was afraid to touch his mate anywhere. His entire back had been flayed, the blood still dripping down to the floor. From shoulders to waist, Luc's back was a gigantic open wound, every bit of skin had been removed. Scattered spots were missing along his sides where whatever tool they were using must have slipped a little farther. Every finger looked twisted and broken, both eyes swollen shut. His arms and legs had black and blue bruising scattered around. His legs had clearly been broken; one had a bone sticking out from the skin.

"Did you find him?" Mac asked, running into the room. He came to a sudden stop at the sight of his uncle.

"Mac. I don't. I don't know what to do. How do I move him without hurting him?" Bert asked, his voice broken.

Mac leaned out the door. "Gina. Find us some blankets. And if you found the club owner, hold him please. I'd like to have a word with him."

Bert could hear the breath shuddering in Mac as he

came closer. Every part of Luc looked damaged. A few healing potions were held out in front of him.

"Don't have him drink these yet, the broken bones would heal wrong, and we need to make sure he doesn't have a rib in a lung or anything," Mac said.

A throat cleared at the door. Gina stood with her back to them, looking into the hallway, holding out some blankets. "These are clean. I can scan him and try to get an idea of how to proceed. I'll keep my eyes shut. I can't tell what I don't know. For all I know, you have some random stranger in there." Bert appreciated what she was saying; if she was questioned, she would be able to answer honestly that she hadn't seen who was in the room. Even a lie potion wouldn't make a difference since she would be telling the truth.

"I'll come guide you in," Mac said, taking the blankets in one hand, laying them over a chair.

Bert guided Gina's hand to a small patch of unmarked skin.

Her breath hissed out. "Shit. He's tranqed with enough to kill an elephant. He's lucky to be alive," Gina spat out. "They started with the normal breaking bones method, I think. Those are older injuries. They tried cutting off his mate mark," she said, tears in her voice. "I think he fought hard for that. I'm getting bits and pieces of memories. They moved to flaying him. When they didn't want to work so hard because he kept fighting back, they drugged him and just kept dosing him, never letting it wear all the way off. It was way too much in a short time, I'm surprised his lungs are still working. Then they. Bert. They." Gina shook her head, swallowing hard, tears in her eyes. "When he finally couldn't fight back anymore, they tied him here and employees...got a turn before they moved him to the wall.

He's got some internal damage from the beating and from the—" Gina stopped as Mac stood.

"I'll be back in a minute," Mac said, his voice completely void of any emotion. Luc wore that same mask when he was going to get bloody. Bert would guess he was going to interrogate the club owner. He kicked the body across the room on his way out the door.

Gina kept her eyes away from Luc but took the healing potions from Bert before he accidentally smashed them in his fist.

"Mac's right, he shouldn't have these until we get the bones straightened. I know you want to move him, but honestly, this is probably the best position for his back. I'm going to help straighten his fingers. See if you can find pens or pencils or something straight enough to keep them in place until we can use the potions."

Bert kissed Luc, whispering to him. "I've got you now, Love."

He found a ruler, a cane, some bamboo skewers that had suspicious stains and smelled like his mate already. He forced himself to ignore it, working quickly to find as many supplies as he could. He stripped the shoelaces off the dead men, as well as their belts.

Gina moved her way past Luc's shoulders, keeping her head averted so she couldn't see his face. Standing next to him, she poured one and a half of the healing potions carefully over Luc's back. It didn't do much, but it did seem to help slow the bleeding. She blocked her eyes as she let some drizzle down the seam of his butt.

"You'll have to get a cream on that later, but that might help a little now." Gina put a hand on either side of her eyes as blinders, moving her way to sit in front of Luc, keeping her head down as she sat in front of him. "These should work," she said, looking at the supplies. She painstakingly straightened each finger, making sure each bone and joint were in the right place before splinting them, all while making sure she never saw Luc's face.

It took a half hour or so before she moved to his wrists, then to his arms, then to his legs. There were a few ribs cracked but not all the way broken.

Mac came back in, covered from head to toe in blood, a few pieces of...something stuck to him. His demon was still raging, the anger flooding the room. He had a small bag in his hand, as well as some sealed cartons.

"Found some gauze that might help protect his back from sticking to the blankets when we move him. Also found this," Mac said, handing over the bag. Bert opened it, staring blankly at the ring he had given Luc. "They were going to hang it on the Netherworld office front door as proof of death. Everyone knew it was Uncle's; he was never seen without it since you gave it to him."

Bert tucked it into his pocket, vowing to put it back on his mate once his fingers were healed.

"Okay. That should be enough for the next part. I have an uncle who is a healer. I can bring him if the potions don't seem to work. He's blind, so he won't be able to say who he worked on. He also won't ask questions if I tell him not to," Gina offered. "I'm going to keep scanning him to make sure nothing shifts internally, but I'm going to turn away. Try to get him upright enough to let him swallow the other potion. It should be enough to keep his bones in place until you get home. Bert, I recommend you carry him like a toddler or a baby, his front to your front. Keep pressure off his back. The bleeding is slowing, but there's essentially no skin there right now. Some of the cuts dug deep into the muscle as well. Once you have him up, I'll help place the gauze and blanket."

Mac stripped down to his boots and boxer briefs. He wore the same type of underwear his uncle did, Bert thought a little hysterically. He wiped his hands on the inside of his shirt.

"I didn't want to get any on Uncle." He shrugged when he saw Bert looking at him.

D came in, also covered in gore. "The rest is cleared. Liam's grabbing the computers, cameras, and hard drives. I'll bring those home to see if we can't find the masked man behind this. What do you need?"

"We need to get Uncle wrapped up," Mac said. "Can you help hold him up on his left side, I'll get his right. Gina, stand behind him so you can't see his face, you wrap the back, Bert you stand in front, pass the gauze between you to wrap him up. When that's done, Bert you stay in front, but squat down and lift him. D and I will help stabilize."

D stripped down as well. Luc was already covered in blood and— Stuff. Blood and stuff. But Bert could appreciate the respect that they were trying to show by not getting more on his mate. He moved into position, resting Luc's lax head on his shoulder. He pressed his shoulders against Luc's, slowly pushing him upright, Mac and D helping support and guide him to a sitting position. Once he was mostly up, Mac and D did all the work of holding him as he and Gina quickly worked to cover his torso and back in the medical gauze. Gina grabbed a blanket, placing it gingerly over Luc's head and back. They were trying to keep him warm but also limit how much anyone could see when they left the room. Even though they were sure they had cleared the building they didn't want to take any chances.

Bert squatted in front of his mate, knowing he had to grab him so they could leave, but also knowing no matter where he touched it would cause pain. Gina grabbed his hands, guiding him to the best spots. Even so, despite all the drugs in his system, Bert could feel a flash of pain over their bond. He had to blink back tears; it was the first glimpse of his mate he had felt since Luc had been taken. Bert had known Luc wasn't dead, but the usual background sensation of his mate had been gone.

"I got some information out of the club owner that I'm going to follow up on when we're done. I'll send it to you all," Mac said, helping arrange Luc a little more securely in Bert's arms. "Get him home. I'm going to make sure all evidence of Uncle is gone before burning this to the ground. We killed everyone here, but who knows if there was someone else in on this. We say nothing. As much as it sucks, as much as you won't want to allow it, he needs to appear at work tomorrow. Act like nothing happened. Let anyone who was involved wonder if he was really taken, if he escaped on his own, if he killed everyone by himself. If they fear him, they may leave him alone. From now on, only ones I trust will guard him. If you know of anyone you trust enough, let me know and I'll add them to the list. I don't give a shit if they're demon, angel, or other. This will never happen again," he vowed.

"He's going to need to eventually process and talk to someone," Gina protested softly. "In no way is any of this okay. I understand the need to keep up the appearance, I really do. To appear weak would be to encourage more bullshit, but he's going to need some kind of therapy."

"I'll send you the details for Viv and Thomas' therapist. She's great and you can do it online, even anonymously," D said.

Mac nodded in agreement, although his jaw was so tightly clenched that Bert didn't think he could speak if he wanted to. Bert knew the feeling. It was all he could do to keep the screams and tears at bay right now.

"You guys don't need to stay. Liam is sweeping it again. I'm sure we can find something to make it burn and I'll do another magical scan to make sure nothing of us or Luc remains afterward. Liam and I will stay here, say we got an anonymous phone call about a drug lab. Looks like it went up in flames. We'll hide the stuff in our car, we have a special compartment no one can sense, and then we'll drop off the cameras and stuff to your house, let Viv and Thomas know everyone is okay enough." Gina said. "May I?" she asked, slowly moving forward.

Bert nodded, swallowing the growl that he hadn't been aware he was making.

Gina laid her hand on Luc's forehead, chanting a few words, before tucking the blanket more firmly around him.

"I don't have a lot of healing power, but it should help until you can get more healing potions."

"Thanks," Bert said gruffly.

"I've got a better plan. Mac, you need to help Bert get Luc situated. Bert ports home first, we get out of the club, and you let your hellfire go. Nothing will be able to extinguish it, and it will consume everything, so get it started and then go directly to the den to help Bert. Gina and Liam can stay to make sure it destroys everything and then take the stuff to our house. I'll port to God and let him know what's going on. I'll meet you at the house with God and the healing potions," D told him.

Mac's eyes were still flaming, but he was incredibly gentle as he leaned over and gave Luc a kiss on the forehead. Bert's heart clenched at the gesture. It was something a parent would do to a sick child; Bert would guess Luc did it for Mac when he was younger. "Love you, Uncle. You keep fighting and we'll make sure all these bastards die. You can torment them later to show them you don't fuck with our family." Bert blinked back the tears at Mac's whispered words.

Bert gave them all a nod, porting his mate home. He could feel the fear leave him as he entered the den. This room was safe. He didn't want to jar Luc and cause injury trying to move him on his own, so he held him, talking softly, just gibberish words until Mac and D could show up to help.

Luc vaguely heard voices talking, but he couldn't bring himself to wake up. He sensed his mate nearby though and knew he was safe. He just wanted to curl up against Bert and sleep. The smell of his mate made everything hurt less. He didn't hear the rest as a buzzing sound drowned everything else out.

"How the fuck could this have happened?" Bert asked angrily. How the fuck was his mate taken, how had they done so much damage in such a short amount of time?

God, D, Mac, and he were on one side of the den, Luc still passed out on the other side. When D had ported to the house, he had arrived on the other side of the den's door with healing potions, a medical bed, and God. Bert was grateful for their friends and family. God had been prepared to rain down vengeance when he saw his old friend. He had reined it in, helping apply healing cream to Luc's back and had kept the healing potions coming.

For now, Luc was slowly mending. The hospital bed was amazing since they could lay Luc down on his stomach so they could work on his back. There was no way he would be completely healed by tomorrow, but Bert would have to support him in any way he could. Mac's argument made sense, as sad and twisted as it was that that was their reality right now.

Viv and Thomas had reached out, offering to come, but Bert didn't want to add to their own past trauma and asked them to stay home and keep the confiscated items safe. He knew no one could enter their home, so he didn't need to worry about their safety. They had Faolán as well. Speaking of... Where were Luc's hellhounds? Luc had been missing for hours, he would think Bal especially would be going nuts. He hadn't even thought to stop and grab them when he went hunting, he figured they would go on their own.

"I stopped by Greg's house. Luc's mentioned him being one of the main Enforcers in the hearing room. He was unconscious, his throat cut, but I managed to get him to the hospital in time. From what I could read of him, he may have found something important and was trying to investigate and it got him almost killed. Until he heals enough to wake up, we'll have to wait to see what that was. His house was clearly searched through," God was saying.

"Where are the dogs?" Bert interrupted. Those dogs would die for Luc, Bal especially. Mac looked up sharply, running out of the room. D chased after him. A wild howl sounded outside, the sound heartbreaking and so sad that goose bumps broke out over Bert's skin.

"Oh shit," God whispered.

D slammed into the doorway. "Potions. We need potions. They've all been poisoned, even the pups."

God ported out, back seconds later with two more large bags. He gave one to D, before looking at Bert. He could tell he was torn between following D and staying.

"Go. We're safe in here. Go save his dogs," Bert urged. Fates knew Luc would be devastated if his pups were killed. Those dogs were part of his family. "Please let the potions work," he pleaded to the universe. Both for his mate and the hellhounds.

It seemed to take forever, but eventually Mac came back into the room, carrying Bal's limp body.

Fuck. Damn it all. "Is he..." Bert couldn't finish.

Mac shook his head. "Not yet. He kept trying to crawl to the house," he said, his voice breaking. "He wouldn't take a potion, too focused on getting here, so I thought if he saw Uncle he would let me save him." Mac carried the huge dog over to the couch, laying him down where he could see Luc. "See? He's here, he's healing too. Please, Bal. You need to heal so you can protect him. He'd be broken if you died," Mac pleaded, holding a vial to the dog's mouth. Bal only looked at Luc, but slowly opened his mouth. They all held their breath, as Mac gave him several more. His breathing eventually evened out and was less labored. He stumbled off the couch, slowly making his unsteady way to lie next to Luc's bed.

Bert fought back the tears and noticed Mac wiping his eyes.

"He's okay," Mac muttered, relief in his voice. "I'm going to go back to help the others."

Bert watched his two patients carefully, jumping up every time he saw Luc twitch. While the others were out of the room, he grabbed a healing potion and a cream and made his way over to the bed.

"I need to do this, Bal. He was hurt—" Bert broke off. He had a small syringe, but without the needle. He was hoping he could somehow squirt the healing potion up Luc's channel. It didn't feel right to try to apply it by inserting a cream with his fingers or anything else bigger. He had already been violated enough and wasn't awake to consent.

Bert gingerly spread his lover's cheeks, clenching his teeth at the state of his mate. They had not been gentle. He was filled with a useless rage, wanting to kill them all over again. Filling the syringe, he gently inserted the small tip, squirting the liquid into his mate's body. He did this a few more times until it started to leak back out. Grabbing the healing cream, he applied it around the outside, hoping it would be enough to help. Wiping his fingers off, he finally broke down in sobs. Huge, ugly, breath-stealing sobs.

His beautiful-souled mate had been betrayed and then violated. They hadn't even had enough honor to stand and face him in a challenge. Until this was settled, he would ask God to put him on leave. He would be by his mate's side twenty-four seven. If something did come up, only D, Mac, or God would be allowed to stand in as a substitute. How had he let his sub down so badly?

A whine sounded and Bal tried to crawl over to him. "No, no. Stay there, Bal. You heal, buddy. I'm okay, I prom-ise." He sucked it back in, not wanting to upset the dog or Luc if he could sense him. He gently put the sheet back over Luc's rear end, leaving his top half uncovered. He took a healing potion and attached the spray bottle top, reap-plying a new layer over Luc's back.

A few minutes later, the rest came back in.

"We lost one of the littlest pups," Mac said, dropping down heavily onto the couch.

"Are they by themselves?" Bert asked worriedly. Maybe they could move them all in here.

D shook his head. "I called my parents in. I didn't tell them everything, just that Luc had been attacked and the hellhounds poisoned. They're staying at the kennels, making sure they get food and water and healing potions if needed. Mom is decent at wards and is putting some more protections around them."

Bert nodded. He knew D's parents were one of the few let into the inner circle and Luc trusted them. D's mom wasn't a fighter, but his dad worked in punishments, so he would know how to take care of himself.

Luc's mind came back online before he really wanted it to. His body was a map of pain, but honestly a little better than he had expected. The last time he had been this conscious, he had wanted to die. So many of his bones had been broken, skewers shoved under his fingertips, some into his eyes. It was a good thing he didn't want kids because the skewers had also been shoved through his testicles and he wasn't sure any amount of healing potion could fix the damage he had felt. All of that he had withstood well, it was when they tried to carve out his mate mark that he had lost his composure. He had no idea how he managed to fight with everything else broken, but he had almost killed one of them before he was shot with another dart. The berserker-like energy had come and gone quickly, and it had sapped all his muscle strength.

They had broken his legs then. The drug had unfortunately only paralyzed him at first, so he was completely aware that he had been raped. Repeatedly. The drug had kept him immobile and unable to scream even if he had wanted to, but it hadn't dulled his nerve endings. He had felt everything. When he heard the plans to use him as the glory hole for the club, he had tried fighting again but had only fallen to the ground. They had tied him down, moved the pummel into place, and dosed him again. As he heard the crowd gathering behind the wall, he had mercifully fallen unconscious. He knew what had happened though, he could feel it. At least he wouldn't have those memories to go with the others.

He wondered if they had forgotten to re-dose him or if

the club was closed it was so silent. He hoped Bert hadn't been able to feel anything over their bond. That would kill him to know his mate experienced that through him. He fought back the tears. No weakness, he ordered himself.

A tongue licked his face. Eww. Dog breath. Dog...what... there hadn't been any dogs. He heard a familiar whine. Bal. That was Bal. What was he doing here? Did Bert find him? He struggled to get up, his body screaming in pain.

"No, Love. Stay there. You're safe. You're home," Bert's voice said. "I'm right here. We're in the den. Mac's sleeping on the sofa. D's downstairs making breakfast. God just left, but he was here all last night. I'm not leaving, I'm just going to grab you a water. Stay put," he ordered.

Luc relaxed, knowing his Mate had found him. He had never wanted Mac to see him like that but at least Bert had backup he could trust. Bal was licking his fingers and Luc tried to move them but found he couldn't. Before he could panic, Bert was back.

"Don't try to move anything," he chided. "They still have splints on them. We had Gina scan you this morning and she said after one more healing potion and an hour, we could take those off."

Well, that seemed like a long time, if they found him last night. There must have been a lot of damage.

"Okay, here's a straw, healing potion first, and then I've got water and a protein drink to get you started. I know those aren't your favorite, but you need quick calories," Bert murmured.

After he drank a potion, the entire bottle of water and protein drink, he had another healing potion. When he was finally courageous enough to open his eyes, he was staring right into his Mate's face, Bert sitting on the floor so he would be the first thing Luc saw. As the tears fell, he heard

Mac quietly leave the room, leaving them together, saying only, "Love you, Uncle. Always."

Luc sobbed, his hand reaching for Bert. "I was careful, I swear. I had my guards with me. They all suddenly dropped. I called for Bal, but he didn't come. I tried fighting, but then they shot with me with something too."

Bert swallowed, gently holding Luc's hand. "The hellhounds were poisoned. Bal was still trying to crawl his way to the house when we found them. We saved all but one of the littlest pups. We didn't get to her in time. D's parents are watching them and his mom put a ward around the kennels."

Luc felt more tears fall, his ribs aching with the sobs tearing through him. "It's my fault. I should have had better wards. I was stupid and overconfident that they wouldn't attack my house, it's surrounded by Enforcers."

"No," Bert said firmly, letting all of his Dom come through. "It is no one's fault except those that attacked and did so in such a cowardly way."

Luc nodded, not really convinced. "How. Did. How bad was it?"

Bert closed his eyes, holding his breath before letting it slowly out. "We found you at an underground sex club. The owner had been working with the masked man, getting paid for letting him use his club. He never saw his face. We could smell your blood and found a glory hole in the wall with a line for it. I just knew that's where they had you and killed the man stepping up for his turn. Mac and the others took care of everyone else while I got to you. You were tied up, obviously tortured. There was blood dripping to the floor from your back and where they. They." Bert swallowed, unable to say it.

"I know. I was still awake for the employees but was

pretty paralyzed. When I fought back they drugged me again. I wasn't awake for the wall," Luc said, trying to reassure his Mate.

Bert surged up, his forehead pressing against Luc's, his chest heaving with his own sobs. Luc tried to hold him, but the bracing kept getting in the way. "I'm sorry I let you down. My job is to protect you and I did a shitty job of it."

"Nope," Luc said strongly. "I have taken care of myself for thousands of years. Your job is to protect my mental state as my Mate, but you cannot take this on yourself. You found me, you saved me."

"And we killed all of them and burned it to the ground," Mac said almost cheerfully from the doorway. "Viv sent some of her banana chocolate chip bread that you love. I haven't told her everything yet."

"She's family, but don't tell her over the phone. And make sure her therapist is on standby," Luc advised.

"I will. I also have her number for you. You can use this burner phone and call in anonymously. We have it all set up. You'll need to talk about this to someone," Mac said, coming closer and sitting on the floor so he could see him.

Luc nodded, although that in and of itself sounded like torture. He wasn't one to talk about his feelings, but if it started interfering with his work or relationships, he would call.

"It's been a half hour, that should be good enough. I need to shower and show up to work today. It already feels late."

Bert groaned, but Mac nodded. "It's a little later than normal, but God was stopping in to make a big deal about a meeting you all had this morning and how he left you with a bunch of paperwork to finish up to buy us some time. I have your breakfast at the table. D made you pancakes and cinnamon rolls. He left for work so it looks like everything is normal. His parents are staying with the hounds."

"Alright, help me up and we'll get this day started," Luc said, not relishing the idea of moving. He could tell not everything had healed all the way yet. This was going to hurt.

33

Luc sat on his chair, grateful Bert had finally given in and applied the healing cream to the inside of his torn-up body. The healing had started last night with the potion idea, but it hadn't been thick enough to really coat the tissue and stay there to finish the job. Luc had needed to convince Bert that it was okay to do, but he had been clenching his jaw against a scream the entire time. He had chanted, 'it's my mate,' over and over in his head. After the tissue and skin had knitted together, Bert had helped him get a shower. That had not been fun with the new skin still growing in on his back, but he needed to get all traces of blood and anything else off of him.

Mac had stayed to help apply more healing cream to his back and wrap him up. They had spelled the gauze to hide odors, hoping it would help hide the scent of any blood that might seep as he moved. His nephew had given him an awkward air hug before he left. Luc was glad to see nothing had really changed between them with this. If this had changed how Mac or Bert saw him, he thought that would break him beyond repair.

Getting dressed had been an experience he didn't want to relive. He wondered if he could just walk around naked, although that would show all of his still healing wounds.

Maybe he could just wear a robe, a really soft smooth-textured robe. He had ported to his office, despite Bert's protests. Bert thought he should save energy and go directly to the hearing room. Luc said he needed to appear as normal as possible. And if God had said he was working on paperwork, it made sense to leave from his office.

Right before they left home, Bert had slid Luc's ring back on his finger. He had swallowed back tears; he had been certain they had stolen or destroyed it. Bert told him he'd had it cleaned, spelled to get rid of any negative energy, filling it with feelings of his love.

As the first souls were brought in, Mac slipped in the side door, standing guard. They were short with Greg in the hospital. Luc wanted to go see him after work, depending on how well his back was healing. He didn't need to look like death warmed over while visiting an injured Enforcer. Knowing Greg, he would blame himself even though he had almost been killed.

Behind Mac came a small pack of hellhounds, Bal and a few of his older hounds. Luc was grateful that they had all recovered so well, but he was mourning the loss of the pup. Bal stood next to his chair, full hellhound mode, while the others were fanned out on either side of his chair. Luc made sure his mask was firmly in place before giving a nod to start the day.

The day was long and he was glad he had made the decision to not attend the dispute hearings today. He had asked Mac to cover those at breakfast. Luc was in pain and knew he needed to stop for the day and was grateful when the last criminal case ended. He stood, locking his muscles to keep him appearing strong.

"There will be a new procedure going forward. I will not be overseeing most of the dispute hearings. I will be appointing someone to take over, but for now, Mac will be taking over for today." He grabbed Bert's hand, slowly walking back to his office, Bert keeping his arm stiff to help support Luc without making it obvious. He staggered to his chair, collapsing. The pain in his back was excruciating at this point and his legs ached with the bones barely healed.

Margo quietly brought him a coffee and a healing potion. He may not have told her everything, but she knew he had been missing and injured in some way.

"Go home, sir. I'll handle anyone that stops in the rest of the day. If I think it's an emergency, I'll call you," she told him. He knew darn well from that tone that she wouldn't call him.

"Keep Spot with you at all times," he told her. He reached out and squeezed her hand. "Thank you for taking such good care of me."

Margo's cheeks pinked, but she shooed him away. "Go on now. Get some rest." She shut his office door behind her.

"I need help, Mate," Luc admitted. His body was calling it quits and he needed to get home. He wanted to scream every time he moved and the thought of having to take his clothes off made him want to run headfirst into a wall to knock himself out.

"I've got you," Bert promised, gently grasping his hips. Luc leaned his head against Bert's shoulder and closed his eyes.

Luc felt them port and opened his eyes to see his den.

"Stay there. I'm going to grab the potions, and I'll help take your suit off. I think clothes first, that way the gauze doesn't get absorbed into any new skin."

Luc nodded. "Can I have a drink first?" he asked, pointing to the alcohol cabinet. Unlike with human medicine, there weren't really any interactions with alcohol, and he needed to numb himself as much as possible before they did this.

Bert brought over the decanter and a glass, but Luc simply uncorked the bottle and chugged the entire thing. It took a minute, but the edges got a little blurrier. "Now," he ordered. The buzz wouldn't last long with his metabolism.

Bert quickly stripped his coat and tie, knowing the pants could wait. The back was the big issue. He gently peeled back the shirt, blood stains splattered about. He dropped it off to the side to burn later. He hesitated, trying to figure out the best way to remove the bandages. They were coated in both fresh and dried blood. "This is going to hurt," he cautioned. "Come around the back of the couch. It'll at least provide some support for you." Once Luc was settled, he didn't waste any time. He cut down the sides of the wraps, letting the front fall away. Quickly, but as gently as he could, he peeled back the layers of gauze. A few were stuck and he tried to ease them away from Luc's body. He swallowed his own alarmed shout when Luc abruptly leaned forward, forcing them to tear away from his back. Bert heard Luc's grunt and knew it had to be incredibly painful.

When the final bandage was removed, Bert wanted to beat the crap out of something. Luc's back was better than yesterday, but it was still a mess of blood and missing skin. Small patches had grown in, but even those looked raw. He quickly grabbed the healing potion and sprayed it, trying to get a good coating.

"Okay, Love. It's all gone. Let's leave it for now. We'll put down a towel and you can lie on your stomach." He didn't want to cause more pain and wanted to give the nerve endings a break before applying the healing cream and additional bandages.

"Can you hold me?" Luc asked, his body swaying. He just wanted a hug and to smell his mate.

Bert nodded, even though Luc couldn't see him. He led him around to the front of the couch, grabbing the healing potions before sitting down. "Sit on my lap, Love, and drink these." Luc guzzled the potions before sitting on his legs, straddling him, scooting down until their chests were together and his head rested on Bert's shoulder. It took a few minutes, but Bert could feel Luc's body slowly relax enough for him to sleep.

He closed his eyes, focusing on the feel of his mate in his arms. Safe, if not whole. He heard Bal port into the room, curling up next to them on the couch.

Luc knew Bert had spoken to God about not being sent out on any assignments until the man behind his attacks was caught. He had to admit that having him in the room was a relief and let Luc focus on the hearings and pretend everything was fine. Once his body had healed, at least physically, he had gone to see Greg. They still had him on restrictions when it came to speaking, but Greg had kept trying to write out an apology. Luc had felt like crying. He had done his best to assure Greg that he wasn't at fault, that Luc was fine, and he had a job when he came back, if he wanted. Greg had written down what he could remember of the attack and what he had been researching.

Unfortunately, he had forgotten several hours around the attack, and they weren't sure if it would ever come back. Any research or notes he may have had, had been taken by whoever attacked him. He was able to give a vague description of the man and it resembled Luc's recollection of the maintenance man who had been in his office. They still had not been able to track him down.

Today Luc had a surprise for Bert when they got to the throne room. He had decided that Bert needed his own chair and had gotten one made to match his, although Bert's was in white leather. He had changed his to his favorite color, purple. Fuck the red. He wanted something to make him smile.

"Ready for work?" Luc asked, finishing his coffee. He hadn't slept again last night, every time he tried, he was back in that damn room, and he was done with seeing it. He had gotten very good at lying still so that he wouldn't wake Bert.

"Yup," Bert agreed, rinsing out his cup before placing it in the dishwasher. "What do you want for dinner tonight? Do you want to go out or stay in?"

"In." He definitely didn't want to go out.

"Okay. We still have some dinners in the freezer. Viv sent so many over. I think the zucchini lasagna is in there still, or Mac made a demon goulash too."

"Lasagna sounds good." He could deal with some cheesy goodness. There was something comforting about it and while he didn't want to admit it to anyone, he needed some of that right now. Bert had offered to listen, but Luc just couldn't do it. He felt like he would fall apart if he started, and he didn't want to relive it in any way. He could take being injured, being tortured. It was the other that was fucking with his head.

He trusted Bert with his life, trusted him to catch him if he fell, but he couldn't open his mouth and talk to him about this. He knew it was worrying Bert, but he shoved it down deep hoping it would work the same way it did when he had to go to work.

"Let's go, Mate. The sooner we go, the sooner we get lasagna," he tried to joke.

Bert looked at him closely, almost as if he could read Luc's thoughts, but finally nodded. They stopped by his office so he could review the files and check in with Margo. He was happy to see the chairs sitting there when he opened the doors.

"What?" Bert asked quietly.

"Go have a seat, Mate. I want you next to me when you're here," Luc told him, smiling for the first time in days. The chairs had turned out perfectly. He slid his hand down and felt his hidden weapons. He'd point out Bert's later in private. For now, it was time to get their day started.

L uc wasn't getting out of bed other than to go to work. It had started with not wanting to go out, but now he came home, crawled into bed and stayed there. It had been a month since they had rescued Luc, and he wasn't getting better. Physically he had healed. Mentally was a whole other story. Mac and Viv had stopped over when Bert mentioned how worried he was, but even the lure of the baby visiting wouldn't get him to come downstairs today. They had all visited in the bedroom for a few minutes but hadn't stayed long. Luc had said he wasn't feeling well, but Bert knew it was more than that.

His lover lay there, curled around his hound, blankets piled around him. Bert was hesitant to try a scene, not wanting to traumatize his mate even more. He needed some way to break through to Luc though. Other than the first time he had woken up at home after being rescued, there had been no tears, no outbursts. Luc had locked it up inside and wasn't letting anything out. Bert knew that it wouldn't last, it would all come out eventually. Bert didn't know how to reach him other than being there for him.

A knock on the door had him frowning. They weren't expecting anyone. He opened the door, seeing Alan standing there.

"There's someone here to see Luc," he told Bert with a frown. The Enforcers didn't know the full extent of what happened, and they never would. The ones who had been poisoned that day had recovered. They had told them that Luc had been taken but recovered within hours. The other Enforcers had been told that there had been another attempt. Their inner circle had debated saying anything at all, but with some of the Enforcers involved, they kept it simple. That was all they really needed to know to be more vigilant.

Bert shook his head. "We're not expecting anyone."

"Please, Sir. It's me. May I talk to Lucifer please?" Sky peeked out around Alan.

Bert nodded to Alan, who stepped aside. He waved Sky inside, looking around for Charles before shutting the door.

"Does your Master know you're here?" he asked quietly.

"Yes. I...I thought Luc could use a friend. It's not the same. But. I had a master before Charles who wasn't...kind. He didn't listen to safe words. I. I thought maybe having someone he knows and kind of trusts to talk to would help," Sky offered, keeping his eyes low, his fingers clenching and unclenching with his nervousness.

Bert thought about it. Sky and Charles were the only other ones who knew what happened. Charles had used some of his shadier contacts to help search for Luc and they had given them the bare bones of what happened. Charles and Sky had also spread word that they had all had dinner together during the time Luc had been missing, helping keep the mystery of whether Luc had actually been kidnapped going.

He wasn't having any luck getting through to Luc and neither was Mac. Maybe Sky would. He gave a nod. "Bal's up there as well. He goes to work when he needs to and then stays in the shower or in bed. He won't talk about it and I'm getting worried. Thank you for being a good friend." He was also afraid to touch him, but that wasn't something Sky needed to know.

"Thank you, Sir. He's my only real friend besides Master and you. I want to help if I can," Sky said firmly before heading up the stairs.

Bert forced himself to stay downstairs and to give them their privacy. Bal would let him know if he was needed. He pulled out his phone and texted Charles.

Thanks for letting Sky come over. I'm at a loss. He kept it vague, knowing that phones could be hacked.

He was very adamant. He views Luc as part of our family now. You call if you need anything. Meet next week? There's been some unrest I've heard about. Charles wrote back quickly.

Yes. If it gets worse, call me. I'll make time. Bert sent the message and started making a snack tray for the boys. Not that Luc was eating a lot, but if Sky was there to encourage it, maybe he would. He tried to make it look appealing but also healthy. Any calories right now would be good, but he would like them to be useful calories too. Some nuts, berries, cheese cubes, chocolate candies. Salty and sweet, something should draw his mate's attention. Oh! Mac and Viv had brought some cookies. Bert added a few of those as well. He knew Viv had made Luc's favorites.

He could hear low murmurs of voices upstairs, although he made a point not to listen to the words. That was their time together and he didn't want to intrude. Sky hadn't confided to him all the details of his own past yet and to listen in would be a break in the trust the other sub had in him. He placed the snack tray in the fridge for now, wanting to give them a few more minutes. He would make some tea, keeping it caffeine free. Although Luc had been staying in bed, he hadn't actually been sleeping much.

When an hour passed, he leaned around the staircase, listening for anything. It was quiet, the low murmurs not present. He walked up the stairs, making enough noise to be heard but not enough to wake someone up. Opening the door, he found Sky on their bed, sitting against the headboard, his legs stretched out in front of him. Luc was lying down with his head in Sky's lap, Bal curled up behind him.

Sky looked up as the door opened, making the sleeping motion with the hand not holding Luc. Bert nodded, looking around for a piece of paper. Finding his notebook, he ripped a page out.

You okay? He left it broad in case Sky needed anything.

The other man nodded, holding a hand out for the pen.

I'm good. We talked. He talked a little. We had a good cry together and he fell asleep.

Bert looked at his mate, seeing tears still on his lashes.

I can sit with him for a while. I don't want him to wake up alone or for him to think I just left. Sky wrote.

Bert nodded, grateful they had such good friends. *I have snacks downstairs when he wakes up.*

Sky smiled, nodding. Bert pulled a blanket over both of them before leaving the room.

He busied himself in his office working on paperwork. When that was done, he finished the newest flower for Luc. He had been working on a sunflower this time and he thought it turned out pretty well. He wanted something cheery. When he was finished, it was still quiet in their bedroom and he needed something to do. He thought about going out to play with the hounds, but he didn't want to not be here when Luc woke up. Especially if Sky got him to leave the room.

He grabbed a dust rag, and the natural-based cleaner Luc liked to use, and went about cleaning the house. Even the baseboards got a good scrubbing. After rearranging the pantry, he started clearing out the freezer. There were a few things shoved in the back that had clearly been there too long based on the freezer burn. That was not a piece of steak he would want to eat.

A couple of hours later, he finally heard movement upstairs. Bert turned on the tea kettle and just as the whistle sounded, Sky was there leading a sleepy-looking Luc into the kitchen. Bert quickly poured the hot water into the waiting cups so the tea could steep. He pulled out the snacks, placing them between the boys. He pressed a gentle kiss to the top of Luc's head, resting his hand on his shoulder.

"I made some snacks for you guys, but if you want anything else, just ask," Bert told them before grabbing the tea. He still kept it caffeine free; the solid two hours of sleep Luc had just gotten was the longest stretch he'd had since the attack and Bert was hoping he could get some more real sleep later.

Sky grabbed a cheese cube first. "Oh, this is good! What kind is it? I'll have to see if we can get some for home. Luc, you should try it," he said, holding a piece out.

Bert loved that boy. He was getting Luc to eat without it being too forced. It took a bit, but Luc managed to eat almost half of the plate which made Bert ridiculously happy. That was good progress.

"Thank you, Mate. That was good. Do you mind if I grab a shower?" Luc asked, looking over at Sky.

"No, of course not. I need to head home anyway. You call me if you need anything, okay?" Sky said, opening his arms for a hug, but not stepping forward, leaving it up to Luc.

Luc nodded, giving their friend a quick hug before heading up the stairs. Sky helped clean up, waiting for something. After the shower had been running for a few minutes, Sky turned toward Bert.

"I think he's going to be okay, Sir. But. You—can I say something?" Sky asked, looking him straight in the eyes. Bert knew he was serious about what he wanted to tell him, and nodded his consent.

"He's been hurt. And I know your instincts will be to not hurt him anymore. But what you two do isn't anywhere near the same. Our dynamics look odd to others, but your marks show him you care and love him. Theirs were torture. Your touch is different, even if his body takes a while to relearn it." Sky looked at him.

Okay. Bert still wasn't sure what he was getting at.

"I'm not sure I understand," Bert replied.

Sky huffed but took a minute to think about his words. "He's going to need you to be his Dom in all ways. The longer it goes without you touching him, either in a scene or intimately, the more he's going to get caught up in his own head about it. He didn't say much, but he mentioned you not touching him since you found him. I think he's worried about it," Sky admitted. "He didn't say as much, but when Charles first found me I struggled with how he would see the scars left behind by my old master. He had to take the time, over and over, to show me how much that would never affect how he saw me. The healing potions took care of most of those for Luc I think, but the mental scars are still there. I know you hold him, hug him, that type of touch, but he needs the other too."

"I don't want to hurt him or set him further back on recovery," Bert admitted.

"So start small. Make love instead of a scene. Add in gentle spanks. He needs his place in your life to be reaffirmed," Sky said firmly. "Make sure he can see you. I—I couldn't stand to not see Charles in the beginning, or I would have a panic attack. Being able to see his face and know who was touching me made all the difference. We worked our way to other positions later, but for a long time I had to be able to see him."

Bert nodded. Sky gave him a quick hug and let himself out the front door. He sent Charles a quick text letting him know his sub was coming home and thanking him.

He took a deep breath. Of course he still desired his mate, but he had been hesitant to do anything to worsen Luc's mental state. Walking up the stairs, he saw Bal waiting by the bathroom door. "I have this," Bert told the hound. "Why don't you go play with the others for a little bit."

Bal huffed but walked out. Bert shut the bedroom door, stripping out of his clothes. He watched his mate through the steam. Luc was quiet, but he thought those shoulders were shaking a little bit.

"Hey, Love. Is there room for me in there?" he asked. Luc's head snapped up and the surprise in those blue eyes hurt his heart. As soon as he nodded, Bert opened the door and stepped in. Shit that was hot. Luc's skin was already red, especially that poor back with the new skin.

He reached out, turning the knob to make it a more reasonable temperature. Bert reached out and grabbed the shampoo, lathering his hands before gently scrubbing Luc's scalp. He didn't say anything, just let his hands gently clean his mate. He heard Luc's breath hitch when he slid over his ass, those muscles clenching tight. Bert ignored it, moving to make sure Luc could see his face before washing his shaft and testicles. He heard the deep breath Luc took, drawing in his scent.

Luc slammed into him, almost knocking them both down as he tried to burrow into Bert. He dropped the sponge, wrapping his arms around his shaking mate. "It's okay. I've got you, Love." He held Luc, waiting for a signal of what he needed. Finally, he reached out, placing a finger under Luc's chin, gently pushing him to look at him. "Love. Eyes on me please."

His heart clenched when he saw the tears in his partner's eyes. "I've got you. Always. You're my mate, my Love. My heart. Always. No matter what," he promised.

When Luc's eyes dropped, he grabbed his face with both hands, holding him carefully in place. "Always. No. Matter. What. I love you and want you. Always."

The uncertainty in Luc's eyes killed him. His lover was the ruler of Netherworld; he had defended his position for years, fighting off challengers, facing the evilest of beings. Nothing had thrown his confidence until now.

"Can. Do you," Luc stopped, huffing.

"Tell me Love," he ordered, letting his Dom voice come out.

Luc stood a little straighter, but his eyes dropped again. "I know you love me. But do you. Can you still—" he broke off with a growl again.

Bert thought he knew what he was getting at thanks to Sky. He dropped to his knees. He didn't give Luc any warning, just drew that cock into his mouth, laving it with his tongue, fingers gently caressing the balls until they drew up tight and the cock swelled in his mouth.

"I will always want you. That will never change. Those assholes and what they did will not change that. You're still my Love, my mate, my partner, my lover. I was afraid to hurt you, that's all," Bert told him before deep throating around Luc's dick again. He made sure to drag the head across the roof of his mouth, giving Luc extra sensations to focus on. He knew the pressure would drive Luc to an orgasm faster.

It took a minute, but Luc finally started thrusting into his mouth, gently at first but he gained more confidence the longer they were there. "Will you fuck me please?" he asked so quietly that Bert almost didn't hear him.

Bert surged to his feet. "No, not today," he said, watching as Luc's face fell. "Today I think we're going to have slow and sweet. I want you to ride me, baby." Luc's face lit back up and Bert knew that was the right move. Slow would be gentle, Luc on top would ensure he was in charge and could see Bert the whole time. He shut the water off, pulling Luc out of the shower. He gently dried him off before quickly drying himself.

Bert led Luc to the bed, pulling out the lube to sit on the nightstand. He lay down first, patting the bed next to him. His fingers played with Luc's hair, easing Luc down to lie on top of him. Their lips found each other, gentle questioning kisses at first, before their lust led to deeper more sensual kisses. Bert kept his needs in check, knowing that this time was for Luc. He sent his fingers gently tracing across Luc's skin, never staying in one place long, but making sure to get his face, down his neck to his nipples, across his back down to his cheeks. The muscles clenched again, but Bert gently patted the meatier part of Luc's ass. A little tap to remind him of who he belonged to.

Luc gasped, his eyes flying open to look at Bert. "Again please." A little moan left him as Bert gently smacked the other cheek. Nothing close to what they normally did, but just enough. Luc's dick jerked, dribbling precum onto Bert's stomach. He slid his hand between their bodies, gently circling and stroking the hard shaft.

"Will you get me ready?" Luc asked, eyes searching his. Bert wasn't sure what was going through his lover's head right then. He always got Luc prepped, unless Luc was putting on a show for him.

Bert pressed a kiss to Luc's lips, reaching out to grab the lube. He got one finger slick, rubbing softly across Luc's hole. When his entire body tightened and his breathing hiccupped, Bert reached out and pinched one of Luc's nipples. "Eyes on me, Love. Only me." Once Luc was looking straight at him, he gently pressed into the tight channel. Luc's breathing sped up, but he kept his eyes on Bert. "Good. Now get your finger slick and help me open you up." Maybe if Luc helped it would make him feel more in control. "That's it, slide in right next to me. Feel how tight you are. You always feel so good," Bert praised him. It was mostly babbling at this point, just so Luc could hear his voice.

Those blue eyes stayed locked on his face as he added another finger. Two of his and one of Luc's were buried deep in Luc's body. Bert crooked his fingers, pressing against Luc's prostate. "Oh!" Luc's surprised shout made Bert smile. Good. This was good. "Alright Love. Ride me," Bert told him.

Luc rose up, straddling his body. He held his dick still so Luc could take him at his own pace. Bert shouted and grabbed Luc's hips as he plunged all the way down, ass touching Bert's balls. "Fates, Luc. I meant to take your time. Fuck. You feel so good." Bert held Luc in place, trying not to come. Luc's body was warm and tight and felt so good around his cock. He loosened his grip, finding Luc watching him, that lovely cock still bouncing above his stomach. Luc rocked slowly, testing different motions.

Bert watched as Luc found one he liked and began moving faster, his hips and legs working hard to bring them both closer to climax. He made sure he kept his eyes on Luc, watching for any signs of discomfort. He planted his feet flat on the bed, knees up, adjusting his hips just the tiniest bit. He grinned as Luc shouted when the next thrust landed on his prostate. Bert gently pinched his lover's nipples, his mouth spewing nonsense praise and words of love. Luc's noises were getting louder, the familiar sounds letting Bert know he was close. He grabbed Luc's dick, keeping tempo with Luc's bounces. As Luc's spend coated his hand, his own orgasm took him by surprise. He wiped the cum off his hand before gently encouraging Luc to lie down next to him.

"Hmm. That was perfect, Love," he praised. He waited until Luc had snuggled in. Drawing a blanket over them, he breathed in their combined scents and was grateful his mate was in his arms. "I missed this. I'm sorry I was hesitant. I didn't want to hurt you. I will always desire you, no matter what. You need to let me know if I mess up and miss something. Okay?"

Luc didn't say anything, but he felt the nod against his chest. "Okay. Can we nap? Let's nap. That's the perfect day; you and a nap," Bert said, gently stroking a hand down Luc's back. On the first stroke he paused before reaching the cheeks, but Luc arched back a little and his hand continued all the way down. He wouldn't shy from touching his mate any longer. And hopefully Luc would get some more sleep. He knew this didn't solve anything really; Luc would still have bad days, and he should talk to the therapist, but Bert was hopeful now.

L uc hung up the phone feeling wrung out. He had finally started talking to the therapist Viv recommended. It was helping, but he was exhausted at the end of each session. He probably still wouldn't have gone, but he realized he was missing a lot of his greatnephew's firsts and he'd be damned if he missed more. Viv had sent him videos of the baby holding on to their fingers trying to take his first steps. He wanted to see those. He was there for Mac's, and he wanted to be there for Declan's.

Mac and Viv had been stopping over a lot more than usual, showing their love and support. Viv had a steady supply of sweets coming into the house and even brought some of her favorite cannoli from the store near her work. Some days she came by herself and sat with him while they played cards or watched mindless TV. Mac did that too, although they tended to watch more action movies.

His other friends, D's parents, had dropped off some casseroles and homemade dog treats for the hellhounds. Sky had also popped in a few more times. He just couldn't pull himself out of his funk. He knew Bert was worried but was trying his best to not be overbearing. There had been many new flowers showing up next to the bed, all of which were added to his growing collection. He couldn't even drag himself to his studio to work on anything for Bert, making him feel like a horrible mate.

At least they were having sex again. There were a few setbacks where they had to stop because Luc freaked out like an idiot, but Bert didn't seem to care, he just held him and talked him through it. Luc had had enough and was sick of feeling like a whiny bitch. He had waited until Bert was in the shower to call the therapist the first time.

When she had asked why he was interested in therapy, he had told her that exact thing. She had been very concerned that someone had said something like that to him, but nope, it was just how he was feeling right now. They had progressed to where he felt like he could speak pretty freely to her, although he didn't mention his real name or job title. As she pointed out, he was a protector and a fighter. Injuries from fights or job-related issues didn't bother him because he was actively fighting, he had some control over the situation, injuries were to be expected. Even torture could be seen as something that was a consequence of his job. The sexual assault that happened had not been under his control in any way, nor was it an expected hazard of his work, and that could be the difference in his head.

They had gone over the nights when he had nightmares or when he couldn't sleep to try to narrow down the triggers. They had spoken about Bert's reluctance to touch him right after. Luc didn't blame Bert at all, but part of him had still been worried. His therapist told him that was pretty normal for significant others. They just didn't want to cause any more trauma. He knew that, deep down, but it had helped to hear it from someone outside of the situation.

He shook his head, trying to shake out the weariness

that came after these talks. Also normal from what he'd been told, but right now he wanted to find his mate and get a hug. There was a knock on the door and Bert's head poked in.

"I have the fireplace going, snacks, and God's on his way for game night. If you still wanted to have it?"

Luc nodded. That was normal and normal was good. "Can I get a hug first?"

"Always," Bert replied, coming over to wrap Luc in his arms. Luc was still sitting, so it put them at a more even level. "I love you. I'm proud of you. I know these are hard, and you might not see it yet, but I can tell a difference already."

Luc pressed his head to Bert's chest, listening to Bert's heartbeat, matching his breaths with his partner's. He breathed in deep, taking in the scent of Bert's body wash, his deodorant, and the unique scent that was all his. There was always a faint hint of leather to his lover and he loved it. He needed something to feel grounded right now, but after his kidnapping was afraid to try.

"Mate. I need my cuffs today, but..."

"You don't know how you'll react," Bert guessed. "I have new ones for you that might be better." Luc's normal cuffs had hooks for chains and tie downs, the new ones were smaller and had been designed without D-rings or hooks so that he could wear them under his clothes at work. Bert was hoping that the lack of obvious restraints would make it a better experience for Luc. "Let's go to our room and I'll show you." Bert pulled Luc up, keeping their hands linked together as they walked down the hall.

Bert sat Luc on their bed, bending over to pull out the box the cuffs had arrived in. He had already looked them over and was very pleased with how they had turned out.

They were a black leather, which would blend well with Luc's suits. There was a silver engraving on the cuffs, stylized initials of B and L. Bert's letter had tiny angel wings and Luc's L had tiny demon horns curving from the top of the L. He had also placed a protective spell over them, hoping to keep his lover a little safer.

"I had these ordered for you a while ago, but they took a bit to make. They arrived a few days ago and I was waiting for the perfect time to give them to you," Bert said, opening the box.

Luc watched as he pulled them out. He didn't say anything, but Bert could see the smile coming over his face as he took in the design. Luc held out his hands, and Bert slowly and carefully fit the cuffs around his wrists. He kept them snug but not tight. As he finished with each one, he placed a kiss on the palm of Luc's hand, keeping the process as calm and loving as he could.

"How do those feel?" he asked, feeling a bit nervous. He desperately wanted to provide Luc with what he needed without triggering anything negative.

"Perfect. They're perfect, Mate. Thank you," Luc said, his voice thick. He pulled Bert's face to his for a kiss, his tongue sliding between Bert's lips to claim his mouth, his tongue twining around Bert's. Luc moaned softly, his body pressing closer.

"I'm here! If you're fooling around, hurry it up or I'm eating all the snacks!" God yelled from downstairs.

"Why is he here again?" Luc laughed.

"He's your friend," Bert pointed out dryly. God was becoming his friend too, but it was still a bit weird transitioning from boss to friend.

"Yeah, yeah. We better go. He's not kidding, he will eat all the snacks. Thank you for the cuffs. I love them."

"I'm glad," Bert replied. He stood, pulling Luc up with him. "We'll finish that thought tonight," he promised.

"You better not have eaten all the cookies!" Luc yelled down the stairs. Viv had dropped off some peanut butter and chocolate cookies earlier and Luc had been restraining himself from eating them. They looked so good.

"Not all..."

Uh oh. Bert recognized that tone from the office. God had certainly eaten some, but not technically all of them yet. Bert burst out laughing as Luc went barreling down the stairs to save the rest. Apparently, Luc also knew what that tone meant.

He entered the kitchen to see his mate hunched over the rest of the cookies protecting them. God had chipmunk cheeks stuffed full of cookies, plus he had one in each hand. He had eaten at least half from what Bert could see.

"Come on, you gotta share," God wheedled to get more once he had swallowed his mouthful. "They're so good."

Bert snorted as God shoved another in his mouth and tried to grab a replacement one off the plate. Luc smacked his hand away.

"Right. To share. You ate your share. Go eat a banana or something," Luc said, pouting, wrapping his arms tighter around the plate.

"You can get them any time, you just got to ask Viv. This is my only time to get them. I got to eat them now or I'll never see them again," God said, turning on the sad puppy dog eyes.

Bert leaned against the doorway watching the two most powerful people in their world argue over cookies. This was fun. He was seeing his boss in a whole new way, and he loved seeing how great their friendship was. You could tell they'd been friends for a very long time. Luc was going to cave, he knew it. He could see it in the slight drop of his shoulders. God knew it too based on how his eyes lit up.

"You can have two more and I'll ask her to make you your own batch next time," Luc said, handing over two more cookies. God snatched them right up, just like a toddler would. Bert shook his head as they were eaten in seconds.

"You should have savored them," Luc scolded, scooting away with the rest of the cookies. Bert reached out and grabbed one, taking a bite. Oh yum. The cookie was a dark chocolate with a peanut butter and chocolate topping. So good. They'd go great with coffee, he thought, moving to get a pot started.

"What games are we playing tonight?" Bert asked, measuring out the coffee grounds.

"It's board game night. I brought Monopoly, Furglars, and a few others," God answered.

Luc threw napkins at his friend. "You have chocolate on your face," he pointed out. "I don't think we've played Furglars before."

God shook his head. "Nope. It looks like it's a quicker game but pretty fun. I wasn't sure what everyone would be in the mood for. I have cards too, if we just wanted to play card games."

"Let me throw the pizzas in the oven. Do you want to go make sure the coffee table is cleared?" Luc asked. He loved his table. It sat higher than a normal coffee table, making it perfect to sit around and play games.

"Sure." God walked out to the living room, bringing his cookies with him.

Luc came over to Bert with the plate. "Quick, get your cookies," he whispered. "He'll be back soon!"

"Oh, Lucifer!" God called out in a singsong voice from the other room.

"Oh shit," Luc muttered.

Bert looked at him. What was going on? That was not a tone he had ever heard from his boss.

God leaned against the doorway, a huge shit-eating grin on his face. "Did you have a good night, Luc?" he asked, mischief in his eyes.

Luc stared at him through narrowed eyes. Bert kept glancing between the two of them. He kept quiet though. He was not getting involved in whatever this was. Luc didn't say a word.

"Look what I found!" God said, a bottle of lube hanging between his fingers as he slowly wagged it back and forth in front of Luc.

Luc's face was bright red as he lunged for it.

"Uh uh," God said, putting it behind his back. "I'll never mention it again if I can have another cookie."

"That's blackmail," Luc pointed out.

God shrugged, holding out the bottle again.

"Fine." Luc grabbed the bottle.

God made grabby hands and Bert tossed his boss a cookie. He might need a drink to keep up with these two. They were ridiculous.

"And everyone thinks you're the perfect good one," Luc muttered.

God laughed, grabbing Luc in a quick hug. "Come on, I'll even let you win a game," he said.

"Let me! I don't need your pity wins. I can crush you all on my own," Luc protested.

Bert followed behind listening to them bicker. He loved their weird little family.

"No! I will kill you all. Stop," Luc shouted, but the last word was more pleading, his voice trailing off into whimpers. Bert jumped out of bed, his gun and knife drawn looking for the danger. Bal whined next to Luc, drawing his attention back to the bed and making him realize that Luc was dreaming. They'd had so many good nights lately that Bert hadn't expected the nightmare. He should have though. The weird delivery to Luc's office probably set this off. Margo didn't realize what they were and took the delivery. To anyone else it looked like bamboo skewers, like they were going to have a grill-out or barbeque. To Luc, they were reminders of the torture he went through. He had brushed it off so easily at the office that Bert had kind of forgotten about it. He felt like a shitty mate; he should have realized it would have triggered the nightmares again.

Bal jumped out of the way as Luc started swinging his arms and kicking out. The blankets were wrapped around him, making him struggle. Bert cursed and quickly ripped the covers off, freeing Luc's limbs. It had to feel like he was being constrained again. Getting close, he used his voice to try to get his lover back.

"Luc, you're safe, you're home. I'm here, no one can get you."

Luc shook his head, his entire body trembling. "No, not my ring. Can't die, won't do that to Bert," he muttered. His voice was hoarse and so quiet. Bert also knew that while Luc was held captive that he hadn't uttered any words like these where his kidnappers could hear them. He had been stoic and hadn't let them see his pain.

Fuck it. He wasn't letting Luc suffer any longer. If he took a punch, he'd heal. Bert jumped on the bed, grabbing Luc's hands, holding them to his chest so he could feel his heartbeat, sitting on top of his lover's waist.

"Luc! Wake up right now. Be a good Love and come back to me," Bert said, putting all the command he could into his voice. "It's not real. I'm real. You're mine and I'm yours. No one else. Come back. Don't let them win."

It took a minute, but he saw Luc's eye struggle to open, his sub doing his best to follow his Dom's orders. "That's it. Come on back to me."

Luc finally opened his eyes and made a choked sound, quickly squeezing his eyes tight again. Bert lowered his body, covering Luc with his scent and weight. Luc buried his nose against Bert's throat, breathing him in. This close to him, Bert could feel all of the tiny tremors in Luc's muscles.

Bert climbed off, sitting on the bed and pulling Luc to sit in his lap. Luc's heart was still pounding, his breathing ragged and uneven. Wrapping his arms tight around his lover, Bert called out his wings, wrapping those around Luc as well. Just enough that he would feel surrounded by Bert.

"Alright Love. Let's get you soundly here with me, yeah? Five things you see?" He felt a bit useless at times like this and relied on the therapy practice they knew from Viv and had been confirmed by the therapist. He had super sour candies in the drawer as well, but those only worked some of the time. He squeezed Luc's hand to remind him of their practice.

Luc inhaled a shaky breath. "You, Bal, picture of Mac, the bathroom, blankets." Bert tapped each one out on Luc's leg.

"Okay, good. Four things you can touch?"

"Your arms, Bal," Luc let out a huff of laughter as Bal tried to climb into both of their laps, squeezing his head between Bert's wings. "Your feathers, my ring."

"Three things you can hear?"

Luc leaned down, placing his ear against Bert's chest. "Your heartbeat, Bal's panting, the fan."

"Two things you can smell?"

"Sweat and Bal's breath." He really needed to brush Bal's teeth, he thought, his nose wrinkling.

"One thing you can taste?"

Bert restrained himself and kept the kiss gentle as Luc pressed his lips to his. "You."

"Good. I'm sorry, Love. I should have expected this after the mail today," Bert apologized.

Luc shook his head. "Nope. If I'm not allowed to apologize that I had another nightmare, then you're not allowed to apologize or feel bad I had one. None of it is your fault." The first several times he'd woken Bert up with screams or yells, he had apologized. He felt mortified he had woken up his lover; no one wanted to be woken that way. Bert had finally told him he wasn't allowed to apologize any more, it wasn't his fault.

Bert held Luc for several more minutes before leading him to the shower. Luc stood under the hot water, feeling his muscles slowly unclench as Bert gently washed him and scrubbed his hair. It was nice to be pampered a bit, he thought. As they got out, Bert dried them both off. Climbing back into bed, Bert pulled him close, Luc's ass against Bert's groin. Luc smiled as he watched Bert gently slide his cuffs on.

"Try to sleep Love, or at least rest. Are you still going to work?"

"Yeah. I'm not letting them win, or even think they got the better of me," Luc replied firmly.

"Okay. I'll be with you," Bert promised, pressing a kiss between Luc's shoulder blades.

Luc lay there for several hours, regulating his breathing so Bert could sleep a little bit longer. It was easier to stay relaxed surrounded by Bert's arms and the feel of his cuffs on his wrists. He rested, but he wouldn't say he fell back asleep, not with the memories fresh in his mind. It was always the fucking sexual assault he dreamed about. It might start off with the torture, but all the nightmares quickly moved to the rape. His body ached with phantom pains from the dream; it absolutely sucked to relive the pain as strange men repeatedly forced their dicks into his body, his body ripping and bleeding, how dirty he felt with their sweat and cum on him, the sounds they made, the few who had talked saying how good his blood felt on their dicks, how some of them had used their hands to rip him open even more, claws tearing at his insides to get more blood flowing before they fucked him.

Luc kept his eyes open, only blinking when it got to be painful. Bal crawled up on the bed and rested near his chest. Clenching his ass muscles, he confirmed he was healed but he still itched with the urge to shower to get clean, but he knew it would wake Bert. Luc gently pulled

Bert's arm closer to his head, breathing in the scent of his mate, letting it calm him.

All too soon his alarm blared, and he reached out to smack it off. He pulled out the suit he wanted to wear for the day and paused to admire Bert's body as he got dressed. At first he had worn suits like Luc to the hearings, but Luc had encouraged Bert to wear his normal clothes. He liked seeing his lover in his jeans and biker boots. It was comforting. Plus, he looked hot as hell, and intimidating to everyone else.

"Are you ready for today?" Bert asked, concern in his eyes. They were tired and Luc wasn't sure how much more sleep he had gotten either.

He shook his head silently, then shrugged. It didn't matter if he was ready or not, he had a job to do.

"Can I help?" Bert asked.

"How?" He wouldn't say no to an orgasm, although he didn't think that would help for more than an hour or two.

"I want to mark you, give you something you'll feel all day so you know you're mine."

"Nothing anyone will be able to see?" The cuffs had been helping until now, but today he thought he needed a little extra. Last night had not been a good one and he wasn't in the right headspace for work yet.

Bert had a mischievous smirk on his face. "No," he said, "no one else will see it, but I'll know it's there and so will you." He reached down and pulled out a plug.

Luc shook his head.

"We haven't tried this at work yet," Bert said.

"I don't know about this," Luc replied, eyeing the plug, both eager and trepidatious. He'd enjoyed them during their fun times, but he'd never worn one more than a couple hours, and certainly never outside of their house or the club.

"Trust me," Bert said seriously, his eyes looking directly into Luc's.

This was his mate, he trusted him with his life. He'd trust him now. "All right," he said.

"Bend over," Bert instructed. As soon as Luc was in position, he felt Bert pull his cheeks apart. He waited for the slide of the plug, but a surprised shout left him as he felt a warm wet tongue lick at his hole. Bert got him just wet enough and begging for more before plunging three fingers in, quickly prepping him. As that huge cock slammed into him, Bert shoved a hand between his shoulders, changing his angle and pegging his prostate, bringing him to an embarrassingly quick orgasm. Luc felt his partner's climax fill him, the heat of it making his muscles clench around the shaft inside him. He protested as he felt Bert pull out, but the plug quickly slid in to take his place. Kissing his cheeks and giving the plug a gentle tap, Bert stood up.

"Turn around," he told Luc.

As soon as Luc faced him, Bert dropped to his knees, licking him clean before sliding a cage around his cock and balls that Luc hadn't seen until now.

"I'll be able to help you during the day and no one will see," Bert said with a smirk.

"Not sure how this is helping, Mate," Luc said dryly, looking down at his bound cock. There was something about the sight of it that made his dick attempt to get hard, but the cage kept him down. That wouldn't be distracting at all, he thought sarcastically. He was smart enough to keep it to himself though.

"Because now every time you move or shift in your seat, either the cage, the plug, or your cuffs will remind you of who you belong to. It's not to any of the voices in your head, it's not to any of the assholes who hurt you, it's not to the jackass who's behind this mess, it's not even to your people. It's to me," Bert told him, standing up to pull him into his arms, holding him tight. "You belong to me; I belong to you. That's it."

Luc nodded, holding tight. He listened to Bert's heartbeat, letting the scent of his lover fill him. "Thank you," he said, finally pulling away to press a kiss to Bert's lips. He kept it quick, not wanting to be late for work. The feel of the cage was maddening as he got dressed. He picked tighter underwear to minimize the amount of movement it would have, although he didn't think it would help that much.

Bending over to lace his boots, he didn't hear Bert come up behind him. Luc shouted as his body lit up in pleasure as the plug nudged his prostate, Bert's fingers tapping against it.

"Let's go to work," Bert said cheerfully, ignoring Luc trying to catch his breath and glaring at him.

Luc grabbed hold of his lover and ported them to his office. Margo was already there, filling coffee cups and setting out the files for the day and some pastries for breakfast.

"Good morning, Margo. Thank you for all of this. It looks delightful," Luc said. "I know your youngest grandson has a school show today, so make sure you leave in plenty of time to get there. Take Spot if your son-in-law won't be able to bring you to school."

"Are you sure, sir? It's at two o'clock," Margo replied, looking surprised he knew about the play.

"Yes. You need to be there to see him. Bert's here all day with me. Just lock up the office when you need to go and set the alarms. I've heard all kinds of great things about the school play. You'll have to let me know how it was." He never went even when he was invited because he drew too many stares when all of the attention should be on the kids. He did miss seeing things like that sometimes; he knew all the kids of his personal Enforcers and had babysat many of them. Maybe he'd get a chance with his great-nephew; after all, most of the people on Earth had no idea who he was.

"Thank you, sir. I'll take lots of pictures. Sam's been so excited. He's a mushroom," Margo confided, her lips twitching as she tried to keep in a smile.

"I'm sure he'll be the best mushroom there," Luc replied confidently. Sam was hilarious and loved being the center of attention. The kid was meant for drama and acting. Luc had been privileged to see many scenes of Sam trying to convince his grandmother to do something. Like the time he would 'simply wither away, completely dried to a husk,' if he didn't get some ice cream soon. It hadn't worked, but it had been very amusing, complete with the slow wavy descent to the floor to mime said withering away.

"Thank you, sir. I'll leave any notes for you on your desk before I leave," Margo said, smiling at him.

Luc grabbed the top file and sat down to study the cases for the day. He had to bite back a gasp as the plug nudged his prostate again. His cock twitched but couldn't get hard with the cage. Oh fuck, he swallowed his moan. There was no way he would be ignoring this all day, it was like they were in the middle of a scene instead of at work. Luc glanced at Bert, who was scrolling on his phone, a very smug look on his face.

It was going to be a damn long day.

37

ert was about to lose his mind. There had been three more attempts on Luc in the past few weeks. One had been a shooting outside of their neighborhood. Luc had been injured. The shooter either had no experience, or the sudden gust of wind had changed the trajectory because it didn't even go toward Luc. His darling loving idiot of a mate had jumped in front of someone else to protect them. Of course, it had been heading straight for a child, so Bert didn't really blame Luc or expect anything different, but he still hated his mate being hurt.

A bomb had been sent to work, but the Enforcers had taken care of that one. The other attack had been a poisoning attempt with a delivery to the office. Both Spot and Bal had growled at the package and wouldn't let anyone near it. Luc had called in one of the Enforcers who also happened to be a Sensor, and they were able to read the magic and poison within the box. They had removed and destroyed it.

What Luc didn't know was that Bert's bike had also had the brake lines cut, but it was a sloppy job and he'd seen the damage right away. He had brought it with him into town to grab dinner one night and had found it when he came back outside. Luckily, he was able to port it home and ordered new parts. He fixed it and kept it locked in the garage at home. His mate had enough to worry about without worrying about him as well.

The one bright side was that Greg had returned to work. His throat had healed, although there was still a very faint scar, which showed how close he came to dying. His voice was a little raspier, but not bad considering the damage that needed to be repaired. Luc had tried to give him more time off or even early retirement if he wanted it, but Greg was having none of it. He still couldn't remember what he'd found before his attack and all evidence had disappeared.

Bert had gone back and looked at all security cameras in the area, but the man had been smart enough to have a hoodie on and his face pointed away. Clearly, he knew the area well because some of those cameras were very hard to see.

When Luc had asked why he wasn't riding his bike more, he had made up some excuse, but based on the look he received, he didn't think Luc was buying it. The next day a new glass motorcycle had appeared on his pillow, this time with a man on it. It looked very similar to Bert, which he imagined was hard to achieve with glass. He added it to his collection and worked on finishing the newest rose for Luc. He was trying to get the same red/black effect out of wood that the Netherworld roses had. It was harder than he had expected but he thought one or two more coats of the special stain blend he created might do it.

Tonight though, they had enchilada pie in the oven for dinner and he may have added a tiny bit of extra cheese knowing his mate loved all things warm and cheesy. He planned on ignoring the rest of the world and loving on his mate. He had a new toy to play with and he was eager to see if Luc loved it. They'd had to give up blindfolds after their last scene. It had been the only time Luc had Red safeworded. As soon as his eyes had been covered, he had panicked, his body fighting the restraints and the cries afterward would haunt Bert for a long time. Blindfolds had been something Luc loved, but now he couldn't stand his eyes being covered.

Luc had been angry with himself because his kidnappers hadn't blindfolded him in the room and thought his mind was reacting stupidly. Bert had pointed out that it had been kept very dark and Luc had been restrained. It was perfectly normal for him to react that way. Bert had held and praised Luc for safe wording, until Luc fell asleep. Inside he was seething that something Luc had enjoyed had been taken away. Maybe they could get back there one day, but Bert wasn't going to push it. There were plenty of other things they could do, even simply ordering Luc to keep his eyes closed would work. That way if Luc was getting close to a Yellow or Red situation, he could open his eyes and see he was safe.

Bert drew in a deep breath, holding it before slowly releasing it. He wanted a calm evening and he was determined to keep his shit to himself so Luc could relax. He'd go to the gym and find the punching bag later. Maybe Mac would spar with him. They both had anger to work out.

A knock on the front door had him frowning. They weren't expecting anyone, and most of their close family ported inside the house. D's parents still knocked though, his mom saying it was rude to simply barge into someone's home. He didn't hear any commotion outside, so the Enforcers must have cleared the person. He turned the oven off so dinner wouldn't burn and made his way to the front door. The shower had just turned off upstairs, so he only had a couple of minutes before Luc came downstairs. Hopefully it was something he could handle quickly and Luc didn't have to get involved.

"God? What are you doing here? You could have ported in. We're just about to have dinner," Bert said.

God's face was livid, his features tense with anger and the energy coming off of him was extreme, almost forcing Bert to take a step back. Bert had never seen him like this.

"I'm here on official business. Someone sent a challenge to Luc."

Alan looked over sharply but held his comments to himself. Bert saw him whip out his phone though, his fingers flying over the screen.

"Are you fucking kidding me?" Luc asked, coming to stand next to Bert, his hair still dripping.

"Nope. I guess since all his attempts at killing you failed, he decided to go straight to the source," God replied, his hand clenching a balled-up piece of paper.

"Why did it go to you?" Bert asked, confused. If they were challenging Luc, wouldn't it have gone to the office?

"That's what the protocol is. It's so the challenge can't be ignored or the challenger assassinated before it's public knowledge," Luc replied. He sighed deeply, his body tense again.

Godsdammit. There went their relaxing, no stress evening, Bert thought.

"Come in, have some dinner," Luc offered.

"I stand with you, no matter what the fucking protocols may say. If they have a problem with that, they can challenge me too. You're my best friend and the best ruler for Netherworld. We've done great fucking things, so they can suck it. Let's make a game plan," God said, walking through the doorway and following Luc to the kitchen.

As Bert went to close the door, Alan stepped in front of it.

"We've got your back. Lucifer is our ruler. We'll keep you both safe," he pledged, arm over chest. As he spoke, several other Enforcers ported in to surround the house.

"Thank you," Bert replied, returning the gesture. Luc's people loved him. He hoped his mate knew that.

He walked back to the kitchen to find Luc dishing out dinner and God setting the table. "Does anyone have a clue as to who it is?"

God shook his head, as did Luc. "All of our sources have come up with zilch. Those that may have known something end up dead. I found one on our side and had them brought in for questioning. It was similar to Keevhan. They said a word and a kill spell was activated. It was seriously a fucked-up spell too because their soul was so damaged that I couldn't read it or communicate with it at all. I had someone scan the challenge and it's been cleaned. There's no traces of the sender on it."

"So we're going into this blind," Bert said flatly.

"Hm. Not entirely," Luc said slowly. "We know it's a man. I'm betting demon and someone close to here. Not that it's hard to port anywhere, but he knew where cameras were located that someone just visiting wouldn't know about. I think he likes control, he's bound to be close by to keep a watch on his little spies."

"That doesn't help narrow it down much," Bert replied. Almost everyone near here was a demon. There were a few that weren't, but the majority were. "We could try investigating everyone who hasn't been here long, but I don't think that will help much."

"It's got to be someone that I would recognize," Luc said suddenly, jumping up and pacing the kitchen. "He hides his face. Part of that would be so he doesn't get caught. If we knew what he looked like, we could hunt for him better. But he hid his face in my office, never turning around. If the poison had worked, which that amount would have if I didn't have the healing potions, I would be dead and at that point it wouldn't matter if his face was known."

"Hm. Maybe," God replied. "I don't know that that helps much. You're pretty available to your people, you see a lot of faces every day, both in the office for hearings and out in the public."

"True," Luc said, sitting down. There was a hint of defeat in his voice.

"Is a challenge to the death?" Bert asked.

God shrugged. "It's up to the participants. Killings are permitted, but so is showing mercy."

Bert looked at his mate, his face and voice as serious as he could be, every bit of Dom coming through.

"You will show no mercy."

God nodded once in agreement. "None. This asshole deserves nothing. His soul should be destroyed as well."

"No mercy," Luc agreed. The man had tried to kill him multiple times, had almost shot a child, and had messed with his mate. Bert may think he didn't know about the bike, but very little happened in his world that he didn't know about. Which made this whole thing very vexing.

"What are the rules of the challenge?" Bert asked. It had been an abstract thing taught in school. They all knew it was in their rules, but no one really studied the details or thought it would happen.

"The challenger and the challenged enter into a ring. The challenged's Enforcers are there as witnesses, as am I. If the challenged loses, the challenger in theory becomes the new ruler of Netherworld and the Enforcers are expected to swear allegiance. I don't see that happening. Luc's love him. No one else is allowed to interfere. They are permitted one weapon each: no guns, no poisons, no spells, no armor. Sword, dagger, knife, whip are allowed. They can fight in human or shifted form. No breaks, no water, no food. They fight until one is killed, surrenders, or is deemed too damaged to continue. I'm the judge of that. Luc would be the judge if I was challenged."

"Can't you—?" Bert broke off, knowing it wasn't possible.

"He can't just declare me the winner, Mate. The rules are there for a reason and I need to uphold them. We fought to bring peace and we established these rules so we wouldn't have another Satan situation. Breaking those rules won't help our people in the long run," Luc reasoned.

"Bullshit. You winning will help our people. But yes, they need to be maintained," God agreed, looking pained.

"When does this take place?" Bert asked.

"One week. It needs to be seven days from the day of delivery," God replied.

It had been a week. A long exhausting week. Luc hadn't been sleeping well and neither had he. The hounds had all piled into the house, sleeping around their bed. There were Enforcers everywhere; Bert loved their support, but he was also craving time alone with his mate. They had been sparring every day, with Mac, D, and God coming over as well. God's fighting style was a lot dirtier than Bert had been expecting. He had never seen his boss fight, but the man was a machine and he was terrifying to observe.

Luc was breathtaking to watch and when he and God sparred, it shook the ground with their strength. It made Bert realize that he had only seen a small portion of his partner's abilities. After watching them, it was no wonder they had held their positions so long. There was no way Luc was going to lose, he thought with a smile as they entered the arena.

The Netherworld Enforcers were already present, as well as Mac and D. They had sent the hounds and D's parents to Mac's house, keeping Viv and Thomas home. It allowed Luc to focus entirely on the fight, knowing Bert and the others could take care of themselves, and the more vulnerable of his family were safe. The hounds weren't allowed at the fight and at least this way they were doing a job to keep them occupied.

"You've got this, Love. Kick his ass, finish this, and come back to me," Bert ordered, drawing Luc's face down for a kiss. He wished Luc was allowed his cuffs but they had been spelled for protection so they were disqualified.

"Love you, Mate," Luc said before stepping away to stand in the marked ring on the ground.

God ported in, standing next to Luc and whispered something to him. He saw Luc nod, a smile lighting his face for a brief second. There was an audible pop as the entirety of Arlysium's Enforcers ported in to stand with Netherworld's. They weren't required to be there and it was a surprising show of strength. God looked proud as he looked over and nodded to his people. There was a crowd, as the challenge was required to be made public knowledge. There were nonhumans from all the realms and of all different species. He had a feeling most were gossipy lookers; although to be fair, it wasn't every day that there was a leadership challenge. It had been hundreds of years, maybe closer to a thousand since the last one and it hadn't even been an official fight.

"The challenger must step forward now or forfeit," God called out. Bert knew he was pushing the timeframe allowed to the bare minimum but couldn't bring himself to care. His fists clenched and he took a step as a figure in a hoodie stepped forward. Mac threw out an arm, holding him back, his own eyes burning flames in anger. Bert took a breath and nodded, stepping back into his place.

"You've got this," God said, bumping their shoulders together.

"If I don't, you've got—" Luc started.

"I've got them. No one will touch your family," God vowed. "It's time. Fucking destroy him."

Luc watched the crowd as his friend called for the challenger. A man stepped into the ring, the hoodie and mask thrown off to the side. An ordinary-looking man, about his height, a little heavier.

"You, Darius?"

He had to admit this was a surprise. He wouldn't have thought of Darius being behind this. He hadn't seen him in years. Like since he took over this position.

"Yes me. You think you're such the big man since you got this job. I should have gotten it. Look at what you've done to the fear and mystique that is supposed to surround the leader of Netherworld. You're making a mockery of this station instead of creating fear and horror. You mated an angel. An angel," he repeated in disgust. "We should be ruling over them like we did in days of yore."

Yore…really? Luc was getting bored of the diatribe, but he'd let Darius spew his hate a little more, try to weed out if there were others involved that he needed to ferret out and kill. He knew they had gotten some, but he wanted to make sure they got all of them.

"All we did was kill each other and weaken our numbers. Which led to an imbalance through all the realms. We've had peace and it allowed for our numbers to grow, for children to be born again. We are not better than any one race," Luc interjected. He knew Darius had held similar beliefs when they were children together, which is probably what discounted him from the position of leader of Netherworld. He wasn't open to hearing any opinions other than his own and his speciest beliefs made him hugely biased against anyone not a demon. He wasn't sure if Darius had been disqualified due to losing a fight or because the Fates told him no, as they had done with a few that came forward during the challenges. There was no way the Fates would have allowed him to lead, as he would have been too much like Satan.

"And now you lower yourself to be submissive to a piece-of-shit angel. You're a pussy and clearly not fit to lead."

Luc could hear God, Bert, and Mac growl at that one.

"What are you talking about?" What did the asshole know?

"I've seen you near the club. Oh, you may wear a mask to hide your face, but we all know what your ring looks like. We all know what goes on there. And your mate is well known to be a Dom. Which makes you the bitch in the relationship."

"That's not how that works," God interjected. Luc could feel the anger pulsing through his family, but he held a hand out and down at his side telling them to settle.

"My personal life has nothing to do with my ability to lead. I've held this position for thousands of years. You've heard the stories. You really want to test me?"

"I, Darius, challenge Lucifer for the right of his position. To rule over the dead and Netherworld. I will bring the realms to war once again and lead the demons into greatness. Come on, join me," he said, looking at the Enforcers gathered nearby. It was written in the rules that they had to witness the fight. It was meant to ensure lineage of the job, but as one, they turned their back to Darius.

"You want to follow someone who is a submissive bitch half the time. How can he lead if he's not one hundred percent dominant? I know of Bert; he likes to spank his boys, whip them, tell them what to do. You want someone to lead you that will let someone do that to him?" Darius demanded.

Greg stepped forward, his eyes flaming in anger. "We shall not serve another, no matter the outcome of this challenge. Lucifer is our leader and we will not follow you," he vowed, cutting the palm of his hand, letting the blood drip to the ground in his pledge.

The hundred Enforcers gathered all followed suit, pledging their loyalty to Lucifer. It wasn't only the demons, all the Enforcers from Netherworld and Arlysium joining in as well.

"No matter," Darius muttered. "I've got some of my own."

Yeah, no he didn't, Luc thought to himself gleefully. What Darius didn't know yet was that he had already lost the few that he had planted in the Enforcers. Luc had made sure of that. Most had willingly taken a truth serum, one that worked on everyone, no matter their species or training. The ones who hadn't shown up, had been hunted down afterward and made to swallow it. When the truth was revealed, Luc's loyal Enforcers had killed the others.

His people had spoken and the majority wanted the peace and stability that Luc's reign had brought. Very few wanted to go back to the old ways and constant war. Even if he lost, Luc was at least reassured that there were enough of his people who wanted peace to make it happen. Of course, Darius was a dead man either way. If Luc lost, God, Mac, or Bert would kill him. If he won, Luc would kill him. He wanted this to end for good.

"No guns, no spells, no armor, no poisons, no food or water, no help. You may bring one weapon. Toss the weapon to the center of the ring for inspection," God instructed.

Luc tossed his favorite dagger to land perfectly in the center of the ring, Darius' falling short. God collected them both, inspecting them and having a Sensor examine them as well. Once they had been cleared, God called them to the center.

"Grab your weapons. The challenge begins when I call it." God looked straight at Darius before adding, "I hope Lucifer destroys you. You are no leader, and I will not align with you. My allegiance is to the one and only Lucifer." He nodded to Luc and stepped outside the ring. "Begin."

Luc was ready, his body tense but fluid. He knew Darius wouldn't fight clean, so it didn't surprise him that the first action he took was to kick sand at Luc's face. He dodged it easily, his body falling back into a rhythm he knew well. His emotions and concerns firmly locked away in their box, allowing him to focus only on the fight in front of him.

Darius spent more time running away from him than actually fighting. When he took to his demon form, Luc switched to his as well, his transformation much faster. Darius was a better fighter shifted, his wings getting him close to Luc quickly. Luc hissed as a hand raked his face, narrowly missing his eye. Son of a bitch. He hoped that didn't scar. He didn't need a reminder every time he looked in the mirror.

Darius grinned at him, his teeth gleaming in his smirk. Luc smiled back, tossing the dagger to his other hand, throwing out a punch with his dominant hand. Darius yelled, stumbling back, spitting out blood and broken teeth. Luc's wings shot out, swiping at Darius with their sharp edges, forcing him back toward the edge of the ring. He had this. This was the easiest fight he'd had in years.

Taking a step forward, dagger raised to finish this, Luc's heart skipped a beat, his feet stumbled. He looked at Darius, pushing his body forward, even though it felt like moving through sludge.

"Not so tough now, are you?" Darius gloated quietly. His wings quickly brought him out of reach, his claws waggling a mock hello.

Luc turned his body, following Darius's movements while trying to conserve his own. It took him a minute, but his brain finally figured it out. The bastard had coated his claws in poison and with it being so close to Luc's brain and a bunch of blood vessels, it probably wouldn't take long. Luc had to finish this quickly, both to save his people from having Darius as their leader and also to save himself from the poison if possible.

He knew from their time together that Darius wouldn't have the patience to wait much longer, and he stood still, gathering his strength for a last push. When the other man came flying at him, Luc waited until the last possible second, grabbing Darius by the throat, his own nails digging into the artery there. If he pulled out, Darius would bleed out. As the other man struggled, it took all of Luc's remaining strength to hold him still.

"You're no ruler. Real leaders don't need to cheat or bribe their people to follow them. You have no honor." Luc plunged the dagger into Darius's gut, pulling it upward. As his body began to fall, Luc grabbed his hair, tilting his head back and slit his throat. He watched as the blood sprayed and dropped the body. The pool of blood grew, soaking the sand beneath it.

"Lucifer is the winner!" God declared, stepping into the ring to officially end the fight.

Luc stood over the body of his challenger, keeping to his

feet by will alone. As his people cheered, their shouts filling the arena, his eyes found his family's. Mac and D were smiling, Bert waiting patiently. Luc saw his mate mouth the words "Good, Love," as he adjusted himself in his pants. If only he were up to that, Luc thought wistfully.

Just as he thought he would have to sit down, there was a static to the air and Lucifer locked eyes with God. This could go so poorly.

"What the actual fuck is going on here?" three enraged female voices said in unison. As the sound echoed through the area, it reverberated, growing in strength until everyone present was kneeling before the single woman as she stood by Lucifer and God. The Fates had arrived. They were three distinct people, but when they made appearances, they took a single form. The amount of power and magic now filling the room made his skin burn. These were the real boss.

"Are you out of your fucking minds?"

"Mams——" Lucifer started.

"Shh, Luc. Not you," the trio of voices said in unison, laying a hand on his bowed head. The gore from the day disappeared, his injuries healed, and the burning stopped. The poison vanished from his body. They laid the other hand on God, saving him from the sensation as well.

Luc could feel the relief from his mate as he was also spared via their bond.

"I try to take a short vacation and the world gets overrun with idiots. Do you have any idea what you could have done?" she asked, kicking Darius' body but holding on to his soul so she could scream at it. "I put the two most capable people in charge of Netherworld and Arlysium. I chose these two. For you to challenge one is to challenge me. Which you do not want to do. I am immortal. I do not forgive easily and I do not forget. Lucifer is The Lucifer. He has this job for life; his life experiences and yes, even his personal life preferences make him the perfect man for the job. He can dish out brutality when needed, as you saw today, but his compassion and love allow him to be balanced and have empathy as well.

"All nonhumans have had relative peace because of God and Lucifer. I do not want that jeopardized again, do you understand? To help you realize just how badly you could have fucked this all sideways if Luc had somehow lost, here's a little taste of what would have happened."

The room was filled with the screams and sounds of war. Based on how some of the people in the room started moaning or sobbing, the rest of the group was experiencing this like it was real life. For Luc and his family and God, it was more like watching a movie. Still completely horrifying as they watched the world burn, but they didn't have the sensations and emotions that apparently everyone else was having.

"I never want you to have a chance to fuck up my plan again," the Fates said, squeezing Darius' soul until it popped out of existence. Well, there was one less thing to worry about, Luc thought. It was kind of comforting knowing Darius wouldn't be able to ever cause problems again.

"From this day forward my chosen leaders, God and Luc, are protected. Their lines are protected. The fated true mates brought into the lines are protected. So mote it be," Fates declared, raising her hands.

A blinding golden light filled the room and Luc experienced what felt like a blast of fresh air passing right through his body, leaving him energized.

He looked up as a gentle hand touched his shoulder. Fates had crouched down next to him.

"Don't worry. It includes D, Thomas, Mac, Viv and any of their children. I know they're like sons to you," Fates said, pressing a gentle kiss to the top of his head.

As soon as she disappeared, the images stopped and people began to rise, standing on shaky legs. Bert rushed over to him. "Are you hurt?" he demanded, running hands over his body.

"No, Mate," Luc replied. "They healed me."

God stood as well, grabbing him in a hug. "I'm so glad you won. I knew you would, but I was still a little worried, old friend."

Luc held on for a moment, hugging his oldest friend back. "Me too," he admitted quietly. They didn't even know yet that Darius had cheated. The poison would have allowed Darius to eventually win. Without the Fates arriving and healing him, he would have been in bad shape. He knew Bert had healing potions ready, but they may not have been enough with how strong it had felt.

"What exactly does 'protected' mean?" God asked him quietly.

"I have no idea."

Bert was ready to be alone with his mate. He had held back until now, knowing that Luc needed to interact with the Enforcers and his people. Viv and Thomas had ported in since it was now safe, and it had been amusing to watch Viv fuss over Luc. Luc had soaked in all the attention. Bert hoped he finally realized how much his people and family loved him.

There had been an impromptu celebration, drinks and food brought in. Margo had personally brought Luc food, ordering him to take a couple of days off. She was rescheduling everything. It had been several hours, but they were finally home. There were Enforcers outside, Luc's favorite cookies and dinner for tomorrow in the fridge courtesy of Viv. Mac had hugged his uncle so hard, Bert almost expected to find bruises. They had all been scared, but they could now put it behind them.

And he could finally focus on his mate.

"I think you deserve a reward for fighting so hard for us, for your people, for your position. I think it's time."

"Time for what?" Luc asked, nerves running through him. They had talked about a lot of things they wanted to do in the future, but he didn't know what Bert was referencing.

"Your Jacob's Ladder. Go lie on the bed. I'll get the equipment."

"Yes, Mate."

Bert came back minutes later, a black box in hand and a healing cream. "I asked Florence to teach me. No one gets to touch you but me. Are you good with me doing this?" he asked, standing by the bed. He had studied it a lot and practiced on mannequins she provided. She had done all of his tattoos and he trusted her.

"Yes, Mate. I trust you," Luc replied.

"Good, Love. Just like everything else we've done. Breathe through it, lean into it, make it work for you. Yes?"

Luc nodded, watching as Bert laid out the needles and rings. He gasped as Bert suddenly deep throated his cock, causing it to harden so fast he got lightheaded. He was glad he was on the bed or he might have fallen. Once he was fully hard, Bert pulled off, making Luc whimper in need.

"Don't worry. I'm not going to leave you hanging. I want to mark where I want the piercings. I think we'll do four," Bert told him, staring at his shaft. "I don't want it too crowded; I want to be able to wrap your dick using the rings. Too close together and we'll lose area for the ribbon to go. If you like these, I think we might add a guiche and a lorum later."

Luc started panting as he felt his lover's hands on his dick. It wasn't even sexual, but his body had been accustomed to what happened when he felt these hands on him. He felt the brush of the marker, his lover holding his dick firmly.

"Hmm, maybe a piercing here too," Bert said absently, flicking the tip of his dick.

"Mate! Yes, anything. Please," Luc begged, his hips thrusting in the air.

"Well, I can't have you hard for the piercing part," Bert replied, giving his cock a few strokes. "Let's fix that. Then I'll clean you up and get started." It only took a few strokes and a deep throat swallow before Luc's orgasm exploded out of him.

Bert licked him clean, quickly wiping him down with an antiseptic and touching up any lines that got messed up. "Now hold still. Once the piercing is done, I'll add the healing cream. I should be able to suck you again tomorrow, but for tonight, I'm taking you when we're done. My reward for not jumping in there when the asshole poisoned you and ripping his head off."

That sounded fair.

Luc clenched his teeth together, keeping in the shout of surprise as he felt the first needle being inserted. It wasn't necessarily a pleasant feeling, the pain sharper than he had expected.

"Good. I'm going to insert all the needles, make sure they're where I want them. Then I'll thread in the rings. If you're still good, I'll give you a piercing of my choice for your tip. I think you'll like what I have in mind."

Luc nodded, breathing heavily through his teeth.

"Luc. Look at me," Bert commanded. He waited until Luc's eyes were on him. "You're not listening. Breathe, make it work for you. You can get your high if you work with it, not against it. Just like the paddle or the whips, yeah? Breathe deep, focus on me, focus on me marking you where no one gets to see, no one gets to know about," Bert said, his voice full of love and the strong undertones of his Dom.

Luc kept his eyes on his Mate, watching as he slid the next needle in. But this time he relaxed, knowing his partner would keep him safe, that Bert marking him as his, that this would lead to even more types of scenes for them to explore. He felt the beginnings of a familiar buzz, his body reaching for his calm zone, the zone where everything else disappeared and there was only Bert and him.

"That's it, that's my good Love," Bert murmured, sliding another needle in. Luc didn't even flinch this time and Bert kept the praise coming. He watched as Luc fully sank into his space, happy he finally got there. He needed the release after the last few months. Bert had decided when marking the lines the first time that there was enough room to add a couple more. It would be a nice surprise when Luc came back to himself. There was still enough space between them to thread the ribbon or leather cord or thin chains, whatever they chose. It would look amazing. The piercing he was most excited about was the one that was a surprise. He had been debating with himself on the best one or even if he should do it, but he thought he had the answer. A Prince Albert would have worked together with a cock cage or tying him up, but it hadn't felt quite right. Nor did a Reverse PA.

Seeing his lover's penis with the markings for the Jacobs Ladder, Bert had finally decided on a foreskin piercing. He would be able to change out the hardware, making it either pleasurable or to act as a chastity device. He grinned at the thought. So much fun to be had. He looked at his sub's face, seeing no stress. This is what he could give Luc. Bert might not be the tallest or the best-looking, or even the strongest, but he was the one that could give him this type of freedom, this type of release.

He finished the ladder, pausing to wipe off the blood and admire his work. Now for the last ones. Bert let his lover float for a little bit longer and took a minute to decide where the piercings would be. He wanted a foreskin piercing on either side so he could link them together. The ladder was on the underside, and he didn't want to interfere with those. Hmm. Three and nine o'clock, possibly, assuming the top of his penis was noon. With the foreskin piercings on the right and left side of the head, they would still be able to be used for chastity but wouldn't get caught up in the frenum piercings of the Jacob's Ladder.

Bert carefully slid the needles through, followed by the smaller rings. Once they were in place, he leaned back and admired his lover. Those looked amazing and he thought Luc would love them. He knew it would be tender and while Luc was still out of it, he gently cleaned the whole area first, then applied the healing cream, making sure to get all around the piercings, rotating the metal so the cream could reach where it was needed.

Luc gasped at the sensation. "Oh! It feels. Mate—"

Bert hurriedly finished. His sub needed him. "I'm here. Feel my hands on you? Give me a minute to finish and I'll get you some water before you're allowed to see." He finished with the aftercare of the piercings, happy to see the cream had sealed the wounds and the redness was fading. He moved to sit beside Luc on the bed, placing one hand on his chest so Luc would feel him there, and reached over to grab the bottle of water.

"Sit up a little bit for me. No looking yet," Bert instructed.

Luc leaned against him, sipping the water, keeping his eyes closed. Bert held him close, loving the fact that they were safe, Luc's job was safe, that they had amazing friends and family surrounding them. He wasn't surprised that Luc inspired loyalty, but it had still been a shock when all of the Enforcers had pledged to Luc before the fight. It had been an amazing sight. Many of them had followed them back home and were standing guard just to make sure nothing else happened tonight. The rest were making sure there were no other Darius sympathizers.

"You were such a good Love for me. Are you ready to see?" he asked several minutes later.

Luc nodded, still looking hazy. Bert gently brought him to his feet and led him over to their bathroom where there was a huge mirror. He stood Luc in front of it, standing slightly behind him.

"Now open your eyes," he instructed.

Luc's eyes flew open and his mouth dropped in an O. "Mate! Can I touch?" At Bert's nod, he cautiously touched his own shaft, counting the rings in the Jacob's Ladder. "More?"

"I added a couple more. Your dick's long enough and there was room with these sized rings. There will still be enough space to add ribbons. Your cock looks gorgeous, and I can't wait to wrap it up. What do you think about your surprise?"

Luc fingered the double foreskin piercings before looking questioningly back at Bert.

"They can stay like this for fun, extra sensation. Or I can change the rings, link them together to create a chastity cage. So much fun to be had with these," Bert grinned at him. He loved it when Luc moaned, his cock trying to get hard, but it was still healing. That was going to look so lovely tomorrow.

"Now I think it's time for my reward, don't you think? Bend over and spread your cheeks for me." He knew Luc probably wouldn't get fully erect as the cream wouldn't have been able to reach everywhere inside, but he may get a dry orgasm if Bert played this right. He slicked his own cock, before pressing two fingers inside of his mate. He barely prepped him, wanting Luc to have all the sensations possible as part of his reward, knowing he liked a little sting with his pleasure.

Gripping his mate's hips tightly, Bert slammed his dick home, groaning at the tight hot feel of Luc's body. He loved the matching moan from Luc as he was filled. Bert took his time, admiring the view of Luc's cock swaying in the mirror. Wrapping a hand around Luc's throat, Bert ordered, "Look at me." When their eyes met, he sped up his thrusts, making sure to angle enough to hit Luc's prostate. "Come if you can." He knew a prostate orgasm was possible, although they had never achieved one without Luc being erect. He moved his other hand to pinch Luc's nipples. Maybe those were next to pierce, they were so sensitive.

Leaning up, he whispered in his lover's ear. "I love you. Forever. You're mine and I'm yours." He pulled down on Luc's hips as he thrust violently one last time, hitting Luc's prostate head-on. Bert's orgasm rushed through him, and he fought to keep his eyes open to watch Luc.

Luc gasped as heat filled him, and a feeling similar to an orgasm erupted. After the day he'd had, he felt shaky as his body began coming down from the adrenaline of the day. He stood, almost asleep as Bert gently cleaned him up and led him to bed. He could feel the new weight in his penis from the piercings and smiled as he climbed into bed. He would always know Bert was with him, even if he wasn't physically there with the new reminders.

He barely stirred as Bert slid on his cuffs before pulling the covers over them. Luc fell asleep, sleeping hard knowing that his family was safe and his job secured. He had employees who were loyal to him and the very best of friends. It was everything he could have ever dreamed of. He had fought for it all and now it was his. Forever.

NOTE FROM THE AUTHOR

Thank you for reading *Demon's Angel*! If you enjoyed the story, please consider leaving a review. Reviews, no matter how short, are invaluable to independent authors. They help with visibility, encouraging other readers to give the book a try. Even a simple star rating is amazing. Thank you for taking the time if you leave one. It means so much to me!

I have a playlist for *Demon's Angel* as well. You can find it on Spotify using the link below. You can also check out my website to see where each song goes and from whose point of view it might be from.

https://spoti.fi/4OYVFmm

ABOUT THE AUTHOR

I have loved reading since I was a child. I also enjoy baking, photography, and seeing new things. The world is a crazy place; sometimes escaping into a great book is the only way I can truly relax. Happily-ever-after romances are my favorite type of book, so my stories will end with an HEA, even if the road is a little bumpy getting there. I currently reside in the Midwest with my family.

If you sign up for my newsletter, you will get a free short story from the Nightwood Clan series! Christmas with the Nightwood Clan is a glimpse into the Clan's first Christmas together and takes place during the Christmas in A Hairy Situation.

You can find me here:

www.HarperDakota.com
www.Harper Dakota.com/newsletter
linktr.ee/harperdakota

ALSO BY THE AUTHOR

NIGHTWOOD CLAN

Bite Me Again

A Hairy Situation

Pointed Love

Forged In Love

Linked In History

The Nightwood Clan's Favorite Recipes (Nightwood Clan series companion)

Hoarded Secrets

Warded Bond

Demon's Mate

Demon's Angel